THE ORPHAN QUEEN

JODI MEADOWS

KATHERINE TEGEN BOOKS
An Imprint of HarperCollins Publishers

ALSO BY JODI MEADOWS

Incarnate

Asunder

Infinite

Phoenix Overture, a digital novella

Katherine Tegen Books is an imprint of HarperCollins Publishers.

The Orphan Queen
Copyright © 2015 by Jodi Meadows
Part opener photograph © iStockPhoto

www.epicreads.com

Library of Congress Cataloging-in-Publication Data
Meadows, Jodi.
  The orphan queen / Jodi Meadows. — First edition.
      pages   cm
  Summary: "In a world where it is forbidden, refugee Princess Wilhelmina's ability to do magic might be just the thing to help reclaim her kingdom, or ruin it forever"— Provided by publisher.
  ISBN 978-0-06-231738-4
  [1. Princesses—Fiction. 2. Magic—Fiction. 3. Orphans—Fiction. 4. Fantasy.] I. Title.
PZ7.M5073Orp   2014   2014022631
[Fic]—dc23   CIP
                                                              AC

Typography by Torborg Davern
15 16 17 18 19   PC/RRDH   10 9 8 7 6 5 4 3 2 1
❖
First Edition

If you wear smiles like armor—
If you put on personalities like clothes—
If you can't show the world all that you are—

This book is for you.

Mirror
Lake

Indigo Valley

LIADIA

THE
INDIGO
KINGDOM

Wraithland

Midvale Ridge

West Pass Watch

SKYVALE

East Pass Watch/
Old Palace

North Bow
River

South Bow
River

TWO RIVERS
CITY

Bracken
Lake

LAKESIDE

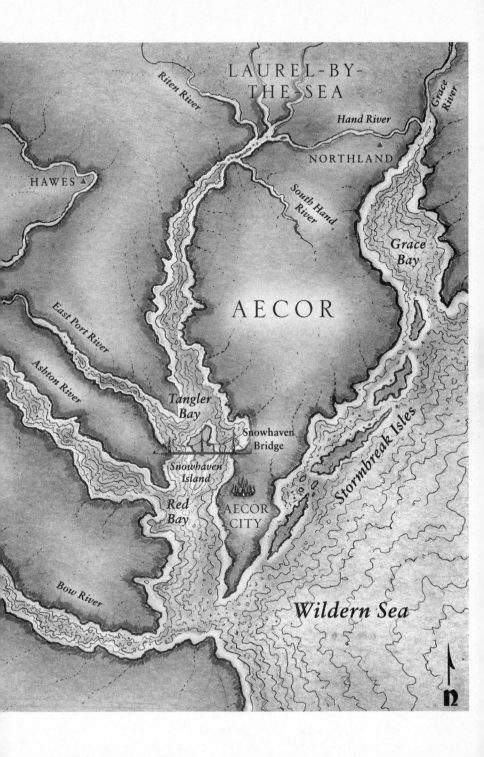

PART ONE

THE
OSPREYS

ONE

THE MIRRORS WERE an expensive superstition.

Not that it mattered to Melanie. Every time we came to the western side of the city, she insisted we stop and look, and I couldn't find it in myself to deny her that pleasure.

"It's beautiful, isn't it?" Wind plucked at a wayward strand of her sleek, black hair. She gathered it all back and tied it with a torn bit of fabric.

"Sure." The city spread below us, shimmering with knots of streetlights in the wealthy districts. Those people were important enough to warrant gas lamps at night, as though light protected like locks or swords or shields. But wealth wasn't the only thing that shone: glass panes hung on the west face of every house and tower and mansion in Skyvale, the mirrored city.

Beyond the houses, factories, shops, and refugee hovels, mountains were silhouetted against the night sky. A heavy, full moon lifted.

"When the wraith reaches the Indigo Kingdom," I said, "all of this will be destroyed. Mirrors won't do anything to stop it."

Melanie shot me a frown as I crept toward the edge of the roof and let out a short whistle.

A sharp trill answered from below. The other Ospreys were in position by the warehouse doors and the nearby intersections, watching for passersby, police, or worse: the vigilante. Black Knife.

For two of the youngest Ospreys, this was their first mission. Though we had been preparing them all their lives, a Black Knife appearance was the last thing Connor and Ezra needed.

Just the thought of Black Knife dragging away Connor—

"You don't have to worry about them, Wil." Melanie touched my elbow. "They're well trained."

I straightened and shook off the anxiety. Everyone, including Melanie, needed me to be strong. "Why should I worry about them? They're only standing watch. We're the ones about to do all the work."

She rolled her eyes. "You've been checking their progress every five minutes."

"I'm being observant."

"You're being paranoid and it makes you look suspicious."

"Well, you didn't see Black Knife drag that old man from his house because he'd used magic to hide his family while the Nightmare gang tore through the neighborhood." Magic was forbidden in the Indigo Kingdom, and Black Knife didn't care how it was used. Self-defense, healing, greed, murder: it was all the same to him when magic was involved.

"You're awfully sensitive about him."

Melanie didn't have magic. To her, he was no more a threat than the police. But to others . . .

I scanned the flat warehouse rooftops again to be sure we were still alone up here, and then jumped down to the lower section of the roof. I landed in a crouch, my fingertips on the cool slate tiles for balance. A moment later, Melanie landed beside me with a quiet *thump* that was masked by the rush of the swollen river nearby.

The clock tower in Hawksbill chimed midnight.

Kneeling before the warehouse's roof-access door, I drew a lockpick and tension wrench from my pocket. In a few seconds, I had the door open. Melanie and I slipped inside, silent as shadows. The warehouse was cool and still, with the dusty scent of neglect.

Moonlight fell through smeary windows, barely illuminating the stairs as we descended. Toe, ball, heel—careful so we wouldn't make a sound. There were no guards here, but one couldn't be too cautious.

We followed the spiral stairs down two flights. Mel went left and I headed right, to the southwest corner where crates from the Indigo Kingdom's famed paper mill hunched in the dark.

There were fifty or more crates, their labels mere outlines in the shadows. I slipped a match from my pocket and struck it against the floor. After I scuffed out any traces, I leaned toward the crate labels, searching for the one I wanted.

My match sputtered out, and I lit another, still edging down the rows of sealed crates.

There. A faded page inked with a lion and Liadia's coat of arms. The crate was stashed in the corner, where other homeless stock had been shoved. Thankfully, the one I needed was still in the front—Liadia hadn't fallen very long ago—but it was too high for me to open and reach inside.

I checked over my shoulder. No Melanie.

What I needed to do was so small that it was insignificant, but still I hesitated. Magic was completely illegal. Unpardonable. Unforgivable. Not many people had magic anymore, as far as I knew, but those caught using it were never seen again.

With a deep, shuddering breath, I touched the crate. *"Wake up."* It was an old command, from when I was little and I used magic without fear. From when I'd believed I brought things to life. *"Do this silently: slide forward and float down to the floor. I will guide you."*

The crate shifted, loosening with a gasp of dust. With my fingertips resting on the wood, I stepped back to give it room. Slowly, as though it were as light as a leaf, the crate floated down and touched the floor without a sound.

"Unseal the lid," I murmured. A faint, fleeting wave of dizziness clouded my head.

The lid popped up, loose now. I bade the crate sleep again before I opened it. I needed only a handful of pages.

"Find what we're looking for?" Melanie's whisper came from behind me, and I stiffened. She was *quiet*.

"It's right here." I pulled several pages from the top and handed them to my friend. "Hold this while I put the lid on. You got the ink?"

"Easily." She lifted the jar so the glass gleamed in the weak light, then shoved it into her bag. The papers followed. "Let's fetch the others and get back."

I lowered the lid, but didn't dare seal it and move the crate up again. Not with Melanie here.

Together, we found a door and headed outside.

Quinn, who was supposed to be the lookout, wasn't at the door. Brittle leaves skittered down the cobblestones; the autumn wind blew from the west, and a sharp, acrid stench rode the air.

Melanie and I looked at each other, our noses wrinkled from the smell. Wraith. It was strong tonight.

A small, guilty part of me twisted. If I hadn't used magic on that crate . . .

No, magic that simple wouldn't bring a gust of wraith. The stink and creatures that blew into the valley, like the heavy winds before a storm, were normal these days.

I whistled for the Ospreys and waited for the reply.

Nothing.

I whistled again. There should have been four lookouts: two at the street-level warehouse doors and two at the nearby intersections. Someone should have answered.

Still nothing.

I rested my hands on my daggers as wariness prickled over my skin.

What if the police had caught them? Or worse, Black Knife? He liked capturing all kinds of criminals, not only flashers: magic users. We'd run across him during three of our last five jobs, and once he'd come close to capturing Melanie.

The acrid stink grew stronger.

"Help!" A shout came from down the street.

I drew my daggers, sprinting toward the shout and terrified

screams, and then the *thud* of a body slamming into a wooden fence.

Ezra, one of our youngest boys, dropped to the ground. His sister, Quinn, shrieked and ran for him. Connor and Theresa stood in the street, blades drawn as they backed away from looming shadows.

I skidded to a halt. Five huge men bore down on the Ospreys.

Connor's round-eyed gaze darted from the attackers to me. "Wil! Mel!"

"Oh, saints."

The strangers turned toward me. They were grotesque, with bulging shoulders and arms, the muscles bursting through the fabric of their clothing. Two were enormously tall, practically giants, while the others were as wide as doorways. All of them were revolting with red-veined eyes, cheekbones like shelves, and fat lips. They stank of wraith and shine.

They were glowmen: men turned into monsters.

I rushed at them. They swung at me with heavy fists, but I kicked and slashed with my daggers, my limbs but blurs of movement. I went for their knees and groins; their throats were out of my reach.

Melanie and Theresa fought with fiery quickness, making their way toward Quinn, who guarded Connor and Ezra near a crumbling wall.

A length of chain whipped through the air and caught my shoulder. Pain cracked through me. I tried to pull away, but the glowmen had me surrounded. Three on one didn't seem very fair. Thankfully, they were stupid.

The first glowman, wrapping the chain around his fist again, didn't notice as I stomped on the bottom links, jerking his whole body forward and into the giant closing in on the other side of me. I ducked beneath them, away from the third.

While they untangled themselves, I crouched and slashed my blade across one's heel, slicing through the leather of his boot to the heavy tendon.

The glowman dropped immediately, dragging one of the others with him.

I jumped toward my friends, but the third glowman shoved me hard against a building, knocking both my daggers from my hands. As he lumbered closer, I groped along the brick wall, and a windowsill came loose. I swung with all my strength. The rotting wood clapped wetly against his head, but did no damage. He jeered and lunged for my throat.

I reached for my daggers, and his hands mashed against the brick.

The glowman reared back. I brought my heel down on the arch of his foot, making bone crack. When I drove my dagger into his thigh, blood poured, hot over my hand. I stepped away.

Melanie, Quinn, and Theresa were dispatching the two glowmen who'd been bearing down on an unconscious Ezra. The glowman with the cut tendon was limping toward them, but they could take care of him.

The fifth glowman . . .

Down the street, he held a dagger to Connor's throat. Blood caught moonlight as it trickled down Connor's brown skin.

"No!" I lunged for him, but the glowman I'd just stabbed caught my ankle and I fell, both daggers skittering out of my reach. Magic stirred on my tongue. I could make the ground bring the daggers to me.

No. Not yet. Magic was a last resort.

I struggled, twisting and yanking my foot, but the glowman's grip tightened.

I slammed my heel against his face. His nose cracked and blood spewed, and he released me.

Daggers in hand again, I scrambled to my feet and ran to help Connor.

But Connor was free. A sword-bearing figure sliced and stabbed at the fifth glowman. Long and slender, he moved like a dancer when he twisted and ducked and disarmed his opponent.

Connor peeled away from the fight and hurtled toward me. "Wil! I'm sorry! I was coming to help you, but he—"

"It's all right." I dropped to one knee and touched his neck. "How bad is it?" It was all I could do to keep from hugging him, checking the rest of his body for wounds. He was old enough that it would only infuriate him. Still, I didn't stop myself from pulling him closer.

He tilted up his head and cringed, but the cut on his neck wasn't deep. "It hurts."

"Put pressure on it. The bleeding will stop." Instead of coddling him more, I turned and rushed the glowman who'd hurt him.

The newcomer had the glowman worn down. The beast was panting, bleeding from cuts all over his arms and chest. His shirt hung in shreds. With a mind to add a few more gashes to his collection, I ripped him away from the stranger and slammed him against a building.

A fantasy tickled the back of my thoughts: the brickwork coming alive, swallowing the glowman whole. A fantasy it remained; I couldn't call attention to my power.

"Why did you attack my people?" My voice was little more than a growl, a knot of rage and fear. If they knew who we were . . .

His gaze flitted beyond me, toward Connor and the others. "The boys looked easy."

Not because they knew us. Good.

Again, I slammed his head into the bricks. His eyes grew unfocused. "Touch us again," I said, "and you die." Maybe he could die right now, for what he did to Connor. I had daggers. I could do it quickly. It wasn't like he was human. Not anymore.

A presence warmed my back, and the glowman tried to wrest himself away. "No!"

"Excuse me." The voice was deep and unfamiliar. "I'll take him, if you're finished."

I spun away from the glowman as he crumpled to the ground, and readied my daggers, but the hooded man didn't look up. Quickly, expertly, he bound the glowman's hands and feet together with a silk cord.

The sounds of fighting died away as the other Ospreys dropped their opponents. Five bodies littered the ground, still breathing for now. My eyes followed the stranger as he turned toward me.

His face was covered by a thin sheet of black silk; only his eyes remained unhidden, though shadowed now.

Black Knife.

"Thank you for your assistance." He stepped closer and

offered his hand, but then paused and let it fall back to his side. "*You?*"

Wonderful. He recognized me from the last few times our paths had crossed. Though he'd never saved one of my friends before.

I threw a glance over my shoulder. Melanie had gathered the other Ospreys and they were already slipping quietly away. I took four long strides backward.

"What's your name?" Black Knife stalked toward me, removing another silk cord from a pouch on his belt. "I've been looking for you. Where have you been hiding?"

I touched my chest and feigned flattery. "You've been looking for me?"

"Who were those children? More recruits for your gang?"

Same group. Younger orphans. Not that I'd tell *him* what we were, or from where we'd been taken.

"Surely we're a waste of your time. There are worse things in Skyvale than a few teenagers trying to feed themselves."

His gaze cut to the glowmen bleeding in the alley. A few of them were beginning to stir. "What are you stealing this time?"

"Do I look like a thief to you?" I reached for a look of innocence.

"You look dangerous."

I smiled. "Thank you." Before I could consider the wisdom, I pulled a dagger and threw it.

Black Knife swore and darted aside. The dagger struck behind him, pinning a glowman's hand to the ground. The broken pipe he'd been reaching for rolled away.

When Black Knife kicked the pipe aside and knelt to tie the

glowman, I ducked around a corner and ran as fast as I could, crossing into the White Flag district and taking to the rooftops. The other Ospreys would be waiting at the inn.

Away from the quiet of the warehouse district, midnight life rumbled on the streets below: drunks staggering home, dogs barking, and babies crying. The moon cast wan light over the district, not yet reflected in the mirrors that hung on the taller buildings. If Black Knife had followed me, I couldn't see him.

I paused on the roof of an apothecary and whispered to the sky, "Thank you." My Ospreys were safe. That was all that mattered.

They were my only family, my only hope for home. When the Indigo Army invaded Aecor almost ten years ago, every adult living in the palace was slaughtered, and the highborn children were brought to Skyvale, the capital of the Indigo Kingdom. We escaped the orphanage a year later and named ourselves after the national animal of our conquered homeland.

The Ospreys, these children, were my life. Without them, I had nothing.

But with them . . .

With them, I would take back my kingdom.

TWO

AFTER DROPPING INTO the apothecary and lifting a few bandages and powdered herbs, I made my way to the Peacock Inn and slipped inside through the open window on the top floor.

We couldn't afford the room, even though it was the worst one in the building; but Patrick, Melanie, and I had once broken up a huge fight that would have ended with five dead men on the floor, police swarming through White Flag, and the Peacock's owner in jail. Now the innkeeper always let Ospreys stay when we were in town.

The others were there, starting a small fire and rinsing their wounds. I shut the window behind me and tossed my bag of medical supplies to Quinn Bradburn.

"Ezra." I nodded at him. "Glad you're awake. That was quite the hit you took."

He ducked his face and shrugged. "I'm better now."

I raised an eyebrow at Connor, who gave a small, frantic shake of his head; he hadn't done anything. A knot of tension in my chest untangled. I smiled and moved on to gathering the stray weapons the boys had tossed everywhere. "Good. Next time, try not to get knocked out or cut, you two. It's embarrassing. People are going to think kittens trained you."

"What was wrong with those men?" Connor winced as he dabbed a damp cloth on his throat where the glowman had cut. "They looked human, but they were *wrong*."

"They were huge," Ezra added. "And strong."

"They were glowmen." The tiny room was packed, three sitting on the bed and two in the only chairs. I perched on the windowsill, ignoring the way the old wood creaked. Muffled shouts and thumps came from the lower stories; the inn stank of waste and smoke and sweat.

Connor finished inspecting his neck in a tarnished silver mirror he kept in his pocket; he'd fallen hard for the whole mirror-and-wraith superstition. With a frown, he set the mirror aside. "What are glowmen? And are there glowladies?"

"There are women like that, but the term is just glowmen." I raised an eyebrow at Quinn—Ezra was her younger brother, after all—and she nodded. We couldn't keep the younger boys sheltered forever, especially now that they'd faced a pack of glowmen. "Sometimes people use wraith to make themselves feel happier, stronger, whatever. Like people once used magic."

"Wraith isn't magic, though."

"Wraith *was* magic. Once." Quinn shook her head at the boys. "Haven't you been paying attention to your lessons?"

Both boys slumped. "Yes," said Ezra. "If magic is like fire, then wraith is like smoke. Magic isn't created or destroyed. It just gets changed."

"That's right." I leaned against the window, the glass cool on my spine. "Wraith is another form of magic—a toxic form."

"Wait." Ezra held up a hand. "We're not finished. We *did* study."

"People once used magic for everything, from building to farming to war." Connor parroted the history papers we'd written for the younger Ospreys. "Radiants had even built a railroad system for transporting goods and people. Magic was *useful,* and families with a lot of radiants became powerful and rich. There was always wraith, but never enough of it to be a danger."

Ezra took up where his friend left off, his voice pitched to mimic Quinn's: his impression of her giving lessons. "But just over a hundred years ago, the western kingdoms noticed the wraith accumulating, obscuring sunlight, and making storms worse. It's been creeping across the continent ever since, destroying everything in its path. Liadia was the most recent victim."

"When the wraith was first discovered as a problem, King Terrell Pierce the Second, sovereign of the Indigo Kingdom, forced most of the surrounding kingdoms to sign the Wraith Alliance, making magic illegal, and now radiants are persecuted and hunted. People call them flashers now, to be rude. The once-powerful families and businesses who'd used magic to gain their wealth were replaced by those who could produce similar results without magic. Lots of people went into ruin, even in Aecor, which didn't sign the treaty. But Aecorians did change their methods of industry, and the kingdom became a safe place for radiants to hide. Until the One-Night War." With a chuckle, Connor snapped and thumped his chest at Ezra—the Osprey salute.

"I'm glad your studies amuse you so much," said Melanie.

Connor turned back to me. "But what does *history* have to do with glowmen?"

I shook my head. "Wraith isn't magic like people are used to, it manifests physically. But wraith is still magical. Sometimes people add certain chemicals to wraith mist and sell it to others to drink or inhale. That's called shine. A little will make people feel however they want to feel. Stronger. Braver. Bigger."

The boys exchanged glances and raised eyebrows. "That doesn't sound bad."

"It's dangerous. If you take too much, the changes become real and permanent. You don't just *feel* amazingly tall or muscled. You *are*. Those people will never be normal again."

"When they're caught, glowmen are exiled to the wraithland." Melanie placed her bag on the small desk and fished out a notebook and pen. "I've seen the prison wagons. The glowmen are sedated, loaded like sacks of grain, and taken as far west as horses are willing to go." Almost nonchalantly, she shook a bottle of ink and twisted off the cap.

Both of the boys were silent.

Theresa nodded. "It's true. They're dumped while they're still unconscious. Sometimes soldiers in West Pass Watch can see the glowmen waking up, if it's still light out. If the wraith beasts don't find them first, the glowmen usually attack one another and—"

"That's enough." Quinn twitched her little finger at Theresa, who just smirked at the rude gesture and unfolded enough bandages for everyone's wounds.

Sufficiently frightened, the boys shuddered and turned

toward creating a paste from the powdered herbs I'd brought. While they were engaged with treating cuts and bruises, Melanie and I wrote a quick report to Patrick, the leader of the Ospreys.

When we got to the glowmen, Melanie paused. "What was Black Knife doing there?" Her voice was low.

"Hunting the glowmen, I assume." I turned a pen in my hands. "He doesn't know what we were doing, and he didn't follow us. That's all I care about." I glanced back at Connor, who was helping Theresa put away the last of the medical supplies. Hard to believe I was *grateful* to Black Knife for something. "Did the boys realize who he was?"

"Oh yes." Melanie hunched, hiding a smile. "Ezra made fun of Connor for getting rescued by *Black Knife*, of all people. Connor made fun of Ezra for getting knocked unconscious almost before the fight began. Then they punched each other."

"Clearly, they've made up," I muttered. The boys now wore matching bandages around their heads and on their necks.

"Clearly." Melanie smiled and shook her head. "Maybe you were right about him being a problem. At least he was more interested in the glowmen than us."

This time. "We see him too often," I muttered. "Maybe he'll trip and fall on his knife."

"Say it again." She glanced at the others, all engaged with their tasks throughout the room. "Hopefully, we can stay clear of him for a while. We have a lot more work to do before our masquerade begins."

I covered a shiver by folding our report. "Now that we have the right paper and ink, our masquerade may actually happen."

She grinned and poured a glob of melted wax onto the

folded paper, and I pressed my thumb into it as it cooled. "You'll make a lovely refugee duchess," she said, making room between us as Quinn approached.

"As long as I'm a *convincing* refugee duchess."

"I wonder if you'll meet the crown prince," Quinn mused. "I hear he's very handsome."

"I won't be there to admire the royal scenery." I dropped our report into the bag with the stolen ink and paper. "I'll be there to learn about the occupation of Aecor so we can reclaim the land and go home."

"I know." Quinn's mutter hardly carried. "That doesn't mean you can't have a little fun while you're working. Admiring the royal scenery might do you some good."

The room grew quiet, everyone looking between Quinn and me.

"In case you forgot," Melanie said, voice roughening, "the *royal scenery* is why we're trapped in a crumbling old castle in the Indigo Kingdom, scraping for food and stealing all the time. If it wasn't for the royal scenery, we'd be in Sandcliff Castle overlooking the Red Bay. We'd be with our parents."

There was a long pause. Melanie had seen her parents murdered in their beds, the fate of so many of Aecor's high nobility. My mother and father had been dragged into a courtyard and beheaded in front of everyone; their deaths meant the kingdom had been conquered. Afterward, King Terrell sent one of his younger brothers to rule the puppet state.

My kingdom. In *their* hands.

I couldn't allow those murderers to continue ruling my land. Reports from our Aecorian contacts indicated my people were suffering hunger, oppression, and crippling taxes, not to mention the sudden disappearances of all known flashers. It wasn't right. I had been born with the responsibility to lead the people of Aecor, and I could not fail them.

"I know." Quinn dropped her gaze. "I'm sorry."

"Don't be." I stood and handed her the bag. "It's hard to remember sometimes." Quinn was fifteen; she'd been only five during the One-Night War and could barely recall it.

My memories of that night were crystalline, and sharp. I would never forget the horror of blood and fire and steel, or that King Terrell and his family were why I was left without a home, and my kingdom was a handful of orphans. With only them and a few rebel groups in Aecor who opposed the foreign military presence, I was expected to resurrect an entire kingdom.

Queen Wilhelmina Korte. It sounded a little ridiculous.

"Why don't you take these back to Patrick? Melanie and I will stay the night in Skyvale to gather more supplies." Food, clothes, and other necessities were hard to come by in the old palace, and it was already autumn. With winter coming, and Melanie and me leaving soon, the rest of the Ospreys needed everything we could bring them.

Quinn apologized again, saluted, and then took Theresa and the boys from the inn. Their footsteps thudded on the floorboards and stairs, all traces of their training vanished like they didn't even know the word *stealth*.

Melanie rolled her eyes. "Ready to get back to work?"

"As long as Black Knife doesn't show up."

"Say it again." She tossed me a backpack, and a minute later, we were out the window.

20

THREE

BLACK KNIFE DIDN'T make another appearance, but we saw evidence of him all over Skyvale. On balconies and in yards, we found discarded hoods and masks, left over from children's games. Everywhere, there were knives carved into fences and walls, smeared with pitch or black mud.

Ugh. Eventually, he'd do something horrible enough that the city would stop worshipping him.

Melanie and I worked the remainder of the night, collecting enough supplies to last the Ospreys three or four weeks, if they were frugal. After sleeping for a few hours in the inn, we left Skyvale, picked our way through the refugee camps that huddled outside the city, and headed east toward the old palace in the mountains, where the Ospreys had lived for almost nine years.

We ascended into cooler air and patches of heavy mist, which softened the carpet of leaves on the worn road. Birdcalls and wind in the trees obscured any sounds we might have made.

Half an hour later, mist gave way to the moss-covered stone walls of the old palace. East Pass Watch was an ancient fort-style castle, with several towers and tiny windows meant to be defensible on the cliff side. Kings of the past had tried to build additions to the castle several times, until it was an awful mishmash of eras, pieced together with pride and sweat and contempt. No wonder it had been abandoned almost two hundred years ago in favor of the newer palace in the valley. Sometime in the last century, a section of the south wing had collapsed, and now ivy crawled into every crevice, camouflaging the castle as it destroyed it.

Drafty and dirty, heavy with the weight of age-old battles, this was the only home we'd known since Aecor. Most of the Ospreys didn't even remember Aecor or the orphanage. Just . . . this.

"Glad to be home." Melanie hiked her bag into a better position on her shoulder, then spent a moment tugging free pinned strands of hair.

But this wasn't home, no matter how long we spent here.

I whistled the four-note signal as we approached the castle wall, and high up in the ramparts a shadow slipped away.

The last few minutes of trudging through the main curtain and bailey seemed unusually long, thanks to my heavy load, but a silhouette in the entrance to the state apartments urged us onward. Patrick Lien waited with his hands behind his back and his shoulders squared. "I got your report," he said as we approached. "I can't believe you let Black Knife live."

"I'm not a murderer."

"You know that doesn't make a difference to him. He'd capture you if he had the chance."

Patrick was the oldest of the Ospreys, and while I was the heir to Aecor, he'd become the natural leader of the group. He didn't know about my magic—I didn't think—but that didn't make his statement any less true. Black Knife would gladly arrest any of the Ospreys. We were thieves, after all. That we'd witnessed our parents' murders, been kidnapped, and wanted only to take back what was ours would be inconsequential to his judgment of us.

When I didn't respond, Patrick's expression grew harder. "Anything else?"

"We checked the guard routes around the King's Seat," I said. "They're the same as before. Sneaking out and back in won't be a problem."

"Good." He glanced at the bags we carried and gave a sharp nod. "Put those away and clean up. We've been working on your documents all morning. They should be ready for your inspection." He held open the heavy door for us before vanishing into the hall.

I pretended not to notice as Melanie gazed after him. Like General Lien, Patrick cut an imposing figure. Unlike his father, he'd never hit anyone out of anger. Of that he'd always been very careful.

But would it have killed him to help carry our supplies?

Biting back weary grunts, we hefted our bags and headed toward the general supply room. This whole wing was ours; we'd appropriated and restored—as much as we could—a large section of the state apartments nine years ago. But there were so few of us, we took up only a small portion of what was once a spectacular and prestigious place to live.

After we unloaded and washed the worst of the grime from our hands and faces, we walked to the common area, lively with the other ten Ospreys' chatter.

The windows had been thrown wide to invite in as much light as possible. The upper frescoes were darkened with age, and peeling, but we'd given the lower walls a fresh coat of white. It made the chamber seem brighter, especially when the sun shone directly through the east-facing windows. When it got cold, we shuttered all the windows and stuffed rags into the cracks, but these days of early autumn were still fine.

The others were huddled around a big, round table with papers strewn across the old wood like memories. Seven boys and five girls: we were a small group, all that was left of Aecor's high nobility.

Ronald and Oscar Gray—the eighteen- and seventeen-year-old sons of a now-dead duke—waved and went back to discussing whatever medical notion had caught their attention this week. Connor sat beside them, wide-eyed and attentive while words such as *arteries* and *blood clots* were used.

Across the table, Paige Kendall, Theresa Markham, and Kevin Walton, the other older Ospreys, were working with Ezra Bradburn and Carl Darby over a handful of maps, asking the younger boys to point out the locations of various lords' holdings.

Melanie and I took seats at the table, both of us restraining relieved groans. Last night's fight had left bruises.

Patrick didn't glance up from the document he was studying. "Now that you're back, we've got a lot to cover and I've just received word of a new hunt." He looked at Quinn. "This one's yours and your brother's."

24

Quinn sat up straighter. "What is it?"

"In a moment." Patrick stood and Quinn shrank a little, but the excited light didn't leave her eyes, even as everyone else quieted and looked up. "Now that Wilhelmina has returned, we'll finish these documents and go over the plan. I want everyone to be absolutely clear on their parts in this, especially Wil and Melanie."

I pulled a pile of forged documents closer. "Good job on these," I muttered to anyone, everyone. The papers still required a few finishing touches to make them appear as authentic as the true residency papers we'd found; that was my job.

"Wil and Mel will infiltrate Skyvale Palace as refugee Liadian nobility," he said. "King Terrell won't be able to turn them away, not with the Wraith Alliance still in effect. Once they're in place, we'll check for their reports at Laurence's Bakery every three days. If you need supplies delivered to the drop or if there's an emergency, we'll check whenever we see the signal. Which will be?" He raised an eyebrow at Melanie.

"A red ribbon in our window." She pulled the silk length from her hip pouch. "We'll tie it up the first day, so you know we're successful and where we're located."

"Very good." Patrick gave a clipped nod. "We're on a deadline for the ten-year anniversary of the One-Night War, so I want us all to have clear goals for this mission. That way, if anything goes wrong, we know who to blame."

His narrowed-eye glance at me meant he counted last night's encounter with Black Knife as something "going wrong."

"Goal one: intelligence. We know the Aecorian terrain and we have people willing to fight for us, but we can't risk them until we know where the Indigo Army bases are located in Aecor, how many troops they have, and what kind of weapons they're using.

"Two: we suspect King Terrell's people also have a list of resistance groups in Aecor—groups just waiting for the opportunity to fight back. We need that list, both for our own purposes, and to keep our potential allies out of enemy hands."

"We already know of a few resistance groups," Oscar said. "And our contacts in Aecor have been scouting for more."

Patrick gave a brisk nod. "But if we're to take back an entire kingdom and defend it, we need to overwhelm the Indigo Army. A force of a thousand people won't be enough. Not against an army that's had a decade to establish its hold."

Everyone looked somber.

Patrick pulled a sheet of paper from the pile in the middle of the table and slid it toward me. "Of course, they'd notice if their list went missing, and they'll have multiple copies. Wil and Mel, your job will be to replace their list with ours, which holds false information. Send 'updated copies' to the forces in Aecor if you can, but regardless, they will spend precious time discovering the problem and reverifying all of their information."

"Meanwhile," I said, "we'll have our contacts reach out to these resistance groups, warn them of the Indigo Army's attention, and recruit them for our purposes." I glanced at the paper he gave me. Names, numbers, locations, all no doubt meant to lead the Indigo Army into a trap.

"Exactly." Patrick rested his forearms on the table, his fingers interlaced. His tone was steady, but weighted with something I would have called grief if he had been anyone else. "As for the third goal, this is a bit more disturbing and crucial."

I held my breath.

"I've heard rumors that the people of Aecor are being drafted into the Indigo Army to fight on the front lines of the wraithland—that they're being used to patrol the borders, fend off wraith beast attacks, and track the wraith's progress. Wilhelmina. Melanie. I need you to verify this as soon as you can." Patrick pressed his palms to the table and stood, leaning forward. "If this is true, those are *our* people sent out for slaughter in the wraithland, breathing in that toxic haze. Those are *our* farmers and fisherman, *our* chandlers and cobblers. Those are *our people*," he said again.

My heart felt like it had climbed into my throat. Those were my parents' people. My people. "I'll find out if it's true." My voice was deep, grave. "If it is, I will deal with it."

"I know you will." Patrick gazed over the assembled Ospreys, and his tone shifted like fire. "We will have our army. It will come from refugees who recognize the Indigo Kingdom's nefarious nature. It will come from the resistance fighters still in Aecor. And it will come from the people being drafted into the wraithlands.

"Most of all, it will come from the people living in fear, without hope, and under the false rule of a conquering king. People will come to our call when they hear we have the most important piece of all: Princess Wilhelmina. She's alive. She's with us. And she's going to take back her kingdom."

I kept my posture straight and my expression stiff as a few of the others cheered and Melanie smiled at me. Maintaining morale was a necessary endeavor, and Patrick was good at it. He was good at a lot of things.

And to him I was a name and a title.

Patrick leaned on his fists and focused on me. The scar over his eyebrow stood out stark and white. "There's one more thing I want from your time in the palace."

I waited.

"A map. I want to know which windows lead to which rooms. I want to know where the armories are, where guards are stationed, and even where King Terrell sleeps at night. I want to know everything about that place, that way, if your disguises are compromised, we can come and get you."

I'd want a map for myself, too, so making a copy for him wouldn't be trouble. "Consider it already done."

"Good."

He wanted me to write a report every three days, gather information, plant false information, free drafted soldiers, and draw a detailed map while disguised at all hours because I was living in the palace of my enemies. It was amazing Patrick didn't want me to stop the encroaching wraith while I was at it.

He tapped the documents in front of me. "How do these look?"

"They're close." I motioned at a smudge of ink where someone had tried to conceal a mistake. "That . . ."

Patrick's voice deepened into a growl. "Close isn't good enough. They need to be perfect."

"Presumably, we'll have traveled for leagues across the wraithland." Melanie's tone was placating. "Our papers won't have survived the trip in perfect condition."

Patrick frowned, but acquiesced. "Finish these, then. We'll put them in the envelope and leave them outside with the rest of the supplies." He pushed himself straight and paced toward the other side of the room. Everyone watched him, as though he were magnetic and their compasses declared him north. "I've gotten word of an army supply caravan leaving Skyvale in one week. It's heading for Aecor."

Quinn's breath hitched. This was the other mission, the one Patrick had said was for her. I lowered my pen.

"Quinn, you will take Ezra and Ronald. You will identify what supplies exactly are being transported, and ride with the caravan until it's four days out of the valley. Then you will take whatever measures you think wisest and halt the wagons. Bring back whatever is immediately useful to us, and hide the rest. We'll need it when *we* march to Aecor to prepare for the anniversary."

"I can do that." Quinn lifted her chin and smiled.

"That is a risky mission, Patrick. Are you sure Quinn and Ezra are the best for this?" I asked. The siblings glared at me, and Melanie winced.

"Everything we do is a calculated risk," Patrick said.

My voice strained. "Quinn is good, but she'll have to look after Ezra. His first mission was only last night, and a glowman nearly killed him. This isn't safe. We could *all* go if we postpone the palace mission another week." We'd gone from nineteen to twelve people thanks to jobs like this. I didn't want to lose more.

"The glowman *didn't* kill me, though. I can do this easy mission." Ezra crossed his arms.

Quinn's glare was deadly. "We can do it."

Patrick shook his head at me. "They'll be fine. We can't put off the palace mission any longer. The anniversary of the

One-Night War is approaching. I want us to be in Aecor before winter is over, so that we can take back our kingdom on the day this all started."

"I realize we have a deadline," I said, "but I'm not willing to unnecessarily risk our lives." I cast my gaze around the group. "Those who vote we postpone the palace mission and send more experienced Ospreys, raise a hand. Those who vote Quinn, Ezra, and Ronald go, raise a fist."

Quinn, Ezra, and Ronald raised fists immediately. So did Patrick, Paige, and Oscar.

I lifted my hand. Connor did, too, of course, and Theresa followed a moment later.

"Carl? Melanie? Kevin?" I lifted an eyebrow. If they sided with me, we'd be tied.

Kevin raised his hand, voting with me. Carl glanced between Connor and Ezra, his two best friends, and heaved a sigh. "I would like to abstain."

"You can't," said Melanie. "Everyone votes. But"—she glanced at me—"it doesn't matter either way. I vote Quinn and Ezra go. Ezra needs the experience. Ronald and Quinn will look out for him." She raised a fist. Seven against four and an abstainer. "The only way they get experience is by sending them out there, Wil."

"Fine." I flicked my little finger at her and smiled like I didn't mean the gesture, but no doubt she could see the truth.

I might have been the future queen, but here, in the Ospreys, Patrick was the leader. Every time we disagreed and the decision was put to a vote, Patrick got what he wanted.

Theresa had once explained it by saying it wasn't so much

that I lost as Patrick won. It was hard to deny him.

At least I'd always been able to count on Connor to vote with me, even when it meant he voted against his best friends.

"Moving on," Patrick said. "Ronald, pass the map. I'll show you all the route the caravan is taking. . . ."

Quinn smirked and returned her gaze to Patrick.

Trying to ignore the tightening in my chest, I focused on the residency papers once more. I added the signature of the priest who supposedly witnessed my birth in Liadia. Fortunately, the sample we had to copy from was still clear and sharp, and recent enough that he could have witnessed both my birth and the birth of some duke born five years before me.

She had been a real person, this Julianna Whitman, the girl I was impersonating. She was my age and her general description fit mine as well, but I'd chosen her because as far as I knew she'd never visited the Indigo Kingdom.

It seemed very morbid, going around with a dead girl's identity.

Melanie was doing it, too, though she was able to use her real first name. We'd found evidence of a girl named Melanie Cole who'd probably come into contact with Lady Julianna a few times. They would be best friends now.

"We need those supplies." Patrick's attention stayed on Quinn and Ronald, while Ezra sat bouncing in his chair, excited for such a dangerous mission. "Our return to Aecor may depend on our having them."

Everyone nodded solemnly; their rapt attention never left Patrick. I finished my work with the residency documents and moved them aside, then let my gaze slide toward the open window where cool light filtered in through the sand-speckled glass.

Far beyond the horizon, past the piedmont and the plains and rivers—past the dirt and cobble roads our prison wagons had bumped over almost ten years before—lay Aecor, a home only a few of us remembered. A home we wouldn't recognize when we returned.

Aecor was my responsibility, but how could I rule a kingdom when I couldn't even lead the Ospreys?

THE FIRST WINTER *in the old palace was awful. In spite of all our stolen clothes, blankets, and the fireplaces we'd cleaned and lit, the ancient castle was always freezing. The wind blew constantly.*

One morning while the other Ospreys were cleaning or looking after the youngest children, Patrick summoned me to the common area, where the big table in the center of the room was covered in stacks of paper, jars of ink, and wooden boxes with rusty latches.

My breath caught at the scribal bounty. "Is this for me?"

Patrick was leaning on the windowsill, his arms crossed. He smiled faintly, an expression that looked out of place on him. It softened him, and eased the sharp effect of the scar above his eye. "I know it's not the best quality, but it's what I could get."

I beamed as I unlatched boxes to peek inside. Pens,

spare nibs, and wax-sealing supplies. "These will work just fine."

"Will you need anything else?" He cast a cool gaze over the table, as though he weren't proud of all this, but there was a light in his eyes, and one corner of his mouth tipped up.

"We'll need lots more paper. Lots of different kinds. Inks. Um." I touched the unlined papers, trying to recall everything that had been on my father's writing desk in Aecor. "Rulers. Candles. Cleaning cloths. A blotter. Perhaps copybooks, if we can find any. Samples of other people's handwriting."

Patrick nodded, keeping everything in his head. He wouldn't forget anything we needed. "You don't actually know anything about forgery, do you?"

I cringed and shook my head.

"It's fine." He pushed off the windowsill and slid a notebook toward me. "Your idea was good. We will be a lot more effective if we can deliver false notes and forge official papers, but if we're going to do this, we need to do it correctly. I'll figure out what else we need and make sure we get it. You get to work actually learning what you're doing."

The simultaneous praise and criticism made my emotions knot up. Patrick rarely complimented, but he was right: I'd rushed into the idea of tricking my way into places, not having a solid foundation of experience behind me.

"You can do this, Wilhelmina." Patrick patted my shoulder awkwardly; he was two years older, but we were the same height, which I could tell annoyed him. His father had been taller. "I'll do anything I can to help you get back Aecor. So will the other Ospreys."

"Thank you." I took the notebook off the table and flipped through the evenly bound pages. Each sheet was lined and unusually perfect, while the cover was rubbed dull from handling. "This looks old."

"It's pre-wraith, I think."

Ah. From before the ban over ninety years ago, when people used magic to manufacture and power everything. It must have been such a different world then, with the freedom to use magic and the ability to get whatever was needed with minimal inconvenience.

If only I'd been born then. It sounded like a better world than this one.

"You should keep it," Patrick said. "Practice writing in it."

"It's too special for practice. That's what all the scrap paper is for." My fingers traveled across the cover, bumping through the shallow grooves where braids or vines had been stamped along the edges, but worn away over the century. "Father kept a diary. I don't know what he wrote in there—he never let me see—but it might be good for me to write about reclaiming Aecor. When I am queen and you are my top general, historians will read what I write here and our efforts will never be forgotten."

A pleased smile turned up the edges of his perpetual frown. "So you like it?"

"Yes." I took a chair and ink and found a pen and nib

that wasn't rusty. The curved end of the nib fitted into the holder perfectly. "I like it very much."

Patrick sat next to me, watching as I shook and then opened a jar of ink, tested the color and flow on a scrap paper, and wrote my name on the inside of the leather-bound notebook.

Property of Wilhelmina Korte, Princess of Aecor.

The following is an account of my return to my kingdom. It is real and true.

The sharp pen nib scraped the paper, making a pleasant scratch scratch *as I wrote the date and location. My pen strokes were slow, careful so that the black lines were an even thickness and had proper spacing, just as my tutor had taught me. In fact, the letters looked exactly like my tutor's.*

"You have nice handwriting."

Well, my tutor had nice handwriting. But I smiled anyway.

Patrick held open his hand for the pen, and I placed it in his palm. "Can you copy mine?" he asked.

"Let's see."

He dipped the pen in ink and wrote on a scrap paper.

I, Patrick Lien, son of General Brendon Lien, do hereby swear my life to helping Princess Wilhelmina Korte reclaim her kingdom, no matter the cost.

I blinked up at him.

"Go ahead." He slid the paper toward me. "Let's see what you can do."

Our writing was very different. Where mine was all elegant lines learned from a patient tutor, Patrick's penmanship was scratchier, with uneven lines, and he allowed letters to fade at the end of words when the ink ran low on the nib. The letters weren't the same height, and they didn't have a uniform roundness. Those were mistakes my tutor would have drilled out of him, but perhaps his didn't care, or his father wasn't interested in his studies.

"It's not as nice as yours." Patrick shifted away a hair.

I dipped my pen into the ink. "I wasn't thinking that. I was just studying the differences. But if you don't like your handwriting, maybe I can help you change it."

The motion was small, but he nodded. "I'd appreciate that."

I hid my smile behind a strand of hair as I began copying his words. It was tricky; my training made his scratchy lines difficult to emulate.

The rough paper caught a tine, and all the ink sluiced out of the pen, making a huge inkblot over Patrick's name.

I slammed the pen on the table and shouted a word I'd heard the older boys use.

"Wil!" Patrick's voice was sharp. "Not as a queen. Would your mother have ever had an outburst like that? Used that word? Over a pen?"

My mother wouldn't have lived in a freezing old castle, but I did. There wasn't another choice. But I shook my head because I didn't want Patrick to be angry with me.

"Try again."

I dipped the nib into the ink and began writing. This time, I focused more, letting the point glide lightly over the paper to avoid the rough patches. I rounded or narrowed my letters like Patrick's, noting which ones he tended to make the same way every time and which ones changed depending on where they were in the word. I caught myself refilling the pen where he'd have let the ink run out, though, so I pressed open the tines and let the black seep back into the bottle before completing the word.

Finished, I sat back to inspect my work.

"That's not bad." Patrick cocked his head. "Your lines are still more even than mine. See how mine taper at the tops and bottoms?"

I scowled. "You don't even do the same things regularly, though. See this g here? You don't curve the y descender the same way, even though they're both at the end of the word."

"That probably makes my handwriting easier to forge, since it's inconsistent."

"Oh. Hmm."

"Try again," he said. "Then we need to go out and train with the others. Our goals won't be easy to accomplish, Wilhelmina, and we won't get Aecor back this year, or even next year. But one day we will. One day you'll take your rightful place on the vermilion throne, and your parents will be so proud."

I muttered a thanks, not sure how to respond to such a heartfelt statement from Patrick, of all people.

When I finished the next attempt at copying his handwriting, he gave a sharp nod and minuscule smile. "You have a real talent for this," he said. "I'll make sure you have everything you need. Maybe I can even find a tutor."

I wanted to hug him, but he was Patrick; he didn't like hugs. Instead, I cleaned the nib, closed the bottle of ink, and said, "Thank you. I hope you know how much I appreciate you, and how happy I am that you're here with me."

He placed his palm on my shoulder, carefully, deliberately. "I'll always be with you, Wilhelmina."

FOUR

WE'D LEFT OUR disguises outside to accumulate mud and grime: Patrick and Oscar—who'd be playing the parts of our escorts—and Melanie and I hadn't bathed since our last trip to Skyvale, either. My skin felt slimy as I wiggled into my dress; my hair wasn't in much better shape, but I'd plaited it into a tight and complicated coronet that would hold up for days of travel.

Authenticity was the key to any deception.

Sometimes authenticity was disgusting.

After a quick rap on the door, Melanie walked in, wearing her dirty clothes. "Ready, Lady Julianna, Duchess of Liadia?" she asked, using an accent that thinned out her vowels. We'd learned it from refugees and had been practicing for weeks. She gave an exaggerated curtsy and giggled.

"Don't look too happy." I slipped the envelope with our papers into the side pocket of my bag, and hid my sheathed dagger inside my dress, at the small of my back. My other dagger, as far as I knew, was with Black Knife, assuming he'd taken it from that glowman's hand. "If Patrick sees you smiling, he'll send you to run laps around the castle until you're *not*."

"If it's a crime to be excited about our future of hot baths, plenty of food, and walks through winter gardens, then I'm definitely a criminal." She tugged at the sleeve of my dress, straightening it. "There. Don't you have a shawl somewhere?"

"Right." I picked up the tattered wool shawl and threw it over my shoulders. "Unfortunately, the war will interrupt our new life of luxury. When we march to Aecor, it will be all dirt, hunger, and walks through bloody battlefields. That's assuming we're not immediately discovered as impostors at the castle and sentenced to death." I winked so she'd know I wasn't scolding.

"Well, now I'm not smiling." She hitched her bag onto her shoulder and together we headed down to the bailey where Patrick and Oscar met us with grim nods.

Day broke at our backs, sending liquid light cascading into the valley ahead of us. Glass windows on the palace and mansions winked in the reflected sunlight.

"We'll walk all the way around," Patrick said. "So we appear to come from the west."

When at last we emerged from the woods on the western edge of Skyvale, the sun was directly overhead, and the famous mirrors were just beginning to reflect its glow.

"Refugees are saying they can see the mirrors' shine from across the valley," Melanie said. "That it leads them to safety. Some even say they can see it from across the western mountains, as far as the wraithland."

"That seems unlikely. The valley is huge, and Skyvale is

hidden behind the Midvale Ridge." The long mountain cut lengthwise through the northern half of the valley, splitting the path of the Indigo River in two. Skyvale huddled between the eastern side of the valley and the lower end of the Midvale Ridge, which looked as though someone had scooped off a chunk of the southern face.

"That's true, I guess."

"It's just a refugee story. They're almost never accurate." I kept my gaze ahead as we approached White Flag, the poorest, westernmost district of Skyvale. "No more out-of-character talking. We're refugees from Liadia. We've been through a great trauma and terrible journey."

Melanie's cheeks darkened, but she nodded. A few minutes later, we entered the refugee camp just outside the city wall.

It looked like every other camp, with people huddling inside dingy tents or under lean-tos. The stench of unwashed bodies permeated the air, along with rotting refuse. Chickens clucked and a pig hurtled across the road. A few children played, though their clapping and hopping games all bore a weary note. Under the tendrils of filthy hair, their cheeks were sunken in from hunger.

In the spirit of authenticity, Patrick and Oscar moved closer to Melanie and me, protecting us as we slipped through the noisy refugee camp.

Above us loomed a pair of guard towers, the dragon standards and Pierce family crests flying above the bright mirrors. Nervousness shuddered through me.

"This way, my lady." Patrick guided me to the gate and the soldier on duty. Sweat streaked his stubbled face as he slouched and spoke in a Liadian accent, "May I present Lady Julianna Whitman, Duchess of Liadia, and her companion, Lady Melanie Cole. My friend and I have traveled across the wraithland to bring them to the safety of Skyvale." Patrick dropped to one knee, head bowed low. His shoulders curled inward as Oscar knelt, too.

The guards eyed me, my dress, and the almost-empty bag I carried. "Do you have papers?" one asked from behind a heavy mustache.

My bag slipped from my shaking hand and landed with a shallow *whump*. "Y-yes." Trembling all over, I started to retrieve the leather envelope with our forged papers, but Melanie touched my shoulder.

"I'll get them." She spoke gently and, although she appeared as exhausted as I, she knelt and drew the envelope from a side pocket.

The guards glanced over the papers, held them up to the light to check the watermark, and slipped them back into the envelope. "You ladies are welcome to enter Skyvale. We'll send for a carriage. I'm afraid the two of you . . ." His mustache twitched at Patrick and Oscar.

Patrick and Oscar glanced at each other, my supposed loyal escorts. "We'd like to wait until the carriage comes," Patrick said. "Just to make sure. We've seen our ladies this far."

Mustache Guard considered a moment, then nodded. "Very well."

The second guard ran for chairs for Melanie and me, then sent a message up to the top of the guard tower to signal for a carriage.

Seated and pretending I was trying not to slouch, I watched a trio of boys racing through the camp. Two in front carried battered sacks that leaked pebbles, while the third wore a black mask and threatened to bring his friends to justice.

Mustache Guard followed my gaze. "They're playing Black Knife."

"What is that?" I asked, though I knew the answer.

"Black Knife is a vigilante," he said, pointing to a tattered poster that offered a hefty bounty for the menace. "We try to discourage Skyvale children from this game, but we aren't allowed to do much with the refugees."

Besides keep them out of the city, of course.

"And this Black Knife does what?" I made obvious glances between the bounty poster and the children.

"He catches thieves, glowmen, and flashers. He's been at it for about two years, since the Hensley scandal."

"It sounds like he's doing good work. Shouldn't you send a thank-you note?"

Mustache Guard shook his head. "Some think so, but no one is allowed to subvert justice. If he wants to stop flashers, he needs to join the police."

"So you hunt for him?"

The guard nodded. "When we can, or whenever there's a rash of mimics. Skyvale is so big that we usually have to focus our attention elsewhere. But don't worry: Black Knife is almost never spotted in the districts where you'll be staying."

"Thank you." Maybe *I* could catch *him*—once I infiltrated the palace, found the resistance fighters in Aecor, rescued the Aecorian men in the wraithlands, and took back my kingdom.

Or maybe somewhere in between all of that. The reward was sizable, and the coming war would have to be funded somehow.

I turned my attention toward Skyvale, watching for the carriage.

We didn't wait long. Once the carriage arrived, indigo with the Pierce crest emblazoned on the side, Melanie and I made a show of thanking Patrick and Oscar for their kindness and assistance.

"This way, my ladies." The soldiers helped us into the carriage and stowed our bags on the opposite bench. "You're being taken to an immediate audience with King Terrell and Crown Prince Tobiah. Tell them your story. The driver will give your papers to the secretary. They'll know what to do with you."

Tobiah.

"Thank you." Melanie slumped into the cushions as the carriage door shut and latched. In the dimness, she gave me a secret smile. "We're really doing this." Her voice was low and didn't carry.

I tried to smile back, but my thoughts whirred.

I was going to see Tobiah. Of course it was inevitable. The mission called for me to live in the palace, the same one where the crown prince lived. But seeing him this soon? *Immediately?*

He'd be eighteen by now, learning from his father. It made sense he'd be there. After ten years, would he recognize me? Surely not.

"Ew." Melanie wrinkled her nose as one of White Flag's more pungent odors pressed through the carriage, even with the heavy wool curtains closed. The clatter of wheels and horse hooves beat a headache behind my eyes, and nothing, not even the throbbing in my head, covered the din of shouts and people banging on pots or walls or one another.

What was I getting into? This had seemed like a good idea months ago when Patrick announced it. Now—now I was going to have to face the man who'd destroyed my kingdom, and the boy who was the reason.

Gradually, the sounds and smells shifted to boys calling out the latest wraith news and Black Knife sightings, and meats roasting and bread baking. My stomach growled; we'd eaten a small breakfast, but hadn't paused for lunch or even a snack on the way here.

Even so, I'd had more than those refugees outside the city.

"We must be getting into Thornton," Melanie said.

"Need anything while we're here?" It was a weak joke. Thornton was the high-class district of Skyvale with several sizable markets, and where we did most of our work. The Flags—Black Flag, White Flag, and Red Flag—were easier and less guarded, but it seemed impolite to steal from other poor people.

Several minutes later, a shadow fell over the windows and the carriage stopped. We'd reached the enormous wall separating Hawksbill and the King's Seat from the rest of the city. After a few moments of men's voices at the driver's box, a guard swung open the door.

My stomach dropped. They'd caught us already.

But the guard only checked inside our bags and underneath the benches, then ducked out, all without saying a word. My head buzzed with uncomfortable energy, and the dagger at my back pressed hard into my spine.

With a rattle, the carriage burst into motion once more. Voices of servants and nobles and guards calling cadence rose above the noise of our vehicle. Cathedral bells pealed in the distance. Every moment brought us closer to Skyvale Palace.

We'd meet King Terrell.

I'd see the prince.

"Are you all right?" Melanie touched my arm. "You look nervous."

I twitched a smile. "I do not."

"Only to your best friend." She kept her voice low. "What's wrong?"

I couldn't tell her the whole truth, but she deserved something. "This mission is so important. We need people in Aecor to fight for us when we return. If we can't find the resistance groups, or we can't protect them—"

"I understand." Melanie kept my gaze for a moment. "We'll do this. We've been training and studying for months. We're as prepared as we can be."

"It's the things we aren't prepared for that I'm worried about."

"Say it again," she muttered.

Shortly, we were deposited at a side entrance to the palace. "So no one gawks at you before you've had time to adjust," explained the driver, all haste to soothe potential offense. He passed us off to a valet, who clutched the envelope with our residency documents, and not very carefully. All our hard work, crushed beneath clumsy hands.

I maintained an expression between weary refugee, aloof nobility, and awe for the palace's magnificence.

And it *was* a magnificent palace, with gilded friezes and

marbled floors. Heavy rugs ran the length of the hall, all blue and gold and patterned with geometric figures. Copper-and-glass oil lamps hung on the walls every several paces. The palace would never be dark.

Uniformed men kept guard over staterooms and studies, while a handful of lords and ladies made their way through the palace. Some glanced at us, but most hardly seemed to notice our presence.

Even indoors where they'd do no good against the wraith, there were glass mirrors on every west-facing surface. We turned a corner and I caught my reflection. My face was thin and hard, smudged with dirt and sweat. The coronet I'd braided my hair into was oily and dusty. Brown strands hung loose in places, as though I'd been running. Melanie, with her pale brown skin and black hair, looked the same. We looked horrible, and hungry.

We looked like refugees.

"This way, Lady Julianna, Lady Melanie." The valet gestured toward a heavy oak door, which stood open for our arrival. "His Majesty and His Highness will see you now."

"Thank you." My voice came out raspier than I'd realized it might. Nerves crowded in my throat, and my whole body was shaking.

In moments, I'd see the man who was responsible for my parents' deaths. For my kingdom's destruction. For my stolen childhood.

In moments, I'd be in the same room with the man I hated most in the world, and I'd have to pretend he was my rescuer.

When the herald announced us, Melanie and I entered the king's office.

The room was well lit with the windows thrown wide. Four men with Indigo Order uniforms stood around the perimeter, their expressions blank. Bodyguards. A middle-aged man in blue livery sat in the corner, writing at a tiny desk.

The king sat behind a massive desk, and a young man stood beside him.

My breath caught. Tobiah.

"This way," said the valet, beckoning us toward the crowded end of the room. He handed our papers to the secretary, and then exited.

The herald cleared his throat. "His Majesty Terrell Pierce the Fourth, House of the Dragon, Sovereign of the Indigo Kingdom, and his son, Crown Prince Tobiah Pierce, House of the Dragon, Heir to the Indigo Kingdom."

My feet moved. I walked. But I couldn't look away from Tobiah. His eyes were lowered toward something on his father's desk. He kept his hands behind his back as he nodded and murmured, and then both the prince and his father looked up.

King Terrell's smile flashed in my peripheral vision, but it was Tobiah's dark gaze that held me.

He cocked his head and glanced from me to Melanie and back. There was something in his eyes—surely not recognition. It had been almost ten years since the One-Night War, and I was a different person now.

The crown prince said nothing, though, offering only a slight nod and cautious smile.

He had no idea who I was. No idea that—because of him—my life was in ruins. And here he was with his palace and father and perfect life. Like the One-Night War had never happened.

I pushed down those thoughts. I needed to work.

"Forgive me for not standing to greet you." King Terrell motioned to a pair of chairs in front of his desk. "Please sit. You must be exhausted."

"Thank you, Your Majesty." The words slipped from me without thought, as though I'd never left my own father's palace. My childhood of court manners hadn't disappeared, even after ten years.

Servants held the cushioned chairs for us, then vanished.

"Lady Julianna. Lady Melanie." King Terrell offered a grim smile. "I'm sorry that you've been forced from your home, and that there was nothing more the Indigo Kingdom could do for Liadia. But I rejoice in your presence here. We'd been informed that there were no more survivors. I couldn't be more glad for incorrect intelligence."

We both thanked him again.

"Tell me," said the crown prince. "Why did no one in Liadia evacuate? Everyone knew the wraith was coming, surely."

Was that a test? Could he suspect?

I repeated the information I'd learned from refugees. "Of course everyone knew that the wraith was coming." I bit back more venom. A little indignity at his question would be natural for Julianna, but lashing out at Tobiah was unwise. I softened my tone. "Of course everyone knew. For months before the wraith arrived, the weather grew more intense. Winter was colder. Summer was hotter. On clear nights, we could see the glow of wraith on the western horizon."

The room was so, so quiet.

"We knew it was coming. And so, the royal scholars and

49

philosophers studied and tested and worked until they announced they had found a way to protect the kingdom. Because he trusted their efforts, His Majesty promised safety for the kingdom, but many didn't believe. They left anyway, so martial law was declared, and borders were closed to keep more people from fleeing." I let my voice sink. "As you already know, the barrier erected did little to halt the wraith."

Seconds ticked by on the large clock on the king's desk, and the prince gazed downward, studying his father. I urged myself to sink deeper into the Julianna Whitman persona. I'd been over her stories. I'd practiced her mannerisms. Wilhelmina Korte's feelings didn't matter right now.

"Is there anything else you can tell me about your journey here?" King Terrell's voice was weak. Raspy. "An account of the state of the wraithland would be useful in our own efforts to mitigate its effects."

I tore my gaze from the prince and focused on his father. Both men were tall and slender, with dark hair and eyes, but the similarities ended there.

The king's face was sunken in, and dark hollows had carved permanent places around his eyes. He was too young to have such wrinkles.

King Terrell was sick, probably had been sick for some time. And he wasn't getting better.

The prince stayed close to his father's side, his hands clasped behind his back. He looked . . . resigned.

This man—this king who'd stolen not just my land, but my parents and childhood as well—was dying. Emotions thundered up inside of me: anger and disgust and a faint sort of satisfaction.

He had destroyed everything I loved. Now, he was finally getting what he deserved.

Melanie touched my arm. A subtle reminder that still looked as though she was comforting me.

"I understand how important your wraith mitigation efforts are." As I began my tale, a pair of servants moved a small table next to me and poured glasses of pale wine. A plate of crackers and cheeses appeared, as well, and at the king's encouraging nod, we ate. "At first it seemed like the barrier might work. There'd been testing, of course, and we were told that there were pockets of unaffected land in the wraithland, thanks to smaller experimental barriers. When the wraith reached Liadia, it seemed the barrier was going to work."

"I remember the announcement," said King Terrell.

"It was almost a year before the barrier fell. Half the kingdom was flooded with wraith overnight. The beasts attacked. The air was—it was—" I drew a shuddering breath and slumped, allowing the Pierces to witness a moment of unguarded weakness.

Melanie reached for my hands. Everyone's expressions softened.

"Forgive me," I whispered, dropping my gaze to my knees. "Everything happened so quickly. So many people were killed. Even our own guards. If not for the help of two men from the kennels, we'd have perished as well." I lowered my eyes, letting my expression fall still and grave. It was easy to show grief; all I had to do was think of my parents slaughtered in a courtyard.

"The air glowed in some places," Melanie said. "It was difficult to breathe. Every night we heard howling, and other noises. Trees had been turned upside down, and buildings were filled with something solid; everything inside was trapped, like insects in amber. People trapped inside—" Her voice broke. "I'm sorry. I can't. It's too awful."

"Father." Tobiah's hand rested on his father's shoulder, and he spoke with a note of tenderness. "These ladies come to us in need of aid. We must provide."

King Terrell reached around and patted Tobiah's hand, and the difference between them was striking. One was strong and whole, while the other was only a wasted memory of a hand, with veins and tendons protruding. "You're right, son. Lady Julianna, Lady Melanie, you're both welcome in Skyvale Palace for as long as you'd like to stay. Our home is your home."

I permitted myself the tiniest of smiles, disguised as relief and gratitude. This was it: the beginning of victory.

FIVE

WE WEREN'T TWO steps out the office door when a tall brunette and slim blonde stopped us, a duckling trail of maids at their heels.

The ladies were not much older than Melanie and me, but the brunette held herself as though she owned the palace. Her air of assurance faltered only a breath as she glanced from Melanie to me and back.

It was the blonde who spoke first, her voice warm and welcoming. "You must be the two Liadian ladies who just arrived."

The servant escorting us stepped in to make introductions. "Lady Julianna Whitman, Lady Melanie Cole, this is Lady Meredith Corcoran, House of the Unicorn, Duchess of Lakeside, and Lady Chey Chuter, House of the Sea, Countess of Two Rivers City."

"Pleased to meet you." I performed a quick curtsy, and Melanie followed. "Thank you for your kind welcome."

Lady Meredith, the blonde, stepped forward and took one of my hands in both of hers. "The pleasure is ours. We're just so happy you were able to make it here."

A cloyingly sweet scent, like honeysuckle, enveloped me as Lady Chey moved next to her friend and took in our dirty, weary appearances. "When we heard two Liadian ladies had arrived at the gates, I couldn't believe it. Lady Julianna Whitman. Your presence is indeed welcome here."

Lady Meredith cast a guileless smile. "You'll have to attend tomorrow night's ball, of course."

Surprise flitted across Lady Chey's face, but she concealed it quickly. "Of course, Your Grace. I will make arrangements. It will be good for you to meet new people, especially if you're going to be staying in Skyvale Palace. Do you have gowns?"

I glanced pointedly at my limp bag and the filthy dress I wore. Did it *look* like we'd brought ball gowns?

Lady Meredith gasped. "Look at them. They've been through a horrible ordeal, Chey. Why would you even ask if they brought gowns?"

"Oh." Lady Chey touched her lips. "I suppose they have nothing at all."

Fantasies tickled the back of my mind: I could make her perfume come to life and suffocate her, or ask her dress to coil around her and constrict until she couldn't breathe. Anything to make her stop talking.

"We'll send a pair of gowns to your quarters," Lady Chey said after a moment. "I think we're all about the same size."

"Thank you." I pretended not to notice her curves, or the way her emerald dress was cinched to display her cleavage. Years of hard work and hunger had kept both Melanie and me from developing much in the way of feminine figures. We could—and frequently did—pass as boys. "I appreciate your generosity."

"It's my engagement ball. It would mean so much to me if you would join in the celebration." Lady Meredith squeezed my hand and released me.

"We'd be delighted to attend," Melanie said. "All our congratulations on your engagement."

Lady Meredith practically glowed as she and Lady Chey offered slight curtsies before turning down the hall, their maids in tow. "We'll find a russet for Julianna. It will match her eyes. And perhaps a teal for her friend . . ."

Melanie and I exchanged pleased smiles as our guide beckoned us farther into the palace.

We didn't have to hide the way we gazed around the palace, but if our expressions were wonder filled, it was by design only. I noted statues large enough to conceal me, and ventilation grates where supplies could be hidden. I kept track of my steps and every turn we took until finally the servant produced a key and opened a heavy oak door.

"These will be your apartments," the man said. "Traditionally, they were kept as quarters for visiting Liadian royalty. We thought it fitting that you receive them now."

I didn't respond, just slipped into the large sitting room to get a good look at the silk-covered sofas and chairs, the lace draped across tables, and a half-dozen full bookcases. There were paintings of people and places, but nothing familiar.

"All the furniture was carved from trees cut from the surrounding forest, primarily. The wood panels on the walls are chestnut, like the rest of the palace." He went on, naming every-one in the portraits and passing along any gossip he knew first- or second- or thirdhand. "Here is the larger bedchamber where the duchess will sleep. The fireplace, you might have noticed, has no back, so the fire can throw its heat into both the sitting room and the master bedroom. For privacy in the summer, there's a lever that will lower a blind."

He guided us through the washroom and Melanie's room. Everything was more spacious and grand than I could have hoped. During our tour, a small army of maids invaded with towels, robes, and baskets of soaps and other toiletries. Skyvale Palace had real plumbing and had been fitted with gas lamps in every room.

"Skyvale Palace is a little over two hundred years old—pre-wraith, like most of the homes inside the Hawksbill wall—which means it was originally built and run using magic. In the last hundred years, we've significantly refined the methods of run-ning the palace using new scientific advancements and modern technology, and we also make use of systems that previously used magic." He finished showing us all the wonders of the palace, and finally left us alone.

I unbraided my hair and indulged in the most delicious bath of my life, lingering until the water grew cold, and then put on a long silver dress to explore while Melanie took her turn.

There were five windows, two of which were actually doors and led to a small balcony; one of those doors was in my room. Thoughtfully, Melanie had already hung our red ribbon in the window: the signal to the other Ospreys that we'd succeeded in installing ourselves in the palace.

I stepped outside and leaned over the edge of the balcony. The air was crisp with an autumn breeze and the scent of turning leaves and the clatter of horse-drawn carriages down wide avenues splashed with red and gold. The private district for Skyvale's nobility, all wealth and extravagance.

Among the autumn foliage, indigo-coated guardsmen walked the perimeter of the grounds. Two men passed the base of the wide staircase, near the entrance gate.

From here, Skyvale was beautiful. The immense wall surrounding Hawksbill blocked most of the view of the other districts: Greenstone, Thornton, and the Flags. From here, the city had no poor, no refugees, no flashers being taken off the streets.

No children living in a forgotten castle in the mountains.

No deadly wraith rushing eastward.

All that could be seen was beauty, prosperity, and people who'd never known anything beyond their own privilege. Children ran under the white cascade of a fountain far below. Their laughter floated upward.

"This is certainly a nice change from the old palace." Melanie stood in my doorway, wrapped in towels and a robe.

"More dangerous." I nodded toward her room. "Get dressed. Dinner should arrive soon, and we've got work to do."

She snapped and thumped her chest, the Ospreys' salute, and vanished into the other room.

After a maid dropped off a heavy crock of soup and a loaf of fresh bread, Melanie and I settled around the table in the sitting room. We devoured the soup within five minutes, and only when we were halfway through the bread did we slow down. Eating was a competition in the old palace, where the slowest often nursed growling stomachs.

The desk in my bedroom had been stocked with pens and ink and palace stationery, so we positioned a few sheets side by side and started with a long rectangle, a huge rounded bulge at the back.

"This is the palace." I drew two perpendicular lines for the exterior doors we knew about, including the one we'd entered through. "And the king's office was . . ." My pen nib hovered over the eastern end of the palace. "Here?"

"Yes." Melanie broke off a piece of bread and chewed. "And that's us." She tapped the western front.

I marked both locations. "What else?"

"There was a glass building near the office, too. I saw it out the window."

I'd missed it, but I drew a glass house where she pointed. "The king is ill," I said, adding outlines of the front gardens and court-yards. A circle and spray for the fountain, an immense staircase, and a scattering of statues: I added everything I remembered.

"Yes. Looks like he has been for a while, but I haven't heard much talk about it. Have you?"

"Nothing." Which seemed strange, but perhaps his decline had been so gradual no one noticed. Perhaps they thought he was simply growing old.

"This is a good start on the map."

I corked the ink and wiped the nib clean using a damp cloth. "There's a long way to go, but it's unlikely we'll find palace plans just lying around. We'll take a walk tomorrow and get a better sense of the layout."

"And then that ball. Perhaps Tobiah will be there." Melanie smiled slyly as she placed our dishes on a tray. "I saw the way he watched you."

So I hadn't imagined his look.

He *hadn't* recognized me. He couldn't have. As far as Tobiah knew, Princess Wilhelmina Korte had vanished years ago. It was unlikely he'd ever thought of me since that night. Perhaps he'd thought me familiar and was trying to place me. I'd just have to give him every reason to believe I was only Lady Julianna Whitman, a duchess from a wraith-fallen kingdom.

I wished I could avoid him altogether.

"I'm sure he will be at the ball. Quinn would be so jealous."

"It's strange that Chey is hosting Meredith's engagement ball," I said.

"Why? They seem to be friends."

I laid the mapping pens back in the writing box and found one more suitable for writing letters. "But Chey is only a countess. Maybe Meredith is marrying down and it's embarrassing."

Melanie snorted. "Regardless, they're our way into society. *Try* to be polite."

"I'm always polite."

"You're always eyeing people's valuables. That's hardly polite."

As evening fell, our discussion moved toward the contents of our first written report to Patrick, and the possible routes we'd take to the bakery, now that we knew our position in the palace.

There wasn't much to write, but we added a few lines about our treatment so far, the upcoming ball, and the king's deteriorating health.

"It seems like a pointless risk to send a report on the first night." I fanned the paper, giving the ink a moment to dry before I folded it in thirds.

"I agree, but Patrick insists. A report every three days or he storms the palace because he thinks we've been discovered." Melanie rolled her eyes and dipped a blot of blue wax onto the edge. I pressed my thumb into the cooling blob, sealing the report with my print. Not that it would look any different from Melanie's, but again, Patrick insisted, and I didn't care enough to fight about it.

"I should go the first few times." Melanie laid her fingertips on the edge of the report. "My absence will be less suspicious if someone comes looking for you."

My hand was still on the letter. "This is a stupid risk."

"But you'll let me do it?" She raised an eyebrow.

I released the paper, and as soon as lights began vanishing across the city, she slipped out the window.

The next day, Melanie didn't emerge from her bedroom until noon. So much for taking a walk through the palace to expand our map. "You were out late last night," I said, not lowering the book I'd been reading. *The Fall of Magic in the Indigo Kingdom* had kept me company most of the morning.

"Just long enough to stick the report behind the loose brick, as ordered. Patrick left a few items for us: spare ropes and hooks, dark clothes, and a few small knives. I've hidden all the things that need hiding." She sat at the table where lunch had already cooled and began filling her plate with bread and slices of chicken and ham and cheese. "You were sleeping when I got back."

But I'd waited for two hours before I stepped onto the balcony, worrying that maybe I should go after her. We'd worked in the city countless times, though mostly together. So what could have kept her?

I could still feel the glass chill my palm as I pushed open the balcony door, still feel the frigid wind as I scanned the courtyards and gardens for signs of Melanie.

Just as I was about to climb over the balcony rail and hunt for her, a shadow on a lower balcony stayed me. Someone else had been staring down at the city. With the streetlamps below, the figure was only a silhouette.

But he'd looked up, right at me.

Shivering, I'd lifted my hand. He'd waved back, then leaned his hips on the balcony rail and watched the city.

I'd come inside. Maybe Melanie hadn't been able to get back in because of him, either.

"Did you see someone on another balcony last night?" I asked.

Melanie was chewing, but she shook her head. After an exaggerated swallow, she gulped down some wine and said, "No, everything was quiet. I didn't even see your friend Black Knife."

"You know you're my only friend."

"I'm sure you say that to all the Ospreys."

My grin disappeared when someone knocked on the door. I stood to answer, but Melanie was faster.

Unease smoldered in the back of my thoughts as a maid bustled in, carrying long, paper-wrapped parcels and a wooden box. "Lady Meredith sends her regards, along with these gowns for tonight's ball. We'll have to alter them quickly to fit you, but we'll make do. Lady Chey ordered a carriage for you; it will arrive with the others this evening."

"A carriage? Where is the ball?" I pressed my eyebrows together, as though uncertain of being taken from the palace already. Attending a ball seemed like expecting a lot of two young women who'd just been through tragedy, but Melanie and I needed the introduction into society. We'd simply have to work harder to maintain our story.

"It'll be at the Chuter mansion, my lady. The family has a home in Hawksbill, like many lords and ladies. They stay in the palace only rarely, though most keep rooms here."

This was good. It meant we'd see more of Hawksbill from ground level. Without having to hide or pretend we were maids, like we usually did.

The afternoon passed quickly as we tried on the gowns and held still while the cloth was pinned. A seamstress came in to make quick alterations while the maid busied herself with our hair and cosmetics and jewelry.

At last, the transformation was complete. I wore deep russet and silver, with a silver teardrop pendant hanging just below my collarbone. The maid had pulled my hair back into an intricate braid, revealing rather severe cheekbones, which she softened with rose powder.

When they stepped away and I finally saw myself in the mirror, it showed what I might have been if I'd grown up in Aecor: a princess.

SIX

THE CARRIAGES ARRIVED as the sun slipped into the west, lighting the city's mirrors with orange flame.

Melanie and I waited in the front hall with handfuls of others, everyone clothed in their most elegant attire. Men strode around in their tailcoats, looking impatient. Ladies glanced at mirrors to make last-minute adjustments to their coiled braids or shimmering gowns. Finally, guards hauled open the heavy glass doors and nobles poured outside, into the waiting carriages.

"This one is yours." A valet led us toward a white carriage at the end of the line, a silver cresting wave painted onto the door: the sigil for House of the Sea.

I tipped up my chin and stepped into the carriage, not bothering with his offered hand. Once Melanie was inside, the door shut and ours followed the other carriages down the palace drive and into Hawksbill.

We drove by columned mansions with intricate reliefs carved into the stone, and long, winding drives bordered by generous gardens and fountains. Roses and ivy hung on iron trellises, and flags bearing house sigils fluttered in the breeze. Dragon. Sea. Unicorn. Sun.

The caravan of carriages turned along the winding streets, and reflected sunlight shone straight through our window, forcing us to close the curtains or go blind. For the moment, we were alone. "We're still reeling from our trek through the wraithland," I said, even though Melanie didn't need the reminder. The *clip-clop* of horse hooves covered my voice.

Melanie nodded. "But we're trying to fit in like nothing's wrong. We don't want to talk about our experiences. We don't even want to talk about home. We're afraid if we do, we'll show weakness."

"Perfect. We'll remain the enigmatic beauties of the evening." I held my face straight for a heartbeat, until Melanie cracked a smile and we both fought off a fit of giggles.

It wasn't a long trip; it'd have been quicker to walk than wait in the carriage line for ours to reach the front door, but walking would have been unseemly. Practicality almost always was.

But when the door opened, the vision of lights was worth the wait.

The Chuter mansion boasted a dozen columns carved from marble, each with a sprinkling of tiny mirrors, which threw off the sun's light. Cold torches waited for dusk, still over an hour away, but the buzzing of crickets already filled the air.

Wind breathed through the surrounding gardens and trees, spurring me to follow the others as they entered the mansion.

The whole place reeked of opulence, and so did Chey's guests. No one stopped to look or admire, like such a display of wealth was an everyday occurrence.

It was for them. Melanie and I were the only ones trying not to gape as we hurried after everyone.

"I didn't see Tobiah," she muttered as we entered the mansion.

Good. "Maybe he wasn't invited. Or didn't want to come. I heard he refuses to attend most social events." Warring scents of rose and honeysuckle filled the mansion's front hall, making my head spin.

"The dining hall is through here." A footman gestured to the left, his tone holding all the enthusiasm of having said those exact words five thousand times tonight; we were among the last to arrive.

One of the house staff led us through the dining hall, resplendent with crystal chandeliers and glossy wood panels along the walls. A string quartet sat in the corner, their music nearly drowned out by the several dozen guests talking.

"Here are your seats." The footman pulled out two chairs at the lower end of the table, next to a handful of men in military uniforms.

A surge of disgust made my face hot.

I saw soldiers of the Indigo Army every time I came to Skyvale, but I'd never been forced to share a meal with men who might have been there during the One-Night War. With men who might have murdered citizens of Aecor City, high nobility, and my parents.

Focusing on calming breaths, I accepted the cushioned chair and arranged the russet gown over my lap.

"Oh, thank saints." A young man wearing the uniform of

the Indigo Order offered a wide smile. His hair was short, in the style of most soldiers, but the top buttons of his jacket were undone, as though he hated even that much confinement.

He was too young to have fought in Aecor. Maybe he'd be all right.

"I was afraid I'd be alone with these old men all evening." He motioned at the four other men surrounding us, who all grumbled good-naturedly. "I'm Lieutenant James Rayner. The old men are Clint, Ethan, Eric, and Bryce. They all have ranks more impressive than mine, so I'll just skip over those, if that's all right with you. I do, however, have the distinction of being Crown Prince Tobiah's principal bodyguard."

Maybe he wasn't all right, after all.

But the last bit of information snapped him into my memory; he'd been in the king's office yesterday. "I'm pleased to meet all of you. I'm Julianna Whitman. And this is my companion, Melanie Cole."

"I remember. My most heartfelt condolences for the loss you've both suffered." James offered a deep nod, almost a bow. "I, too, know the pain of losing someone close."

Rayner. That was the queen's maiden name, which made James Tobiah's cousin. If I recalled, there was a scandal around James's birth, which was why he carried his mother's name, rather than his mysterious father's. Later on, his mother had married a prominent lord, but he'd died in a fire at the Rayner family home; that must have been the loss James spoke of.

"It seems you've had no trouble securing places in society," said one of the other soldiers. He looked about the king's age, though he wore the years with more grace. It was entirely possible he'd been in Aecor ten years ago. Any of the four older men, actually. They all wore medals on their jackets, but I couldn't tell what they represented.

My stomach turned over, but I managed to say, "Thank you." I wanted to make the tablecloth slither alive and hurl dinnerware at the soldiers. I wanted to instruct forks and knives to—

Melanie reached for my hand under the table, and squeezed. "We're fortunate for Lady Meredith's and Lady Chey's consideration. We don't know anyone here, but we're eager to make friends."

"I don't think that will be a problem for either of you." The soldier smiled easily.

"Lady Meredith said this is an engagement ball. Who is her fiancé?" she asked.

Everyone swung his head around, eyebrows lifted and mouth slightly agape. "You don't know?" James looked incredulous.

Melanie paled slightly. "Unfortunately, our invitation came only minutes after we arrived, and we weren't informed of any details." She shot a glance toward the head of the table, where Lady Meredith sat. "I suppose we'll find out soon, won't we?"

At her easy, palpable charm, the men seemed to relax. "That you will, my lady."

"We're also eager to see the whole palace and the parks behind it. If only we could find someone willing to give us a tour or two."

James grinned. "Well then, you've been seated with the right people. If I'm ever given a day off duty, I will beg for your company."

"Aren't you off duty now?" she asked.

James gestured toward the head of the table. "At events like this, I'm not important enough to sit by the crown prince, but I can see him from here. If anyone threatens him, I'll just cut down everyone between us. I'm not worried." He winked as though it had been a joke, but there was a hardness to his expression that revealed otherwise.

"We'll be sure to stay out of your way, in that case."

So the prince was present after all. I glanced in his direction and saw the distracted, sullen expression of someone who didn't want to be here. He sat between Lady Meredith and his father, who looked very gray this evening. The queen sat on the other side of the king, her face turned away from me.

James caught the prince's bored look, too, and flashed an awkward smile at me. In a low voice, as though sharing a secret, he said, "His Highness doesn't usually come to balls and parties. He'll make an appearance when he must, like tonight, but often he spends his evenings alone with his father." James cast another look toward the crown prince and shrugged. "His preference for staying in gives me plenty of nights off, but it is good for him to be out in society."

"Ah, the scandal there would be if he'd skipped *this* event!" Clint chuckled to himself.

Why should I feel sorry for him, even if he was watching his father die a lingering death? By my count, he'd had nine years more with his father than I had with mine. And he would get to say good-bye.

I shook the thoughts away—I was Julianna tonight, not Wilhelmina—and let myself be pulled back into James's company as he indulged Melanie and me with the names and ranks and current gossip of everyone at the table.

This, if nothing else, was an excellent time to study my enemy.

A glass clinked at the head of the table, and Lady Chey rose to her feet; a servant spirited her chair back, out of her way. She smoothed her elegant lavender gown, with finely cut diamonds arranged in an elaborately stylized wave that crested on the bodice, which accented all her best feminine qualities.

"Thank you all for joining me this evening." At Chey's greeting, the remaining murmurs faded and the quartet played a soft chord before lowering their instruments. "I hope we've all had opportunities to catch up with old friends and make some new ones." She glanced at me, eyebrow lifted in falsely sweet acknowledgment.

It took all my self-restraint not to flip my little finger at her.

"Tonight, we're here to celebrate the engagement of two people who I admire greatly, and who are some of my closest friends." She made a welcoming gesture toward Crown Prince Tobiah and the young woman sitting next to him. "His Royal Highness Tobiah Pierce, and Lady Meredith Corcoran, Duchess of Lakeside."

The prince smiled politely, though he managed to make it look gloomy. Lady Meredith was radiant as she gazed up at her fiancé.

Well. *That* was bound to be a loving marriage with no problems whatsoever.

Lady Chey continued with her speech, mostly recounting all the time she and Meredith spent together, and how privileged she was to host their engagement ball thanks to this close friendship. A few of the guests began shifting in their seats, and a woman—her mother, perhaps—glared pointedly, a clear signal for Chey to stop talking.

Finally, the first course was announced and served. After the blessing, everyone began picking at the crab puffs, and it was all I could do not to shovel the food into my mouth as quickly as possible.

Melanie moved just as stiffly as she speared a puff, and soon the conversation turned toward favorite dishes and desserts. James and his friends kept up a steady chatter, which allowed Melanie and me the space to observe them, as well as the rest of the guests.

A few people flashed us curious looks, but I didn't acknowledge the accompanying whispers of gossip as the meal progressed into the second and third and fourth courses.

I had to stop myself from eating everything, or risk revealing my real life as an orphan, but I hated myself for wasting food. While I ate more than my fill in here, children in the Flags went hungry tonight. Knowing that, how could I enjoy the meal?

The music stopped a little while later; the players took their instruments and quit the room, which seemed to be a signal.

At the head of the table, Lady Chey stood again and tapped her glass. Everyone quieted. She and several others delivered speeches congratulating Tobiah and Meredith, wishing the best for the Indigo Kingdom, and hinting there should be no fewer than a dozen children after the wedding. Even the king managed to say something, though he remained seated for his part.

"The night is not over," Lady Chey said. "If you'll proceed into the Crystal Room, the orchestra should be finished preparing for dancing."

Several people clapped and began rising. My companions all finished their glasses of wine before standing. James offered his arm. "Allow me to escort a beautiful lady?"

I reminded myself he was too young to have been part of the One-Night War.

"Thank you." I placed my gloved hand on his forearm. Now that dinner was over and the men were tipsy, Melanie and I would separate and begin asking more probing questions.

"May I beg the first dance?" James guided me from the dining hall, after the others.

"I'd be honored. I should warn you, though: I'm a terrible dancer."

"I don't believe it. Surely, you're too modest."

There was no modesty about it. I'd learned a few dances as a child, and every Osprey had received instruction over the last several years, but we'd had little opportunity to practice. But I just smiled at James and allowed him to lead me onto the dance floor where several other couples were already arranged.

As its name implied, the Crystal Room glittered from floor to ceiling, though most of the crystals were actually just glass and mirrors. There was plenty of space for all of us, but the reflections made the room seem bigger. The orchestra had set up in a small balcony overhead, so when the music began, it soared above the crowd.

"If you're as terrible a dancer as you claim"—James drew me into the line of flushed-faced nobles—"then please just follow my lead. I'm a fantastic dancer."

"If that's true, it seems I'm doomed to embarrass myself." But in the first few measures of music, he proved himself correct. James held his frame tall, but relaxed and comfortable with the movements. The music carried us along as we spun through the room.

"So." James held my gaze as we stepped close, then far. His eyes were brown, as warm as his smile, but sharp with wariness. Readiness. Though it was true he wasn't old enough to have been part of the One-Night War, he'd seen other battles.

"Yes?" I'd have to be careful around this one.

"What do you want to know about Prince Tobiah?"

I lifted an eyebrow. "I didn't ask about him."

"Not aloud. But I saw you looking yesterday."

"Oh." He thought I was interested in Tobiah? A sour boy with a perfect life he couldn't even see? Well, as long as the prince's bodyguard thought I *liked* the prince it was better than knowing I'd been imagining punching that sullen prince in his sullen face. "I wasn't well yesterday. I was exhausted and dizzy from the journey here, and His Highness just looked so familiar. It was rude to stare. Forgive me."

"Ah." James stepped closer, his palm slipping over my upper arm. "I'm sorry. I shouldn't tease you."

I let my expression turn soft, forgiving. "I'd rather be treated like you'd treat any other young lady. I do not want to forever be the sad duchess from a fallen kingdom, too fragile to befriend or tease. That's why Melanie and I came here tonight: to show that we won't allow our tragedy to define the rest of our lives. The pain of what happened—it won't last for eternity."

A lie. I knew very well how pain could last, and fester, and shape a person in unnameable ways.

But James squeezed my arm. "Tobiah's miniature was sent to many families a couple of years ago, including some in Liadia. Perhaps your family received one."

"I wasn't yet out, so probably not, but I must have had an older cousin or friend who received one." I shivered. "Details like that are hazy now, like they're filled with wraith."

"It's all right." James's voice was soft and comforting, and if I'd been the real Lady Julianna, I might have fallen for him right there.

"So." I made my voice a little husky. "You were concerned that I might be interested in Prince Tobiah. Even though he's engaged, apparently."

Color rose up James's throat and cheeks. "I wasn't *concerned*, but I *was* thinking that the fastest way to get your mind off him and on to me would be to tell you something truly appalling about him."

"By all means, tell me something truly appalling about him."

James glanced across the room, and for a heartbeat his smile fell away, revealing a young man too used to checking on his prince to make sure nothing was wrong. "Well." He gave an exaggerated sigh and spun me. My gown flared, a desert of silk at my feet. "I bear a great burden. As Tobiah's bodyguard and best friend, I know all his worst faults."

Best friend? That made me doubly glad I'd concealed my real feelings. "You do know how to keep a lady in suspense."

He grinned. "Prepare to be scandalized. The prince is a *terrible* swordsman. He sleeps through breakfast almost every day.

And once I saw him chew with his mouth open."

"Just the once, though?"

"He was ten."

I nodded solemnly. "I see. These are unforgivable offenses and I'm deeply scandalized."

A smile lit his eyes. "At last, I'm not the only one to see his true nature."

"And now he has a fiancée. What will she do when she discovers these dark truths? Didn't you warn her?"

"The fair duchess would not be swayed from her decision to accept his proposal. No matter how often I complimented her beauty, she still chose him. Ah, to be a prince." He pressed his hand to his heart.

"Lieutenant Rayner, do I perceive that you are something of a flirt?"

"My heart is simply more open than most people's." As the first dance ended, James offered a deep bow. "You're not as terrible a dancer as you claimed, Lady Julianna." He offered his arm.

Face ducked as though to hide a blush, I let him lead me off the dance floor. "You're so kind."

"So kind I'd like to get you a drink while we wait for the next dance, if you'll honor me again. Wine?"

"Please."

He left me by a gilt-framed mirror, which showed couples pulling closer and others seeking conversation partners. I caught glimpses of Melanie smiling shyly at a man, Lady Chey parading around in her exquisite lavender gown, and Tobiah listening to someone speak, a thin mask of politeness across his features.

He looked ready to drop from boredom, in spite of Meredith's presence beside him. She looked lovely, her hair all in tight coils, save a few pale tendrils that brushed her golden gown.

No doubt she was engaging in the long-celebrated tradition of marrying up, but what did he get from this? A lovely wife? Her family's wealth?

"Her name is Julianna," a woman nearby said. "She's a duchess from Liadia."

I continued my admiration of the room as the woman repeated my manufactured history, occasionally shooting pitying looks my way. As long as they believed my story, it didn't matter that I was in a palace filled with enemies, biding my time until I could go back to my ruined kingdom and scrape it off the ground.

James returned and handed me a glass of wine. "My lady."

I thanked him and took a tiny sip, just enough to wet my mouth. The room was warm, and being Julianna, pretending that I didn't hate everyone here, was exhausting. But I couldn't risk getting drunk and revealing something I shouldn't, either. I needed to stay sharp. Focused.

"You've said you don't do much dancing," James said. "What *do* you enjoy doing?"

Forgery? "Writing letters. Drawing." Picking locks? "Puzzles." Fighting? "Sewing." I kept my tone pleasant—as pleasant as Julianna might, given her recent trials.

"I'd love to see some of your artwork." James sipped his wine. "I've never had much opportunity to learn, but we have many fine artists in Skyvale. Many pieces are in Skyvale Palace, but I don't have the knowledge to tell you anything about them. I simply enjoy looking."

I dulled my tone a little. Just enough. "Unfortunately, all of my drawings are still in Liadia."

James pressed his mouth into a line and nodded. "Of course. If you want to take up drawing again, though, I'm sure supplies would be provided."

"I don't want to be an inconvenience." But really, what did I care about inconveniencing anyone here? Some other time, I'd reference this conversation when I asked for large sheets of paper and a selection of colored inks. The prince's best friend and *cousin* said I should ask, after all.

"I'm sure you wouldn't." He continued inquiring about my hobbies and favorite things—animals, seasons, paintings—until the next dance was announced and couples began assembling on the floor. "Ready?"

We set our wineglasses on a shelf, and once the dance began, I circled my questions around his job and habits and promise to show Melanie and me around the palace.

The song ended, but as James and I returned to our wine and settled into conversation, another tall figure approached.

"James. Lady Julianna."

James flashed a pale smile and turned a fraction to include the newcomer. "Your Highness."

I curtsied and murmured a greeting.

Prince Tobiah stood beside his bodyguard. The two were of similar height, both with lanky frames and hidden strength. But James stood with a fierceness the prince didn't possess; he stood like someone ready for an attack at any moment.

"I was hoping I might beg a dance from Lady Julianna." He offered his hand, palm up and fingers extended. The wool jacket he wore must have been stifling, but if he was uncomfortable, he didn't show it; his expression remained somber. Bored.

James's eyebrows arched up, but he stepped aside.

"I'd be honored, Your Highness." I smiled at James once more before placing my hand in Tobiah's.

A memory welled up, like blood from a thin cut, of standing on a ledge and watching my city burn. My hand in Tobiah's.

Tobiah Pierce and me: this was why the Indigo Kingdom had won the One-Night War.

SEVEN

I SWALLOWED HARD and reminded myself where I was and when—and who I was pretending to be.

"Watch out," James called as the opening chords played. "She's a terrible dancer."

I forced a chuckle and fell into step with the prince, in time with the tempo. "Your cousin is quite the gossip." When his expression didn't change, I urged lightness into my voice. No matter how I felt about him, I needed him to like me—Julianna. "He was just telling me about the time you chewed with your mouth open. I admit, I am horrified."

"And I am horrified that a lady of your rank cannot dance." Hints of a smile tugged at his mouth. "Unless James is simply spreading his disgusting lies again. Did he tell you I'm a poor swordsman? Because it isn't true. He's jealous, that's all."

"I have no idea what to believe at this point." I let my smile fade and lowered my eyes. This was almost too easy. "Your

Highness, I want to thank you again for your hospitality."

"It's nothing." His tone fell bored again. "Were our situations reversed, I know your family would have taken me in as well."

My family—birth and Ospreys alike—would have been clever enough to spot a spy, but I nodded. "I understand the Indigo Kingdom has been making efforts to mitigate the wraith's effects."

"It has. As part of the Wraith Alliance, we have Liadia's research and construction plans for the barrier, as well as several other kingdoms' work. Obviously, they've not been successful, but they have been educational. We're confident that something will prove useful."

Did he believe that? I couldn't tell.

"Your Highness." I pressed my lips together, glanced up, and met his eyes as we took slow, steady steps around each other. "I'd like to help. The wraith destroyed my home. I don't want to see it destroy another."

"That is incredibly brave of you."

"I want to see the wraith stopped. I *need* to help." The idea of spending more time with Tobiah and the Indigo Order made me need to vomit, actually, but this might be the fastest way to learn whether the Indigo Kingdom was drafting men from Aecor to fight in the wraithland.

And when I took back Aecor, I'd need to know if there was a way to protect my kingdom from the wraith, too.

Tobiah bowed his head. "I'll see what I can do. Though do keep in mind we all hope you will be able to rest and recover from your journey. I'm sure you're eager to see this stopped, but your health comes first."

I made my voice raspy. "At least until the wraith arrives."

"It won't happen tomorrow." He said it like a prince, like someone who'd never known uncertainty. Like he could command tomorrow to be wraith-free.

He'd never known the horror of seeing his people shoved into a courtyard to witness the execution of his blindfolded king and queen. His parents.

He'd never known the fear of the orphanage, with bigger children who stole food and bedding, and beat the younger ones for fun. And minders who didn't care.

He'd never known hunger in a winter-frozen castle, trapped with other starving children.

The dance ended, and everyone applauded the musicians. I clapped as well, but my thoughts were far away.

"Are you well?" Tobiah studied my face. "You've gone pale."

"It's warm in here. I'd like to sit, if you don't mind."

There were chairs placed all around the ballroom, many with occupants already, but Tobiah led me to a seat under the orchestra's balcony and helped me settle.

"May I get anything for you?"

Information. Lists. My kingdom.

"No, thank you. I'm so embarrassed."

"Don't be." Tobiah took the seat next to me and though his tone was all compassion, his posture announced otherwise: he leaned slightly away from me, rather than toward, and his hands rested too stiffly on his knees. He couldn't wait to get away. "Perhaps it's too early for you to be out yet. You just arrived, after all."

I tilted my shoulders toward him, clasped my hands together

in earnestness, and repeated the same excuse I'd given James: I refused to be the sad duchess doomed to friendlessness. "I desperately want to know more about the Indigo Kingdom and its people. This is my new home."

He waited.

"For example"—a cresting-wave sigil caught my eye—"the Houses. I've seen them on flags and carriages, and anything else that can be labeled. What do they mean?"

He shoved his fingers through his hair, upsetting the slight curls. "They represent birthplace. Those born in the Indigo Mountains or Valley claim House of the Dragon."

"You're Dragon."

He nodded. "And my mother claims Sun, as she was born northeast of here. Chey is House of the Sea, from directly east. House of the Unicorn is to the southeast. My fiancée is House of the Unicorn." He rested his elbows on his knees and linked his hands together. "It has little to do with family and more to do with the location of one's birth, similar to the belief in Liadia that the month of one's birth influences personality. There are stories about those four regions, and how the Houses influence people born under them, but it's not commonly discussed anymore. It's more tradition than anything."

"Oh, my apologies, then. I didn't mean to be rude."

"I don't mind. Most people view the stories as too magical, though." He glanced at me from the corner of his eye, like waiting to see whether I'd break down again. I held my spine straight and my chin firm. "With magic being the source of the wraith, anything related to magic—even legend—is taboo."

Lady Julianna would be supportive of this. "I understand."

But still inquisitive, perhaps. I dropped my voice. "The Indigo Kingdom has a *complete* ban on magic?"

He nodded. "To assist in our efforts to stop the wraith."

"And the people comply?"

Tobiah turned his head, studying me. "Most. They've had a hundred years to get used to the ban."

"But not everyone."

"Not everyone." He leaned back, arms crossed over his chest. "There are some who persist. The Indigo Order finds them."

"Or Black Knife does."

He cocked his head. "Has he made a name for himself even in Liadia?"

I bit back a laugh. "No, but I hadn't even stepped foot in Skyvale before I heard tales. Refugee children pretend to be him."

"So do some of the nobility." Tobiah jerked his chin toward a tall, handsome man dancing with three ladies at once. "Notoriety means never being lonely at night."

I twisted my face into a conspiratorial smile. "It seems to me that kind of notoriety might mean never having time for that sort of company."

Tobiah chuckled. "As long as it keeps Lord Daniel out of worse trouble."

After a quiet moment, I said, "I was curious. . . ."

Tension wound up in the prince's shoulders. When had it left?

"What happens to them? The flashers arrested by the Indigo Order and Black Knife?"

"They don't use magic anymore." Tobiah shrugged as though he truly did not care. "That's what matters." He pushed himself up and gave a slight bow. "If you're recovered, my lady, I'd better excuse myself and dance with my fiancée."

"Of course. Congratulations on your engagement, Your Highness."

The sullen expression broke for a minuscule smile. Then he turned, bumped into someone, apologized, and made his way through the ballroom.

Alone under the balcony, I studied the dancers as the next song began. Lady Julianna might have been a fool to come out tonight, but it had been a wise move for me. James and Tobiah were wealthy with information. I just had to ask the right questions.

From across the dance floor, Melanie caught my eye, a silent query in her lifted brow. I cast a faint nod and smile, and went back to my observations. Learning dance steps. Who spoke with whom. Who seemed to be the most important members of society. The king and queen were present, though halfway through, Terrell doubled over with a coughing fit, and both Tobiah's mother and father left early.

A few men here and there asked me to dance. I accepted, gleaning bits of information from them as well, and at last the orchestra played the final song.

Together, Melanie and I stepped outside, pausing to admire the glittering night as carriages pulled up and out of the drive. Couples and families left in groups, laughing or yawning or gazing suggestively at each other.

Before I could start toward our carriage, though, Prince

Tobiah stepped in. "My ladies. I'd be honored if you rode back to the palace with me."

I caught James's smirk behind Tobiah as I accepted. Soon, we were tucked inside a large carriage with heated stones placed beneath the benches, and heavy wool shawls over our shoulders. A lantern provided a feeble illumination over the blue-and-gold interior, but cast more shadows. The prince and his bodyguard sat across from us, loosening their collars and buttons as the carriage lurched into motion and the candlelight jumped.

"The duchess is returning home with her family," James explained when he caught me eyeing the prince's fiancée as she glided by outside with a pair of adults. Her parents, presumably.

"Ah." No suggestive gazing for them. Well, few in this world had the luxury of marrying for love.

"I hope your first full day in Skyvale was satisfying." Tobiah steadied the lantern, and light struck the angles of his face. "I can't promise every day will be as exciting, but there do tend to be many parties in autumn."

"The company was enjoyable." When I smiled pointedly, both boys offered polite thank-yous. "As for less exciting days, I'm very interested in learning more about the Indigo Kingdom."

"Anything in particular?" Tobiah lifted an eyebrow.

"Its history."

"That's not a light subject." Tobiah gripped the bench to brace himself as the carriage jostled. "Why history?"

"My father maintained that the history of a kingdom contains clues to the kingdom's future." At the prince's nod, I continued. "He said people tend to fall into patterns, even over hundreds of years. They make the same mistakes as their ancestors. The only way we can avoid that fate is to learn from what's come before."

"That is an interesting philosophy," said the prince. "I can't say I disagree with it."

"Besides, the Indigo Kingdom is my home now." The words sat sour on my tongue. The Indigo Kingdom could *never* be home. "I want to know everything about it. As much as those who were born here."

James, who'd been quietly observing the exchange, leaned forward. "You strike me as an incredibly clever young woman. Somehow, I don't think you'll have trouble catching up."

"Indeed." Tobiah smiled. "Whatever you require for your studies will be provided."

Later, alone in our rooms, I turned to Melanie. "The Indigo Kingdom is *so* kind to us. Whatever we require for our reclaiming of Aecor will be provided."

She laughed and began unpinning my hair. "Did you get anywhere with the prince or his bodyguard?"

"Tobiah promised to get me into his wraith mitigation talks sometime, and James is a river of gossip."

"Not a good trait for a bodyguard."

"But good for us." I recounted the conversations and when my hair hung loose, I turned to help with hers. "What about you? Anything?"

"I made friends out of a few ladies-in-waiting. I'll use them for information on people we're up against. They were horrified that we'd been seated with the military guests, so we have potential allies against Chey if we need them."

"I get the impression Chey doesn't like us, and I'm not sure why. We should be careful with her."

"Meredith is friendly, though." Melanie shrugged. "She invited us to her engagement ball."

True, but she hadn't spoken with us tonight. That was a little strange.

The clock tower chimed as we ran through the people we'd met, who might be useful, who could be ignored for now, and how we'd behave around all of them. We were refugee nobility, after all; we could get away with quite a range of behavior, if we played our characters right.

And we were nothing if not good at being exactly what others expected us to be.

EIGHT

THE NEXT SEVERAL days blurred. Dress fittings, introductions to other palace residents, and a dizzying number of formal dinners, though none as grand as the first. The king was paying for all of it, though, so I didn't complain.

One evening, we returned to our quarters and found a stack of large paper and bottles of colored inks resting on the sitting room table.

"Perfect." Melanie circled the supplies, giving them a predatory smile as she dragged her fingers along the edge of the table. "This is even more than we need for the map."

"Which is good." I locked the door and took inventory. Large sheets of white, fine-grained paper. Richly colored inks. I'd be hard-pressed to steal something better. "Really good, considering we'll have to show off all the drawings we promised."

Melanie grinned as she lifted the lid of a hand-carved box; it smelled of rosewood. "Pens. Dozens of nibs. They really are trying to make us feel at home." She removed an ebony-handled pen and turned it in her hands. "What else do you think we could request? The king's head on a pike?"

"Hmm." I gave an exaggerated tap on my chin. "How does one word that kind of request?"

"With liberal repetition of the word *please*, I expect." Melanie shut the box. "I'm ready to begin transferring the map right now, if you are."

I glanced at the mantel clock, hands drawing toward twenty-two. At the window, darkness peeked around the edges of the curtain. "This late?"

"You're imagining we'll have a convenient time tomorrow?" She shook her head. "Between dress fittings, social meals, and our gossip-collecting efforts, we're scheduled every moment. We have four tasks. The faster we get through them—including this one—the faster we can return to the old palace."

I cast a quick, longing gaze toward my bedroom before I sat at the table. She was right. There was no better time than now.

Melanie fished the draft of our map from its hiding place behind a bookcase, and we got to work.

An hour later, everything was transferred to the larger paper, though we were still missing portions in the royal wing and details about who lived where. We'd get more over time, but for now . . .

"It's almost a respectable map." Melanie folded the smaller papers in with our collection of reports for Patrick, and a letter from me to Connor. "Think he'll appreciate having the draft?"

I rolled my eyes. "It won't be enough to please him."

"Perhaps it will placate him for now."

As I finished cleaning the pens, I mimicked his favorite disapproving tone. "You're not working fast enough."

Melanie deepened her voice into his, too. "We should have had the entire palace infiltrated with Ospreys by now."

I couldn't cage my laugh. "Yes, all twelve of us against thousands of them."

"Nine. Quinn took Ronald and Ezra to raid that supply caravan."

"Oh right." Worry settled in my stomach again. "Nine."

"Wil." She leaned forward. "You know I only voted with Patrick because I *do* think they're ready for that job."

"Sure." A shiver passed through me. Why had Patrick sent Ezra on such a dangerous mission? "I disagree, but I understand."

"I know." Melanie pushed herself to her feet. "Unless you need help with your hair and dress, *Lady Julianna*, I'm going to change and get these documents to the drop."

"You just took a scheduled report last night." Again, she'd stayed out later than necessary and denied it in the morning.

"Last night we didn't have the spare map."

"Very well."

She beamed and pranced toward her bedroom.

I slipped the new map-in-progress in between other sheets of paper to hide it, then hurried into my bedroom and shut the door. I pulled the pins from my hair, letting the brown strands tumble down over my shoulders. A quick braid later, I was shimmying into a dark shirt and trousers when Melanie called from the other room.

"I'm going." Her voice was high, almost giddy.

The sitting room balcony door clicked open and closed as I

grabbed my dagger and waited by the door in my room. With the curtain nudged aside, I could just make out Melanie's form moving across the courtyard, guards none the wiser.

Well. This should be fun.

I tucked my braid under a black cap and followed her.

The night was cool and breezy, with a pale odor of wraith on the air. After a quick survey of the nearby balconies—no one was out tonight—I grabbed the rail and swung myself over, one side pressed against the palace wall. My legs dangled, boot-clad toes scrabbling for purchase. I found a ledge and readjusted my weight, then wedged my grappling hook around the balcony rail. Cautiously, I climbed three stories down to the gentle sloping roof below.

I gave the line some slack, shook it, and coiled it so that it fit in a clip on my hip.

The tiles on the roof were slick, but the treads of my boots gripped and my footing was secure. One more climb down to the ground. My toes hit the courtyard with hardly a sound. The whole night held its breath as I raced after Melanie.

She was far ahead of me by now, a slim figure keeping to the shadows, nearly invisible. If I hadn't been looking for her, I'd have never known she was there.

But she and I had the same training. I knew all her tricks.

I followed her through the King's Seat and Hawksbill. The mansions were hulking shadows in the dark, glimmering here and there with mirrors. Fountains splashed and wind chimes rattled. There was a party in one of the houses; laughter carried from an open window. Farther away, dogs barked, and the clock tower chimed twenty-three: an hour before midnight.

When Melanie climbed over the wall surrounding Hawks-bill, I followed a minute later.

In Thornton, she stayed on the streets, but I ascended to the rooftops where I could keep an eye on her. While most of the shops were closed this late, the inns and taverns were brightly lit with candles and lanterns. Gas lamps hissed at intersections, making it impossible for anyone to hide, but Melanie slipped through the crowd, unnoticed. A few times, her hand flashed out and into someone's purse. She pocketed her prizes.

At last, we reached Laurence's Bakery, its windows dark now. Melanie stole around the back of the building and wrestled out a loose brick near the chimney. She stashed our reports and map inside the hollow, then replaced the brick.

It hadn't taken her three hours to get here, so—

Melanie glanced over her shoulder before she climbed onto the roof and headed south, deeper into Thornton. *Now* what?

Maybe she was bored not being able to steal things in the palace and simply needed to scratch that itch. But she wouldn't hide that from me, surely.

I followed, keeping my distance as she crept across peaked roofs, climbing and leaping and scrambling where necessary. Thornton's architecture was such that anyone with the skill—and who didn't mind heights—could use the roofs as a second and secret road. People almost never looked up, but we had to be careful in daylight; the mirrors scattered across the western faces of buildings could give us away.

In one of those mirrors, a shadow darted across the reflection of the slender crescent moon.

Someone was behind me.

Maybe someone from another gang. Soon, they'd go somewhere else and be out of sight, so I didn't turn around and alert them to my knowledge of their presence. They probably hadn't seen me.

Still, I checked my stealth as I continued after Melanie. She headed into less crowded areas of the market district, where being noticed wasn't such a danger, but I kept lower to the rooftops and wished the darkness were a palpable thing I could gather around me like a cloak.

It *could* be.

No. Fantasies were one thing, but actually using the magic would always remain a last resort.

Minutes later, the shadow appeared in a mirror once more, gone so quickly it might have been my imagination.

Someone was *following* me.

I stuffed down my indignation. I was following Melanie, after all. Still, I didn't want to lead this person to wherever she was going. Not when I didn't know. It could be something Patrick had asked her to do.

But why wouldn't he have told me, too? Unless he knew it was something I wouldn't like.

With one last glance at Melanie's vanishing figure, I slipped behind a chimney, its bricks warm with smoke and fire from below, and I waited.

My pursuer would slow, would watch for me in the direction I'd been heading, wondering if he'd missed seeing my leap onto the roof of the next building. He'd be curious whether I'd somehow spotted him. Because he'd been careful. Quiet. Only chance had let me see him.

I steadied my breathing and strained my hearing beyond the pounding of my heart and the wind that kicked up dirt and trash. Paper scraped the side of the building, and a door slammed down the street. Wind moaned around corners. Chimes clattered.

The chimney seemed to blur as a darkness moved forward.

Without hesitation, I grabbed my pursuer's wrist, yanked him forward and around, and slammed him back against the chimney where I'd been hiding. My hand was splayed out across his chest, pinning him, and my dagger gleamed against the black skin of his throat.

No, not skin. Silk. It covered his entire face, save his eyes.

"Black Knife." My blade stayed steady at his throat.

"You won't look, but I hope you'll believe me when I say there's a dagger at your stomach." Darkness obscured what little of his face was visible, but his eyes remained on mine.

"I believe you." Neither of us moved, maybe both of us thinking about how we'd react if the other attacked. Or how we could attack first, without getting killed. For either of us, it would take only a quick flick of the wrist to make the other bleed to death. Even if I cut his throat, he could gut me in his last moments of life. And the other way around, too.

"So what do we do?"

"Why were you following me?"

"You were sneaking around on rooftops. Only dangerous people do that." His arm shifted and the point of his dagger caught my clothes and scraped my skin. I adjusted the angle of my blade on his throat, and neither of us moved. "We both know how a fight would end." His voice was low and menacing.

A fair fight, perhaps. But I could bring our weapons to life.

I could bring this roof to life. I could make them fight for me.

"I suppose." My eyes watered with the need to blink against the cold wind, but I couldn't look away from Black Knife. Now that we were practically nose to nose, my perception of him shifted: he was young, not a grown man like I'd thought.

"You're a very interesting thief. I've been trying to find where you and your gang stay, but no one seems to know. No one seems to know even your first name."

"I treasure my anonymity. I'm sure you can appreciate that."

In his *humph*, I could almost hear a smirk, but the black cloth concealed the expression. "I've never seen you alone before," he went on. "Usually, you have quite the entourage. Or at least that black-haired girl. You two seem close."

Why was he talking so much? To confuse me? To trick me into relaxing? Whatever he was up to, it wouldn't work.

"I don't need my friends to protect me from you." Wind picked up, howling now. A faint, acrid stench rode the air. A trash bin clattered and a cat yowled.

"No. That is obvious." He broke our stare, glancing toward the street below. "I have a proposition. We both agree that standing here with blades at each other's bodies is not going to accomplish anything but cramped muscles. So why not back off and sheathe our weapons? And if we decide to fight, we can get right back into this position. I prefer this to potentially falling off the roof."

I narrowed my eyes. "I don't trust you."

"I don't trust you, either."

"So we don't move."

"Ever?" He met my eyes again, and seemed to search me.

"You may not believe that I have things to do besides chase you around the city, but it's the truth."

"Doesn't change that I don't trust you."

"If I dropped my dagger?"

I let the corner of my mouth curl up. "You'd pick it up and throw it at me as soon as I retreated."

"If I handed it to you?"

"I'm sure you have more weapons." That sword he used so much.

"So you'd rather stay like this." When I didn't answer, he pulled back his blade and my clothes shifted straight again. "I'm not going to stab you. I'm lifting my hand, see? I'm going to put the hilt by your hand. You can take it."

His movements were slow, both of us waiting to see if I'd slice his neck open, but when the dagger came into view, he'd shifted his hold so the weapon hung between his first two fingers; it would be impossible to get a good grip on it before I attacked.

"That's *my* dagger."

"I know. In your haste to escape our last pleasant meeting, you abandoned it in a glowman's hand." His eyes never left mine. "Take it."

I snatched the hilt and took several strides backward, keeping the edge of the roof to my left.

But before I could decide to run or attack or *anything*, Black Knife drew a miniature crossbow from his belt and leapt off the roof.

I reached the edge of the roof just in time to see him hit the ground, crouched and balanced on the balls of his feet and one hand. Like the jump didn't faze him, he lifted the crossbow and shot a bolt into the darkness across the street.

The darkness roared and reared up, assembling itself into the shape of a huge black cat, all pale scars and sinewy muscle. Crates and beams clattered aside as the beast charged Black Knife, who reloaded his crossbow and shot again. The bolt struck the cat's throat, making the cat stumble, but it didn't halt.

With another yowl, the beast pounced. Black Knife rolled away as immense paws thudded on the ground, making even the building shudder under me. The cat seemed to be *growing* as it prowled around Black Knife, who shot it again and again.

Small black bolts protruded from the beast like whiskers. It let out another bone-shaking roar as it closed in on Black Knife, trapping him against the wall.

That hardly seemed to concern him. From a sheath along his back, he produced a black-handled sword and pressed his attack.

The cat swiped at Black Knife, who raised his sword and blocked the fan of claws. A fine spray of blood coated the ground between them, and the cat roared again.

In the nearby houses, candles and lamps were doused. A child's scream rose up and was hushed. The clatter and shouts and roars of a boy fighting a beast were the only sounds on the dark street, and they were piercing.

This creature was a nightmare from the wraithland in the west. It had been normal once, but wraith seeped into its body and mind, reshaping it into this horror. When the wraith reached the Indigo Kingdom, these creatures would be everywhere, not just here and there, blown in on storms.

Black Knife ducked another swipe of the cat's claws and deep gashes appeared in the wooden fence, just behind where his head had been. He leapt onto a stack of crates, lithe and limber as he climbed upward.

The cat pounced, and Black Knife's sword flashed in the gleam of a gas lamp. The cat jerked back and out of the way. Black Knife let out a rough, frustrated sound and pursued the cat without apparent distress.

A pungent, wraithy stench filled the street, wafting up as the cat growled and lashed its tail. With a ripple of muscle, the beast struck. Black Knife blocked, but his wrist wrenched sideways, and the sword went spinning beneath the creature. The crossbow was nowhere I could see. Black Knife drew a pair of knives, but they had no reach. The wraith beast crouched and growled.

"Hey, cat!" My voice sounded shrill and strange against the night, and the wraith beast looked up and yowled.

Black Knife lunged for his sword.

I fixed my grip on my daggers, jumped, and slammed onto the cat's back. The beast screamed as I drove my blades into the back of its neck and dragged them across its spine. Another *thump*, this one from below. Black Knife plunged his sword into the cat's throat, and the tip of the blade pierced the back of its neck, shining wet with blood.

The creature shuddered as Black Knife withdrew his sword, and I yanked out my blades. As the wraith cat fell to the street with a heavy *thud*, I hopped to safety.

The neighborhood remained utterly silent as the dying beast lay between Black Knife and me.

His sword point rested on the ground. His breath came in hard gasps. "Thank you."

"For what you did in Greenstone. For saving the boy."

He wiped his bloodied sword on the cat's fur before sheathing it, but when he started around the beast, I took a step backward and he stopped.

"Who are you?" he asked.

"No one." I glanced between the black-clad boy and the shallowly breathing cat. It groaned and gurgled, and the stench of blood and wraith flooded the street. I swallowed until the urge to gag passed.

"Your group is called the Ospreys, right? What does that mean?"

"It's just a name."

"You'll admit to that name, but you won't tell me yours?" He tilted his head. "I suppose you'd just give me a false name."

He was definitely right about that.

"I like the way you fight."

Was that a *compliment*?

"It's very efficient. Who taught you?"

"Your grandmother." Patrick Lien had taught us, as well as men he'd brought back from Aecor. Those men hadn't known my identity—it was too much of a risk—but they'd been well-compensated.

"That seems unlikely. My grandmother preferred sewing to fighting." He stepped closer, all stealth and dancer's grace. His hands stayed at his sides, not touching weapons, and if his wrist hurt from the fight, he didn't show it.

My daggers were still clutched at my sides, the hilts digging into my skin. "Why were you following me?"

"Because you're a criminal. I'm trying to figure out what you're up to."

"It's not really your job, is it? The city has police."

He shifted his weight and shrugged. "They underperform. They work hard, but it's not enough. There are still thieves everywhere." His tone was pointed. "Clearly."

"If I were a thief, I'd steal only what I needed."

"Like paper?"

Chills ran through me. Not even Black Knife was crazy enough to search all the warehouses in the vicinity of our previous encounter and find one misplaced crate with a loose lid.

I eyed his black shirt, trousers, and knee-high boots. His sword. His *mask*. Well. Maybe he was crazy enough.

"Are you going to tie me up and leave me outside a police station?"

"Eventually. Once I know what I need to know." He looked at the wraith beast. Soon the neighborhood would realize it was safe. People would come out to look at the defeated animal. "Better go."

I started to back away, still keeping Black Knife in my sight.

Between us, the wraith beast gurgled one last time and died. White mist spewed from the body, a viscous miasma that filled the street.

I coughed and gagged and dropped to the ground. Tendrils of mist swirled around me, suffocating me, drowning me. Darkness shoved at the edge of my vision.

Then it was gone. Dispersed, I guessed.

I was flat on my back, and a shadow leaned over me, touching the pulse at my throat.

Black Knife.

I kicked, but he pressed one palm to my sternum, then twisted and caught my ankle. "I was just checking to make sure you're alive." His grip loosened a fraction. "I'm going to back away."

When I didn't move, he released me and took several long strides.

"I'm fine." I grabbed my daggers and scrambled to my feet. "What was that?"

"They release wraith when they die." Black Knife gave a deep nod, almost a bow, and sidestepped into a shadow. Metal skidded on the cobblestones—his crossbow, perhaps—and then there was only silence.

I peered into the darkness for a moment longer, but caught no movement, no sounds. Either he'd slipped away or he was waiting for me to leave first.

As much as I hated turning my back on a boy with a crossbow, I had to get back to Skyvale Palace. I couldn't let Melanie return before me.

I spun and ran down the street, keeping to the darkness where I could. I climbed up buildings and used the roofs to get around more quickly, being sure to stop and check for pursuit often. It was bad enough Black Knife had followed me tonight. He *couldn't* know where I was staying or the truth of my mission.

By the time I reached my room in the palace, my whole body shook with adrenaline and exhaustion. My daggers clattered to my bedroom floor as I shut the balcony door behind me and then stood listening for Melanie's presence. Straining to hear her voice, her breathing, the soft way she snored when she slept.

I shouldn't have worried about returning before her. When the window finally opened and she crept inside, dawn was just touching the sky.

NINE

CROWN PRINCE TOBIAH might have been a spoiled, sullen boy, but he kept his promise.

A few days after Black Knife and I killed the wraith beast, I walked into a large study, all polished wood and paintings, with a heavy desk at one end and conference table in the center. There were six men in the room: four in military dress at the table, James standing at ease in the corner, and Tobiah at the desk.

"Lady Julianna." Tobiah rose, the others following suit. He gestured to the table. "I'm glad you could join us. Please take a seat." His tone was cool.

All around the table, polite smiles fell.

"Thank you for the invitation, Your Highness." I gathered up my gown, a high-waisted creation of midnight blue silk, and prepared to sit. The whole room went quiet. Waiting.

A lady never scooted in her own chair if gentlemen or footmen were present. But now, the men at the table stared at me like they'd never seen a lady before.

Maybe they hadn't. Not in here.

Just as I started to sit without the luxury of fitting comfortably at the table—as if I hadn't been scooting my own chair for years—Tobiah shot James a look and nod, and the bodyguard stepped from his post.

The room was held-breath quiet as I picked up the ends of my gown, and James pushed my chair as I sat. "I'm happy to see you again, my lady." His voice was soft. So was the way his fingertips grazed my shoulder blade as he stepped away.

"You all know of Lady Julianna Whitman of Liadia, I trust." Tobiah strode away from his desk, a small stack of papers in his hands. "Please treat her with as much respect as you'd treat one another."

That seemed unlikely to happen. Not when I was invading their world.

"Lady Julianna has done what few of us have dared: she's traveled through the wraithland and survived. Her knowledge will be invaluable and her determination to put a stop to the wraith problem is no less than ours."

Part of me wondered if those praises should make me feel guilty. But while I hadn't trekked through the wraithland, I *had* lived through something horrific, and I *did* want the wraith problem solved.

But more immediately, I had those four tasks: information, misdirection, rescue, and map.

"I'll make quick introductions, and then we'll catch up Lady Julianna on our efforts." Tobiah sat—the rest of the men followed—and gestured around the table. "This isn't the full committee; some members have been called away recently. But I'll start with Captain Clint Chuter, House of the Sea."

"I remember. We were seated close together at the engagement ball." I nodded toward the captain, who looked a little abashed by his staring earlier. He sent a faint, apologetic smile.

"General Adam Goldberg, General Fredrick Goldberg, both House of the Sun. Adam commands the Indigo Order, while Fredrick oversees the Indigo Army."

The generals, brothers presumably, were both solid-built men with thinning hair. They eyed me warily.

I put on a shy, hopeful smile. "I'm afraid I'm not clear on the difference between the two divisions. The Order and the Army: they're both military, yes?" I knew, of course, but Lady Julianna probably wouldn't. Men like these enjoyed explaining things. They liked being helpful, so I would put them at ease.

Adam cleared his throat. "The Order is a highly selective military branch. We accept only highborn soldiers."

I nodded toward Tobiah's bodyguard on the other side of the room, standing stoically. "Like James?"

"Lieutenant Rayner is one of many young men trained to guard the King's Seat and the royal family, as well as deal with anyone practicing magic in the city. Lieutenant Rayner's scores on the Academy final examination, as well as a recommendation from His Highness, earned him this position." The general sat back. "It's a small, elite army, since there are so many qualifications."

It hadn't been the Indigo Order that had come through Aecor nearly ten years ago, unless Tobiah's previous bodyguard had followed. They were dangerous for an entirely different reason.

No doubt they had whole divisions dedicated to ruining the lives of anyone caught using magic.

I turned to Fredrick. "And the Indigo Army?" Which *had* been there. Maybe even this man. I pressed my hands to my knees.

"We accept anyone, so long as the young man has all his limbs, though, like the Order, we do comb through the records at Bome Boys' Academy for the highest-scoring students to be considered for officer positions." He shot his brother a wry look, an indication of a long-standing argument that might never be won. "It's not as prestigious, but my soldiers and officers have an opportunity to travel. We have men at West Pass Watch, under the command of Prince Herman Pierce, and all along the western border of the Indigo Kingdom, protecting people from the wraith."

Along with men from Aecor?

I bowed my head solemnly. "Both seem like selfless pursuits. I'm sure your people must be grateful for both the Order and the Army."

"Isn't she delightful?" Clint asked the others, as though I were a secret he was finally allowed to share.

I'd never been called delightful before.

After a bored shake of his head, Tobiah turned to the last man in the room. Though he wore a uniform of the Indigo Order, the buttons strained, and he appeared to have seen little fighting in the last decade. "Finally, my uncle, Prince Colin Pierce, House of the Dragon, Duke of Skyvale, and Overlord of Aecor Territory."

I blanched. Overlord of Aecor.

Overlord of *my* kingdom.

"My lady?"

My breath was too short; I could feel it, but I couldn't fix it. Men leaned forward, studying me. Someone said something about me not being fit for this type of work, but his voice came from far away.

The prince pushed himself up and started around the table. "James, call for a physician."

"No. It's all right. I'm fine." I wasn't fine, but my ailment wasn't anything a physician could cure. I forced my expression into something resembling calmness, struggling to recapture the mask of Lady Julianna before I ruined everything.

Tobiah rounded the table toward me and crouched at my side, pressing one hand flat against my spine, an incredible breech in manners. "Are you certain?" He touched two fingers to my throat. Our eyes met for a heartbeat before his gaze shifted to somewhere over my shoulder. "Your pulse is racing."

"I'm fine." I reached for an explanation. Anything. "I'm afraid I haven't fully recovered from my journey through the wraithland. I suppose I was thinking too much about the necessity for this committee." I needed to control myself better. Even now, the men exchanged unimpressed glances.

James hesitated by the doorway. "Your Highness?"

The moments lengthened, but at last the prince stood and waved James back to his position. "Let's continue. If the lady says she's fine, we won't disrespect her by calling the physician against her wishes." His polite words didn't quite disguise the withering look he gave me.

James returned to the corner where he'd been standing, but

his eyes, filled with concern, stayed on me. As though I needed his protection.

Tobiah took his seat and slid a pile of papers across the table to me. "I thought you might like to study these. In addition to statistics and reports from West Pass Watch, they detail the different ways members of the Wraith Alliance have attempted to mitigate or halt the wraith, as well as the varying levels of success reached."

None of the attempts had been truly successful, though. Like Liadia, some countries held off the wraith for a few months or a year, but eventually, it broke through. "I appreciate this, Your Highness."

"What can you tell us of your time in the wraithland?" Fredrick's tone turned patronizing. "If discussing it won't be too difficult."

Clint cleared his throat. "We do realize you've only just escaped. The horrors you must have endured would mark anyone. But we learn so much every time we speak to a survivor. If it weren't so dangerous, we'd send more teams to study it. That you survived something that many trained men haven't—that speaks very highly of you."

It was nice of him to try to stick up for me, but I'd already made myself look weak. I'd have to rectify that.

Everyone listened, taking notes as I described the same events I had for King Terrell and Prince Tobiah my first day here. I kept my voice strong, letting it slip only when I spoke of the harrowing escape from my home—Julianna's home—and nights in the wilderness with beasts prowling all around us. I needed my performance to be realistic and inspiring.

"We've heard reports of violent storms," Tobiah said. "Did you notice an increase in activity after the wraith came through?"

I nodded. It was better to confirm these things. Everyone knew the wraith was terrible, and that it was coming. I didn't want to give them a reason to underestimate it. "Before it arrived, summers steadily grew hotter, and winters colder. I'm sure you've noticed the same changes here. When the wraith hit the barrier and halted, we didn't notice a drastic change, but when the barrier collapsed, the night immediately grew hotter." I laced my fingers together and allowed my expression to harden, like armor against memories. "I couldn't sleep much during the journey here. The howling. And it was so, so hot. But it snowed sometimes, too. Flakes as big as your hands. They melted as they hit the ground."

That was one of the more uncommon rumors about the wraithland, but I'd heard it from a few different groups of refugees. It was legitimate enough for me.

They asked about other phenomena in the wraithland, questioning the same details multiple times from different angles. Each time I gave the same answers, biting back frustration over the repetition. They were only trying to be thorough, to coax out details I might not be aware I'd overlooked. Their questioning would have been more useful if I'd actually been to the wraithland.

At last, they were satisfied I knew nothing more.

I sipped the wine someone had set in front of me, then leafed through the papers from Tobiah. "The wraith began after centuries of industrialized magic, correct?" That was what my parents had taught me, and what I'd taught the younger Ospreys when it came time for them to learn.

"That's the theory," Clint said. "The overuse of magic triggered a cataclysmic reaction we haven't been able to reverse."

"But it has slowed," Tobiah added. "If you put out the fire, it stops producing smoke. Maybe not immediately, but given time . . ."

"Hasn't magic use ceased, though? The Wraith Alliance has been in effect for a hundred years, after all." I pushed away the memory of my hand pressed against an old crate, magic on my lips as I bade it awaken. Any wraith created would have been minuscule.

Tobiah shook his head and gazed out the window for a moment. "When I was younger, I met a girl who told me that it was safe to use magic for emergencies."

Me. He meant me.

"She'd grown up in Aecor, where people used to believe it was only great amounts of magic that contributed to the wraith problem. I was young, about eight, and curious. I became obsessed with learning all I could about wraith. I spent hours in the library, studying. Over the next few years, I met with every expert on magic and wraith in the kingdom, but they all said the same thing: *all* magic contributes to the wraith problem, even a little bit. And they all agree that magic is still being used. Today. Now." He glanced at the men around the table, who nodded. Then, to me: "Ten years ago, Aecor was an independent kingdom in the east, not just a territory of the Indigo Kingdom."

I held my breath.

"It wasn't part of the Wraith Alliance. Then, though people were cautioned to use only small amounts, most didn't listen. There were no consequences, so they used what they wanted."

No, that wasn't what I'd been taught. That wasn't what I'd *done*.

"With Aecorians using magic as they wished, the wraith approached quickly. But since we conquered Aecor, the laws there have changed. Magic is forbidden, just as it is everywhere else." Tobiah glanced at his uncle, the shadow of a frown flashing across his face. "And the wraith has slowed its approach. It has measurably slowed."

My voice was hoarse. "This fact is confirmed?"

Everyone at the table nodded.

"That's why the Indigo Kingdom is doing better than it has in almost a century," said Colin. "There's hope that the wraith will stop. The economy is stabilizing. There's less violence."

If there was hope, I hadn't seen it. The Skyvale I'd always known was dirty, hungry, and flooded with refugees. And that didn't seem to be changing.

"How are you measuring its movement?" I asked.

Clint rose and revealed a large wall map of unfamiliar landscape, with hashes of colored ink in bands across the plains. "Here. Once a month, we send a rider to place a marker at the edge of the wraithland. We track its progress on maps like this."

Ah, now I recognized the land. There was the Indigo Kingdom's western reaches—West Pass Watch—and Liadia and other fallen kingdoms covering most of the paper. The bands of hashes were twelve different colors, one for every month of the year, presumably. "The bands get narrower."

The captain tapped the map. "Because the wraith's progress has slowed. It doesn't cover as much new ground every month as it did previously."

I dragged my gaze over the colored ink. There were small scribbles on the northwestern end of Liadia, hard to read from this distance. "What's that in Liadia?"

"Unfounded rumors." Clint returned to his seat. "Nothing you need to worry about, Your Grace."

The crown prince glared at the map a moment longer before he continued his earlier lecture, as though I'd never interrupted. "There are pockets of magic use in Skyvale and the rest of the Indigo Kingdom. They're why the wraith magic still creeps toward us. They're why it hasn't halted its approach. But if those pockets were stopped—well, smoke eventually dissipates."

"Dissipates, yes, but that doesn't mean it's vanished. Like magic, it cannot be destroyed."

He regarded me with a carefully neutral expression. "That is true. However, we have no reason to believe the wraith won't settle or ease, and the world will be safe to live in again. The fact remains that magic use will only draw the wraith closer until the Indigo Kingdom *is* the wraithland."

Could that be true? It seemed unlikely wraith would ever just *go away*, but could halting all magic really allow the wraith to settle enough so the world became livable? It was hard to believe there was anything but darkness in our future.

"Not everyone with magic will want to stop using it," I said, and the others nodded agreement.

Some people *couldn't* stop. Though it sometimes took all my will to avoid using my power selfishly, there were others compelled to use their abilities selflessly—to help and heal. Surely, healing couldn't be wrong.

"That's why they're arrested when they're caught," said Clint. "Because they won't stop."

My voice came as thin as silk. "What happens to them?"

Silence fluttered through the room.

"They're dealt with." General Adam Goldberg's voice was gruff. "Let's move on."

I drew a shaky breath. "Beyond putting a stop to magic use, what is being done to combat the wraith? General"—I turned to Fredrick—"you said you have men at West Pass Watch and all along the western border."

He nodded. "Brave men from all over the Indigo Kingdom."

"Supplemented," added Colin Pierce, "with draftees from Aecor Territory."

My mouth went dry. Patrick had been right. "They're taken against their will?"

If my question offended him, Colin didn't show it. "Aecor was responsible for so much wraith. If they'd joined the Wraith Alliance when it formed one hundred years ago, Liadia might still be here."

I couldn't speak. Lady Julianna wouldn't be able to, either. But for such different reasons.

My fingernails dug into the seat of my chair, aching.

"We're giving Aecorians a chance to redeem themselves. We're giving them a chance to help keep the Indigo Kingdom—and Aecor, of course—safe."

Dizziness pressed inside my head. Hearing the horrifying

rumor confirmed made me sick. My people. Thrown onto the front lines to be slaughtered.

"My lady?"

I held up a hand, but couldn't speak. Angry tears crowded my throat, and I had to look down before someone saw them threatening in my eyes.

The prince stood. "We'll adjourn until next week. I'm certain by then Lady Julianna will feel more able to withstand these talks."

There was grumbling, but a few minutes later, the generals, Colin, and Clint filed out of the room; the last paused just before laying his hand on my shoulder, like he thought better of it at the last moment.

Finally, the room was empty, except for the prince, his bodyguard, and me.

Tobiah didn't move from his place. His tone was hard and unimpressed. "I invited you here because I believed you could handle the discussion."

I mustered my voice, because I had to give some kind of excuse for my reaction. "It will never be safe." The words came roughly. "Not the Indigo Kingdom. Not Aecor. Liadia has already shown that kind of faith to be a lie."

Tobiah and James exchanged a look, and finally Tobiah said, "I know how difficult it can be to move beyond traumatic points in your life."

"Not everyone has the luxury of being able to move beyond them," I rasped.

"When I was younger," said the prince, "something happened to me."

113

Oh yes. I knew. But Tobiah had had a family to return home to. He'd lost nothing beyond his innocence of what people could do to one another, and that innocence had only fallen away on the ledge with me while we watched *his* people massacre mine.

"It isn't something I speak of often, but it left a mark. I don't know that we ever fully move past that kind of trauma."

I pushed myself up, palms flat against the table. "I think I should retire to my quarters for now."

The prince gave a curt nod, and James stepped away from the wall. Both of them watched me, one annoyed, and one wary. "Shall I escort you back?" Tobiah asked, making it clear that he didn't want to.

"I can make it on my own." I gave a small curtsy and gathered up the papers he'd given me earlier. On my way out, I glanced again at the wall map, and the mysterious scribbles on the western border of Liadia.

They read *confidential* and *debated*.

What did *that* mean?

TEN

HALFWAY BACK TO my rooms, my head still full of *confidential* and *debated*, I ran into Lady Chey.

She was as resplendent as ever in a yellow gown, a fashionable split down the middle of the top layer and an intricately embroidered pattern at the bottom. With a quick curtsy, she said, "Oh, Lady Julianna! I hope you were on your way to the ladies' solar. We were all gathering for needlework."

"How kind of you to invite me. But I'm afraid I don't have anything to work on." The very last thing I wanted to do was join Chey and all her friends for *needlework*.

Chey shook her head and tutted. "Don't be silly. We'll find something for you."

Before I could escape, she'd hooked her arm around mine and begun guiding me through the palace. Mirrors flashed in the edges of my vision, lit by sunlight streaming through windows.

Chey was a fountain of chatter as we walked, listing

upcoming celebrations and balls she was excited to attend, and what she would wear to each of them. "There are several plays coming to the Saint Shumway Theater. You should try to attend a few." At last, she paused to breathe. "Here we are."

We were not far from the Dragon Wing, where the royal apartments were held. I could see nothing of them, however: just a pair of guards and a long, empty hallway beyond.

Chey pulled open the door to the ladies' solar, revealing a chamber occupied by a dozen women seated in large chairs with sewing baskets beside them. The walls were covered in brocade silk, and hissing gas lamps lit the room with a cheery glow. But at my entrance, every face turned toward me and became cool, guarded.

Second time in one day. My skill at ruining moods was truly incomparable.

Lady Meredith set aside her needlework and rose. "Julianna. Welcome." Her smile measured equal parts suspicion and genuine pleasure. She smoothed her palms along her sky blue day dress, embroidered with gold filigree around the hems. The gold matched her hair, all coiled braids and artfully arranged tendrils.

I offered a pale curtsy. "Thank you for your invitation, my lady. I'm afraid I haven't anything to work on, though."

Chey stepped forward. "I told the duchess we'd find something for her."

"Of course we will." Meredith gestured to an empty chair. "Please."

After Chey and I were both seated, introductions were offered, and a maid had poured everyone glasses of sweet wine,

I was given a hand spindle and a cloud of soft lamb's wool. I left them on my lap, touching the pages of wraith research instead, like reassurance they were still there. I didn't have *time* for these ladies.

Meredith adjusted the canvas on her lap and pressed a blue-threaded needle into the work. "Julianna, I think you've just come from a meeting with my fiancé's committee. How interesting. Ladies don't typically attend those meetings."

"I think the duchess is not a typical lady," mused Chey.

"Perhaps." Meredith didn't look up from her work. "Julianna, I hope he didn't pressure you too much to recount your time in the wraithland. You must forgive him. He wants only the best for the Indigo Kingdom."

Several of the other ladies nodded agreement as they worked on needlepoint and knitting and sewing together embroidered canvases.

Meredith noted my attention on everyone's projects. "We, too, want what's best for the kingdom." She turned her needlepoint to face me, revealing an emerging pattern of house sigils and lines of holy scripture. A silhouette of the Cathedral of the Solemn Hour appeared in the background, in cloud-silver thread. "We make tapestries, shrouds, and other items for chapels all around the kingdom. It's said that patterns made by innocent hands can soak up wraith, trapping it in the smallest spaces between the fibers."

"Indeed?" I eyed the spindle in my lap and tried not to think about all the things I'd done; no doubt I didn't qualify as "innocent." "Does it work?" I asked.

Meredith smiled sweetly. "What matters is the hope our

work brings. Soldiers of West Pass Watch sometimes wear our creations on their backs, or wrap them beneath their uniforms, against their skin like armor. What matters is that the people protecting us feel we've given them something in return."

"I see." I trailed my fingers along the spindle whorl, feeling the ridges of the wood and the hammered metal spirals twisting around the edge. It had been a decade since I'd held a spindle, and I wasn't sure I could make my hands remember what to do.

"Don't you want to spin?" Chey asked.

I clasped my hands and pressed them to my lap, as though hiding a tremble. "I'm afraid the committee meeting took a little more out of me than I'd like to admit."

"I'm sorry to hear that." Chey set her mouth in a frown. "We've heard such wonderful things about your spinning."

Was that true? Could Julianna be known for her spinning? It wasn't something that had come up in my research of her, though I hadn't been able to find much on the duchess in the first place.

"I'm sorry to disappoint," I said at last, setting aside the spindle and wool. "Perhaps I should return to my chambers to rest. I'm sure my companion is wondering what's become of me."

"Of course." Meredith gestured toward the door. "Please accept my best wishes, and again I apologize for my fiancé. He simply does what he thinks is necessary for the good of the kingdom."

And now that she'd told me twice, I was *certain* to remember.

I curtsied and said my farewells before gathering my papers and hurrying out the door.

* * *

Lunch waited on the sitting room table when I returned to my apartments. Steam obscured the contents beneath the glass-lidded trays. Books and papers surrounded them, and our map in progress lay across the back of one of the chairs. Melanie glanced up from the notes she was writing and grinned. "Well?"

"Well, what?" I shut and locked the door behind me. "What's all this? Osprey papers?"

Melanie's smile dropped.

"If I'd been anyone else, we would be in the dungeon by now." I strode toward her.

Her pen fell to the table as she scrambled to her feet. "I—I'm sorry. I figured anyone else would knock."

"You were willing to risk the entire mission on politeness?" I was overreacting, I knew. About this anyway. "Tobiah offered to walk me back here. And Chey tried to attach herself to my hip. If either of them had joined me, they would have seen this." I thrust my hands toward the map, bright with streaks of color denoting the gardens and fountains and offices and *bedchambers* of nobility. If anyone saw that . . .

Melanie said nothing, but her eyes were round.

"And why is it taking you so long to deliver reports? Where else are you going after?"

Her eyes grew wide and hurt. "Nowhere. I come right back here."

I held her gaze for a moment longer, but she didn't so much as squeak. Finally, I turned away and took a seat.

"Sorry." Melanie lingered beside her chair, as though unsure whether she was allowed to be here anymore. "I'll put everything away."

"Take notes during the day. Remember that we could be interrupted at any moment."

Her eyes cut to the door. "Sorry, Wil." A few minutes later, she had everything back in hiding, except a notebook and a couple of books we'd been reading. *The Lost Art of Architecture: Skyvale Palace* and *The Valley within the Valley: The Exploration of the Midvale Ridge.* The latter was a pre-wraith book, with incredibly even lettering and realistic art. It was worth a fortune.

Lunch was a small bowl of soup, half a loaf of bread, and a pile of sliced meats and cheeses. It was only stock, whatever they had in the kitchens, but still so much more than what we called lunch at the old palace. Not to mention the setting; the price for just one of these glass lids could have fed the Ospreys for a week.

I glanced out the window, watching clouds drift in the breeze. I hoped the Ospreys were well. I hoped Connor was in control of himself. I hoped Quinn and her team were safe. I hated so many of us being spread out. Already there were so few of us.

Melanie nodded at the papers I'd brought back. "Those look important."

We Ospreys prided ourselves on our powers of observation.

"From His Surliness. It should be wraith research. Thanks to Chey practically kidnapping me in the hall, I haven't read them, but perhaps it will provide us with some answers."

She nodded. "Good. That will be useful."

Awkwardness pulled at us.

"There was some kind of monster attack in Thornton the other night. That's why I was back late."

We both knew *that* wasn't true, but I didn't call her on the lie, because here our secrets overlapped. "A wraith beast? What happened?" I was pretty sure I'd left before anyone else arrived, but I wasn't ready for Melanie to know I'd followed her.

As she told me about Black Knife's victory over the wraith cat, with no mention of a second fighter, I relaxed.

"That guy is everywhere, isn't he?" I sipped my wine.

"I doubt he ever sleeps." She flashed a pale smile. "I keep seeing posters asking for his help. They want him to stop a gang in Red Flag, or find a missing child in White Flag. I even saw a few demanding he stop the wraith before it crosses into the valley. The police keep tearing them down."

"He's a menace." He took flashers and did who knew what with them. Something bad enough that no one would dare tell a lady. I couldn't let that happen, not to myself, and not to . . . others I cared for.

"Did you learn anything at the meeting?" she asked after a few minutes.

I learned that the Indigo Kingdom didn't have any more of an idea of how to stop the wraith than anyone else.

I learned that the *Overlord* of Aecor was here in Skyvale Palace.

And I learned that my people were being used to fight King Terrell's war.

"Yes," I said at last. "I learned that we are going to win this."

ELEVEN

IT WASN'T LONG before a maid came to collect our dishes, and a young boy followed close behind with an envelope. "For Lady Julianna."

"Thank you." The envelope was sealed with the royal crest. The wax snapped in half and the envelope released a single, heavy card with thick script.

> *Please join His Majesty Terrell Pierce, Sovereign of the Indigo Kingdom, for breakfast tomorrow at the ninth hour. Dress is formal.*

Frowning, I flipped the card over, but that was it.

"Someone looks unhappy," Melanie said, once the maid and courier were gone. "Bad news?"

"No. Probably a good opportunity. Just"—I flicked the card onto the table—"I hate being here. I hate that we're expected to jump and run because he says."

Melanie picked up the card and skimmed. "We're expected to jump and run for the Ospreys, too."

"Yes, but Patrick *earned* our respect when he freed us from the orphanage. What has King Terrell done for us?" And there was an interesting question about monarchs, but it was one I didn't want to ponder now.

"Well." Melanie sat on the arm of a sofa and folded her hands. "For *Julianna*, he's provided shelter, food, an entire wardrobe, and anything else you ask for. He's probably fantasizing about who he'll marry you off to, once he deems enough time has passed that it's not inappropriate."

"All his kindness would mean more if I were really Julianna, not Wilhelmina." I'd begun answering to her name, though, without pause for thought. Responding quickly was good for the mission, but I wasn't sure I liked it.

"Even so, you should enjoy the wealth while we have it." She gave a liquid shrug. "As you said, soon it'll be all dirt, hunger, and walks through bloody battlefields. The anniversary is in the spring."

"And we'd best complete our tasks." I tapped the lid of the writing box. "Our map is in progress, which leaves the other three tasks. Intelligence about the Indigo Army's locations in Aecor, the list of resistance groups, and the Aecorian draftees on the front lines of the wraithland."

Melanie paled. "So you have confirmation they're being drafted?"

"I heard it straight from *Overlord* Colin Pierce. And I know what I have to do." During lunch, I'd been flipping through Tobiah's papers, and a few important signatures stood out.

With a spare sheet of paper in front of me, I dipped my pen into black ink and began practicing the first signature.

Melanie's expression shifted into understanding. "That's not quite right." She poked through the collection of nibs. "Try this one."

The second nib was stiffer, forcing my writing cobweb thin, same as General Fredrick Goldberg's. "Better. Thanks." I sent her to fetch the appropriate paper from his office while I practiced the second signature, and then we drafted a letter recalling the Aecorian troops from the front lines.

We worked through dinner, triple-checking the handwriting and word choice against official documents, and finally signed it with Colin Pierce's and Fredrick Goldberg's names.

I was Julianna, a general, and occasionally the orphaned Princess of Aecor. I was anyone I needed to be.

"How will we deliver this?" Melanie asked.

"Tonight, go to Colin Pierce's office and seal it closed with his sigil. Then, find out who the military uses to send their urgent messages, and hire him. I'm sure you can obtain the money for his usual fee as well as discretion." I grinned. "Just don't let anyone catch you."

She feigned offense. "I'm practically invisible."

"Say it again." I snapped and thumped my chest, and she did the same. "Don't forget to poke around for the lists of resistance groups and Indigo Army locations in Aecor."

"What Patrick wants, Patrick gets. Are you going to rest here for a while?" She glanced at the sofa where I'd left a book about the Indigo Kingdom's history. Tobiah had sent it shortly after the ball.

"I'm going for a walk. I need to clear my thoughts."

She flashed a sympathetic smile and nodded. "I know this is difficult, but we're making progress. We're about to free hundreds—maybe thousands—of our people."

"We still need to make home a safe place for them."

"We will." Conviction filled her voice. "I know we will."

It was hard not to wonder about her faith, though. Did she believe in me? Or just Patrick? He was the leader of the Ospreys. I was a title.

When she was gone, I changed into a black sweater and pants, and laced my boots tight. Cold air hovered near the window, hinting of the frigid evening, so I pulled a cap over the braids and coils of my hair. My daggers fit neatly at my hips, comforting weight I missed in the palace.

I left our apartments a few minutes later, sneaking out the window same as before, and cutting across courtyards and gardens. The night air smelled sharply of conifer trees and smoke, and cold slithered down my heavy wool sweater no matter how I adjusted the collar.

Cheerful noise came from one of the Hawksbill mansions, fading as I ran past. Gas lamps glowed in swirling patterns all through the district, so I couldn't linger.

In a quiet area, I threw my grappling hook over the wall separating Hawksbill and the rest of the city, and climbed into Thornton.

I took a different route to the baker's than the last time, keeping to the streets rather than the roofs. This way, I could avoid the mirrors—at least for now.

The streets were busy, even hours after dusk. With mirrors covering every western surface, the occasional gas lamp was much more effective than it would have been alone. Light shone everywhere.

"Black Knife will save us from the wraith!" shouted a man holding a rotting wood board up in the air. The words painted onto the wood repeated his claims about Black Knife, though they were misspelled and several of the letters were drawn backward. "Black Knife will journey to the wraithland! He will battle the wraith and free us from our impending doom!"

Though most people stayed clear of the man, a few stepped in as though to ask questions—and then pulled back when a police officer approached.

"I have a right to speak!" the man yelled. "You can't stop me."

"If you have information on the vigilante Black Knife . . ."

Their voices faded into the din of the crowd as I moved past.

When I reached Laurence's Bakery half an hour later, I slipped into an alley, pulled my cap toward my eyes, and climbed onto the roof. With my body pressed against a chimney, I scanned the area to make sure I was alone. Nothing. Just starlight and mirrors and the pale glow of the city slowly falling to sleep.

I darted south, keeping myself small and quick so the mirrors wouldn't catch me. It wasn't hard to retrace Melanie's steps; my memories were sharp and clear.

I leapt onto the roof of a chandlery and stopped.

This was it. I was standing in the last place I'd seen Melanie before Black Knife interrupted my pursuit. *Now* what? Though

I was on my way out of Thornton, the Flags were enormous, and there were three of them. She could have gone anywhere, even doubled back into Thornton or Greenstone.

A deep voice came from behind me. "You're just everywhere, aren't you?"

I spun and had my daggers drawn before his question was half finished. "Black Knife."

"Nameless girl." He stood on the edge of the roof I'd just left, with only a small jump between us. His hands hung at his sides, no weapons, but his crossbow and sword were only a quick reach away. "Again, without your entourage. I know you're not out here to stop thieves or gangs, so you can just tell me the truth. What are you doing?"

My grip on my daggers didn't slacken despite his apparent ease. "Taking a walk."

"Most people use the street."

"Standing on a roof isn't illegal, is it?"

"There was a robbery in Greenstone a couple of weeks ago. Right around the time I saw you, actually."

"And you think I'm responsible?" I feigned affront.

His gaze dipped to my weapons before he sat, letting his legs dangle from the roof. The leather of his boots shone in the weak lamplight from below, and the silk kept his face perfectly concealed. Still, with the relaxed set of his shoulders and the easy way his hands rested on his knees, he looked comfortable. Cocky. "I don't think a robbery like that is beyond your skill."

"A compliment and an insult in one sentence."

"Would you like to sit?" He leaned his weight onto one arm, glancing down into the quiet alley. "People rarely look up, but we're not the only ones to use the rooftops as a second street. I'd rather not be seen."

Cautiously, I found solid footing and crouched, keeping my daggers in my hands. "Are you following me?"

"How can I when I don't know who you are?" The words sounded like a sneer.

"That makes us even. I don't know who you are, either."

"Good."

What did he want with me? "Why do you wear a mask?"

"To hide my face. That's the function of a mask, after all."

I rolled my eyes. "Why do you hide your face?"

He went still for a moment, almost a statue's shadow. "I think the more pressing question is this: why don't *you* wear a mask, considering your suspicious proximity to crime?"

I repeated Patrick's belief: "The best mask is a face no one will remember."

"Oh," he said, and looked at me as though I were a mystery. "I don't see how anyone could forget your face."

Compliments again. Why couldn't he just chase me, like normal? Unless—no, he couldn't know me from the palace. If he recognized me, I wouldn't still be there. "Are we going to fight?" I asked.

"Do you want to?"

"Not particularly." But fighting would be a lot more straightforward.

He shrugged. "Then we don't have to. As you said, standing on a roof isn't illegal, and I can't prove you're responsible for the warehouse robbery."

"Is that how it works? You prove that the people you

capture were breaking the law?"

"Sometimes."

"What about the rest of the time? What if you caught someone about to break into that warehouse, but they hadn't actually succeeded yet?"

"I'd bind them and leave them where the city police would find them."

"With no proof they'd done—or were about to do—anything?" When he didn't respond, I said, "Who gave you the authority? If you have your heart set on stopping violence and crimes, there are less dramatic ways to do it. Or do you enjoy the reactions to your theatrics?"

"I have my reasons. As I'm sure you have your reasons for fighting and stealing."

Wind howled through the alley below, bringing only the normal odors of the city: sweat and smoke and waste. The thuds and squeaks and cracks of humanity's presence softened as Skyvale residents headed to bed.

"I'm not admitting to anything—"

He laughed. *Laughed.* "No, I don't imagine you ever would."

I hefted a dagger in his direction, and he held up his hands in mock surrender.

"Sorry. You were saying?" There was still a hitch of laughter in his voice as he made himself comfortable again.

"If *I* were going to fight and steal, it'd be because I had no choice. It would be for survival."

"When does fighting and stealing become more?"

I lifted an eyebrow. "Like what? Murder?"

"How interesting that's where your mind turned."

"Well, it was recently suggested that my life might be easier if I'd let someone die." I squeezed my dagger hilt. "But I left one of these in a glowman's hand to keep that from happening, you see."

Black Knife shrugged. "I thought that was simply a diversionary tactic, to allow you time to get away."

"It served two purposes." I smirked. "But I'm not a murderer, and I wouldn't just *let* someone die. Even a menace like you."

He cocked his head, leaving his hands motionless in his lap. "Do you think others feel the same way? About stealing and whatnot, I mean."

I hesitated. "Some. Maybe most. There are parts of Skyvale where people feel they cannot afford to be civilized. Desperation makes them dangerous. But I've seen others who would fight and steal regardless of their circumstances. Like those glowmen, and the gangs that supply them with chemicals and wraith. They just like the thrill of violence. They like hurting people, even children. They like making things burn."

"That's a very bleak outlook."

"No. It means I know to be careful. You can't always tell which way someone leans." I shifted my weight to keep blood flowing through my limbs.

"And you lean toward desperate danger."

I scoffed, gesturing at his black uniform and the array of weapons. "I suppose you think your reasons for fighting are nobler than mine."

"I was going to ask about your circumstances. What led you to this life." He paused. "Hypothetically, that is."

Not that it was any of his business: "Hypothetically, I fight and steal to help others."

"The other Ospreys. The children I saw."

The Ospreys. The victims of the One-Night War. The people still of Aecor. Yes. I leaned toward desperate danger; I would do anything for my people.

In Hawksbill, the clock tower chimed midnight. Starlight, and a sliver of moonlight, set the mirrors aglow, half illuminating the boy across from me. His long, lanky body appeared relaxed, but I'd seen him spring up and fight frighteningly quick before. I could not relax.

"I think I agree with you," he said at last. "Most people want only to survive. Perhaps, if they were able to afford to be civilized—as you put it—even the gangs and glowmen would be kind and generous and law-abiding."

The thought made me snort. "That's an optimistic view."

"You make optimism sound like an accusation."

"Maybe you haven't seen as much of the city as you think." Hadn't he heard the glowman the other week? When I'd asked why he attacked my people, he'd simply claimed they looked *easy*.

Black Knife waited a moment before asking, "What about flashers? Do you think they're deliberately using their magic to bring the wraith closer? Do you think they like making things burn?"

Every muscle in my body tensed. I wanted to leap to the other roof and strangle him, but that would get me nowhere—except maybe shoved to the street below. I took measured breaths until I could speak calmly.

"I need to go." My thighs ached as I stood.

In only a heartbeat, Black Knife pushed himself up and crossed the gap. I raised my blades, but he grabbed my forearm and twisted me around, bending my wrist so the dagger fell to the rooftop. With one arm around my waist and his free hand clutching both of my wrists, his breath came in harsh gasps by my ear. "Who *are* you?"

Trembling with how easily he'd disarmed me, I hissed, "Take off your mask. Then we can discuss identities."

His breathing grew deeper and even. "No. I don't think so."

"Let me go." Dull pain throbbed through my wrist where he'd bent it.

"Once you tell me what you think about flashers. Do you think they're just like gangs and glowmen, and eager for the end?" His body was warm against mine, even as the night cooled around us. Gusts of wind brought the scent of an oncoming storm. Veils of clouds blew eastward, shrouding the stars.

"No," I said. "I think most are desperate. Everyone knows about the wraith, but it's hard to care about that when your children are starving or cold or sick, or when gangs are demanding tolls for traveling streets you can't avoid. They have nothing but this one ability, and the people in power forbid it. They're terrified to use magic, but more afraid not to."

"Even though it's destroying our world?"

"Several problems are immediate. One is not." I shivered. "Everyone knows about you."

He was quiet.

"You *seek* flashers. And once you find them, they're never seen again. What do you do with them?"

"Good night, nameless girl." Black Knife released me.

I staggered away, scooped up my daggers, and spun. The tip of one blade rested under his chin.

His eyes found mine, and he stilled.

I could turn the dagger blade vertical. Cut a slit in the silk that covered his face. Maybe find out who hid behind that mask.

He'd disarm me as soon as I moved. We'd fight, and I'd have to explain away strange cuts and bruises when I returned to the palace.

"Are we going to fight?" he asked, echoing my earlier question.

My voice grew hoarse. "What happens to the flashers?"

"Good night." He reached up, as though to shove away my dagger.

"Black Knife."

He held my gaze and didn't move. His black-gloved hand hung suspended in the air, just breaths away from my wrist.

I licked my lips. "Are they killed?"

Carefully, gently, Black Knife took my hand and pulled away from the dagger. His tone turned darker. "I will find out."

Then he stepped off the edge of the roof and vanished into the shadows.

TWELVE

"LAST NIGHT WAS a success," Melanie said, beckoning me to sit in front of the mirror. As she brushed and braided my hair, she described sneaking into the general's office and navigating his haphazard organizational system.

"So he's messy."

"Say it again. I was embarrassed for him." Her mirror-self grinned. "But there's good news. The letter recalling the Aecorian troops will go out this afternoon. I used money from Colin Pierce's own box to pay the courier."

"Very nice."

"While I was snooping around, I found a map of Aecor with Indigo Kingdom troops marked. I took note of the locations and numbers. I haven't found the list of resistance groups in Aecor, but I did see a few references to it in other notices."

"But that covers most of the intelligence on the Indigo Army?" Excitement fluttered inside me. We'd been here not even two weeks, but we'd completed nearly half our tasks.

"Almost. Patrick wanted to know what kind of weapons they're carrying and other details like that." She finished plaiting my hair into a swirling coronet, leaving just a few tendrils hanging to my shoulders. Every time I turned my head, a thin whiff of rosewater lifted off my hair; it was in the soap. "I'll keep looking for more information, as well as the list of the resistance groups."

"Good. I need to do some snooping, too. I saw something interesting at the wraith mitigation meeting that made me curious."

"Oh? Something interesting like the *royal scenery*?"

"The royal scenery?" I made a gagging face at her.

"But it would make Quinn so happy if you'd at least write her a letter and describe him. Maybe the bodyguard, too, while you're at it? I'll add them to tonight's report."

"Shut your mouth! I will not waste precious ink on that bore!"

She laughed. "Does this have anything to do with the long walk you took last night? Maybe you were meeting someone?"

Before I could make up an answer, a footman came to whisk me toward the Dragon Wing, where the king and his immediate family lived.

After traversing a maze of halls, I was deposited in a dining room large enough to seat ten or twelve people. The room was lavishly decorated, with a heavy oak table and matching chairs, and a lace tablecloth that gleamed like silk under the mid-morning light falling through the open window. Gold-framed paintings hung on all the walls, portraits of the Pierce family going back several generations. The fashion changes over the centuries might have been interesting to study, but movement caught my eye.

"Lady Julianna." On the other side of the room, King Terrell stood, one hand bracing him against the table. His arm trembled with the strain, and his breath came in slow, heavy gasps. "I'm glad you decided to visit me this morning."

As though I'd been given a choice.

"Thank you for inviting me." It wasn't hard to play the part of a nervous young noblewoman, unsure of her place in this palace. Not right now. When the king beckoned me forward, I took the offered chair. "Will your wife or son be joining us?" I asked as the footman slid my chair closer to the table.

"Francesca often has breakfast with her ladies, and I'm afraid Tobiah sleeps rather late."

Of course he did.

King Terrell sat and signaled the servants waiting by another door. "Which is good for us, because I'd like to discuss him."

That sounded bad. "With me?"

He nodded deeply, then waited as we were served dishes of blueberries and strawberries, with small crystal bowls of cream and sugar. There were peeled orange sections and bananas, and other fruits I couldn't identify.

"Your greenhouses must be impressive," I said, "with such a selection." Did anyone beyond the Hawksbill wall eat so well?

"Thank you." He dipped a strawberry into his bowl of sugar and seemed to ponder. "The Pierce family has been collecting seeds and plants from traders for generations. Our gardeners are the best on the continent."

"Indeed?" At last, I knew where his son had inherited his pride.

His mouth pulled into a line. "I suppose there's not much competition. Not anymore."

With wraith covering everything in the west, no. There were countries north and south of here, and Aecor, but this sliver of land was all that remained.

I fought a surge of embarrassment at my unkind thoughts. Why should I mind?

"Forgive me," King Terrell said. "I wanted to speak to you because you know the horrors of the wraithland. Because you know what is at stake."

I spooned cream over my fruit and stirred, waiting for him to go on. The fruit was sweet and perfectly ripe. I hadn't tasted anything so delicious since I was a child.

"You requested to join my son's wraith mitigation committee."

"I did. He explained the committee's position on magic and wraith." But not what happened to the people caught using magic. How strange that I was suddenly relying on Black Knife to help me find the truth. "His Highness believes that ceasing all magic will cause the wraith to dissipate."

"As I'm sure you were taught in Liadia. It's the same theory we've been using for a hundred years."

"Of course."

"In many ways, Tobiah is very like me." He turned his gaze on the window, its curtains pulled back to reveal a late-flowering garden. Ivy-covered trellises arched in the morning sun, while hedges framed walkways and chrysanthemums and helianthuses. Small bells and chimes tinkled in the breeze. "He is idealistic. He dreams up lofty goals. He wants to make this world better, though he's only now starting to understand the horrible things that people can do to one another."

"I thought—" No, maybe I didn't want to ask about the One-Night War.

But the king waited, his eyes dark and tired. He looked *so* different from the king in my imagination, the one who'd ordered his army to invade Aecor almost ten years ago. The one who'd allowed my parents to be slaughtered in the courtyard while my people—and I—watched. The one who'd taken the highborn children and had them put away in an orphanage.

His current illness didn't change his past actions.

Wearing my Julianna persona like armor, I made my voice strong, curious. "He mentioned that something happened to him when he was younger."

Terrell deflated. Though it was only midmorning, exhaustion dragged at his expression, and his skin was gray and waxen. "This is all tied up together. The wraith, Tobiah's abduction, the One-Night War."

My stomach turned and tumbled. I couldn't eat anymore.

"Forgive me," he said. "I'm getting ahead of myself. You know of the Wraith Alliance."

"Of course. That's why I'm here: nobility from one of the allied countries must give shelter and aid to nobility of a wraith-affected country."

"So long as they agreed to the terms. Which included, of course, that every participating country would immediately cease the use of magic. The Alliance was created in nine hundred and one by my grandfather, who recognized that action must be taken against the wraith threat."

Where was he going with this?

"I'm sure you know that not all countries were willing to give up use of magic. One of these was our neighbor to the east, Aecor, and I spent the early part of my reign urging Phillip and Angela to reconsider their predecessors' decisions."

My parents' names stole my ability to speak. I hid my shaking hands in my lap.

"The Kortes and I were friends in our youth, before we understood the scale of the wraith problem, and the animosity between our kingdoms. If we hadn't all attended a royal wedding in Laurel-by-the-Sea, our northern neighbor, we might never have been so close." He gave a weak chuckle and spoke toward me, rather than to me. As though he were somewhere else. His sickness had addled his brain; it was the only reason he was telling me all of this. "We always said that our children would marry and unite the two kingdoms, and the conflict between our parents would be left in the past. It was only when we inherited our thrones that we grew apart. They refused to consider that they were *wrong*, that their decisions would lead to the end of our world."

My face felt numb, as though all the blood were draining from it. He'd been friends with my parents, and then had them killed?

I should have brought a dagger with me.

"Over and over, I tried to make them understand the importance of ceasing magic. I repeatedly sent our latest reports and evidence, and reminded them that the Indigo Kingdom wouldn't always be between the wraith and Aecor. Just as"—the king focused on me for a moment—"Liadia could not remain between the wraithland and the Indigo Kingdom forever. But they were adamant. They insisted magic wasn't as harmful as we believed, so they would not sign the treaty."

My thoughts spun. This was too much. Too much.

"That I could not persuade them will always be one of my greatest regrets." His chair creaked as he leaned back. "Then, almost ten years ago, Phillip's men abducted my son."

I couldn't speak. Couldn't move.

"It was because of the Wraith Alliance again. I wanted them to sign. Their representatives were unreasonable. They refused to outlaw the practice of magic in Aecor, even though they knew the consequences. When I tried to force them, making sure they knew they were surrounded by allied kingdoms, my son was gone—taken by Phillip's General Lien. Tobiah was only eight years old."

I wanted to ask, "Why would General Lien take Tobiah?" and a million other questions, but I couldn't make the words come. His words paralyzed me.

"I'm not proud of what happened after. The Kingdom of Aecor is gone. Phillip and Angela are gone. Their daughter, Wilhelmina, is gone, in spite of my orders to spare her, along with the other noble children. Their children deserved mercy, and I would have given them a home, but they never made it to Skyvale. I searched for them for months, without success. Princess Wilhelmina was killed in the chaos, and the children were lost. But I got my son back."

"Yes," I whispered. "You did."

And I'd always wonder what might have happened if *my* actions had been different that night.

"That was the One-Night War, the night the Indigo Army arrived in Aecor City and rescued my son. It was the worst night of my life since we lost my first son, Terrell the Fifth."

But the Indigo Army hadn't rescued Tobiah.

I had.

"My life is quickly coming to an end, Lady Julianna. I know you noticed my illness when we first met."

"Yes."

"When I die, I want to know I've left my kingdom a better place than when I inherited the crown. In some ways, I think I've succeeded. Crime is lower. The economy is better. People seem more hopeful."

Terrell saw only the Skyvale with elaborate balls and gardens and greenhouses with the best fruits on the continent. Only the Skyvale inside the Hawksbill wall.

"But crime and the poor economy and hopelessness were symptoms of the real problem: magic and wraith. Those things, I've done very little to deter. My son is trying, though, and I must believe he will succeed where I have failed. But he needs someone like you to teach him about the world beyond these palace walls, because, in hindsight, I've done him a disservice by keeping him so close ever since his abduction. I hired Academy professors to come to him, instead of sending him to school. Tobiah graduated well, of course, but was never permitted to experience the equally important social aspects of an education."

Well, *that* explained a lot about the crown prince's attitude.

"Tobiah is a good young man," said the king. "And he will

be a good king one day. I'm afraid that, though I have the best physicians in the Indigo Kingdom treating me, I won't be here much longer. As such, I cannot stop the wraith. Tobiah might be the savior of future generations, but if he's to succeed, he will need someone to temper his blind enthusiasm. An adviser. A friend."

Tobiah and I had used up all our friendship during the One-Night War.

The king seemed to have talked himself out; we spent the rest of the meal in silence, breaking it only to comment on the breakfast I could no longer taste. When I was excused, a footman guided me to one of the public areas of the palace, and then left me alone with *debated* and *confidential* just across the hall.

I waited until the way was clear before I slipped into the wraith mitigation committee chamber and shut the door behind me.

A banner of sunlight streamed through the window, so I didn't need to turn on the gas lamps to see the map, which still hung on the wall, unchanged from yesterday. I followed the bands of color across the land, dragging my fingertip from the far end of some long-forgotten kingdom fallen to wraith, all the way to the western border of Liadia. Plains and rivers and forests and fields: all caught in the haze of wraith.

It would be the Indigo Kingdom's fate.

And Aecor's.

Tobiah was right: something *did* need to be done. But what? Could halting magic really change anything at this point?

I shook off the thoughts. I was here to work, and quickly, before anyone caught me.

"A lake?" I murmured. A small body of water near a border village was circled, but it didn't look like there was anything special about it.

I took note of the coordinates and the surrounding area before heading to the desk. There was nothing useful, though, not in any of the drawers or files, or even in the locked false bottom.

Just as I was slipping my lockpick back into my shoe, the doorknob rattled. Should I hide? A noblewoman like Julianna would never huddle under the desk. I hurried to stand in front of the map again, just as the door swung open.

"My lady?" Clint Chuter paused when he saw me.

I'd posed with my hands behind my back, my shoulders straight, and my head cocked at a contemplative angle. My expression was a mask of sadness and nobility as I looked at him. "Captain. How nice to see you." I offered a forced-looking smile, as though trying to hide my grief. "My apologies, if I'm not supposed to be in here. I was just looking at Liadia."

"Oh." He left the door open as he came to stand beside me. "You must think about it often."

I allowed my voice to break. "Every moment."

He gave me another minute before he said, "I'm afraid this room will be needed shortly."

So please leave was the implied conclusion to that sentence. "Of course. A question, first?"

"Certainly."

I pointed to the lake in Liadia. "What does this mean?"

"Wishful thinking." He shook his head. "It's only a rumor, and not a reliable one. It's nothing for you to worry about."

I bit my cheek to keep from frowning. Clint was supposed to be the one who liked me. He thought I was *delightful*. If he wouldn't tell me, no one here would.

"Thank you for your time, Captain." I gave a small curtsy and quit the room. Clearly, no one was going to *tell* me what was out there, and there'd been no information in Tobiah's desk. But I wasn't discouraged. I *would* learn this secret, even if I had to go to the wraithland to do it.

PART TWO

THE
WRAITHLAND

THIRTEEN

IN OUR APARTMENTS, Melanie was reclining on one of the sofas, a book in hand. *A History of Mirrors*, read the cover in gold foil. There were ink smudges on her fingers, and her braid was askew. She'd been hard at work.

"Did you know that King Terrell Pierce the Second was the one to declare mirrors the answer to wraith?" Melanie didn't look up from her book as I let the door fall shut behind me. "One of his men returned from the wraithland claiming a mirror had scared off a wraith beast, because it saw itself and was terrified, so Terrell the Second had mirrors hung on every west-facing surface in the city. He declared the mirrors would frighten the wraith into never invading Skyvale. At first it was just polished tin, but eventually they moved on to glass and the wards grew more extravagant. Lots of people use them as displays of wealth."

"I did know that, but thank you." Sunshine lit the sitting room, all honey gold and warm. Books and invitations and half-finished drawings of the view lay scattered on the table. Peeking out from the bottom was the beginning of a black-and-white drawing of a gloved hand gripping a black-hilted sword. I hurried to stuff it back under the others.

"What about this? Terrell the Second was called the 'Mirror King.' The Third and Fourth didn't use it, though they could have."

"I didn't know about that. It doesn't seem like a very special title if they all get it." The window drew my gaze, but all I could see from here were mansion rooftops, the clock tower, and the cathedral spires. The wall rose up behind them, blocking the rest of Skyvale from view.

Melanie snorted. "No, it's not. I think it's not supposed to be special, though. It's another name passed down. Not like 'Terrell the Scum' or 'Terrell the Sloth.' Those names are earned. This one doesn't have to be, I suppose. There are mirrors. And there's a king." She flipped to the next page. "Tobiah's older brother would have been yet another Mirror King when he inherited, but—"

"He died when he was an infant." I crossed the room and sat down by her feet.

"I wonder if Tobiah will get the title, too." She shrugged and set aside the book. "What happened to you?" Amusement and worry twisted her face as she smoothed back a lock of hair. "Did the king turn into a glowman and try to bash in your skull?"

"Not quite." I let my head drop back.

Melanie sat up and scrambled over the sofa so her shoulder bumped mine. "Did you learn anything from Terrell?"

My stomach turned over. I'd completely forgotten to ask the

king about Aecor. Instead, I'd been lost in emotions and confusion.

I forced my voice steady. "Unfortunately, he didn't have much to say about Aecor. Not beyond a few details about the One-Night War, which we already knew. Terrell is a very sick man. He just rambled about wanting to be a good king and giving his son the best chance to rule. He didn't leave much opportunity to question him."

"That's too bad."

I closed my eyes, haunted by Terrell's earnestness, and Tobiah's determination to rid the world of wraith.

They were good lessons for a future queen.

If I ever made it that far.

"What about you?" I asked. "Did you do anything useful this morning?"

"As a matter of fact, while you were off breakfasting with the enemy, I was busy working." She pushed herself up and began to pace, her green day dress fanning about behind her. "We've received a number of invitations for dinners and dances. We should respond yes to the most prestigious ones. Meredith Corcoran has been particularly solicitous, which I'm beginning to find suspicious. No one is that nice when her best friend seems to despise you. But I've organized the invitations by date."

Ugh. More social engagements. "Meredith isn't that bad. Just . . . *friendly*."

"Maybe she's keeping an eye on you for Chey."

"Wouldn't surprise me."

"I also did a little snooping." She winked and swiveled around to pace back the other way. "Our letter recalling the Aecorian troops went out, just as planned. I added a few more details to our map, which I did in your room—you have the desk—so no one would notice if they barged in."

"Good. Is that all?"

"No." She halted and stuck out a hip. "General Fredrick Goldberg's office held the very thing we've been searching for."

I raised my eyebrows. "The list?"

"Yes, indeed, Your Highness." She curtsied deeply. "A list of resistance groups in Aecor, just waiting to hear of your triumphant return."

I sat back and grinned. "The list is real."

"Yes." She withdrew a sheet of paper from her pocket. "I took the liberty of copying it and lifting a few blank pages of his stationery. The list is in Fredrick's handwriting, which we already have samples of, and regular black ink, so you should be able to write the false list this afternoon. I'll go back to plant it when you're finished."

"Excellent. Melanie, you are amazing." I stood and hugged her tightly.

"Yes, I do try."

I bounced on my toes as giddiness surged up inside of me. We were on the verge of completing our objectives. The draftees. The resistance list. The map. The intelligence on opposing forces. Soon, we could return to the old palace and begin contacting the resistance groups in Aecor. Patrick would tell them that I was alive. That I was coming to save them. Aecor would be mine.

But what about the lake in Liadia? It might be nothing—just a rumor, as Clint had said—but if the rumor were meaningless, why wouldn't he tell me more about it? What was so secret there wouldn't even be a record of it in the crown prince's desk?

Once we returned to the old palace, Patrick would initiate the next phase of his plan. I'd be taken to Aecor to meet with various groups, giving them hope and confidence and inspiration to fight the overlord's rule. I'd be spirited from place to place, quietly igniting a revolution among my people.

And then, on the tenth anniversary of the One-Night War, we'd strike against the Indigo Army. There'd be no time to investigate rumors once we left Skyvale Palace.

Let alone rumors that might take me to the wraithland.

"I also took the initiative of writing tonight's report for Patrick." Melanie held her hands behind her back and flashed a pert smile. "I've told him that we've accomplished all of our goals, except for the map in progress, but I don't think that will take much longer. If you'll write an addendum with details about your meeting yesterday and breakfast this morning, I'll deliver everything tonight."

I leaned my hip against the table and watched Melanie flutter about the room, pointing out the most valuable books and trinkets she wanted to take when we returned to the old palace.

Maybe her post-delivery excursions were nothing. She was working so hard on our mission—harder than I was, it seemed. Maybe she'd just needed time to get away. To breathe. I couldn't fault that.

Maybe I could trust her with the mystery of the Liadian lake.

"I'll finish the report tonight." I forced my tone neutral, not at all like a test. "And I'll take it to the drop."

She spun, annoyance flickering over her face before she

smoothed it into a calmly raised eyebrow. "But if anyone comes looking for you—"

"No one visits that late at night." I stood straight and crossed my arms. Silk slithered over silk. "Or is there another reason you need to be the one to take it?"

I just wanted the truth.

Her sour expression as she turned away said everything. There was no reason to *insist* she make the drop if she weren't intentionally hiding something.

"Fine," she said. "Let's both go."

"Fine."

FOURTEEN

I SPENT THE afternoon in my room, rewriting the report to exclude mentions of the resistance groups. Instead, I said simply that we were closer. I left in the parts about the Indigo Kingdom troops in Aecor and the Aecorian soldiers being sent home from the wraithland; their recall was already in motion and would be difficult to hide from Patrick once the men began returning to Aecor.

Besides, he needed to think we were getting something done here.

Once I sealed the new report, I wrote several copies of the false list in Fredrick Goldberg's handwriting. There was no reason to wait; the sooner the Indigo Army moved away from the real groups, the better.

As long as Patrick didn't know we'd succeeded.

Finished with the forgery work, I pulled out a fresh sheet of paper.

The palace stationery was fine paper that absorbed ink nicely, with no bleeding or feathering. I mentally sorted through the different handwritings I'd acquired over the years. The general's was fun, with lots of spiderweb-thin curls, but I'd just used that. Once, I'd used a tailor's handwriting to rewrite a delivery card—the clothes had *mysteriously* ended up at the Peacock Inn where Ospreys stayed—but I wasn't as familiar with that one, since I'd used it only that time.

After a moment's more thought, I selected a pointy, flexible nib from my collection and dipped it into thick, blue ink. The handwriting had belonged to a priest in one of the Flags. He had a fondness for wild flourishes on almost every letter; the writing always made Connor smile when I used it, and we could both use a smile now.

> Connor,
>
> The palace is boring. I spend a lot of my time moving from social function to social function. The other day, I was expected to spin yarn with a bunch of the palace ladies. You're not missing anything good except the food. This morning, I had fresh strawberries and cream. It was so rich my stomach hurt, but you would have liked it.
>
> I hope you're still practicing those exercises. Don't forget to work on them every night, and keep up your medical studies with Oscar. I want to hear about everything you learned when I get back.
>
> With affection,
> Wil

I folded the letter, sealed it, and wrote Connor's name on the back. Then, trying not to think about how I was intentionally delaying my return to the Ospreys, I cleaned pens and organized ink jars until the clock tower chimed an hour before midnight.

Melanie knocked. "Ready?"

I nodded, and we changed into black sweaters and trousers, armed ourselves, and slipped out into the darkness.

Without speaking, we made our way through Hawksbill and climbed over the wall, then kept to the streets in the market district. Perhaps she was working on an excuse to break away once we delivered the report.

It didn't matter. When I wiggled loose the brick at the back of Laurence's Bakery, there was already a note inside.

Both of you to the Peacock Inn. Bring the report.
—P.L.

My heart sank. Patrick arranging a meeting in the middle of our deception—that could only mean bad news.

While Melanie fitted the brick back into the hole, I checked the area for observers.

A dark silhouette stood out against a mirror. Black Knife raised his hand in a wave, and I could almost hear him calling me "nameless girl" and his snide comments about my entourage.

"Ready?" Melanie pulled up her hood. "I guess it's a good thing we both came after all, or one of us would have had to go back and fetch the other."

"Sure." When I glanced up again, Black Knife was gone. I'd seen him only because he'd allowed it.

That answered the question of whether he was following me.

We'd have to be extra careful on our way in and out of the palace from now on.

"Is something wrong?" Melanie touched my shoulder. "You look distracted."

"I'm fine. I just thought I saw someone." Why didn't I tell her about Black Knife? Well, she wasn't exactly honest with me, either. "Let's make sure we're hard to track, just in case."

She smirked. "As though we're ever not."

And still Black Knife had spotted us. We'd have to change our drop location.

On our way through Thornton, we threaded through crowds, lifting hats and scarves to disguise ourselves from rooftop pursuit. I jostled someone, nicking a silver bracelet as I apologized; the Ospreys could sell it and buy the younger boys new boots. Once we entered White Flag, though, we kept our hands to ourselves. People here were as poor as we were.

There were no gas lamps in the Flags, which meant most of the decent people headed indoors soon after dark, if they could manage. Only gangs, drunks, and homeless people stayed on the streets at night, and to the latter we tossed the hats and scarves we'd picked up in Thornton. All throughout our walk, I kept an eye on the rooftops, watching for the familiar silhouette of Black Knife. But there was no one, at least as far as I could see.

That didn't mean he wasn't there.

The Peacock Inn wasn't much to look at. The brick building boasted deteriorating columns and fading peacock feathers painted on the shutters. The windows here were just holes, no glass, so the patrons' shouts and laughter and boasting fell from the inn like punches. Along its western face, the required mirrors were cracked, their reflections distorted.

I checked the rooftops one last time as we ducked inside the hot, noisy taproom. The stench of smoke and stale beer made my stomach roll as we wove through the crowd. A man's hand strayed toward my leg, but retreated when I flicked my dagger from its sheath.

"I hate coming in this way," Melanie muttered as we made our way to the stairwell at the back of the taproom.

"Me too." Besides a few battered weapons and trinkets, there wasn't even anything good to steal. But with Black Knife out there, we needed to stick to the ground. We needed not to draw attention to ourselves.

The stairs groaned and creaked as we ascended. A heavy, musty scent huddled on the top floor, all dust and disuse; lots of people didn't stay the night here, but came for the cheap beer and general camaraderie.

Weariness tugged at me as I knocked in a quick pattern, then pushed open the door.

A single candle lit the room: Patrick studied a stack of papers by its light, the knifelike planes of his face made sharper in the shadows, while Theresa and Connor dozed sitting up on the bed. Tattered blankets and old clothes covered them.

"I wasn't expecting you for a few more hours." Patrick didn't even look up from his work. We'd receive his attention only when necessary.

"We both went to the drop," Melanie said. "We came right over."

"It takes two of you to deliver a report now?" Patrick shoved his papers to the other end of the desk and looked up at us, palm flat up and waiting.

Theresa and Connor yawned and sat straight at the sound of voices. Theresa's eyes were bloodshot, and the skin around them puffy and irritated. She'd been crying. Connor had, too.

A chill swept through me as I dropped the report into Patrick's hand. "What's wrong? Why did you send for us?"

"There's been some news." He cracked the report seal and began reading, ignoring the curious way Melanie looked at him. Whatever his news was, we wouldn't hear any more about it until he was finished with our report. It was bad, though, whatever it was. Undercurrents of unease flowed from all of us—except Patrick. He was as stoic as ever.

I lit a few more candles and checked that the window shutters were fastened, then took my perch on the windowsill. Theresa looked stricken as Connor scurried over to stand beside me. His curly hair was too long, and rumpled from sleep. Red splotched his face.

"Hey," I murmured, slipping him the folded letter I'd written earlier. It seemed so pointless now. "Are you all right?"

He shook his head, and his voice was rough with threatening tears. "Patrick said not to say anything until he was ready."

Because only Patrick got to make announcements.

I pressed my hand onto his bony shoulder, the only measure of comfort I could offer now.

Melanie and I exchanged glances as she dropped to the bed beside Theresa. Before, they'd looked as though they could be sisters, with their lean bodies hardened from work and a constant hunger that was never sated. Now, the difference between them was startling. Melanie's skin was clean of the ever-present grime that covered the Ospreys, and her face and arms were filling out, thanks to regular meals. In contrast, Theresa's collarbone stood sharp and shelflike.

We waited in tense silence while Patrick flipped pages and sighed. Finally, he pushed the report away and looked from Melanie to me, disappointment clear in his expression. "That's it? You didn't find anything about the resistance groups?"

My stomach dropped. In my annoyance over the summons and catching Black Knife spying on me, I'd forgotten that I changed the report.

"What?" Melanie surged up from the bed, shock written on her face. "We *did* find the resistance groups. Rather, *I* did."

Everyone stared at me. Seconds stretched.

"What did you do?" Melanie grabbed for the paper. Her mouth hung open as she skimmed through the letter written in her handwriting. The pages fluttered to the ground. "Wilhelmina. Did you change my report?"

I lifted my chin. "Yes." There was no denying it, and trying to explain would accomplish nothing. It would make me look weak. Heart hammering, I faced Patrick. "I wasn't ready for you to know about the groups."

"You thought I wouldn't find out?" His face showed no trace of his emotions, but his eyes revealed the calculated way he studied and reevaluated me.

"I knew you would find out." I slipped off the windowsill and linked my hands behind my back. "I've even done all the work to ensure the Indigo Kingdom will no longer pursue them."

159

"So you simply didn't want *me* to know." He stood. "It isn't your decision whether to withhold information. If I'm to resurrect Aecor—"

"I do get to decide." My voice trembled, but only just. "I do get to decide, because I'm going to be queen. Aecor is my kingdom."

Patrick turned to Melanie. "Do you have the list?" He was so calm, as though I hadn't just betrayed him, betrayed Melanie, and betrayed the Ospreys.

"Not with me. I'll include it in the next drop." Her shoulders were tense, and her voice tight. Normally, she was one of the best at disguising her feelings, but around Patrick, she was transparent. She worshipped him. They all did. And I . . . I wasn't sure what I'd just done.

He was angry. He wouldn't show it, but there was a hardness about him. *More* hardness than usual.

I put aside that worry for now, but didn't relax my posture. "What is the news you mentioned earlier?"

Patrick leveled his gaze on me. "Later. I have further instructions for you regarding your time in the palace."

Further instructions? Did he not hear me say that *I* was going to be queen? Not him?

"I want you to kill—"

"No." There was so much force behind the word that I hardly recognized my own voice. "I will not kill anyone. I've told you before: Ospreys are not murderers."

The room was silent again. Connor was back on the bed, sitting close to Theresa, who just looked on with red eyes.

"I will be Queen of Aecor. Infiltrating Skyvale Palace is one thing. Because of what Melanie and I have done there, Aecorian soldiers will be returned to their families. Resistance groups will be safe while the Indigo Army searches incorrect locations."

Patrick's stare was piercing. "You've done well. But that does not mean your work is finished."

No, it wasn't finished. Not even close.

"I won't kill anyone."

Patrick bowed his head. "I can see you will not." He stepped forward, his voice low and clipped and menacing. "But before you decide you no longer need my help, I want you to remember who freed you all from the orphanage nine years ago. When we return to Aecor and you sit on the vermilion throne, who will fight the war to keep you there?"

My jaw ached from clenching it.

"I will fight your war, Wilhelmina, just as I swore to you years ago. And if you are as wise as you think you are, you'll take me as your king so that Aecor will have at least one strong leader."

What?

He stood before me, his eyes level with mine. "One true heir, lost in the heat of the One-Night War. A queen risen again. The kind of triumphant return that shines in the history books. And at her side, a hero of the Aecorian Revolution."

"You will not be my king."

His eyes narrowed. On the bed, Theresa and Connor held deathly still.

"You will be my general. My adviser. Perhaps even my friend. But never my king."

Drunks shouted downstairs. Wind howled outside. Dogs

barked in the distance. But the room was an island of tense, smothering silence.

I stood my ground, my jaw clenched so tight it ached.

Patrick's expression remained hard. "We shall see, Wilhelmina."

The rustle of paper broke our stare. Connor was looking at the note I'd written for him.

"Tell me why you summoned us here tonight." I motioned at Theresa and Connor. "Why have they been crying?"

"They were the ones who wanted you here for the news." Patrick held himself straighter, as though he'd won. "I've received word from Ronald regarding the supply caravan mission."

"Quinn's assignment." The words were a breath.

"The mission was a success. The supplies have been captured and hidden." Patrick's tone betrayed no emotion. "Unfortunately, Quinn and Ezra are dead."

FIFTEEN

"WHAT DO YOU mean they're dead?" The words sounded hollow in the small room. Cold crept through the cracks around the window, hardening me. Connor and Theresa both looked at their folded hands.

Patrick heaved a sigh as he rifled through a stack of papers. "Here's Ronald's report."

I snatched it from his hand and moved toward a candle to read. Ezra had been caught stealing supplies, Quinn had run to help, and they had both been killed. Ronald had seen everything from his station, and though he'd tried to save them, he'd been too late. The siblings had already been stabbed through their guts by the time he arrived, and he'd needed to pretend he didn't care about what happened—that he was part of the caravan guards. . . .

The paper fluttered to the floor as I turned my glare on Patrick. "You did this. You sent them on that mission. I *told* you it was too dangerous, and you sent them anyway."

"We all take risks—"

"Yes, I know. *'Everything we do is a calculated risk.'* Start calculating better, Patrick. We don't have many Ospreys left."

Patrick straightened. "We will need those supplies, and we couldn't let the Indigo Army have them."

"No!" I banged my fist on the desk. "This was a stupid risk for a few supplies the Indigo Army will barely miss. You should have let them take the supplies to Aecor and had our contacts already there steal them. There are a hundred different things you could have done instead—"

He turned on his heel and left the room. The door slammed behind him.

Melanie folded her arms across her chest, her shoulders hunched over. "Great. Are you happy? You've hurt him."

My jaw clenched around the words. "Meanwhile, Quinn and Ezra are *dead*. Somehow, Patrick's *feelings* aren't that important to me. And you! You voted with him. You're both responsible."

Her eyes went wide, as though I'd hit her, and she spun and left the room after Patrick.

My heart ached with her betrayal, but I forced myself to stand tall. Theresa and Connor were still here, both of them sitting on the bed and making themselves small.

I took a long breath and let my posture soften. "I'm sorry, Rees. Connor."

Theresa lifted her eyes. "Do you think this is worth it? Is reclaiming the kingdom worth this kind of life?"

I didn't know what to say—if there was anything *to* say. I wasn't good at comforting others, even when I wanted to try.

We'd all seen too much death to believe the pain would ever go away, to believe that these emotional wounds would ever heal. No, for us, there was only revenge.

"We'll make it up to them, Rees." My words tasted sour. Quinn and Ezra were *dead*. How could I make up for that kind of sacrifice? It wasn't as if they'd know we succeeded one day. I couldn't bring them back and give them the life they deserved. "When we take back Aecor, memorials will be built in their honor. There will be weeks of mourning. Annual days of remembrance. We won't forget them, just like we haven't forgotten the others."

"Maybe if I'd gone with them—" Connor bit his lip. "I could have done something to help."

"No." I squeezed his shoulder, trying not to imagine what could have happened if he'd gone, too.

"He was my best friend."

"I know he was." Fiercely, I hugged Theresa and Connor. I hated to leave them, but Melanie's voice sounded outside the door—she was talking to Patrick—and I didn't want to be here when they returned. I couldn't look at Patrick right now.

With a whispered good-bye, I threw myself out the inn window and took to the rooftops.

My heart and soul and mind grew numb as I wandered through the night. Aimless. Rooftop to rooftop. Quinn and Ezra were dead.

Dead.

Because Patrick had sent them on a mission I'd *known* they couldn't handle. I'd backed off because of the stupid vote, but I should have pushed. I should have insisted Patrick wait, or send someone more experienced, or not try at all.

I should have protected them.

They must have been so *terrified* as the guards swung down their swords. As the pain cut hot and deep and then stopped hurting altogether. As they held each other in their last moments.

Patrick had been wrong to send them.

He was wrong to think I'd allow him to be king alongside me.

And if he was wrong about those things, what did that mean about our method for taking back Aecor, or even my ability to be queen?

The uncertainty was a fog, heavy and blinding. I wanted to do what was best for my friends and kingdom, but what *was* best?

If only my parents were alive to help me.

Wearily, I climbed to the highest point in White Flag and listened to the faint notes of a fiddle somewhere below. Quinn had always wanted to learn to play. Thunder rumbled in the west, and a fast, cool wind tugged at my clothes. I closed my eyes and breathed in the scent of the oncoming storm. A thread of wraith wove through the air, enough to mask the putrid odors of White Flag.

The fiddle strings screeched, and a scream cut through my fog.

I stumbled, barely catching myself as a gust of wind almost tore me from the roof, and the scream came again from the street. A high-pitched girl's scream.

Desperately, I threw myself downward, into the almost empty streets. A fiddle bow went skidding across the cracked cobbles, just in front of where my feet hit the ground. Some of the hairs had been sliced apart, but the stick was still intact.

I snatched up the bow and ran toward the screams.

A wiry man bore down on a girl—a young woman not much older than Quinn had been. "We agreed to thirty. If you give me twenty-five, you still owe me." He sneered when she staggered backward and her back hit a shop wall.

"I don't have more."

"What about that?" He nodded at her fiddle, lying on the ground like a discarded toy.

"But then I can't work—"

He slapped her hard across the face. Red welts had already formed from previous blows.

My footsteps were silent from years of training, so they noticed me only when I peeled from the shadows, fiddle bow in hand like a weapon. I slowed my steps as I came within striking distance. "Leave her alone." Mine was a stranger's voice, all deadly calm in the spaces between peals of thunder.

"What are you going to do?" The man didn't even look amused, just angry at the intrusion as he glanced from my face to the bow and back. "Another fiddler?"

"I've never tried the fiddle, but I think I'd be good at it." I smacked the bow across the man's neck. Wood stung skin with a loud *clap*. "That was a nice sound. Let me try again."

He swore and staggered back a step.

With long, steady strides, I advanced on the man, striking his cheeks and throat and shoulders in quick succession. He grimaced each time until his hand shot out and he gripped the bow before it hit him again. The wood snapped.

I tried to jerk back, but he was stronger and yanked the bow out of my grasp.

"Who are you?"

I didn't want to talk. I wanted to fight.

Wraithy wind gusted through the dark streets, and I pushed aside all thought of consequence and let instinct take over. I punched him hard in the jaw. Kicked him in the gut. Shoved him against a building like he'd done to the girl, and brought the heel of my palm against his teeth. Something cracked in his mouth, and blood oozed down his chin.

He grunted and drew back to hit me, but I grabbed his wrist and shoulder and kneed him between the legs. With a shout, he doubled over, clutching his groin.

I smirked and scooped up the broken fiddle bow on my way back to the girl. "You're going to need a new one." I tossed her the bow parts and the silver bracelet I'd lifted earlier, and she caught everything in fumbling hands. "Now run."

"Thank you!" She stopped only to collect her instrument before racing down the street.

Pain flared across the back of my head, and white flashed in my vision as the man hit me.

I drew my daggers and spun to face him. Nothing could stop me now.

The sharp odor of his blood dripped through the street, a contrast to the putrid stench of waste and rot and decay. I left thin slices in his hands and forearms, anywhere I could quickly reach as he struggled to block his throat and face.

The man had no proper training; he was just a thug who liked intimidating people with the palm of his hand. He didn't back off, though, even when I laid a gash in his chest. His shirt hung in tatters.

Harder and harder, I kicked him and sliced him, driving him back against the stone wall of a shop. He was wearing down, gasping and gulping for air. He wouldn't last much longer. Already he slumped, and blood smeared across his face and soaked his clothes. The copper stink of it filled my nose.

"*Hold him,*" I whispered to the wall. "*Wake up and hold him.*"

The surface of the stone heated and liquefied. The man howled wordlessly as the wall grew hotter, boiling against his body. The reek of scalding cloth and flesh made my eyes water, but I swallowed the faint nausea as the rock cooled again and became solid, holding him by his shirt and the outer layers of his skin. He groaned, and was unconscious.

"*Sleep,*" I told the wall.

Thunder rattled the street as I drew back my dagger and steeled myself. The tip pointed to his abdomen. All I had to do was thrust.

A black-gloved hand caught my wrist.

"Don't." It was a man's voice, low and dangerous.

I spun and kicked, connecting with a lean figure all in black. He stumbled backward and drew his sword from his back; he was but an outline in the darkness. I lunged for him, and metal clashed against metal as he blocked. My dagger slid down the length of his sword as I reached around to stab with the other. He caught my wrist again and heaved me away.

With a wild cry, I charged him again. His sword arced through the air, forcing me back again. I couldn't get inside his guard.

"Stop!" He took three long strides so that my back was against the stone wall, next to the thug.

I kept my eyes on the sword as I feinted and ducked beneath his guard. Pebbles dug against my palms and thighs as I rolled to my feet again. Strands of sweat-dampened hair obscured my vision. I dragged my arm across my forehead to peel back the hair, and the figure in black took advantage of my distraction and batted my dagger out of my right hand.

"Stop," he said again. "You're not a killer." He knocked the other dagger away from me. Both of my blades whumped onto the hard-packed dirt.

My hands fell to my sides as clarity shrieked through me.

It was Black Knife.

And I'd just used magic.

I swayed on my feet and stared at him, heart hammering with the surge of adrenaline. "Stop following me."

"Are you all right?" He stayed where he was, sword loose in his grip. I wanted to run, but it wouldn't take much for him to pin me against the wall, sword point at my throat. The man already stuck there—stuck by *my magic*—groaned. His head lolled, but he didn't wake.

Lightning flared and thunder rolled through Skyvale. I willed my legs to move, to get me out of here before Black Knife realized what I'd done.

Could he have seen it? No, it was too dark. Heard? Unlikely, given the wind gusting and cutting around corners. The air was heavy with moisture and that *waiting* sensation. Waiting for the storm. Waiting for Black Knife to make a move.

"What did you do to him?" Only the vigilante's eyes were visible as he stepped around me—toward the man I'd almost killed.

As Black Knife sheathed his sword and inspected the man, I gathered my weapons and backed away. Long, silent steps. Shoulders hunched. Daggers ready. I kept my breath slow and quiet, desperate to soothe the frantic beating of my heart. No matter how I tried, I couldn't force myself to calm down. Not with Black Knife right there, with evidence of my magic.

I made it five steps: across the street, to where the fiddler had been.

"He's been fused to the wall." Black Knife swore and spun around. In heartbeats, he closed the distance between us. "Did *you* do this?"

"I'm leaving." I dared another step away, but Black Knife caught my elbow and ducked my dagger when I swung it around. "I'm *leaving*."

"I can't let you." He trapped both of my wrists in his hand as he drew a length of black cord from a pouch on his belt. "You could have killed him. He'll probably die anyway, if I don't find someone to help him."

My whole body trembled as I tried to jerk my arms away. I couldn't even pull my dagger around to cut him.

When an icy wind cut through the street, I shook so hard that my blades fell from my hands again, and Black Knife had me bound—wrists and ankles. He was *fast*.

Or my mind was slow. Maybe both.

The man melted to the wall, the girl with her fiddle, the report about Quinn and Ezra, Patrick's declaration of our future together—

It was all too much.

A heavy sob choked out of me.

At least if Black Knife turned me in to the Indigo Order, I wouldn't have to face Melanie. I wouldn't have to bother chasing the rumor about the lake.

I wouldn't have to worry about ruling a kingdom when I didn't know how.

"What's wrong with you?" He stood and looked down at me.

I sat in the street, hunched over myself. I couldn't remember dropping, but now my thighs were pressed against my chest, and my wrists and ankles were bound together. When I tugged, there was no slack. It wouldn't be long before I lost feeling in my hands and feet.

"What happened?" He loomed over me, a tall, dark shadow in the night. The sky shuddered with another peal of thunder. Black Knife knelt, sighing heavily. "I'm going to find help for your friend over there. If he dies—" The vigilante shook his head. "Pray he doesn't die. Then I'll come back and decide what to do with you."

I pulled against my bonds, but they only tightened.

"Stay put."

It started to rain as Black Knife vanished down the street. Heavy drops soaked my clothes, making me shiver, and the man on the wall groaned loudly.

I'd never used my power to hurt anyone. I'd thought about it—sometimes letting the fantasies play a little too long—but I'd never given in to the impulse before.

If he died . . .

As rain fell in deafening sheets, I pushed my face into the crevice between my body and my knees, taking deep breaths to clear my thoughts. I couldn't worry about that man—whether he'd deserved it or I'd crossed a line. I had to free myself. I had to get back to the palace and form some kind of plan.

I had to *think*.

Carefully, I felt around the cords binding my hands and feet. The knots were unfamiliar, though, at least by touch, and it was too dark to see. Pulling on any loop or end might result in a worse tangle. Dare I use magic again? No; he'd smell the wraith on the air and know what I'd done. He'd begin developing a theory about what, exactly, I could do.

If only I could reach my daggers.

I could scoot. I pulled up my head and waited for the next flash of lightning.

It took two flares before I spotted light shimmering off the rain-dulled metal. Scooting with my hands and feet tied was incredibly awkward, but eventually I began to make progress. The distance to the nearest dagger grew shorter, even as the rain grew harder. Water soaked my clothes and plastered my hair against my head. My teeth chattered as I stretched my fingers and brushed the hilt of my dagger.

"Trying to cut your way free?" A dark shape detached from the rest of the shadows, and Black Knife knelt in front of me again. One toe of his knee-high boots pinned the blade to the ground, and my fingers scraped off the wooden hilt. "The police are coming, so answer me quickly."

I stared at him, my jaw tense as I forced myself motionless.

"What did you do to that man?"

Silence had always been my favorite response, but if I kept quiet, he'd leave. I'd be arrested for magic.

"I hurt him." Rain clattered all around us, steady and unceasing. A chill-wrought shudder in my chest echoed. "I tried to kill him."

This, not even an hour after insisting to Patrick that Ospreys weren't murderers.

"I saw what you did, saving that girl." He shifted his weight and braced one knee on the muddy ground; he kept my dagger pinned, and out of my reach. "You are an intriguing puzzle. A thief. A sister. A warrior. More than that." He paused and cocked his head, as though to study me from a slightly different angle. "Now you rescue a girl and maim her attacker with magic. I don't know what to do with you, nameless girl."

"Let me go." In spite of my best efforts, my voice shook with cold. My hands and feet ached as blood circulation slowed. I clenched and unclenched my fists, struggling to maintain feeling in my fingers.

"Are you going to use your magic again?" His voice deepened, and his words were almost lost beneath the cacophony of rain and thunder. "Do you like burning things? Because this didn't look like a last resort."

"I have as many reasons as you to want the wraith stopped." Maybe that was true. I didn't know his reasons, after all. But mine were strong. I had an entire kingdom to protect.

"Perhaps so." He touched my bonds, a pale contact I could barely feel through the cold and wet. It took all my will not to jerk back, away from him. "I'm going to free you," he said almost gently, "but I want something in exchange."

"I'm not telling you my name unless you tell me yours." A shiver racked through me.

A note of weary humor touched his voice. "Fortunately, I wasn't going to ask your name. No, I want something else. I saw the way you rushed to help that girl. You were fast getting there—faster than I was. And she'll live because of what you did."

Quinn wouldn't live, though. Neither would Ezra. They were my people, and they were dead.

The rain slammed harder and I fought off another violent shiver. Black Knife shivered, too.

"That girl will live, and she doesn't have to be the only one." Black Knife leaned closer, lifting his voice to be heard over the pounding of rain. "Come with me. Help me tonight. Help me save others."

I *had* saved that girl. It had been selfish, driving pain that had compelled me down from the rooftops. Knowing she would live to fix her fiddle and play again because of my intervention—I liked that. Not enough to want to accompany Black Knife, but if it was the vigilante—who didn't seem to want me arrested—or the police, I'd choose the enemy I knew.

"You won't turn me in for what I did?"

He hesitated. The percussion of rain made the seconds linger on, but at last he shook his head. "Not this time. I think you deserve a second chance."

I nodded toward my hands and feet, still caught up in the silk. "Untie me."

There was something in his tone, like relief. "I hoped you'd say that." He got to work quickly.

A few moments later, I stood, stretching my arms and legs. Sharp sensation assaulted my hands and feet.

Rain obscured the man fused to the wall, still unconscious, thankfully.

I'd almost killed him.

I'd almost *killed* him.

"The police will get him out." Black Knife grabbed my daggers, flipped them, and caught the flats of the blades. He offered the hilts to me, like he believed I wouldn't attack him. "You should, perhaps, wear a mask."

I took my daggers and slid them into their sheaths at my hips. "I don't have one."

"I have an extra." Black Knife felt around his belt and pulled free a damp slip of pitch cloth. He pressed it into my hands, this thin, delicate thing; it was a hood that went over the whole of one's head, not just the face. "I keep a spare in case I lose mine."

When I slid the silk over my head, it smelled faintly of boy and musk. It was light enough to breathe through, even when waterlogged, and kept the bite of chill off my face and throat. I adjusted my hair under the hood. "Thank you." The words were strange and soft under the rumble and racket of the storm, but he must have heard anyway, because he nodded.

"Let's go find someone who needs our help," he said. "Before the police arrive."

I looked at him, both of us in black masks, and struggled to reclaim the usual hostility that bound us together. "Sure. But if you try to talk to me or ask me anything, I'll stab you."

He started down the road. "That sounds fair."

As the thunder of police boots joined the thunder in the sky, Black Knife and I ran deeper into the Flags, disappearing into the shadows. We fought thieves and thugs, gangs and glowmen.

We didn't speak, but there was nothing to say, not when there was so much work to do.

When the storm passed and dawn touched the eastern horizon, I offered back the mask.

"Keep it." His tone warmed, even as howls and animal cries rose from within the city: wraith beasts, blown in with the storm. "You might need it again."

SIXTEEN

MORNING MADE MY head pound. My body ached from last night's adrenaline and grief, but I hauled myself up to sit on the edge of my bed, listening to Melanie move around the apartments. After a few minutes, she left.

The clock tower chimed ten as I dragged myself from my room, feet shuffling on the floor. Breakfast was already on the table, Melanie's half eaten. A note rested by the empty plate, as well as a small pile of invitation cards with today's date. In spite of last night, Melanie had organized my engagements.

I poured myself a cup of over-steeped tea and sat, letting the bitter black taste work its miracles while I eyed the note in her tidy handwriting. No flourishes, except the first letter of each paragraph, and her pen strokes were always dark and even. Her handwriting was just like her: familiar, safe, and reliable.

At least until lately.

J—

I received an invitation to take a walk about the palace gardens and a tour of the greenhouse. You know how much I enjoy horticulture.

You were invited as well, of course, but I thought you might want to accept the one from Lady Meredith instead. She, Lady Chey, and several others are meeting in the ladies' solar for needlework.

Perhaps I will see you over lunch.

M—

I flipped through the invitation cards. Indeed, there was the one from Meredith.

Quickly, I ate the rest of my breakfast, dressed, and arranged my hair in a long, simple braid—since the person who was supposed to help me with making myself look presentable had already left.

With times and locations of other engagements in mind, I headed to the ladies' solar where the women had met before.

When I arrived, the solar was already filled with women, most of whom I'd seen last time. Meredith was busy with her needlepoint again, and Chey sat at her right, knitting in hand. A chair on the other side of the duchess held the spindle and wool I'd neglected before. Wonderful. They hadn't forgotten.

Both women smiled brightly as I entered, and Meredith patted the chair beside her. "Welcome, Julianna! We're happy you could join us."

I took my seat and listened to the women discuss their projects—how they'd sew pieces together or make other objects from them. Meredith was turned toward Chey, and the others all paid careful attention to their conversation.

"There's a rumor that last night's storm blew in several wraith creatures." The girl who'd spoken was one of Meredith's ladies, young and flighty sounding. "They say Black Knife was out killing them all night."

I lowered my eyes to inspect the carded wool.

"That's not his duty and you know it." Meredith shook her head. "He'll be arrested if he's ever caught."

"He's a ghost," said the girl. "The police can't catch a ghost."

"He's real." A lady named Margot lowered her needlepoint and leaned forward. "I think Lord Daniel is Black Knife."

Chey's tone went teasing. "Weren't you with Lord Daniel last night?"

Margot blushed, and suddenly I recognized her from Meredith and Tobiah's engagement ball; the prince had said some people—like Lord Daniel—enjoyed *saying* they were Black Knife, even though everyone knew better.

"And did he leave you to kill monsters?" Chey asked.

"Well, he did leave once to fetch more wine." Margot tittered and returned to her needlepoint. "He does have the best stories about defeating the monsters and glowmen."

"Because they're made-up stories." Meredith shook her head. "No, the real Black Knife is no one as innocent as your Lord Daniel. What sort of man disguises himself and becomes a vigilante? One who wouldn't make nearly as charming a bedfellow as Daniel, no doubt."

"They say Black Knife will put an end to the wraith. I've

heard that priests all through the Flags are making prophecies about him!"

Another rolled her eyes. "They're *Flag* priests."

"Indeed." Chey held herself straight. "When the palace chapel priests start having prophecies—or anyone from the Cathedral of the Solemn Hour—then you may entertain the idea. But ignore anything that comes from the Flags."

"What about the belief that *Crown Prince Tobiah* will stop it?" Someone snickered, and everyone looked at Meredith.

"If he does," Meredith said, "it will be because he works hard. Not because of a silly story about a king from all four houses."

"What story is this?" I asked. "I don't believe I've heard anything about His Highness being the one to stop the wraith."

"Oh, it's just a story some of the commoners made up." Meredith shook her head and flashed a smile. "You know about the four Houses, right? It's more to do with where you were born than who your family is—though families do tend to stick to the location, if they own property."

"Yes, that's been explained."

"The rumor began when His Highness Prince Tobiah took over the wraith mitigation committee. It's well known that King Terrell and Queen Francesca are from two different houses, and his grandparents on each side are from the other two. Prince Tobiah is House of the Dragon, but he's descended from people of all four, if you take his grandparents into account." She gave a liquid shrug. "It's not exactly *rare* for this to happen, but it is unusual. The fact that Prince Tobiah will be king one day makes him even more unusual, and you know common people.

They will find signs and superstitions in anything. They need to believe someone will save them before the wraith destroys everything, so they've placed their hope in their future king."

Signs and superstitions—like the mirrors that covered every western surface of the city, courtesy of King Terrell the Second. How very *common* of him.

"I see. Thank you for explaining." I turned my spindle in my hands, judging the weight, the sturdiness, and the sharp end. If I needed to bash in any of their heads, or my own—whichever would help me peel real information from their inane chatter more quickly—the spindle would serve as an adequate weapon. "What are the Flag priests saying about Black Knife and the wraith?"

"Some say he works for Prince Tobiah, but that's ridiculous because he's a vigilante and—"

The solar door opened and all the ladies abandoned their work to stand. When the queen stepped in, they performed small, deferential curtsies. I rose, too. Murmurs of "Your Majesty" fluttered through the room.

Queen Francesca was a thin, stern-looking woman, immaculately dressed in a high-waisted gown of blue silk. Intricate embroidery, patterned with stylized suns and birds in flight, swirled over her sleeves and shoulders and bodice. When she spoke, however, her voice was soft. Meek, almost. "Good morning, ladies. Would you mind if I worked with you?"

Immediately, servants were ordered to fetch an appropriately comfortable chair for her, and better wine.

The queen came farther into the room, out of the servants' way, and in the doorway, two young men hovered: Tobiah and James. Escorting the queen, apparently.

Both boys looked as though they'd been up late, with bags under their eyes. But while James wore an expression of careful neutrality, Tobiah's mouth was pinched and he appeared deeply unhappy as he noticed my presence next to his fiancée.

His expression *almost* persuaded me to spend as much time as possible with Meredith, just to annoy him.

"Lady Meredith. Good morning. You look radiant, as always." He kissed her hand, an odd softness about him as he admired the work she was doing and praised her skill with the needle; she glowed with his attention. But his smile was stiff, overly formal as he greeted the rest of the ladies by name. Then he turned to me. "Lady Julianna, may I speak with you in the hall?"

All eyes turned toward me as I placed the spindle and wool on the chair, and followed the prince and his bodyguard. The queen's eyebrow lifted as I passed her.

Tobiah left the door open for propriety's sake, but motioned me down the hall a few paces, where we could speak without being overheard. "I was going to send you a note," he said. "I think that might have been easier."

And I would have had a sample of the prince's handwriting. I tried not to let my disappointment show; he probably had a boring hand anyway.

"After the committee meeting the other day, several of the members approached me separately with concerns."

I tilted my head and offered a quizzical look.

"They're concerned that the meetings might be too difficult for you to continue attending. Because the majority of those in attendance carried identical misgivings, I'm afraid I must—"

"I understand." It was rude to interrupt, and a duchess would never dare, but one nursing wounded pride might be that bold, so I risked it. I set my mouth in a line and directed a glare across the hall, on a framed mirror reflecting a portrait of some long-dead queen.

"Not because of your gender, I assure you, but because you've endured something incredibly traumatic. The gentlemen are simply concerned for your peace of mind. We all wish you nothing but healing."

Beyond the prince, James stood with his hands behind his back, shoulders straight, and a slight frown on his face. When our eyes met, he shook his head just barely.

We both knew why the committee didn't want me. Fortunately, I'd already learned everything I needed for the Ospreys. But what about the lake?

I'd simply have to continue my own research, and follow it wherever it took me.

"I understand," I said again, and met the prince's eyes. "I'm disappointed, of course. Though I appreciate the concern, I know I could be useful."

The prince's expression was unreadable. "I'm afraid the decision is final, but I will keep you apprised of any developments. I hope that will suffice."

That sounded unlikely. "Thank you." I put no effort into sounding genuine.

"Have a good morning with the ladies." At that pointed dismissal, he turned and headed down the hall. James flashed an apologetic smile before following.

When I returned to the ladies' solar, the women were already hard at work once more. The queen sat in a tall chair with half a dozen pillows squeezed in with her, and she worked right alongside the others. She spun on a spindle—a much finer one than I'd been given.

Meredith cocked an eyebrow as I took my seat. "Is everything all right? You look upset."

I gave a prim smile and took up my spindle, keeping one eye on the queen as she spun. "I'm well enough. Thank you." All eyes were on me, though, and perhaps there was an opportunity here. I allowed my chin to tremble and made my voice small, but trying to be strong. "Well, I'd wanted to join the wraith mitigation committee. I thought I might be able to help."

Meredith nodded. "That's quite brave of you."

"Unfortunately, the majority of the committee believes I am unsuitable, thanks to the very thing I believe makes me valuable: my experience in the wraithland."

A few of the ladies hissed, and several scowled. The queen simply focused on her work—or appeared to focus. Chey shook her head and met my eyes. "Women are constantly underestimated. Women can be just as cunning and clever as men, and oftentimes are. Our triumph is simply overlooked or unnoticed, because men do not expect it or know to look for it." She offered a strange smile. "Use your perceived insignificance to your advantage. It's what we all do."

There was a small chorus of yeses and a ripple of nodding, making me wonder for the first time what they were hiding. All these ladies with their own lives, their own goals.

Perhaps I'd misjudged them earlier. Their inane chatter was

a small theater, meant to disguise their true selves from me: an outsider.

The queen smiled gracefully as she wound yarn onto her spindle.

"Thank you for the advice," I said after a moment. A strange sense of kinship welled up in me. We all wore disguises, and now I understood theirs.

Not that I trusted Chey—or Meredith or the queen or anyone else in this room—but that didn't make her advice any less true. Maneuvering beneath notice was what I'd been doing since my arrival here.

This incident with Tobiah was a setback, but it wouldn't keep me from my goals.

As soon as the ladies disbanded for the day, I set about haunting the halls around generals' offices, and anywhere else I might find answers. But I found nothing.

There was no getting around it. I was going to the wraithland.

Days were getting shorter. By the time the clock tower chimed nineteen, the sun dipped below the western horizon and the city's mirrors glowed with twilight until the sky faded to purple-black, and finally turned dark.

Melanie hadn't returned to our apartments, and even if she'd been here, I wouldn't have known what to say to her. Would we talk about last night with Patrick? Or pretend we didn't know about Quinn and Ezra? Act like she hadn't voted with Patrick, and now two of our friends were *dead*?

Black silk gleamed in the lamplight; the mask peeked out

from beneath my mattress, where I'd shoved it this morning as I staggered in, exhausted.

I tugged it from the hiding place and turned it over in my hands, looking for hints of Black Knife's identity. A piece of hair, a scent, or a seamstress's embroidered mark. But there was nothing. The mask smelled like me now, and there was nothing to indicate it hadn't been my mask all along.

Keep it, he'd said. *You might need it again.*

Earlier, the palace ladies had said there were more wraith beasts in the city. If that was true, Black Knife would be hunting them.

I changed my clothes and slipped my weapons from their hiding places. As exhausted as I was, I wasn't ready to sleep, to think about my wretched life, or to *question* what I'd always known and believed.

Instead, I shoved Black Knife's mask into my belt and made my way into the city.

Unsure exactly where I wanted to go, I roamed the market district, rooftop to rooftop, until I found myself above a small chapel with a bubbling fountain in its tiny courtyard. Half a dozen people knelt on the cobblestones, circling the splashing water. Quiet chanting rose into the night.

"They're waiting to be healed." Black Knife's voice came from just behind me. "They were told to fast for a week, drinking only water from that fountain, and to pray ceaselessly. If they did that, they'd be healed of whatever ails them."

"Has it ever worked?"

He shrugged. "I haven't heard the good news yet, but I hope I will one day."

"Huh." He was optimistic, for a boy wearing a mask.

"I didn't expect to find you here," he said.

I stood and slipped behind a chimney, out of the way of the mirrors. Black Knife followed, utterly silent in his movements.

"Or perhaps"—he pulled the mask from my belt and held it between two fingers—"you didn't come to pray."

Wind tugged at the mask, a banner of black shadow against his dark body. "Are you going to arrest me?"

"Not today. We have too much work to do." He offered back the mask, and when I didn't move, he said, "Unless you'd rather I arrested you."

If he knew how I spent my days, disguised as a dead girl and snooping about the palace, no doubt he'd change his mind.

"Not today." I took the mask just as an immense roar sounded from the chapel courtyard, followed by screams. "Like you said."

SEVENTEEN

WE SPENT THE night together, fighting wraith beasts and capturing glowmen. When we were in danger of being spotted by passersby or victims, we traded off who revealed themselves so that no one would suspect there were two of us.

No, there was no *us*. He had an uncanny ability to find me, and I owed him for not turning me in to the Indigo Order when he discovered my magic. I hadn't brought myself to ask why yet. He might still turn me in.

Nevertheless, we fought together, and we fought well. We followed leads painted on walls and fences, black knives with requests for help scrawled below. We found bounty posters that had been altered to alert him to the presence of a dangerous gang, and hints about where dealers were selling shine.

"That one." Black Knife pointed at the street of linked houses below. All was dark and quiet. This neighborhood had no gas lamps, and the crescent moon had set below the horizon already.

"How can you tell?"

He folded the posters and slipped them into his pocket. "The smoke stains on the house. If there'd really been a fire here, other houses would have the damage as well. No, that's a marker. It tells shine users that they can purchase here."

Now that he'd pointed it out, I could see the smoke stains on the off-white walls. "Do you trust the information?"

"Yes." He didn't take his eyes off the house. "But I'm not going in until tomorrow night. There are a few more tools I need for this."

I was glad we weren't going in tonight. I'd already hidden a few yawns, and I had more work to do on my own before I could go to bed.

He stood and turned in the direction of Thornton. "Are you coming tomorrow?"

"Probably not."

"Good. I'll meet you right here at midnight."

I pulled off my mask and tucked it back into my belt. "No promises."

"Of course not." He hopped across the gap between rooftops and faced me. "Oh, what would you like to be called?" If tones could be expressions, his would have been a cocky grin.

I narrowed my eyes.

"You should choose something you like. Eventually, someone will see the two of us together, and if you don't choose a name, one might be chosen for you."

"You're assuming I'll stick around."

"I think you like the mask. It's irresistible."

I'd never met anyone so arrogant. "Is that how you ended up

with Black Knife? From people who couldn't tell the difference between a knife and a sword?"

He made a noise almost like a chuckle. "No. I actually did this to myself. But that's a story for when we're better friends."

"We aren't friends."

"That's why I'm waiting." He performed a deep, graceful bow. "Until tomorrow, nameless girl."

Then he was gone.

Of course I went back.

We took out the shine house easily enough, and then tracked down the supplier and manufacturer. Black Knife had an entire network of informants, signs people left on fences and windows—messages that looked like random scrawls to me, until he explained them.

During those hours of darkness, my thoughts cleared and I focused only on fighting and surviving. Black Knife was reckless when he fought, like he trusted me to keep him out of wraith beast jaws. Or maybe he'd always been like that.

Our only uncertainty came in the moments after killing a wraith beast, when a blast of mist rose up from the body, leaving both of us woozy and confused. But it always passed.

The lights of Skyvale silhouetted Black Knife as he cleaned the blood from his sword and sheathed it. "Usually, I can finish any wraith creatures within the first couple of nights after a storm. But not this time, even with your help. I think it will just get worse from here."

"What do you think will happen when the wraith gets here?"

"Chaos," he said. "Every refugee I've talked to has said so."

He talked to refugees?

How interesting.

When we parted ways, I slipped through the Flags and over the city wall, well clear of the guard towers. Dawn was still hours away, but weariness tugged at my eyes and clouded the edges of my thoughts.

As I stepped into the dark camp of Liadian refugees, I shifted my stride to mimic Black Knife's. I didn't have his sword or gloves, but I doubted anyone would notice. I didn't have his voice, either, but I could disguise mine. He was probably doing the same already.

Cool, sharp air twined through the tents and lean-tos. Within a circle of shelters, a small fire crackled, throwing a fractured glow among the handful of men guarding the camp. There were ten of them, all armed with clubs or other blunt objects. A few had short blades at their hips, and likely hidden within their clothes.

Sheep bleated at my passing, and one of the guards spun around to face me. "Who are you? Show yourself!" At his shout, the others snapped to attention, weapons raised.

My hands palm-up and out to my sides, I stepped into the light, and pitched my voice deeper. Raspier. "Who do you think I am?"

"Black Knife," one breathed. The men all lowered their weapons.

"I'm chasing a rumor."

The men gathered around, lowering their weapons. "What

rumor?" A few narrowed their eyes as they took in my height. Tall for a girl, but not as tall as people expected Black Knife to be.

"A map in the palace shows a lake in Liadia marked with questions. What's out there?"

The men exchanged glances. "No one at the palace believes," said a boy not much younger than me. Small round scars dotted his face. "We were told not to speak of it."

"I will believe you. Tell me."

"It's just a rumor," said the boy. "I didn't see it."

"Take me to someone who did."

The guards led me to a nearby tent with a goat tethered outside. One man darted inside, and I caught the edges of his whisper. "Black Knife is here. He's going to stop the wraith. He's going to save us all."

I entered the small space, which was lit with a few candle stubs. Next to the guard who'd shown me in, a woman sat amid a mountain of blankets. Though she appeared young enough to be my mother, she was hunched, as if she'd hurt her back, or had carried heavy loads for many years. Her expression was grim, with traces of kindness. "Black Knife."

I stepped away from the shelter's door and assumed Black Knife's posture. Shoulders back, feet hip-width apart, arms over my chest.

"You want to know what I saw."

"Every detail."

"I was forbidden from speaking of it."

"By whom?"

"The Liadian king. His men."

"They're dead now. Tell me."

She offered a slight bow. "Before the wraith hit, I was a maid in a lord's country home. Everyone was talking about those barriers like they were the answer, but I knew the truth. The supposed alchemists the king hired to build the barriers were all flashers taken from their homes and put to work pouring magical energy into the walls. I was one of them. But"—she held up her hands, as though trying to appease me—"I don't use magic now. What use is making myself float? I did only what my king ordered. I could not refuse."

She could have refused, but he might have had her killed for it.

"What happened then?" I asked.

She lowered her hands. "When the walls were finished, we were sent home. The magic barrier seemed to work for a time, but eventually, the wraith broke through. People were angry. Afraid. Many fled immediately, but some of us were trapped by the very barriers we'd helped create. From the house where I was trapped, I watched the wraith break through the walls. Pieces flew into the nearby lake. It was called Mirror Lake."

There were probably a hundred lakes called that. It didn't mean anything. "The lake with the pieces of the barrier is the source of the rumors?"

"Yes." She slumped deeper into her blankets. "I saw the water erupt. It cleaned the wraith right out of the surrounding land. That's everything I remember."

The guard cleared his throat. "I heard that the light of another world shines through the lake now. Others have said the water boils all year around, or the water sucks in the wraith every night so the surrounding land is clean."

"I see. Is that all?"

They plied me with a few more nonsense rumors before I left the tent and refugee camp. When I was sure no one was watching, I climbed over the city wall and made my way through the Flags.

By the time I reached Thornton, the eastern horizon had turned purple and the silhouettes of mountains were just visible. I had to hurry back to the palace, but first, I needed to grab a few supplies.

I stopped in quiet shops, lifting a sleeping roll and sturdy breeches and bags of dried travel rations. I was out of the area just as the clock tower chimed five and owners began making their way toward their businesses.

Hawksbill was trickier, with maids and servants awake to prepare for the day, but the deep gold rays of dawn left pockets of shadow. I stayed to those, ascending to my palace balcony just as light broke over it. I slipped into the room and let all my new belongings fall to the floor as I staggered into bed. Everything I'd learned tonight spun in my head, even as tension eased from my body and I fell closer to sleep.

No wonder the prince's wraith mitigation committee wanted to keep that place on the map confidential.

Liadia had broken the Wraith Alliance, but did anyone even know what the results were, let alone what they meant?

It seemed no one was interested enough to find out.

No one but me.

EIGHTEEN

PALACE SOCIAL LIFE kept me engaged most days, but a few times I managed to disguise myself and sneak into the city to secure travel aboard a caravan to West Pass Watch. But for my plan to succeed, I needed Melanie's help.

It had been a week that we'd been avoiding each other since the incident in the Peacock Inn, and I'd seen only traces of Melanie's existence: food eaten, notes lying on the table, invitations sorted. Once, we'd run into each other in the sitting room and stared as though we were strangers, until we awkwardly edged around the perimeter and went opposite ways.

I couldn't let that happen now. I had to catch her. I had to speak with her.

With twenty minutes until a maid came to finish preparing us for dinner—one we both had to attend—I sneaked into her room and waited.

"We need to talk," I said as she pushed opened the bedroom door.

Her room was half the size of mine, dominated by a large canopied bed and wardrobe. Light streamed in through the window, reflecting in a handful of mirrors. Melanie crossed the room quickly and sat on her bed.

She pushed aside a few books about the origins of the Houses and didn't once make eye contact with me. "I've already had the drop location changed." Her tone was stiff.

"That wasn't what I—Wait, when?" I gripped the split outer layer of my day dress. "When you went out of the room and spoke with Patrick last week?"

She stacked the books onto her nightstand and lined up the corners. "No. The other night." Her chin tilted up a hair. "After you left the room, I left, too. I went where I always go."

My breath caught. After weeks of avoiding the truth, was she finally going to tell me where she'd been going after delivering reports? "And where is that?"

Melanie stood, long, black hair framing her face and delicate features, now pulled down with distaste. "It's Patrick. We meet at the inn."

"You and *Patrick*?"

"Why not?" She folded her arms over her chest. "Do you think he doesn't get lonely?"

"I never even considered it." He was always so practical and calculating. That was why so many Ospreys followed him without question.

"Of course not." She rolled her eyes, tilting her head back. "I doubt you've ever *considered* he might be capable of feelings, or that anyone could see through the armor he wears every day. You've probably never considered that someone might actually love him."

Love?

My mouth hung open. My best friend had been falling in love—with *Patrick*—and I'd missed it.

"It's that impossible for you to even comprehend?" She twisted her little finger at me and started out the door, but then looked back, her eyes hard. "And after all of that, he decided he should be *your* king. Oh, we could still have a relationship, but we'd have to keep it discreet, because he wouldn't embarrass you by having a public mistress."

"Mel, I had no idea—"

"We can't really be together because of *you*." Her knuckles were white where she gripped the door handle. "Because he needs *you* on the throne, and he needs to stand by *you* to keep the kingdom strong. Everything he does is for *you*."

She stalked out, slamming the door shut behind her.

I followed and reached for her shoulder just as she was rounding the sitting room table. "Melanie. Wait."

She shook me off, tears shining in her eyes. "After everything he's done for you, all that he's sacrificed, you said no to him. You might as well have told him he wasn't good enough, just like his father always did."

My heart thudded. I wanted to be nothing like General Lien. "I'm sorry."

"Your rejection won't stop him, you know. He's determined to see Aecor rise as the glorious kingdom it once was. Your manipulation won't change any of that."

"My manipulation?"

She threw her hands up. "You changed my report. You tried to hide important information from him." Her shoulders curled in and her expression set into a frown. "All he cares about is you and Aecor and putting the kingdom right again. That's the *only* things he cares about. And me. A little. Not as much as he cares about you."

"Patrick makes his own decisions," I said. "Don't blame me for anything he's done, because I never asked it of him."

"But you never said no."

"I said no at the inn."

Melanie closed her eyes. "You did. And it hurt him."

"I wasn't trying to hurt him."

"He's done so much for you. Doesn't that mean anything to you?"

"It does," I said. "I care about Patrick. And you're right: he's done so much for me—for all the Ospreys. But I won't marry someone I don't want to marry, and Patrick shouldn't, either. If you love each other, then you should be together. You don't have to hide that from me."

Her words came soft. Pinched. "He told me to hide it."

Maybe Patrick did love her—I couldn't know his heart—but demanding their love stay a secret seemed unfair to both of them. "I'm sorry," I said at last. I should have seen what she was going through, rather than stew in my suspicions.

She held my gaze for a minute, followed by a slow nod. "All right."

I twitched the corner of my mouth upward into a hopeful smile. "I was actually hiding in your room for a reason. I needed to talk to you about something. Why don't you sit?" I pulled out one of the chairs and patted the back.

She took the very edge of the chair, sitting stiffly as she smoothed the layers of her dress down her thighs. "Talk."

My heart thundered as I struggled to find the words. "The list of resistance groups . . ."

Her frown deepened. "Yes?"

"I wanted to hide the list from Patrick because I thought he was going to pull us from the palace once he had it. I didn't expect"—I couldn't hide the scowl—"his other mission."

"You mean to kill someone?" She said it neutrally.

"Right." I swallowed hard, not sure I really wanted to ask. "Do you know who the target is?"

"No. He didn't tell me." She shifted, but her discomfort seemed to be from not knowing, not because she was lying.

I leaned against the table, focusing on the floor for a moment while I collected my thoughts. "The truth is, I'm not ready to leave Skyvale yet. Not because of any of this." I gestured around the sitting room, opulent with all the silk curtains and books and portraits. "I've learned about something that could be important to Aecor's future."

She lifted an eyebrow.

"I'm going to the wraithland."

"Why?"

"There's a lake in Liadia. If the rumors about it are true, parts of the Liadian barrier fell into it. And the barrier—Mel, it was made with magic."

Her eyes grew wide. "Liadia broke the treaty?"

"Yes. And there are a million rumors about what the

magical barrier did to the lake. Whatever happened there could help solve the wraith problem before the Indigo Kingdom and Aecor fall."

"And you have to be the one to go look?"

"Who else is going to do it?"

"Anyone else!" She slapped the table and leaned forward. "Don't be stupid, Wil. This isn't worth your life."

"No doubt that's most people's attitude. And that's why I have to do it." I held up a hand, forestalling more questions. "I don't want Patrick to know. This is for Aecor, but he wouldn't understand."

"He might!"

"Would he let me go?"

"No, and with good reason."

I crossed my arms. "Mel, I know you want to defend him, but listen to what you just said. He *doesn't* understand. He doesn't think the wraith is a problem yet, and he wants to put off dealing with it until after we take back Aecor. But by then, we'll be occupied with stabilizing the kingdom and fighting off the Indigo Army. And Colin Pierce is going to want Aecor back, of course. By the time we have Aecor under control, it could be too late to do anything about the wraith. We have to do something now, whether or not Patrick approves. And since I'm going to be queen, it's my responsibility. If I'm not willing to take risks for my people's well-being, I don't deserve to be queen."

"Isn't it your responsibility to stay alive? Where will Aecor be if you die?"

I didn't want to think about that. "I'm sure Patrick would come up with some way to cope."

She heaved a sigh. "So what are you going to do? What do you need me for, besides keeping your secret from Patrick?"

"*Will* you keep my secret?"

"I haven't decided." She inclined her head toward my open bedroom door, to where tonight's gowns hung. "We don't have long before dinner, so just tell me your plan."

"All right." I took a seat and met her eyes. "I need you to cover for me while I'm away. With Patrick, but also with the palace."

"I thought as much."

"I've already gathered supplies and gotten myself on as a guard in a merchant caravan heading to West Pass Watch. It leaves in the morning. Tonight, I'm going to fall very ill. I will need you to bribe or otherwise persuade a physician to claim he's seen me."

The familiar light of mischief shone in her eyes as she nodded. "I'll turn down all of our invitations, make excuses for you, deliver reports, and finish our map. But I don't want to lie to Patrick."

"I know." I squeezed her hands, urging her to understand. "But I need to do this. I need to do everything in my power to put a stop to the wraith before it gets to Aecor. The Indigo Kingdom isn't any closer to stopping it, and they won't be between it and Aecor forever."

"Are you sure you can't find answers here?"

"I tried. I've searched every office and records room, but nothing tells about the lake, or whether all the things we think we've learned about the wraith are actually true. I have to know. I have to see for myself."

"Wilhelmina, what makes you think *you* have a chance where everyone else has failed?"

The truth balanced on the tip of my tongue, but I'd kept my magic a secret so long that the words died there on my breath. Anyway, I wasn't even sure whether confessing my ability would be an explanation for why I thought I had a chance to do something about the wraith.

Before my hesitation stretched too long, the maid knocked and entered the sitting room, tutting about how little time we had before dinner with the Pierce family, Lady Meredith, and several other members of the royal household.

It would have been a great honor to be invited, if we'd truly been Liadian refugees.

But for us, it was simply an opportunity to study the Pierces and their extended family, and sow seeds for my upcoming deception.

"Time to work."

"Say it again," she said, and offered a tiny salute.

Throughout dinner, I coughed into my napkin and pretended to have trouble focusing, as though faint. My apparent condition grew worse over each course, and I forced myself to eat very little, though the food was delicious and it was all I could do not to devour every scrap of roasted duck.

"Lady Julianna?" James leaned forward, his voice low while the others discussed how the Saint Shumway Theater had been *designed* for magical effects, and what a shame it would be to remodel the building now.

"We didn't rip up the palace and start over when crisis

struck." Meredith shook her head. "We should respect such a historic building."

"My great-grandfather didn't tear down the palace," Tobiah said, "because all of the original fixtures could be renovated for nonmagical use. Besides, building the palace nearly bankrupted the kingdom, thanks to Kelvin Geary. Can you imagine the riots if the Pierce family constructed another palace, after the Geary fiasco?"

Meredith sniffed. "That doesn't mean—"

James touched my hand, drawing my attention again. "Lady Julianna, are you well?"

"I'm fine," I breathed.

"Don't fib, my lady." Melanie frowned and felt my forehead and cheeks. "You've been holding back that cough for a week now, and you're flushed. If you don't get some rest, you're sure to develop a fever."

Tobiah glanced over, wearing an odd mix of boredom and concern. Meredith abandoned her defense of the theater and began inquiring whether I was getting enough rest.

By dessert—the most delicious-looking torte with cream and raspberries that I wasn't allowed to eat, thanks to my *condition*—I gazed around listlessly until Melanie begged an excuse for us, and after a round of good nights and get wells, she helped me back to our apartments.

A few hours before dawn, I got up to finish packing.

Melanie plaited my hair, pinning and tucking it so that the length could be hidden beneath a cap. A tight tube of silk to flatten my chest and a borrowed jacket later, I was William Cole, a young guard hoping to pay his way into Bome Boys' Academy; I was reaching above my station, no doubt.

"You look very handsome," Melanie said, adjusting my hat once more. "All the ladies will swoon."

"I don't think ladies are allowed on this trip." I checked myself in a mirror. The only thing missing was a sword, but I knew where to get one. "Just don't tell Patrick where I am, right?"

"I won't. I promise." Melanie hugged me. "You'd better come back on time, or I'm going after you."

"No," I whispered. "I don't want you to enter the wraith-land or risk revealing yourself here."

"But—"

I shook my head. "Swear you won't."

She let out a small sigh. "All right. I won't."

It was still dark when I hefted my pack onto my shoulders and climbed out the window, leaving Melanie staring after me.

I hoped I'd been right to trust her.

NINETEEN

IN THE PREDAWN hours, the caravan clattered into movement. Guardsmen shouted and vendors cheered as horse hooves clopped the packed dirt. The larger wagon wheels had been folded up, allowing the smaller set to run along the grooves of the old railroads. A deep, metallic hum filled the air.

Trains, of course, hadn't been used in one hundred years— not since magic was banned—but the Indigo Kingdom had found a way to make the old tracks useful anyway. The route curved around the Midvale Ridge; autumn washed down from those heights, all red and gold and russet. On foot, the journey to West Pass Watch took two days, with an extra half day added for the wagons.

I was assigned to the rear guard, following in the caravan's dust. Lovely. But I kept my silence and mimicked the way the men walked, one hand on my stolen sword as though I could cut down anyone if they dared threaten the merchandise. The sword wasn't my *best* weapon, but it was a requirement for this job.

The other men chatted amicably as morning wore on, discussing the rations they'd brought and the previous guard work they'd done. Many, it seemed, had made a habit of working as hired guards, and knew one another well. It paid better than the Indigo Army; that much I knew.

"What brought you here, boy?" one of the men asked.

I shrugged and let my voice fall deeper—but not so much that it sounded like I was a girl pretending to be a boy. "It's work." The words rattled around in my chest as I adjusted my stride.

"Is this your first job?" he asked.

"It is."

"Huh. You hold those weapons like it isn't." He eyed my belt, heavy with my daggers as well as my sword. My pockets and hidden compartments in my pack were filled with my usual equipment.

I shrugged again.

"Get in lots of fights back home?"

I shot him an annoyed glare. "Are you here to make friends or do your job? I'd rather not die in a refugee ambush, so kindly shut up."

One man flicked his little finger at me, and the others grumbled among themselves for a moment before one said, "There was a caravan ambushed by refugees not two weeks ago. It was a caravan heading east, and they killed several merchants and guards. Refugees died, too, at least."

Revulsion washed through me. Those hadn't been refugees. Those had been Ospreys, posing as guards.

Just like me.

They must have been so frightened when the other guards brought down their swords.

I pushed away thoughts of Quinn and Ezra. Right now, I needed to work.

Eventually, the men lost interest in me, letting me lag behind. I kept close watch on the trees, listening for any sounds out of the ordinary. Ospreys practiced stealth in the woods as much as in the city, keeping to the shadows, keeping our voices low, and keeping alert because anything could happen to a handful of children—now teenagers—alone in the woods.

In contrast, the caravan was noisy with the hum of wheels on steel, hooves striking dirt, and the voices of men unworried about attack. The forest animals had gone quiet with our passing and would be no use as indicators of anything else.

Our shadows shortened before us and we paused to eat rations and let the horses drink from a stream that ran down from the mountains.

"There are caverns that way." One of the men sat next to me and pointed northward. "Black as pitch in there, but if you bring a good light and mirrors, you might have a chance of seeing some amazing structures. You'd think a sculptor went in there first. Air's so clean, too, it almost hurts to breathe when you come back out."

"Don't tell him about that one, Josh," said another man. "There's better ones north of Skyvale. Some of the stalagmites are hollow tubes, and you can blow over them like flutes. Those are better."

Josh threw up his little finger at his friend. "Just trying to show young Will what's around *here*. Your singing rocks aren't anywhere near here, are they?"

"Er."

I glanced between them, chewing on a last bit of my jerky. I wasn't much interested in stories about caves.

The caravan stretched into the west, all wood and metal wagons painted with merchants' colors and examples of their wares. The horses milled around in tiny herds, each group near their designated wagons as they munched on the browning autumn grass. Some of the guards had horses as well; their bridles and clips clang-clanged as they ambled around.

The air was still and crisp and, for once, free of the acrid stench of wraith. Only the odor of people and horses and autumn filled the road, and with the sun slipping past noon, there were few shadows.

One of the shadows moved.

Just a fraction, but movement nonetheless.

I peered harder, tuning out the guards' voices. The shadow in the trees resolved itself into a black-clad young man. When he lifted a hand in greeting, I rolled my eyes and sat back.

Once the caravan rumbled into motion again, there wasn't much of a chance to sneak away. A few of the older guards hung back in the forest, making sure no people—or wraith beasts— were following, but as a new and young guard, I wasn't permitted.

At nightfall, I took first watch, and adjusted my weapons before I climbed a tree.

Moonlight filtered through the canopy of copper leaves, and rained silver-blue on the railroad where the wagons had been removed from the tracks and now waited in formation for morning. The caravan leader and merchants slept in the middle, while off-duty guards dozed on wagon rooftops, their weapons close beside them.

The road was dim. Empty. Only a breeze disturbed the stillness.

"Do you even know how to use that sword?" Black Knife appeared out of the shadows, crouched on a branch above me, one tree over. He was *so* quiet.

"I know which end to stick where." I smiled as I scanned the road again. Nothing. Only the faint scent of wraith blew in from the west. "What are you doing here?"

"I just wanted to take a walk. That's not a crime, is it?"

"You're the one who decides whether people are criminals."

"*I* don't decide. Other people are the ones going around taking things that aren't theirs." When he stood, the tree groaned and a leaf fluttered down, but that was all. He braced himself on a high branch, then maneuvered and stretched until he sat beside me, just a breath of air between us. "So, Will."

I stiffened. "What did you call me?"

"Will. I heard one of the guards call you Will earlier, but I can go back to calling you 'nameless girl' if you prefer."

My whole body sagged in relief. "Call me whatever you want."

"Will, then. What are *you* doing here? Don't you have important things to take care of elsewhere?"

"I have important things to do here."

"In a tree? With a merchant caravan?"

I shrugged.

"Wraithland." His tone was low. Dry.

"Yes," I said. "I'm going to the wraithland."

Wind gusted through the trees. At the acrid stench that followed, both of us stilled and our eyes met. "Do you hear anything?" His whisper was so soft I almost didn't hear *him*.

We listened, waiting, but night birds chirped and nocturnal animals skittered through the trees. A wolf howled in the distance. After a few minutes, we relaxed.

"Don't go to the wraithland," he said. "It's too dangerous."

I smirked. "Why, Black Knife. You almost sound worried."

He seized my hands; the leather of his gloves was cool against my skin, and I could hear the faint rasp of his breath as he drew me closer. "Don't go. Come back to the city with me."

I leaned away. "I must go." I hesitated, but pushed out the words in pale gasps. "You know what I did to that man. You know what I am." Since the One-Night War, I'd never said even that much aloud. Even hinting at my ability would draw unwanted attention—like Black Knife's—and here I was, laying myself bare. "I have to see what's out there, what it means. Unless . . ."

"Unless what?"

"Have you been there? Do you know what it's like?"

"Just the stories." The admission sounded like defeat. "Maybe a few more stories than most, but no firsthand experience."

"What kind of stories?" An owl hooted, filling my pause. "There's a secret out there."

He raised his eyes to the sky and drew in a breath. "What are you looking for?"

Could I trust him? Probably not. He called me dangerous, but he was just as much of a threat. Still . . . "I saw a map, which made it very clear there's something hidden out there, and I want to know the truth."

"Ah." There was amusement in his voice. "For someone who lies and steals and impersonates others, you are awfully concerned with the truth."

If only he knew about my other great talents, like forgery. Then he'd be really impressed. "Do you know anything about that location?"

He sighed. "Only rumors. What have you heard?"

"Oh, I don't think so, Black Knife. You haven't said anything to hint that you actually know what I'm talking about."

A small, warm chuckle came from behind the mask, and the black silk shifted with his smile.

"I'm so glad my suspicious nature amuses you."

"It's delightful." He adjusted the collar of his shirt. "Very well. I will take the risk of revealing what I know, in hopes of convincing you of my trustworthiness.

"You saw a map with a location marked 'confidential' and 'debated.' Further investigation revealed that it was on the northwestern border of Liadia, where there was little more than a village, a lake, and a nobleman's country home. Now you've got a mind to go see this lake for yourself to determine what is actually out there, though I can't figure out why *you* care about it so much you'd risk your life and sanity."

He didn't think very highly of me. "What do you mean I'm risking my sanity?"

"There's a reason why your lake is so debated: few people are willing to make the journey into the wraithland, and even fewer return. Those who do bring such wild and unbelievable stories that most end up in institutions for the mentally unsound."

"Oh." I swallowed a heavy lump in my throat. "I don't suppose you have statistics on that."

"The chances aren't good, Will. What makes you think you can survive the journey?"

"Nothing, I suppose. But I must discover the truth."

"It's not your responsibility."

Nice, coming from someone who didn't see why I would bother. "Whose is it, then? Yours? The king's? Any of the other kings who've tried and failed in the past?"

"It should be a worldwide effort, not just the effort of one girl pretending to be a boy."

"Kings and princes sit over councils and pretend they have a plan, but the truth is, they don't. And the rest of the world is weary, just waiting for the end." I hesitated around the dangerous truth. "Liadia broke the Wraith Alliance."

Black Knife stilled. "How do you know that?"

"A refugee told me."

"Who?"

"I didn't ask for a name. I didn't want you to go after anyone, if you found out."

He tilted his head a fraction. "You don't trust me?"

"Of course not. You're a vigilante. But I'll tell you the story I heard." Leaving out identifying details, I repeated what the refugee maid had told me. "If it's true, and there really is an area unaffected by the wraith, I owe it to the people I care about to find it and determine whether there's any way to survive when the wraith hits."

"Don't you owe it to them to stay alive?"

I eyed him askance. "Do you have friends, Black Knife? Family? People who care about you? Don't you owe it to them to stay safe and alive?"

His voice was soft, and he dragged one gloved finger down the side of his mask. "It's for them that I wear this."

"Then you understand. I need to do this because of what I am, and who I have to protect." A queen who wouldn't protect her subjects was no queen at all.

"Because of your magic. And the children you watch out for." Heartbeats thudded between us. "If you're determined to be foolish and brave, at least tell me your plan."

The implied sentiment was clear: *at least tell me you have a plan.*

I dared the smallest of smiles. "While everyone else stays in West Pass Watch, I'm going to hike down the mountain and into the wraithland. I need to *see* that lake. I need to touch it. Maybe I'll find that it's exactly like the rest of the wraithland. But maybe I'll discover something beyond that—something that changes everything. Maybe there's something I can do to halt the approach, not just *mitigate* the effects. If I can stop it, don't I have an obligation to try?"

Black Knife's gaze wandered into the forest beyond me. "I hear myself in your words. Asking you again to reconsider would be horribly hypocritical of me."

"I'm glad you finally realized that." My tone was light, but I was relieved he'd said it. I didn't need his approval, but it was nice that he understood.

He turned back to me. "What is your magical ability? To heat things? The stone on that wall had been melted."

I closed my eyes. Talking about my magic out loud was too much. Especially with *Black Knife*. Naming my ability would shatter this tentative truce. He would never be able to overlook what I was. When I was a child, I'd believed I'd brought things to life. The truth was that I could animate objects, and command them, but there was no real life involved.

Still, it was a dangerous power. "What happens to flashers, Black Knife?"

He seemed to deflate. "They're taken to the wraithland to be killed in the very thing they helped create."

"Oh."

"It used to be a longer journey, and the Indigo Kingdom passed them off to Liadia and kingdoms beyond in order to reach their punishment. Now it takes just a few days to reach the wraithland. They're deposited at West Pass Watch and sent in along with glowmen."

I balled my hands into fists and squeezed my eyes shut.

"They can't use their magic to escape because they're given an injection. It keeps them barely conscious, unable to focus enough to use their power."

And when they were delivered to the wraithland, the glowmen would tear them apart. The beasts would devour them. The air would suffocate them.

"I wish I hadn't investigated. It was easier not knowing." He shivered, and he sounded—upset? Hurt? Confused?

"Are you still capturing flashers?"

"No," he whispered. "I haven't been. It's why I couldn't take you in that night, and why I wanted you with me after."

"Even though the man—"

215

He nodded, shifting toward me, and our shoulders brushed. "Even though."

His shoulder against mine was a faint, barely there warmth. I didn't move away. "Why are you here?" I asked.

"I like sitting in trees." There was tension in his voice, and weariness.

"Admit it." I leaned away from him, keeping my tone hard as our eyes locked. "You're following me."

He laughed and ducked his face. "Very well. I'm following you."

"Why?"

"You keep getting away from me. That never happens."

"I don't think you're even trying to catch me anymore."

His chuckle came again, warm and muffled, but real enough that something inside me melted. "I'm still trying," he said.

"And as part of this never-ending quest, are you going to follow me into the wraithland?"

His posture shifted—shoulders down and slightly turned— and he glanced west, as though conflicted. "I can't."

Disappointment rippled through me. I hadn't realized I'd hoped he would come along. So we could argue more? Fight? "You have important things to do in Skyvale. Thieves to catch. Wraith beasts to kill. I know." And what else? Who was he when he wasn't Black Knife? "The caravan is scheduled to stay at West Pass Watch for two weeks. That gives me a week to get to the lake, and a week to get back. I'll return to Skyvale the same way I left: as a guard."

"It's probably the first honest work you've done."

"It's not completely honest. Where do you think I got this sword?"

"*Will.*" He dropped back his head in exasperation, and a tiny sliver of his throat peeked between his shirt collar and mask. "Well, you'd better come back alive, and in your right mind, because when you do, I'll be waiting for you."

I lifted an eyebrow. "To arrest me?"

"No. To—" He hesitated. As soft as a breath, he closed his hand over my arm. "To welcome you home."

Trees shivered in the wind, sending spirals of leaves hissing downward. I looked at his gloved hand, unmoving over my sleeve. Why was he touching me like that? What was he thinking? He'd followed me out here from Skyvale and now . . .

I held very still so that he would, too. "Skyvale isn't my home."

"It doesn't matter. I'll wait for you anyway." He squeezed my arm, just lightly, and withdrew. "Please be careful—"

A shriek and howl interrupted him. Screams sounded from the caravan. Without another word to Black Knife, I leapt to the ground and ran.

TWENTY

I RACED THROUGH the narrow stretch of forest separating my post from the road.

Already, torches illuminated the clearing. Sleeping guards rolled off the rooftops, and inside the barricade created by the wagons, people shouted and cried out in terror. The reek of smoke and wraith flooded the area, chased by the metallic tang of blood.

Nausea tumbled through me as I drew my sword. It was a strange, heavy weight, and not as comfortable in my grip as my daggers, but it had a better reach.

"Where is it?" Black Knife stopped next to me, breathing hard. His sword was already out, a natural extension of his arm.

"I don't—"

A terrible *click-clack* and shriek came from the far side of the caravan. We both ran toward the sound, following the other guards.

An enormous scorpion—as big as a wagon—scuttled down the road, pincers clacking as men surged toward it.

Black Knife swore and charged the beast, and only then did I notice the most terrifying part of all: chains around the scorpion's head, pincers, and tail. Chains that had snapped and were now dangling like jewelry.

From the chaos, glowmen emerged. They carried the broken ends of chains, torches, and long staffs that they must have used to prod the beast into the Indigo Kingdom.

I drew my dagger in my left hand and hurled myself into battle.

Most of the men concentrated on the scorpion; it was heading straight for the wagons.

I focused my efforts on the glowmen, the grotesque wraith-mutated men. There were five of them. No, ten or twelve. They emerged from the forest with shouts of rage.

I swung my sword down on the nearest glowman. He blocked my sword stroke with his staff, and fire raced up my arm and shoulder from the impact.

With a grunt, I staggered back and into another glowman. He kicked me back toward the first. I adjusted my grip at the last moment, ducked, and sliced a wide arc with my sword. Blood sprayed from the glowman's stomach, but I didn't have the luxury of watching him flail. I turned and attacked the second one, but he lifted his forearm, wrapped in chains, and steel struck steel with a spray of sparks.

I stabbed with my dagger, hitting the large artery in his thigh with a long, clean cut. Blood poured out of him in wraith-stinking torrents.

Smoke choked the air. I coughed into my sleeve and turned for my next opponent, a third glowman. Then a fourth and a fifth and a sixth. The fight became automatic—cut and block and duck and slice and *do not die*—and the glowmen kept coming, wearing horrifying faces that reminded me of hounds and birds of prey.

My right arm burned as I raised my sword again and again. Cacophony filled my head, all clank of steel, rush of fire, screams of horses, shouts of men, and the *click-clack* of the scorpion. I saw it only between glowmen trying to behead me. The wraith beast was black and glossy, its carapace barely scratched in spite of the guards throwing themselves at it.

Glowmen littered the ground around me. I used a dead one as a stool so I could slice open the inner-thigh artery of another, who'd been fighting Josh or Jack or whatever that guard's name was. The man gave a curt nod before turning to his next opponent.

The scorpion's tail slammed into the ground as people hurried out of its way. Men stood on top of the wagons, brandishing torches to keep the beast away from the merchants and merchandise, but a giant glowman with a sparking metal rod jabbed at the scorpion, keeping it from retreating.

I pushed toward it, elbowing my way through guards and glowmen, using my blades where necessary. Blood and sweat coated my hands, drying into a dull armor under the heat. Someone had thrown a torch at the scorpion, but overshot. Now flames licked the edge of the forest, working into a full blaze. The scorpion screeched, shying away from both fires. Its stinger struck the ground, remnants of its binding chain flailing along with it.

People screamed as the chain hit the edge of a wagon roof. Wood splintered and the wagon tipped, but men raced to right it.

I forced past a clutch of guards taking out a glowman with rough skin that looked more like alligator hide.

"Will!" Black Knife appeared beside me, both of us just out of reach of the wraith scorpion. "You're hurt?"

I shook my head. "Not my blood."

"Thank saints." He bumped my arm with his and jerked his chin toward the wraith beast. "Remember the giant cat?"

"With horror." But I knew what he was going to suggest. "This one has no neck."

"Not long ago you claimed you knew which end of your sword to stick where."

Ugh. Using my own words against me wasn't fair. "Taking me out to robberies, bar fights, and wraith houses isn't enough for you anymore? I thought we were happy."

"Only the best for you, my lady." He tugged my arm. "Let's go."

We split up. I headed for the scorpion's back end, looking for a way to climb onto the dancing beast. There were men all around, hacking at its legs and underside, but the stinger came down again and again, the chain striking men aside.

I sheathed my weapons and waited as close as I dared. When the stinger hit the ground, I darted in and grabbed the chain with both hands.

The tail whipped up, nearly catapulting me into the forest, but I clung to the chain so hard my knuckles ached. I screamed as I whirled over the tail, swinging within a gasp of the stinger.

All my breath whooshed out of me when I dropped onto the scorpion's back.

I groaned and forced myself to sit up. The scorpion probably wouldn't sting itself—if it even knew I was up here—but its exoskeleton was slick and difficult to grip. I braced myself with one boot tread against the shell, getting my bearings. The glowman at the scorpion's rear prodded it toward the wagons again, but the torches made it duck backward—not too close to the fire growing in the forest. The scorpion struck with its tail, driving back the guardsmen.

I couldn't see Black Knife in all the chaos, but he was somewhere in front, trying to get beneath the wraith beast to spear it. But the scorpion was too big—much bigger than the cat—and it had enormous pincers just waiting to snap that reckless vigilante in half.

There was no other way.

I stood, clutching the upright tail for balance, and stretched my hand to touch the chain. "*Wake up. Be heavy.*"

The tail went crashing down and I scrambled out of its way, farther up the body of the beast. When I reached the chain wrapped between its head and abdomen sections, I said, "*Wake up. Squeeze.*"

Dizziness spun through me, and I slipped as the beast shuddered against the living chains. Pincers snapped out at nothing, and its legs scrambled across the blood-slicked ground. Men screamed and backed out of the scorpion's way as it began turning in a circle.

Fire in the trees roared, stirring the beast into a frenzy. It banged against wagons and trees, shrieking, and I kept myself low and steady on its head. Where was Black Knife?

There. He'd either killed or disabled the giant glowman with the prod and seized it for himself. "Will!"

"Ready!" The shout tore from my throat as I drew my sword and drove it deep into one of the top eyes. A moment later, Black Knife thrust the prod into the creature's scissor-like mouth parts.

The beast spasmed. Its back half pulled against the immense weight of the chains. It twitched, and everyone cheered as the giant body hit the earth with a *thud*. Black Knife disappeared into the crowd, somehow avoiding everyone's notice.

Quickly, I drew my sword from the eye and tapped the chains on my way off the beast. "*Go to sleep.*"

Men clapped my back and congratulated me, but my whole body shook with adrenaline, and the exhaustion of animating those enormous chains. I managed to pull myself away—I didn't want to get caught in the wraithy mist like I had in Skyvale— and for the first time I got a look at the rest of the caravan.

Guards and glowmen lay motionless on the road, their bodies illuminated by the blaze growing in the forest. There were so many people on the ground.

The scorpion's body hissed, and a miasma of wraith poured into the air above it. Then, the white mist split and snaked around a few men, hitting three or four men in the chest. They all dropped to their knees and coughed, but a moment later, they were fine. Back on their feet, as though nothing had happened.

The mist was wraith, that much I knew, but why touch some people and not others?

My head spun with confusion and weariness, but there was still a fire to put out, so I wiped my sword clean and sheathed it, and accepted a section of the heavy, rigid hose that syphoned water from the nearby river.

Water sprayed onto the forest fire, and heat and steam rolled off in waves. Within minutes, the flames were out.

The fight and fire had left me nauseous. I staggered down the road a ways and heaved, doubting I'd ever be able to sleep again after that nightmare.

When I straightened, a black silhouette stood down the road, motionless as our eyes met. He sheathed his sword and lifted a hand in good-bye.

I stayed planted as he stepped backward. I should have said something. Done something. But while I stood there with all these strange emotions boiling inside me, Black Knife vanished into the smoke and steam and darkness.

"See you when I come back," I whispered. But he was already gone.

TWENTY-ONE

THE CARAVAN WAS determined to arrive in West Pass Watch on schedule, in spite of the attack, and so it resumed the long journey over and around the mountains.

As we trudged up the winding roads, some of the guards worked on the lyrics to their new song, "Will Makes the Kill," and I ducked my head in embarrassment. Maybe that was another reason Black Knife wore a mask: so he could escape the people's adulations by simply removing that slip of silk.

Anyway, it seemed wrong to take credit for killing the scorpion when Black Knife had done half the work. And I'd cheated by using magic. The very thing that had made that creature.

"You ever been to West Pass Watch, Will?" asked Josh Blue. The guard had been one of the men I'd saved during the scorpion attack, and he'd made it his priority to look out for me—since he still believed I was a young, inexperienced boy trying to pay for my education.

"Never been out of Skyvale," I said, squinting against the early afternoon glare.

"You're in for a sight, then." He pointed up at the weathered, gray bricks peeking out from the autumn foliage. "The castle was built long before Skyvale Palace. That one is only two hundred years old, a baby palace. But this one is from centuries before Skyvale ever was. It was built with magic, by some of the original settlers from the old land across the sea. West Pass Watch and its twin castle, East Pass Watch, were the first kings' homes, back when the Indigo Kingdom was much smaller."

"How small?"

"The whole thing was inside this valley, everything the House of the Dragon claims. The rest came during a series of wars with ancient kingdoms you've probably never heard of. They were incorporated as territories for a while, given overlords who were all related to the king of the time, then made official parts of the Indigo Kingdom."

"Like what's happening with Aecor now?" The words caught in my throat. "The king's younger brother is Overlord of Aecor."

Josh shrugged. "Hard to say with times like this, with the wraith just beyond the mountains. Before, I'd have said yes. But now, it'll be a miracle if we're around long enough to see any changes in our world."

I checked the woods, but this area was heavily patrolled; it seemed unlikely we'd run into any difficulty just outside West Pass Watch. The only trouble was the ever-present stink of wraith, which grew stronger every day, though it seemed my nose was becoming accustomed to it.

"So this castle." I motioned upward. "This one and the other guarded the western and eastern borders of the Indigo Kingdom?"

Josh nodded. "King of the time lived at whichever end he was fighting a war on. It was usually the east, as their attentions began focusing on what is now the eastern areas of the kingdom—from those mountains to Aecor. West Pass Watch was pretty neglected until the year eight thirty-five, when the Pierces seized power from the Gearys. Terrell the First gave the keep to one of his top supporters, but it went back into Pierce hands when the wraith problem was discovered."

"You know a lot of history."

He grinned and waved away my comment. "We all have our passions. I do my reading on these trips, once we get to West Pass Watch. There's a lot of off-duty time coming up. The merchants need fewer guards in the Watch, so most of us spend time training with any in the Indigo Army that won't look down on us for being hired. I split my time between training and looking through old journals and history books."

"Old journals and history books are only as good as the people who wrote them."

Josh laughed and patted my cap. "You've got a wise young mind. How old did you say you were? Fourteen? Fifteen?"

Nearly eighteen. "Old enough to work." I added a defensive note to my words, but I didn't mean it.

He grunted, but talked my ears off the rest of the way up to the Watch, pointing out specific bits of architecture he liked, or where a king once drunkenly lost a fistfight with one of his daughter's suitors.

The caravan leaders guided the wagons off the tracks and—once the bigger wheels were on—directed them around the lower bailey. Soldiers on the ramparts cheered and trumpets blared. A caravan of merchandise was as good a reason as any to celebrate out here.

"When will we have time off?" I asked Josh. "I'd like to see off the western wall."

"They don't like us wandering around too much." He pressed his mouth into a line. "But I know a few people who won't care about my showing you around, if you don't mind the company."

"I'd appreciate it, in fact."

The castle itself was deceptively familiar. Now that I knew it was twin to the old palace—East Pass Watch—I could see the similarities of the core structures, though centuries of upgrading had marked the ancient keeps in different ways. While the old palace was regal like an aged queen who tried to disguise unfortunate sagging by dressing in ever-more elaborate gowns, West Pass Watch had aged gracefully, with additions that complemented the original design.

After an hour, we finally made it to the west-facing ramparts, and I had my first glimpse of the wraithland.

"There it is," said Josh. "That glow just beyond the mountains."

"There are so *many* mountains." I hadn't expected that, though I should have. I'd seen the maps.

"The mountains are what protect the Indigo Kingdom from the worst of the wraith storms and beasts," Josh said.

Probably so, but if the mountains we'd already crossed had seemed endless, these looked even more formidable. Though they were all dressed in their autumn best, what had been beautiful and rolling before became unbearably severe. Some of those peaks were higher than the one West Pass Watch stood upon. To get to the wraithland, I'd have to go through all of that.

"I guess the stories about glowmen—soldiers here watching them fight one another when they're dumped in the wraithland—that's just fiction, then?"

He nodded. "Lots of stories about the wraithland are just stories. But there are even more things out there than are conceivable—things too awful to be stories."

"Have you ever been?"

"Once," he said softly. "To the very edge of it. I was hired to map its progress just a few months ago. At first I wasn't sure how I was supposed to know when I'd reached it. But I did. I knew the moment I stepped into the wraithland, and I don't mind saying that I stepped right back out. Just placed my marker and left."

"How long did it take to get there?"

The older guard just studied me for a moment, like he could see through to all of my plans. "About three days, walking. I suppose it'd have been much faster on horseback, but I couldn't imagine doing that to an animal. I wished for one, though, on my way back. I don't care how well it pays. I'll never take that job again."

I lowered my eyes, as though ashamed for making him talk about it. "I see."

He patted my shoulder. "I'll let you be for a while. Go on

to the southern apartments when you're ready. We'll get dinner there in"—he checked a pocket watch—"two hours."

I thanked him again, and when he and the others were gone, I slumped against the wall, already regretting my decision.

I could almost hear Melanie and Black Knife now: I didn't *have* to go. I could wait the two weeks here in relative comfort, read some of Josh's books, and head back to Skyvale.

But how could I come all this way only to turn back?

What had I told Melanie? A queen who wouldn't take risks for her people wasn't worthy of being a queen at all.

I would take this risk.

Before I headed down to dinner, I found the map room—just a brief wave on our earlier tour—and went to studying. There were several roads into the wraithland, many well maintained—and well guarded—which meant I had to find a less desirable route if I didn't want to get caught.

It took an hour and a half of searching and comparing routes with maintenance and surveillance documentation, but at last I found something I could live with—hopefully—and carefully wrote out detailed directions, copying maps and lifting any papers that looked useful.

Armed with a plan, I went to dinner late and took my bunk in the spare barracks meant for visiting caravan guards. When snores resounded through the building, I gathered my backpack and map, stole as many rations from the kitchen as I could carry, and hurried through the keep to take a few other supplies I might need.

In the stables, I liberated a gelding horse from his stall, along with a sack of oats. There was still enough grass on the ground to supplement his feed.

I adjusted my cap and put on the small Indigo Army jacket I'd just stolen, and on my way out of the keep, I told the gate guard that I was a new messenger; I showed him a sealed paper I'd nicked from the map room. Without comment, the guard waved me on.

Dawn was still hours away, but the wraithland's glow shed plenty of light to see by. The chestnut horse picked his way down the road, keeping close to the old railroad tracks that wound through the mountains.

The first day was much like my journey to West Pass Watch, but much faster. I managed to spear a rabbit for dinner, but when I began skinning it, I realized how big and heavy it was—much larger than normal rabbits. Swirls of dark, dark blue crawled up from its hindquarters; I'd thought they were shadows before.

With an acid tingle in the back of my throat, I heaved the wraith rabbit back into the woods and ate some of my rations instead.

The second day, I entered the wraithland.

Josh's warning had been good; I knew the moment I stepped across the border.

Cold prickled over my face, like I'd stepped into a fog bank. The air was wetter, heavier, and the sun dimmed as though it had receded a great distance. Gray tinged the sky.

"It's as though half the color has seeped out of the world," I muttered to my horse. His ears flickered back, but the muscles in his neck remained taut as he stared into shadows so deep they looked like night.

I petted him and murmured reassurances, but he didn't acknowledge me.

Fingers of white mist reached through the waist-high grass, rustling the browning blades until they sounded like voices. *"Who's watching?"* it sounded like. *"Someone's watching."*

I twisted around, horse tack squeaking as I scanned the forest around me and the base of the mountains behind me. There was nothing unusual, though; just that vague, growing tension and sensation of being followed.

As the sun arced across the sky, West Pass Watch became invisible among the russet heights of the mountains. I was truly alone now.

My heart felt like it fluttered in my chest. "Do you have a name, horse?" I reached forward and scratched his ears. "Not that you can tell me, I suppose. What about Ferguson?"

He shook his head and grunted.

Good enough. "Ferguson it is."

It was stupid, but having a name for the horse made me feel a little better. A little.

Hyperaware of every gust and gasp of wind, I pushed deeper into the wraithland until nightfall. With Ferguson tied to a wilting tree, enough slack on his lead so he could chew on the yellowing grass, I climbed into the cradle of an oak tree's branches.

Deep slashes marred the trunk and branches, evidence of huge predators nearby. The wooden ridges pressed against my spine as I settled in, then forced down a small meal of deer jerky and water. I didn't feel safe exactly, but with a hundred golden leaves veiling me, I hoped I'd get a little rest.

Acrid-stinking wind cut through the forest. Something—a leaf?—caressed my cheek with a dry scrape. I jumped and scrubbed my palms over my face, but whatever had touched me was gone, and the area was too dark to see anything.

I bit back a panicked *meep* and dug through my bag for Black Knife's spare mask. When the cool silk covered my head and the eye slit was faced forward, I tried to breathe more deeply to slow my racing heart.

"There's nothing out there," I whispered.

The only sound was the wind in my ears and the soft thumps of my horse moving below.

I lit a candle stub and pulled out my notebook, pen, and a flat bottle of ink that I'd found would sit in my packs without getting in the way. By the flickering candlelight, I wrote about my first day in the wraithland, recording detailed notes about the smell and wind and ailing vegetation.

It's watching me, I wrote, and closed my notebook.

Trees groaned all night in the wind. Every time I closed my eyes, something crashed in the woods. Part of me wanted to find it and face it.

Instead, I pulled my blanket higher and my mask lower, trying to ignore Ferguson's grunts and sighs. In the fits of sleep, my body grew stiff and tense, overwhelmed with this unfamiliar place and unfamiliar sounds. The night had never seemed so long.

Sometime before dawn, a shout tore from the north. A *human* shout.

I jerked awake and peered through the darkness.

"The trees told me there's someone here." Brush crackled

and the man stomped through the forest.

A jumble of other voices replied, too many to distinguish their words or number. If they spotted me—or my horse—I was in trouble.

Torchlight broke through the trees. The light floated higher than any normal person would hold it. When shapes began to appear between the trunks, it was clear:

They were glowmen.

TWENTY-TWO

I MOVED AS quietly as possible, shimmying down the side of the tree opposite from where the glowmen were approaching. My belongings were already in my bag, and I hadn't unsaddled Ferguson the whole way. If I could get down, tighten the girth, and adjust the bridle without being spotted . . .

My toes breezed over the ground. I felt around for a heartbeat to make sure I didn't do something stupid like step on a twig and alert the whole wraithland to my presence. But my footing was good, and I lowered myself from the tree and crept around the trunk.

Torchlight silhouetted my horse. Metal clanked on his bridle as he swung his head around to look at me.

"Hush," I whispered, running my palms over his sweat-dampened neck. Reins snaked around my fingers, alive.

Strangling a gasp, I jerked back my hands and stared hard at the leather straps, but they hung against Ferguson's withers, inanimate again. Maybe the motion had been my imagination.

Even if it had been real, I had to hurry.

"I heard something!" The crashing of glowmen was louder and nearer.

Quickly, I tightened the bridle and girth, but just as I hooked my bag onto the saddle, enormous hands grabbed me from behind and lifted.

"Got it!" The giant hands squeezed my torso.

Air whooshed from my lungs. I flailed, blindly groping for the saddle, as though I could still pull myself onto the horse, but Ferguson was straining against his tether, fighting to get away from the glowman.

"Hold it still. We want to see." The rest of the pack crashed through the woods, waving their torch around as though they didn't care about setting the whole place ablaze.

I kicked backward, but I couldn't reach him. I was high above my horse—almost as high as I'd been in the tree. These glowmen were bigger than the ones I'd fought in Skyvale, probably from being out here in the wraith so long. Already, dizziness buzzed in my head. The giant's grip tightened, making my ribs ache.

"It squirms." His voice was like thunder, vibrating through my bones.

Blackness swarmed in my vision. My breaths were shallow gasps.

The others came nearer and peered at me, their huge, mal-formed faces gaping. The stink of sour breath rolled over me. I couldn't reach the weapons at my hip.

"Let me see it." One of the others grabbed for me. The fingers around my waist loosened and I sucked in a lungful of air as I was passed from one monstrosity to the next. But it wasn't enough. My ribs ached, making every breath like fire. "It has no face. Only eyes."

"I want to look." Another glowman plucked me from the other's grip, this time by my elbow.

Torchlight burned my eyes as I swung through the air, but finally I could breathe and had one arm free.

With a hacking cough, I drew my sword and sliced open the glowman's wrist. Blood sprayed and I dropped, my knees and knuckles slamming into the ground. But I kept my grip on my sword. Nothing could make me drop it.

"You're so stupid!" One of the glowmen shoved the one who'd dropped me. "You have to hold on to them."

I scrambled to my feet, out of the way of grasping hands, and drove my sword deep into a giant foot.

The glowman yowled and staggered into the others, knocking over some. One reached for me, but I was faster. I stabbed another in the knee. Blood oozed down the length of my sword.

The ground shuddered and brush cracked. The night was chaos: glowmen fighting one another, grabbing for me, and the sudden howling of a beast nearby. It had scented blood.

I swung my blade high once more, slicing knees and calves. The nearest glowman tried to bat me into the woods, but I lifted my sword at the last second; his fingers came off.

The baying of beasts grew closer. I spun and ran for Ferguson. The poor thing shied, but there was nowhere for him to go. Already the rope stretched and creaked.

I heaved myself onto the saddle and cut the tether. We snapped away, galloping at full speed as an enormous, bear-shaped shadow descended on the pack of glowmen. Screams chased us down the road, but I kept myself low over Ferguson's neck as his body stretched and folded in a panicked run.

We didn't stop when droplets of horse sweat misted across my face. We didn't stop when the sounds of the dying glowmen faded into the distance. We didn't stop when the sun lifted into the violet sky.

Only when Ferguson had run himself out did we slow to a shaky-legged walk while he caught his breath.

I could have died. My horse, too. We could have died, and no one would have known where I'd gone, except Melanie and Black Knife. She had threatened to come after me if I didn't return on time, and he . . . I didn't know.

But they'd been right to worry, right to be afraid for me. What happened if I died? What would happen to the Ospreys, especially the ones with secrets they didn't understand? Or Aecor? I'd been so flip when I told Melanie that Patrick would figure out something to do.

It was midmorning by the time I halted Ferguson at a stream and let him drink. I trembled all over as I freed him from his tack and set about rinsing the blood and sweat that covered both of us. The work steadied my thoughts, if not my body, and by the time we were on the move again, walking toward the setting sun, I knew one thing for sure:

I would do anything to survive out here. Anything to get back to the people I cared about.

I moved deeper into the wraithland over the next few days, stopping to draw and catalogue the things I saw and heard: a rosebush with thorns for petals; whispers in the wind, urging one another to run and hide; grass with serrated blades so sharp Ferguson whinnied and had to go around; and the distant rumble of wraith creatures—dogs and hawks and all manner of other beasts turned sour by magical waste.

At night, I slept in trees to avoid the glowmen that roamed the woods, and the mice as big as cats. Not that trees meant safety, as I'd already discovered, but they were still the best option and I trained myself to doze for only a few hours before moving a league down the road to doze again.

Once, a tree began to nibble at my shoulder in the middle of the night, and I tumbled to the ground. No, the trees weren't safe.

My sixth day out of West Pass Watch, I reached the village I'd set out to find. Or what was left of it.

The buildings rose out of the dust like a giant's toys. They stood haphazardly, where they stood at all. Bricks had toppled over under the siege of storms, or something worse. If scorpions and cats grew to horrendous proportions when affected by wraith, what about larger predators?

I swallowed hard as Ferguson clip-clopped over the dry dirt road and stopped. The road ahead lifted into the air, curling around like a ribbon, with nothing supporting it before it dove back into the earth. It didn't look safe, and if my horse didn't want to put his hooves on it, I wouldn't make him.

Still, I needed to look, because according to my map, the mysterious lake was nearby. Indeed, a liquid glimmer shone beyond the shops and houses, near the high brick walls of a nobleman's country estate.

This was what I'd come to see.

Gathering my nerves, I nudged Ferguson to walk closer to the shops and houses, away from the road.

The buildings were stone, but many had the texture of wood. They'd been petrified. Glass windows had melted and run down the walls like tears, freezing that way.

I peered inside the first building we reached.

Faces stared back out at me: grotesque, horrified faces of the dead, like insects in amber. They grasped for windows and doorways, never reaching safety. Whatever they were trapped in, it was transparent, so every detail of their death was unsettlingly preserved, but it was also solid and hard, and sheered off at the windows or doors, as though it had known where it reached the boundary of the building.

One of the women trapped inside blinked.

I yelped, causing Ferguson to scramble away, but when I guided him toward the window again, the woman looked as dead as ever. I'd imagined it. Maybe.

Trying not to heave, I moved on, following the gleam of the lake behind the far buildings. My goal was so close; if there was anything out here that might give insight to a way to *stop* the wraith rather than simply *mitigate* the effects, I would find it.

Unseasonably bright green leaves sprouted from a tree in the center of the village, but its trunk was twisted and bent so that the top branches dug into the ground; the roots reached up through the earth to touch the pale sunlight. It was strange; even though there were no clouds, a thick haze obscured everything. Even the mountains in the distance were lost to the fog of wraith.

It was as though the world ended with that fog. There was nothing beyond. I was alone on an island of wraith and horror.

But the lake was close by.

Halfway through the village, I dismounted Ferguson and collected my weapons and writing utensils. It was hard to say what information might turn out useful when I returned to Skyvale, especially information from around the rumor-rich Mirror Lake.

I grabbed a snack and left some oats for Ferguson, and headed toward the lake and the large country manor beyond, keeping clear of the levitating road.

Several times, I paused and balanced my notebook on my knee in order to sketch and make notes on the state of the village. How far was I from the lake? Not very far, so if there were any unusual properties to the water, they didn't extend into the village.

A low, metal wall ran along the western side of the village, curving around the lakeshore and manor. Once, it had been pieced together in scales, giving the illusion of an immense snake. After the wraith had broken through, huge sections had been flattened against the earth, while others had been pulled off as if by giant hands. Several sections were just gone—tossed into the lake.

My heart pounded as I made my way toward the lake. Bare, scraggly trees grew around its still surface, though there was something odd about their branches hanging over the water.

I stepped over rocks and rubble, around brush with twigs that reached like fingers. This shore was covered with brown, brittle grass that crunched under my boots as though coated with frost. The lake spread out before me, motionless even with the breeze that rustled across the rest of the world.

"How strange," I whispered as I moved along the edge of the lake.

Palm-sized scales of metal gleamed in the weak light. I plucked one off the ground. It was silver, tarnished with time, and warm, though not from sunlight. Haze still obscured the sky.

But when I glanced up, there was a hole in the haze, the exact shape of the lake beneath it.

The lake was blue, reflecting bright sky. The branches that hung over the water looked healthier—more alive in spite of the oncoming winter. I couldn't even say *what* exactly looked different about them, just that they did.

I pocketed several scales and wandered over to the barrier to inspect it more closely.

Where it was still intact, the wall was only waist-high and a few scales thick. Most of this area of the barrier lay scattered across the lakeshore, though, or beneath the water. I could almost hear echoes of the panic the refugee maid had described, with people trampling one another to escape the flood of wraith.

This part of Liadia must have been hit first, and the hardest. It was on the western edge of the country, and right on the barrier. When the barrier failed, there'd have been no warning.

Some had been trapped. Others had gone mad. Most had likely died.

Precious few had escaped across the terrifying remains of their kingdom and into the neighboring mountains, only to be forced into refugee camps in the Indigo Kingdom. Dirty. Hungry. But alive.

I let my gaze follow the length of the barrier, running north. It curved around the manor house and grounds, and then was lost beyond the fog and forest.

This was what magic use created. This was why Black Knife hunted flashers, and why the Indigo Order was merciless, and why the Wraith Alliance had been written. This was terrible, the worst thing I'd ever seen—and I'd seen so much—so why had my parents refused the treaty? Why had they allowed magic use to continue, if *this* was the consequence?

Because they believed magic was acceptable in emergencies, as long as it wasn't relied upon? That was what I'd always thought, though with little proof, but what if there was more to it than that?

I returned to the very edge of the lake until the toes of my boots grazed the water. The depths were crystalline, offering a perfect view of fish and plants and barrier scales scattered along the green bottom.

The water was cold with autumn, but it didn't feel strange or magical when I dipped my fingers in, then shook off the droplets. The only thing unusual about Mirror Lake was that there was *nothing* unusual about it. It reflected a clear, unblemished sky, with healthy branches hanging over the water. And these things were normal outside the reflection, too.

It was as though the wraith didn't touch the lake. Because of the barrier pieces?

Maybe my parents had wondered if there was a magical solution to the wraith, and didn't want the Wraith Alliance to prevent them from pursuing that option. That seemed possible.

For an hour I roamed around the edge of the lake, pausing

to fill pages with notes and drawings of the landscape.

In the village, Ferguson gave a loud, annoyed snort.

"Just a minute," I muttered. Bossy horse.

Wind picked up as I was sketching the shape of the silver scales. My paper rustled, and the ink dried on my pen. I shivered and found another angle, protecting my work from the wraithy grit that rose, but the wind followed me, twisting around my body like a serpent.

Run away, the wind whispered. *Hide now.*

Ferguson whinnied and yanked at his lead. Whites shone around his eyes and his cries grew more panicked.

Hands shaking, I wiped off my pen nib, closed the ink bottle, and threw them in their case. Wind tugged at my clothes, dragging everything sideways. With my supplies secured, I scrambled to my feet and adjusted the black mask, scanning the area for anything dangerous—anything the wind might be warning me about.

There was nothing.

Ferguson stamped and jerked against his lead as rain hissed all over town. But the sky was still that hazy blue.

Rain flew upward from the earth, and the sky became a wide, sucking mouth. Clouds shot up from the ground and became teeth.

I screamed and ran for Ferguson. Water poured up my trouser legs and jacket, caught inside my mouth and nose, even through the silk mask. I grasped around my face, struggling to keep from drowning as I ran toward the edge of town.

Run away. Hide now, the wind chuckled in my ears.

Ferguson wrenched himself free from the tree where I'd tied

him. Hooves thumped, coming closer, louder and louder as rain drove harder.

Blackness swarmed in from the west, and the sky went dark—everywhere except directly over the water. Dots of darkness flaked off where they flew too close over Mirror Lake, and then I could see nothing beyond my outstretched arm. Just rain.

For a moment, the only thing I could hear was my ragged breathing as I ran. My footsteps pounded the wet ground as I reached for Ferguson. He'd been close just a moment ago.

Then came the buzzing. It was loud, low, and a constant drone that filled my ears completely.

Something small hit my arm, like a pebble. Another struck my cheek. A lump crunched under my boot and then the swarm descended.

Bugs—thousands and thousands—hurled themselves onto the village. They flew down in torrents, thudding and beating in the rain. Prickly legs scratched at my hands and forearms, climbed up my jacket and trousers. They caught on the silk of my mask, creeping in through the eye slit to touch my face.

I screamed and scratched at the bugs, but they poured into my mouth. I spat them out, but I couldn't breathe against the hard little bodies all trying to crawl up my nose. Their legs pried at my lips. They skittered around to the back of my neck and into my hair.

I turned back and ran for the lake, but the bugs and rain were so dense I'd lost all sense of direction. I slammed into a building, bugs crunching between my body and the wall, long legs pricking at my skin.

My heart raced as the droning grew deafening. I stomped

and kicked, but there were so many bugs and they were every-where. Panic brought one note of clarity: I would die.

No.

I had to do something.

Anything.

I coughed, spitting bugs. My voice was garbled. *"Air!"* I thrust my hands out, though leggy little bugs just caught on my fingers and crawled up my sleeves. *"Wake up!"*

Thunder joined the droning. Drumming built inside my head as the bugs crept inside my shirt and into the strip of silk binding down my breasts.

I clawed the bugs away from my mouth. *"Save me!"*

"Wilhelmina!"

Wind blew from all directions, harder than the rain, more relentless than the bugs. I staggered and fell as the wind shouted my name again and again.

And then everything went silent.

TWENTY-THREE

I AWOKE FLAT on my back with my limbs splayed akimbo, resting on a prickly bed. Sunlight beat into my eyes. My clothes were dry, though I vividly recalled rain. And insects.

The bugs shifted beneath me when I sat up and pulled off my mask. Small, hard bodies dropped out of the silk.

As far as I could see, there was nothing but long-legged bugs covering the ground. They half buried the houses and stores, all the remnants of this town. The lake, too, was spotted with patches of bugs floating on the surface, obscuring the reflection of morning sunlight.

Morning sunlight. It had been afternoon when the swarm descended, but now it was morning. How long had I been unconscious? Where was my horse?

My breath grew short as I scrambled to my feet, shaking grasshoppers from my clothes and hair. Something scraped my throat when I inhaled—and my stomach flipped. I gagged and spat grasshopper legs until there was nothing left and my mouth was raw.

"What did I do?" The words tasted sour. This was wrong. All wrong.

Adrenaline buzzed through my limbs as I dropped back to my knees, bugs crunching beneath me. Ferguson was missing, and at least one night had gone by.

I'd done this. I'd shouted for the air to save me, and it had, but now there was nothing to touch, nothing to put back to sleep. The wind had done as I'd bidden, and now it was gone, leaving behind thousands of dead locusts.

And me. Alone.

"Oh, saints." I'd never prayed much before, but this seemed like a good time to start, with the mountains standing in the distance, so far away now that I'd lost my horse.

Strange, though. The mountains were sharply defined with sunrise and shadows in the contours; yesterday they'd been obscured by the wraith. The sky, too, was bright and empty, and a lovely shade of blue. The haze was gone.

The *wraith* was gone.

The whole village was like the reflection of Mirror Lake: as normal as the Indigo Kingdom.

Frantically, I dug through the grasshoppers at my feet, finding my notebook and other things I'd been carrying. With everything tucked into pockets or my belt, I waded through the drifts until I found the house where the people had been trapped. The door was blocked, but the windows were still uncovered. I peered inside.

Everyone lay dead on the floor.

Released from their prison, they'd dropped into broken heaps; if they hadn't truly been dead before, they were now. Even the woman who'd blinked at me—maybe—had that stillness of lifelessness.

I wanted to be sick again, but there was nothing left in me.

It was time to go. The information I'd already gathered would have to be enough. With a horse, the trek had taken six days. Without, it would take much longer, especially considering I had no food or water—which I'd left hooked into a ring on the saddle—or even a change of clothes. If I didn't reach West Pass Watch and meet up with the caravan again, I'd never make it back to Skyvale in time to keep Melanie from following me out here.

Clutching my few belongings, I stumbled through the dead insects and aimed myself at the mountains.

The wraithland was different now, at least this part, and it was certainly because of what I'd done, though my brain was too sluggish to sift through the facts.

I just had to stick to what I knew: if I didn't get back to the Indigo Kingdom, Melanie would come after me, the Ospreys would erupt in chaos, and Aecor would have no queen.

If I didn't make it out of the wraithland—even this seemingly tamed wraithland—everything I cared about would be lost.

I pushed myself to walk through the near-freezing night, stopping to rest only when the quarter moon set and I had to wait for daybreak or risk losing track of the road. I shivered inside my jacket, which was suddenly too thin for this journey. I'd never be warm again.

My feet throbbed and my hips stiffened. My stomach felt hollow and my mouth was so dry that my lips cracked. When I finally stumbled over a stream, I didn't even worry about whether it was wraith polluted; I just stuck my head in the fast-moving water, gasped at the cold, and sucked up as much liquid as I could.

A few minutes later, I vomited up all the water I'd just drunk.

I tried again, this time slower, and my head began to clear.

Everything hurt, and any time I closed my eyes, the prickling sensation of locusts returned. I scratched at my arms and neck, rubbed my face red, but the memory never abated. There was no way I'd sleep, maybe ever again, so I drank my fill of water and returned to the road. I had to keep moving to stay warm.

The mountains grew in the distance, but not quickly enough. Though I walked through the night, using a small branch to help me keep my balance, I never seemed to get closer to my destination.

With luck, mostly, I caught a squirrel my second day out of the locusts. Its fur was of a normal color and it seemed to be a normal size.

I gathered up a small pile of twigs and peeling bark, then speared the squirrel with another stick.

I had matches in my pocket. There were only two, but I needed to eat *now*. Carefully, to keep from spoiling it, I struck the match and lit a curl of paper on fire, then laid it across the twigs to let them catch. I cupped my freezing hands around the fire, pulling in its warmth until it was big enough to cook with.

The squirrel was the best thing I'd ever eaten. It was gone by the time I realized I should have saved some for later, but I felt stronger, so I fed the fire more wood and went hunting.

Any real hunter would have laughed at my methods, but I managed to catch two trout and snare a few rabbits—a miracle, as far as I was concerned. After checking to make sure they weren't visibly contaminated with wraith, I cooked them all and hovered by the heat of the fire before pulling myself up and throwing dirt over the embers. Sitting in the meager heat and marveling over the thought of food wouldn't get me back to West Pass Watch.

The days blurred as I pushed east. I drank from the stream, ate tiny bites from the meat I'd cooked, and rested only when it was too dark to see. Once more I lit a fire, and then I was out of matches. A third fire would have to be started with magic, and I couldn't use that. Not after what I'd seen. Anyway, I wasn't sure I had the strength.

Mostly, as I walked, I thought about Melanie and what she'd do if I didn't come back. I thought about Connor carrying the burden of his secret alone. I even thought about Black Knife and that last conversation we shared. If I died out here, would he care?

Maybe. After all, he wasn't the nightmare I'd originally believed. I owed him for saving Connor's life, and not turning me in for magic use. He'd even chased down the truth about what became of flashers. He'd taken me fighting with him, and trusted me with secrets. He'd been an unexpected ally, even though I was a thief and he was a vigilante. And the way he'd touched my arm . . .

I missed my Ospreys. I missed Black Knife, too.

My thoughts wandered, never settling anywhere for more than a minute. Or an hour. Time was fuzzy and meaningless when I hadn't truly slept since waking in the locust field.

Though all this land I walked through had been filled with wraith before, now the forest seemed almost normal. Not poisoned. Too late, I wished I'd looked around the town more, after I'd awakened. I should have looked at the floating road, and the upside-down tree.

I'd used a lot of magic and I didn't know what the consequences would be. Especially since I hadn't been able to put anything back to sleep.

Over a week after the locusts, Ferguson found me. Or I found him.

Too thirsty to be picky, I was drinking from a suspect-looking stream when I heard the slurp of a horse sucking up water. And there he was.

His saddle and bags were still on, though they'd been twisted, and twigs and pine needles had caught in the tack, evidence of his rubbing against trees.

"You poor creature. I'm sorry." Once he was hitched to a tree, I liberated some oats and let him feast. He allowed me to unsaddle him without complaint. I brushed him down as best I could, then devoured half of the rations I'd left in my bag, eating until my stomach ached with being so full.

When we were both finished eating and drinking, I wanted so much to saddle him again and gallop all the way back to the castle, but that wouldn't be fair to Ferguson. I settled for resting the saddle and tack on him, and leading him up the mountain.

Only after he'd had a good night of rest did I tighten the straps and let him carry me. Not walking was bliss.

It wasn't long before we reached the railroad tracks that had once run between the Indigo Kingdom and Liadia.

"*Wilhelmina?*" The voice came from behind me, and I spun.

Only trees and dirt and birds waited.

"*Wilhelmina.*"

Ferguson's ears twitched; he heard it, too.

We'd left the wraithland—the *changed* wraithland—behind before climbing the mountains. Nevertheless, the feeling of something watching me grew stronger in the woods.

"*Wilhelmina.*" It sounded like the wind, all breathy and suggestive, but there shouldn't *be* anything here.

"The wraithland is back there!" Like reminding it of its place would do any good. I kicked Ferguson into a gallop up the twisting mountain road.

"*Wilhemina!*"

"Go back to sleep! Go to sleep, whatever you are!" I cried. If the command had any effect, I couldn't tell.

I hunched over Ferguson's neck to make myself smaller as he worked into a gallop. The stench of wraith pushed at us from behind, making my stomach roll in time with the steady rhythm of hoofbeats.

"*Wilhelmina!*" The voice chased us faster. Sweat on Ferguson's flanks grew into a stinking lather. He panted; I could feel the expansion of his ribs beneath my legs.

We ran. Whenever I peeked up, I caught glimpses of a castle rising above the trees. The road cut its way upward. All we had to do was get there.

"*Wilhelmina!*"

I kicked Ferguson harder, but it wasn't necessary. He gave another burst of speed at the blast of wraith stench. A finger of white mist crept behind us, relentless as it filled the width of the road and navigated the curves with ease. Steel screeched: the railroad tracks bent where the wraith touched.

Light flared ahead as the sun began to set behind me. The wraith screamed and called out my name again, but when I looked over my shoulder, the mist was retreating down the mountainside, leaving only the twisted metal of railroad tracks to mark where it had been.

What had scared it? What *could* scare wraith?

Above, the light flared again, and I laughed.

Mirrors.

A hundred mirrors hung on West Pass Watch; the setting sun had made them glow like fire.

Giddy, weary, and aching all over, I urged Ferguson to slow as we approached the castle. I traded Black Knife's mask for the cap to hide my braids, still piled up on top of my head from the night I left Skyvale.

Skyvale. I'd see Melanie again. The other Ospreys. I'd get a *bath*. A delirious giggle escaped me. I'd made it out of the wraith-land.

As my horse trotted into the lower bailey, several men in Indigo Army uniforms came out to meet me.

One glanced at a sheet of paper. "Will? William Cole?"

"Yes, sir." I dismounted when Ferguson came to a stop. "Where's the caravan?"

The lead man was tall, sharp featured, and vaguely familiar, though I was certain I hadn't seen him before.

"The caravan is gone, son. They left four days ago."

I let my shoulders slump. Now I'd have to walk by myself,

without the protection the caravan offered.

"I'm Herman Pierce, House of the Dragon, Lord of West Pass Watch." He didn't offer his hand. Of course. I was just a lowly hired guard. "You will address me with 'Your Highness.' Is that clear?"

He was one of the king's younger brothers—Tobiah's uncle.

"Yes, Your Highness." I dropped my face, taking note of the number of men surrounding us, the fading sunlight, and a silhouetted figure in the doorway to the barracks. My heart thumped. Was *he* here? Had he come?

"I'm going to take you where we can talk about what happened, why you went down the mountains, and why you came running back up like the very wraith itself was chasing you."

Hadn't he heard the voice?

"I'm also sending a letter to the caravan master requesting that you never work another job," he said. "And when I send requests, they're taken as orders."

I heaved a sigh as though I actually cared. "Yes, Your Highness."

"Your employer sent someone to collect you. He got here mighty fast. I'd have let you stew here for a while."

I glanced toward the silhouette in the doorway again. The slim figure wasn't tall enough to be Black Knife. My heart sank.

He strode toward us, mountain lion grace and mountain lion eyes.

Patrick Lien.

PART THREE

THE KNIFE

TWENTY-FOUR

HIS HIGHNESS HERMAN Pierce had dragged me into an interrogation room, Patrick marching along behind us, and then he proceeded to question me for hours about my disappearance into the wraithland. The king's brother was the kind of man who enjoyed watching people squirm, and I hated giving him the satisfaction. But young William Cole, who'd never been faced with royalty before, wouldn't have been able to stand up to the prince.

"Why did you go in? You could have been killed."

"I was sent."

"By whom?"

"He didn't tell me his name, just that I was to deliver a letter." I flinched, as though afraid the prince was going to hit me, but no blow came. "Your Highness, he looked important. He told me it was urgent and that I had to deliver the letter to a twisted old oak tree. He said he'd pay me when I got back."

"Well, you aren't getting paid." The prince thumped his fist on the table. He asked again about what I'd seen or done in the wraithland, and my answers were always the same. I gave as many detailed descriptions as possible—though I left out the locust attack and what I'd done. I still wasn't sure what had happened, but I definitely didn't want him to wonder, too.

"There was a voice as you rode up the mountain," Herman said. "Yelling a name. Do you know anything about that?"

I shook my head, keeping my eyes wide and frightened.

He blew out a breath. "I have no more time for this. Get out of my sight."

As though I were truly a lowly messenger boy, I ducked my face and scampered from the interrogation room.

Patrick had already gathered my belongings and acquired a pair of horses, so we were on our way out of West Pass Watch by dawn. We rode toward Skyvale in silence.

At night, in the same tense silence, we dug a fire pit as the forest gloom closed in and birds settled into their nests. Nocturnal creatures awoke, trees rustled in the breeze, and the faint scent of wraith stirred up a deep unease. Now that I knew just how potent the wraith stench could be. Now that I'd seen what kind of threat the wraithland posed.

Stones showed more emotion than Patrick as he settled on his bedroll and arranged a pot of water to boil over the fire. In stoic silence, he added dried meat, vegetables, and a packet of powdered spices. His glare never left me.

I refused to flinch.

When we reached Skyvale, Patrick led me to the Peacock

Inn, where he ordered a large dinner of pork chops and bread and wine. While we waited, I unpinned my hair to let the braids hang down, removed the cloth ties, and slowly began unraveling the plaits Melanie had spent hours putting together. With a wide-toothed comb Patrick tossed at me, I untangled the grimy lengths of my hair and picked out broken locust legs, twigs, and pine needles. There'd be no real washing my hair until I got back to the palace, but letting it down now felt good.

While I finished transforming back into a girl, Patrick fetched our meal and set a plate on the bed beside me. I cleaned the plate within minutes, and then Patrick's calm rumbled into the beginnings of a storm.

"What happened?" His voice was low and dangerous. It was that danger that had made him an attractive leader for the Ospreys, like he wore a thin film of control over everything he could do.

I pulled my jacket tighter, warding myself against Patrick and the autumn chill that blew in through the window. "I wasn't sent to take a letter to anyone."

"Obviously." He crossed his arms and kept my gaze. "Someone was yelling your name. Your true name. Who were you meeting?"

The memory of something calling me back into the wraithland shuddered through me, but now, back in Skyvale, with Patrick scowling at me, everything from the wraithland felt . . . as though it had happened to a separate person, or in another life.

Patrick would outwait me if I refused to answer. He'd easily stare at me all day, even if I fell asleep. I'd wake up to find him glaring at me. Forget the wraithland; his watchfulness would be a nightmare.

"I don't know who—what—was yelling my name." But didn't I? The wind? The air? Something more?

"I see. And what were you hoping to accomplish by risking your life, your friends' safety, and your kingdom's future?"

"It was for my kingdom's future that I went."

"So you abandoned your post."

"I didn't abandon it." I balled my fists, letting my fingernails dig into my palms. "I moved on for a little while, and now I'm going back."

"This is why you tried to lie to me about the resistance groups—why you didn't want me to know that you'd almost completed your work in the palace."

"It's my duty to see what will eventually destroy my kingdom." I didn't want to tell him about the lake. I wasn't even sure what it all meant.

"Your kingdom is already destroyed." His words came as a low growl, and his stare was unwavering. "Nothing else can destroy your kingdom until you raise it back up."

"You're wrong." I'd never had the courage to say that to him before. It was one thing to lie to him, and to declare I would not marry him, but Patrick hadn't been *wrong* since he was nine years old—since before the One-Night War. But surviving the wraithland made me brave, or foolish. "You're wrong. My kingdom is far from destroyed."

Patrick stiffened, and smoldering anger in his eyes warned that I should back down. "Have you forgotten the night the Indigo Army forced their way into Aecor City, burning shops and homes? Have you forgotten how they murdered highborns and commoners alike? Have you forgotten how they executed your parents in the courtyard? How can you say Aecor isn't destroyed when there's nothing left?"

"I could never forget that, the memory that haunts me every day. Especially when you've sent me to live among the very people responsible for the slaughter." My voice broke, but I forced strength back into it as I continued. "But Aecorian people still live there, and more are returning home from the wraithland. It's under Indigo Kingdom rule right now, but the land remains. The people remain." I climbed to my feet, shoulders thrust back, and swept one arm toward the wraithland. "I've seen destruction, Patrick. I've seen what Aecor will become if the wraith *doesn't* stop. I don't know what the answer is, but I know something must be done."

He was on his feet, too, all panther grace as he stalked toward me. "I'm bringing Aecor back the way *your parents* left it. Or don't you care about their legacy anymore?"

"Of course I care about their legacy, but I don't know what plans they had for the wraithland. I don't know how they expected to keep the country safe when wraith came pouring in. Maybe they thought it wouldn't happen. Maybe they believed there was another way. But maybe they were wrong." My ears rang in the deafening quiet and I whispered, "Maybe resurrecting Aecor the way they ran it . . . maybe that is wrong."

Patrick slapped me.

I staggered back, clutching my cheek. He stared at his hand, his mouth hanging open and horror written across his features.

For a heartbeat, he'd become his father.

"Wil—"

"Don't." I held my palms toward him, and he pulled back until he bumped the desk. I grabbed my pack and shoved my things inside it.

"I didn't mean to." His tone had softened, and he still clutched his hand like it was some kind of foreign thing. "I don't know what happened."

"I know." I hitched my pack over my shoulders and headed for the window. When I glanced back, he hadn't moved. "Be a better man than your father."

Then I left.

TWENTY-FIVE

THE SUN STILL burned high. I couldn't just walk into the palace in my current condition—trousers and messy hair and ten layers of grime all over me—so I roamed the Flags and let my mind wander.

Everywhere I went, I found knives carved into fences or painted onto walls. Some were merely in support of the vigilante, while others had pleading messages underneath them:

HELP ME FIND MY BROTHER. HE DISAPPEARED FROM
UNDERMARKET STREET.

THE NIGHTMARE GANG IS EVERYWHERE. PLEASE HELP.

SOMEONE ON REDWINE STREET IS USING MAGIC. IT
SMELLS LIKE PEE ALL THE TIME.

STOP. NO ONE WANTS YOU HERE.

You saved my life. Thank you.

Please stop the wraith. Everyone says you'll do it.
I believe in you.

I walked past more drawings, messages, and bounty post-ers with hastily sketched silhouettes of a man in a mask. Some notes were familiar, now worn away under wind and rain, while others were fresh. Down several alleys, I caught children playing Black Knife; they battled one another with sticks or pipes or wooden swords.

What would happen when I saw him again? He'd *come after me* when I'd left Skyvale, and not even to arrest me. What did that mean?

The clock tower chimed every hour, louder as I made my way toward Thornton, where carriages emblazoned with crests flitted from shop to shop. I kept my face turned away in case anyone recognized me. Unlikely, given my current state, but I didn't want to be too cavalier; coming into Thornton was already a risk.

Evening descended, announced by the peal of cathedral bells in Hawksbill. Smaller bells chimed in the market district, and a small army of homeless people from the Flags wandered through, shouting.

"The heir to four houses will end the wraith!"

"Wraith is coming! The end approaches!"

It wasn't long before police swarmed in and began making arrests.

Wanting to avoid the eyes of authority, I scrubbed my face on my sleeve, then ducked into a bakery where I could watch the commotion from the open door with a cup of hot tea, though the proprietor didn't look overly happy about serving me.

Midway through the evening, a thunder of carriages with dragon sigils and Pierce crests drove by.

At last, night fell. When the bakery closed, I waited for the clock tower to strike midnight, and then I climbed over the wall and into Hawksbill. The fading perfume of flowers and roasted chicken and autumn foliage welcomed me as I crept through the courtyards and gardens. Laughter chimed like bells from mansions, and horses whickered in their stables. This district was deceptively peaceful.

Weary, I sneaked through the shadows of the King's Seat and climbed up to my window. My fingers touched the handle just as Melanie pushed open the door, and we stared at each other for a long minute.

"Wil," she breathed, and threw her arms around me. "Oh, Wil. I'm so glad you made it."

I hugged her back, and a knot of fear loosened inside of me. She didn't hate me for going. We were still friends.

"Come inside." She grabbed my hand and dragged me in, kicking the door shut behind us. The sitting room was warm, thanks to the small fire burning. Vases of flowers filled the end tables and bookshelves, and dozens of envelopes waited in a basket on the table.

"What's all this?" I dropped my bag on the floor, doing my best not to wilt back into my friend's arms.

"You've been very ill for over three weeks." Melanie motioned at the closed door to my bedroom. "Too ill for visitors. There was some improvement and people were looking forward to seeing you again, but your recovery wasn't as swift as I'd hoped."

"Oh. Right." I moved through the room, glancing at the notes pinned under vases. From King Terrell. From Crown Prince Tobiah. From Meredith. Three from Lady Chey, of all people.

The letters were just as numerous, but I'd look at those later. I almost felt guilty that people had been so worried for my health, and I hadn't even been sick.

"Are you going to tell me what happened?" Melanie asked. "You're late. And I was so worried. I thought about you every moment."

I managed a smile. "You sent Patrick after me."

She went pale. "I—he knew. Somehow he knew that you weren't here. I didn't tell him anything."

"I believe you." Patrick had a talent for that, knowing things without being told. He could just *see* the truth in people's eyes, and hear it in their breath. "It's fine. I'm back."

"So." Her voice dropped. "You went into the wraithland."

"I did. And it was—" I shook my head and considered giving her my notebook to let her read everything. But I wasn't sure I wanted to confess all of my secrets. Not yet.

My knees buckled and I collapsed onto one of the sofas. I bent over my legs and cradled my head in my forearms.

"Oh, Wil." Melanie dropped next to me and draped her arm over my shoulders. "Let's just get you cleaned up. We can talk later about what happened."

I didn't think I'd be ready later, either, but I let her guide me to the washroom, where I ran the bath as hot as possible. While

I scrubbed and rinsed and scrubbed some more, Melanie went to my room. From the tub, I could hear the *whoomph* of sheets as she remade my bed, and the *screech* of hangers in the wardrobe.

"Here." She came back in bearing a warm nightgown as I wrapped a dressing gown over myself. "Oh, your cheek. What happened?"

I hesitated, but if she was going to be with Patrick, she needed to know. "Patrick."

The nightgown fluttered to the floor. "He wouldn't."

"We were arguing. He lost control."

Melanie closed her eyes, reeling, but I didn't have the energy to comfort her.

I finished dressing while Melanie ordered a crock of soup, and we discussed the wraithland as we ate. I told her everything—everything except what I'd done, commanding the wind with my magic, and then the voice that had chased me.

But I knew what it was. I couldn't deny it any longer.

Somehow, with that single command, I'd brought the wraith to life.

And it knew my name.

TWENTY-SIX

MY PRESENCE WAS required at King Terrell's birthday ball. Two invitations had arrived in our apartments the day I'd left for the wraithland, and a letter from the king himself had appeared shortly after; in it, he all but pleaded for my return to health and attendance.

I'd *just* made it in time for the celebration. I slept through the night and most of the morning, but it wasn't enough. When Melanie woke me to prepare for the ball, dancing was the last thing I wanted to do, but declining such an invitation would have been a terrible insult—likely, we'd have been shunned from palace society.

In anticipation of my return, Melanie had ordered a pair of gowns made for us. Hers was a pale pink creation with pink sapphires sewn into the neckline and high waist. She looked beautiful in it; she'd look beautiful in anything.

The gown she'd chosen for me glimmered when the maid

brought it out. Silver silk rippled and shone in the firelight, like scales, while diamonds and silver embroidery graced the bodice in a flowing, intricate pattern. They weren't random patterns, though. When I looked closer, I caught ospreys taking flight, swords and daggers dangling from their talons.

I lifted an eyebrow at Melanie. "You ordered this?"

She peered at the gown. "Not exactly that. I ordered ospreys. Well . . . it's all too stylized to see at a glance, at least. No one will notice."

"I hope not. It's a little odd for a duchess of Liadia to wear ospreys. Lions would have been more appropriate." Nevertheless, I put on the gown, strangely relieved to wear something so fine again. "I wonder what His Majesty thought when he saw the bill for these gowns."

"He probably thought about marrying you to someone very quickly. Then someone else can provide for your expensive tastes."

I smoothed the silk and wool over my ribs, down my hips, then sat for the maid to conceal the yellowing bruise on my cheek. She didn't comment on it, of course. As far as she knew, I'd been ill; my gaunt appearance only added to the illusion.

Melanie pulled a tiny strand of my hair, freeing it to curl down from the elaborate coils and braids. "Perfect."

What she meant was that the tendril of hair would distract from any bruise that showed through the cosmetics.

"Mel," I whispered when the maid stepped away. "We weren't on the best of terms before I left. . . ."

She shook her head. "We are now, though. I've had a lot of time to think, and to miss you, and to see the Ospreys how you must. It's over between Patrick and me."

I held my fingers just over my bruised cheek. "Does he know?"

"Not yet. But he probably suspects." She dropped her eyes.

I wanted to ask if she still loved him, but the maid returned with a small dinner and the promise of a generous buffet in the grand ballroom later. Shortly after the clock chimed the hour, a footman came to escort us. Light spilled through the wide double doors, and music twinkled in a delicate melody.

The herald took our names, guided us to our positions, and then announced us. "Duchess of Liadia, Lady Julianna Whitman, and her companion, Lady Melanie Cole."

I stepped into the immense ballroom and was dazzled by the lights. Melanie touched my elbow to steady me.

Iron dragons twisted around the grand chandelier that hung above. Mirrors and faceted gemstones glittered in the light of the gas lamps, throwing rainbows across the room. Candles sat on every surface and in sconces along the walls. There was even an illuminated dragon statue, with a candle set into its lower jaw. The beast stared a challenge into the large crowd assembling on the dance floor.

A few faces turned up at our announcement, and I caught the king's frail smile from a high-backed throne at the far end of the room. He gestured for us to approach.

The throne area was a crowded place. Princes Herman and Colin stood beside their brother and the queen, chests all puffed out as they surveyed the ballroom.

I hoped Herman wouldn't recognize me from West Pass Watch.

On the other side of the throne, Crown Prince Tobiah, Lady Meredith, and Lieutenant Rayner stood tall. The prince wore a jet-black tailcoat and trousers with deep blue stripes down the sides, and his cousin displayed his formal Indigo Order uniform, medals pinned on his chest and a sword hung at his waist. While the prince hardly seemed to notice my approach, his bodyguard flashed a smile and minuscule nod.

"My lady." King Terrell reached for my hand as I curtsied. "I'm so glad you've recovered. I was quite worried when I learned of your illness."

"I'm much better, Your Majesty." I forced my voice even. "And I wouldn't have missed your birthday celebration for anything."

The king smiled again. "I believe you've met my wife, Queen Francesca, House of the Sun."

I curtsied again. "Of course, Your Majesty. I've had the honor, and I'm glad to have it again."

The queen sat tall and lean, like her son and nephew, with pointed features and a sharp look in her eyes. But she smiled and dipped her head.

"And you've met my brother Prince Colin Pierce, I believe. He is Overlord of Aecor Territory."

It took every drop of my self-control not to clench my jaw and fists as I curtsied. Overlord of *my* kingdom.

"And my youngest brother, Prince Herman Pierce, Lord of West Pass Watch."

This time, I made sure to keep my posture open and feminine, but if the prince recognized me, he gave no indication. People saw what they expected to see.

We moved on to greet Tobiah and Meredith, and the latter offered a warm smile.

She was resplendent in her peacock blue gown. Gold-embroidered unicorns paraded across a band of silk around her ribs in an exquisite display of her wealth, and her seamstress's skill. Sapphires and other gemstones glittered as she curtsied and offered a warm smile. "We're both so happy you've recovered, Julianna."

There was an odd note in her voice. Suspicion? Amusement? She and Chey had both sent lots of flowers and well-wishes. More than made sense, considering our short acquaintance.

"Thank you." I pushed a little, to study her reaction. "I'm so looking forward to spending more time with you and Lady Chey in the solar. I've missed our talks."

Her expression was nothing but politeness.

Tobiah cast an uninterested glance and turned to murmur something to James. The lieutenant grinned, first at his prince, then at me.

Meredith and I exchanged a few more pleasantries, and then Melanie and I were dismissed.

Several more lords and ladies and prominent merchants wealthy enough to keep the king's attention were announced, and the ballroom grew stiflingly hot.

Melanie leaned toward me, her voice low. "Meredith seemed delighted to see you."

"An act, I'm sure. She's probably annoyed that when I join her in the solar, she and her ladies will have to stop gossiping about me. I wonder what they say. Did you go while I was ill?"

"I'm not important enough to go without you. But we could

bribe some of the guards to repeat conversations. No one ever notices them, let alone important ladies." She wore a pleasant smile as she gazed around the room. "Oh, the prince is watching you."

I glanced over my shoulder, catching the prince's eye before he leaned toward James again.

"Careful, there." Melanie gave a low chuckle. "Meredith seems nice, but if she thinks you're interested in him, I bet she'll find a way to remove your head."

I nodded with exaggerated seriousness. "She's fiercely good with a needle. I wouldn't want to anger her."

Melanie grinned.

We mingled with the other guests until the music began, then took our partners in the lines of dancers. I still didn't feel as confident in my dancing as I'd have liked, but this time I knew more of the steps and kept up with my partner, a count from another region of the kingdom.

He rambled on about his control of sheep farmers and wheat mills, and I responded where appropriate, but my mind kept wandering. A tree, maybe, or a rooftop. Somewhere dark and dangerous. In my mind, my partner was a boy in all black, and our music was the clashing of blades. Our dance was leaping and cutting and pulling the other back to their feet.

After the first dance ended, Tobiah helped his mother and father stand and the room fell quiet.

"Thank you all for joining me tonight." Terrell's voice wasn't quite feeble, but he was certainly struggling to make himself heard. Several people in the back of the room shifted forward, and others began repeating his speech for those who couldn't hear. "There are so many people to be grateful to: firstly, my wife, Francesca, and my son, Tobiah. I wish I could say they are my life, but as a king, that hasn't always been true. There have been so many times when my wife and son have come second, or third, or worse. Nevertheless, they've stood by me, and now my son prepares for his marriage and eventual reign as king. As a father—and as a king—I couldn't be prouder."

Francesca and Tobiah gave Terrell warm smiles, and the audience clapped politely. The applause didn't last long; the king continued, and everyone had to strain to hear again, if they were interested at all.

I spent the remainder of his speech observing the guests. There were many I didn't recognize. Perhaps I'd be able to pry James from Tobiah's side and receive a bit more of his gossip.

The speeches went on. Tobiah and his mother each spoke, droning about how much they loved and appreciated Terrell, what a great king he was, and how hard he worked to serve the people of the Indigo Kingdom.

The crowd grew restless and, from across the room, I caught James's eye. He quirked a smile and subtly scratched his ear with his smallest finger. At the rude implication, I hid a chuckle under a fake cough. The bodyguard's smile widened.

Melanie elbowed me. "Stop it."

I signaled for James to dance with me once the speeches were over. His eyebrows lifted, but he nodded.

From beside his father, Prince Tobiah frowned in my direction.

At last the speeches were finished and the music began. I tried to catch James's eye again as dancers began pairing off, but Tobiah had him cornered. Melanie had already accepted someone's invitation to dance, so I wandered alone toward the terrace. The glass doors were closed against the night chill, and it was too bright inside to see anything outside, but I pretended I was studying the stars, while really watching the reflections of dancers behind me.

"Your Highness. My lord," I said as they appeared on either side of me. Tobiah offered a glass of wine, which I accepted. "Thank you."

"I must caution you about venturing outside," said the prince. "It's cold, and you've been ill."

"But Lady Julianna was wise enough to bring a shawl and gloves. We won't keep her long." James pushed open one of the large doors, and a gust of wind made all the candles flicker, but we were all three outside a moment later.

The terrace faced west, toward the wraithland. The odd scoop of the Midvale Ridge stood silhouetted in the night sky.

I walked ahead of the boys, past the glass tables and cushioned chairs, hardly realizing I was moving. I held my shawl closed with one hand, and rested my wineglass on the twisted iron railing.

What had I *done* in that desolate place? I couldn't have brought the wraith to life; my magic didn't work like that. The life it gave objects wasn't true life. It was just . . . temporary animation. A temporary compulsion for otherwise inanimate objects to do my bidding.

But I couldn't deny that something had happened, and it was different. Dangerous. The wraith knew my name.

"Do you think of it often, my lady?" James asked.

"Too often." I turned my back to the wraithland. The boys stood side by side, identical in their postures, and so similar in features that they might be mistaken for brothers. They were silhouetted by the brilliant lights shining through the terrace doors, through which I could see the sway and swell of dancers in glittery gowns and perfect black tailcoats. Around the door, mirrors hung on every opaque surface, reflecting starlight.

Out of habit, I shifted out of the way of the mirrors. The boys were already standing where they wouldn't reflect.

"Is there something you wished to discuss?" I sipped my wine, hoping the alcohol would warm me.

"Go ahead, James." The prince broke his stance to move toward the railing behind me.

Having him where I couldn't see him made me wary. I adjusted my position so the prince filled the corner of my vision while I focused on James. "My lord?"

James's shoulders dropped. "I feel it's only fair to warn you. There's been some concern regarding your residency documents."

My heart stumbled. "Excuse me?"

The lieutenant nodded. "It seems a warehouse in Greenstone was recently robbed. The only items taken were ink and a few pieces of paper—paper with the Liadian watermark."

I caught a glimpse of Melanie dancing inside. Her gown swirled, and the black lengths of her hair gleamed in the illumination. "Someone believes our documents are forged?" My voice was hoarse.

"No." James shifted his weight. "Well, not yet. The police will search the warehouse for clues, while our records-keepers and secretaries make further inquiries into your past. They'll also begin verifying your documentation against others. I'm sure there's nothing to worry about, but I wouldn't want anyone to catch you off guard."

As if I hadn't been caught off guard already. My documents were flawless; I'd gone over them and added the final details myself. But who would have known about the warehouse in Greenstone?

Black Knife.

Unease and disappointment tightened in my stomach. "Thank you." I cleared my throat and sipped my wine. "What prompted this inquiry, if I may ask?"

James began. "Lady Ch—"

Tobiah cut him off with a lifted hand. He'd been staring westward so thoroughly I hadn't realized he'd even been aware of the conversation. "I'm afraid we're not at liberty to say. Regardless of the outcome, you'll hear your accuser's concerns when this is all over. For now, it's probably best to keep the peace."

When the prince turned away again, James mouthed, "Chey Chuter."

Of course. That day in the ladies' solar, when she'd counseled me about using my perceived unimportance, Chey hadn't been offering advice. She'd been warning me that she knew I wasn't who I claimed, and I'd been too foolish to understand it. She'd been playing games with me the whole time.

It didn't matter. I'd figure out a way to call off the inquiry and reestablish my place here. We'd succeeded in our goals thus far, but I wanted to know more about their plans to stop the wraith. Having seen the wraithland firsthand, I might actually be able to help.

But first, I had to figure out how to tell them that the wraith was alive.

Alive. Aware. In pursuit.

"You're shivering, my lady. I'm afraid we've kept you outside too long; I'd hate to undo all the recovery you've made from your illness." James offered his arm, and the heat of his body warmed me. "Shall we go back inside? I believe you owe me a dance, and then one for Tobiah. He got jealous earlier."

"James." The prince's tone was light. Friendly. Something shared with only his cousin.

"I'd be honored to dance with both of you, as long as Lady Meredith doesn't mind." I offered the prince my free arm, though I still held my wineglass with that hand. He took it from me and placed all our glasses on a table. After the smallest hesitation, he hooked his arm with mine.

Two boys at my sides: one as warm and genuine as a summer day, and the other as cold and deceptive as winter night.

James grinned at me. "What a scandal we'll cause."

"It wouldn't be a ball if someone didn't take it upon themselves to be wildly inappropriate." I put on a smug smile and we strode back into the ballroom.

TWENTY-SEVEN

IN SPITE OF the promise—or threat—of a dance, the prince was called to attend his fiancée immediately, which left me alone with James.

"So much for our scandal." I watched Tobiah's stiffly retreating form for only a moment before I turned back to James and smiled. I could get a lot more information out of James without his cousin there to censor him.

James grinned and adjusted his collar against the warmth of the ballroom. "Shall we take the next dance? I'm willing to put my life into your hands for the honor of your continued company."

I put on a coy smile. "The prince won't mind if you're not shadowing his every move?"

"He'll no doubt be proud of feeling he's shaken me, but have no worry: I can see him from here." His eyes focused beyond me for a moment, and he offered a satisfied nod. "See? He's just there, shadowing Lady Meredith's every move."

"Ah." I didn't take my eyes off James. "How fortunate for me. I get, what, half of your attention all to myself?"

James shook his head. "Perhaps a third. His Highness takes a *lot* of looking after."

I feigned a dramatic sigh. "I'll forgive you if you escort me to the buffet before the next dance begins." The table was across the room, and sadly neglected. The thought of all that food going to waste at the end of the night made me sick, but it wasn't as though I could single-handedly eat all of it, or deliver it to the Ospreys or refugees.

James took my arm as we walked around the edge of the ballroom, out of the way of dancers. The whole place was a wash of movement, with couples on the floor, flames on candles, and the vibrations of music on the air. Elegant gowns swished and flared, their gemstones catching the light.

This was almost my life. It would have been, before the One-Night War. Before Tobiah and the fighting and the Indigo Army murdering my parents in the courtyard for all to see. And now that I'd seen the source of the contention between the kingdoms—the wraithland created by industrialized magic—everything grew muddled and murky in my head.

I paused, closed my eyes, and breathed against the tide of memories and emotions.

"My lady?" James touched my wrist gently. "We can rest, if you're not feeling well enough to dance."

"I'm fine." I had so many questions about my parents' plans for Aecor and magic. There was so much I needed to consider, but this wasn't the time. This wasn't the place. "I'm fine," I said again, as though I could command away all my uncertainties.

We moved to the buffet, a long table draped with a white cloth. House sigils covered the front, mostly dragons. My stomach rumbled as I spotted platters filled with salads prepared as intricate and colorful mosaics, sandwiches of every kind, and tiny desserts: pies, tarts, and puddings.

Music and laughter covered the sound of my hunger, but James flashed a knowing smile. "I hope you're enjoying your return to palace society."

"I suppose the company is adequate." I tried to keep my voice light. "Honestly, I'm very relieved to be here. I was afraid I wouldn't be able to attend."

His expression turned unreadable as he offered a small plate of canapés: egg, cheese, and salmon. I took one.

James shifted closer to me, his voice low. "Are you concerned about what I told you?"

I shook my head. "Why should I be? A warehouse robbery is unfortunate, but has nothing to do with me. I'm certain an inquiry will find my residency documents completely authentic."

"It's just that you arrived so shortly after the robbery. Some would find it suspicious." James shrugged. "But as you said, I'm sure your papers are without fault."

I finished the canapé.

"Will you confront Lady Chey, once your name has been cleared?"

"I would hate to embarrass her by drawing attention to the scandal."

"That's very forgiving of you."

"Perhaps." How many people suspected, though? Chey,

certainly. Meredith? They'd been awfully insistent for me to demonstrate my ability to use a hand spindle. It must have been a kind of test—one I'd failed.

I wasn't ready to leave, though. Not until I'd shared my experience in the wraithland with someone who had a chance of using the information for good. Maybe the pieces of the barrier would help, too; I could say I'd been keeping them all this time as talismans against the wraith, like Connor and others did with small mirrors.

"Do you think His Highness would reconsider allowing me back onto the wraith mitigation committee?"

James lifted an eyebrow.

"While I was ill, I did a lot of thinking and remembering. I might have more information we didn't cover before."

"I can't promise anything, but I will ask." The dance finished with a flute trill and flourish. The dancers bowed and curtsied. James checked on the prince, then offered his hand. "Shall we dance the next?"

As the musicians began playing, I took my place before him and curtsied. He bowed.

"Last time we danced," James said, "you mentioned you enjoyed sewing."

Had I? So much had happened since then, but I had a vague memory of saying sewing when I meant fighting.

"But I've heard rumors from certain ladies you hardly participate when they meet in the ladies' solar. Have you given up such pursuits?"

"Of course not." I summoned a blush. "Though my focus has shifted toward stopping the wraith, since my experiences in the wraithland." How strange, being able to reference my time in that nightmare and have it be true.

James nodded, sympathy in his eyes. "I imagine it has. My grandmother enjoyed knitting and needlepoint, and she made many fine things. But she tended to do that only when she was working on a separate problem. She said it helped her focus."

My thoughts flashed to another boy mentioning his grandmother and sewing. But certainly lots of grandmothers enjoyed that.

"Do you still draw?" he asked.

"Yes, of course." That was something I had prepared for: there was a pile of drawings in my apartments, ready as evidence. Part of me wanted to mention the Black Knife drawing to James and see his reaction, but I kept its existence to myself.

Still, they moved alike, and James smiled as much as I imagined Black Knife did.

I shook the thought away. James's voice was softer than Black Knife's. Certainly, he could change it, but wouldn't he have slipped during one of our conversations? Anyway, he was Tobiah's bodyguard, and Black Knife had declared me dangerous. If James knew I wasn't Lady Julianna, he'd have never let me get close to Tobiah.

James and I took the next few dances, talking about the music, the food, and palace gossip. As I laughed at one of his jokes, I caught a glimpse of Tobiah across the room. His jaw was clenched, and his chest expanded with a deep breath. A moment later, he leaned down to whisper in his father's ear.

"I believe your cousin is jealous that you're spending so much time with me," I whispered as James walked me in a slow circle. "Not that I want to give up the best—and most forgiving—dance partner, but I suspect he would appreciate your attention after this."

James chuckled and rolled his eyes, then cast a casual glance over his shoulder. He stiffened. "He's gone. Excuse me."

The lieutenant departed, pardoning himself as he slipped between dancers. His eyes stayed on the empty space where Tobiah had been a minute before. The king was gone, too.

Abandoned on the floor, I hesitated only a moment before following. With my gown, it was more difficult to squeeze around dancers, but I caught a flash of James moving out the door.

I emerged into a familiar hallway; the king's study was nearby, and raised voices fell from the open doorway. James hurried into the room, his movements clipped with annoyance.

With my gown gathered up to hide the rustle of silk, I crept up to the door and parked myself with my back against the wall where they wouldn't see me if they looked out.

"I can't." Tobiah's voice was a growl.

The king's words came significantly softer, weaker. "She'll make a fine queen and a fine wife. You must."

This wasn't my business, but I was already eavesdropping. Might as well keep listening.

"I've done everything you ever asked. Studied, trained, and made decisions on your behalf. You *know* I'm willing to do whatever it takes to be a good, strong king. Meredith has nothing to do with my being king."

"But she does." Terrell heaved a sigh. "I know you will make fair and wise decisions as a king. I know you will be thoughtful and patient. But I've never met anyone so opposed to interacting with society. You come across as dismissive and uninterested. I know that's not who you truly are, but if that's how your subjects perceive you, they won't see your strength and wisdom."

"Father—"

"Meredith is kind and well loved. The people respect her because she respects them—and she shows it. You *need* her."

I cringed, but it wasn't as though the king was wrong. Tobiah had a most unfortunate personality for a crown prince. Well, no. He could be worse. I didn't know him well, but I didn't think he was reckless or abusive. Just . . . *bored*.

"I don't," insisted Tobiah. "I can get better."

"Is there something objectionable about Lady Meredith?"

Tobiah hesitated. "No. I just—I don't love her."

There was a long pause, and I imagined the king rubbing his temples or performing some other delaying tactic. "Son, I'm dying. You know that. The kingdom needs a strong pair of rulers—and it needs an heir."

"Don't speak so brazenly about dying." Tobiah's voice turned rough. "Don't tempt fate, Father."

"I'm not tempting anything. I've already made peace with what I have and haven't accomplished in my time. The only thing I have left is seeing you and Meredith married and ready to take the throne when I go."

"Father." The prince's voice broke. "Father, please."

"I won't change my mind. You've given me no *good* reason to reconsider. You need Meredith for your image. She's of high rank and will make a good queen." Though his voice was weak, Terrell sounded immovable. "Set a date. We won't have this conversation again."

A heartbeat later, Tobiah stormed out of the office, his fists curled at his sides. His expression was raw. Wrecked. Then his glare locked on me standing there with my back pressed against the wall, obviously having listened to every word. His face turned frigid.

James strode out after the prince, and stared when he saw the prince staring at me. Then Tobiah jerked his head down the hall, and James placed his hands behind his back, the prince's obedient servant.

The prince bowed stiffly in my direction. "My cousin and I have something to discuss, but I'm sure you won't have trouble finding a new dance partner."

I curtsied. "Good evening, Your Highness. Lieutenant."

TWENTY-EIGHT

THE BIRTHDAY CELEBRATION was long over and Melanie had fallen asleep in her room, but I couldn't put my mind to rest. I kept thinking about the ball, about the inquiry and the silver ospreys carrying swords and daggers into flight, and whenever my eyes closed, my imagination conjured images of immense creatures with strangely colored fur, trees with teeth, and swarms of locusts beating down on me.

"*Wilhelmina.*"

It wasn't real. I'd been dreaming.

I shoved my blankets to the bottom of my bed and sat up to braid my hair. A black sweater with a hood, silk scarf tucked into my shirt, trousers, and a few of my favorite weapons later, I was out the window. I told myself I was going to return to the warehouse and make sure there wasn't *actually* evidence of my being there. But by the time I was over the Hawksbill wall and scanning the Thornton skyline, I admitted the truth:

I was looking for Black Knife.

The city was quiet this late, two or three hours after midnight. Thornton was silent, and even the Flags stirred with but a fraction of their usual activity. Black Knife must have been working for hours already, and I had no idea where to find him now. In the week I'd gone on patrols with him, he'd taken us in different paths every night. If he had a routine, he hadn't shared it with me.

With no better idea of where to start, I planted myself in the street where he'd stopped me from killing a man. The area was dark, with no gas lamps to push back the shadows. I shivered, wishing I'd worn a jacket. A sinister thought bubbled up in the back of my head: I could tell the air to warm itself for me.

The idea fizzled as quickly as it arrived. After what I'd done in the wraithland, I never wanted to use magic again.

Since I'd *experienced* the wraithland, everything was different.

A shadow peeled from the others. Black Knife gestured upward.

I followed him onto the rooftops, relishing the feel of using my muscles. This was a familiar exertion.

When we stood atop a tea shop, Black Knife studied me without speaking. Shadows cloaked his eyes as he circled me—I turned only my head to watch him—and there was something heavy and thoughtful about the way he moved. Then, he must have worked out whatever he'd been trying to decide, because he motioned for me to follow.

We took off at a quick walk at first, and then faster until we were running through the city, as though on a chase. He leapt; I leapt. He ducked under an overhanging beam; I ducked, too. Over apothecaries and chandleries and inns, we raced into Thornton where we dodged the bright streetlamps and mirrors. Cold air stung the back of my throat, and breath misted white.

Out here in the city, I felt real. Alive. There were always questions with Black Knife, but still, I knew what to do: we squabbled, fought criminals and wraith beasts, and made the darkness our cloak and armor. Though we constantly threw ourselves into danger, these nighttime excursions felt safe.

Safer than my life with the Ospreys, or at the palace, or my uncertain future as queen.

Black Knife vanished around the corner of a bank.

I followed only seconds later, but he was gone. Gasping for breath, I paused under a stone-and-glass breezeway that connected two shops, and checked the dim rooftops. There was nothing.

Darkness gaped above me as gloved hands reached down through a trapdoor in the breezeway. I laughed and took his hands, and after some pulling and hushed laughter, we both tumbled inside the breezeway. He pushed the door shut.

Ambient light bled through the glass windows, which rattled in the wind. The breezeway wasn't large, only wide enough for two people to walk abreast, and about five strides long where it arched over an alley.

From the center of the walk, I could see several familiar shops, plus the roof of Laurence's Bakery.

So *that* was how he'd caught me so often.

"What happened to your mask?" Black Knife stood at the other end of the breezeway, unstrapping the crossbow from his hip, but he was watching me. "Did you lose it?"

"It got dirty in the wraithland."

"Hmph." He dug through a pouch on his belt and tossed me a small paper-wrapped parcel. "I brought you a new one anyway. It will fit better."

I snatched the package out of the air and pulled a flap of paper from inside a crease. The paper unfolded, and a delicate silk mask tumbled into my fingers, followed by a pair of leather gloves lined with wool and silk. All black. Of course, I'd known Black Knife must be someone wealthy enough to afford all of his weapons and perfect black clothes, but not so rich that he was too lazy to spend his nights as a vigilante. "They're beautiful."

"They're useful. You need to hide your identity out here."

All I did was hide my identity.

Even this, fighting and bickering with Black Knife, was hiding. But I loved it. I loved it more than Julianna Whitman's life, definitely more than William Cole's life, and even more than the life I'd planned for myself.

And how often did I get to keep things I loved? Never.

"I'm not like you." Carefully, I wrapped his gifts back inside the paper.

"I thought you liked this. What we do." He cocked his head. "Was I wrong?"

"No." That was the problem. "You weren't wrong." I pressed the parcel to my chest. "I used to hate you, you know. I thought you had a vendetta and that innocent people were paying the price. But then you saved my friend, and you showed me mercy. You gave me a second chance."

"I believe you're a better person than you think you are."

"You're so optimistic. It's not what I expected from a vigilante who calls himself Black Knife."

"Well, I considered Optimistic Knife, but I didn't think anyone would take it seriously."

The paper crinkled against my chest as I shook my head, not bothering to hide my weak chuckle. "I've seen the notes people leave you. The city needs you. They want your help."

He shifted his weight toward me. "The city could need you, too."

What was he imagining? That we'd just continue for the rest of our lives like this, fighting crime and not knowing each other's real names?

"I'm not like you," I said again. "I can't give this city what it needs. I have other obligations."

Black Knife was motionless, a shadow statue across the breezeway. His silk hood glimmered in the faint light. "Did you find what you were looking for in the wraithland?"

Could I tell him the truth? He knew I had magic. What would he think if I told him about the wraith wind, and how it had called my name?

When had *Black Knife* become someone I considered confiding in? If I wasn't careful, I'd want to tell him about my parents and the Ospreys and how everything was so confused now because I wasn't sure we were doing the right thing anymore.

And all I wanted —all I *really* wanted—was this. The mask. The hunting. The night.

His footfalls were whisper quiet. "Will?"

I turned away.

"What happened here?" Gloved fingertips brushed my cheek,

so, so gentle. "Someone hit you. Who?"

I covered the fading bruise. "It's nothing. I handled it."

"I'm sure you did." He pulled away. "You said you're not like me. Who *are* you, then? What kind of trouble are you in?"

"The kind you can't help with." The words came out more harshly than I intended, but he didn't even flinch.

"I might," he said. "Or I might know someone who can help."

"I don't *want* your help. Not with this."

"With what?" He was relentless.

I leaned my forehead on the glass. "I hate you." It didn't sound remotely convincing.

"You like your secrets, I know. I like mine, too." He leaned closer and whispered, "I'm good at keeping secrets."

Maybe telling him just a little wouldn't hurt. He already knew so much about me. What would a little more change? "I'm part of a group. The Ospreys."

He waited.

"I'm supposed to be a sort of leader—eventually—but I'm not right now. Someone else is. He's the one who hit me." I closed my eyes and hugged myself. "I've certainly taken worse injuries, but I never expected it from him. He's always been so careful."

"What made him change?"

"The wraithland. I wasn't supposed to go. He didn't know until I was already there."

"You really don't like to tell people your plans, do you?"

"Not if I can execute the plan on my own." I straightened and wiped my forehead smudge off the glass. "I'm not interested in being rescued or saved. I've been part of the Ospreys for almost ten years and I'm committed to our cause."

"It was for the Ospreys that you went to the wraithland?"

I nodded. "I had to know what would happen when the wraith reaches us. And if there was any truth to the rumors about Mirror Lake."

"Is there?" There was a hopeful tilt to his voice.

"It's complicated." I touched my pocket, and the ridges of the barrier scales I'd taken from the village. "The truth is, I found something much, much worse." The voice calling my name haunted me.

"Can you tell me about it?"

"Another night. I can't right now."

"Very well." He was quiet for a moment, letting the silence between us soak in. "Do you still think what you're doing with the Ospreys is right?"

"Yes." At least, I hoped. "I'm not as sure about our methods anymore."

"What methods are those? Stealing? Something worse?"

"We stole to survive!"

He held up his hands like surrender. "I know. We had this discussion. I'm just trying to understand, and you won't give me anything but vague answers."

"Because I can't!" I slammed my fist against the window, and he stepped back. "If you don't want vague, don't ask questions. Don't bother trying to understand."

"I'm sorry. I didn't mean to upset you." He hesitated, then touched my hand on the glass. The fingertips of his gloves were soft against my skin. "Will, I think we are more alike than you realize."

"What do you mean?"

"Black Knife. I started this fight because I was angry. I wanted to show certain people that I wasn't a puppet." An embarrassed chuckle escaped him. "Of course, I wore a mask, so no one ever knew it was me. But eventually all my anger was burned away by a deeper understanding of Skyvale and everything that was wrong with it. I still do this because it's right. Because Skyvale needs *someone* and no one else was stepping up. Now I'm Black Knife because it's the best way to help my kingdom," he whispered.

Maybe we were alike after all.

Our eyes met. Strange, how familiar he'd become. "Who are you?"

His eyes were gentle, as though he smiled beneath that mask. "You know I can't tell you any more than you can tell me who you are."

His hand was still on mine. Our shoulders brushed. Our arms pressed together. I could hardly breathe against the swelling in my heart. I turned up my face, overcome with a wild recklessness.

"Will." He spoke hoarsely, but he didn't stop me.

I cupped my free hand over his cheek, letting the cool silk slide beneath my fingers; his face was sharp and angular, and his jaw tensed, as though he was worried I'd lift the mask. But I left it as I rose to my toes and pressed my mouth against his, only that thin silk between our lips.

He gasped and pulled back. "I don't—"

Shame welled up inside me. "You're right. I shouldn't have. I'm sorry." I was such an idiot.

I shouldn't be here. I needed to get back to the palace, offer as much information about the wraith as I could, and then return to my real life as an Osprey. As a future queen of orphans. It would be best if I never saw Black Knife again.

Black Knife closed his eyes. His mask puffed as he exhaled through his mouth.

The packet with his gifts dropped as I retreated toward the trapdoor. "I'd better go."

I'd barely taken three steps when he grabbed my arm and spun me around. His hands were tight around my forearms; his body angled toward mine. When I stepped back, my shoulders hit the window with a *thud*.

He kissed me, just another touch of our mouths through silk. His breath came hot and ragged. "Don't leave."

"I'll have to, eventually."

He couldn't rescue me, and I didn't want him to. I'd chosen my path long ago.

"Don't leave now, though." He released my forearms and touched my face, gloved fingertips gliding over my temple and cheekbone and chin. "Stay here a while longer?"

"For now, I suppose." When I closed my eyes and let my head drop back, he kissed me again, light and sweet and restrained with the silk of his mask still between us. It wasn't enough.

Haltingly, I slid my hands up the sides of his neck, beneath the base of his mask. The barest hint of stubble scraped my fingertips as I folded the layer up.

"Will—" He touched my hands, halting my progress.

"I won't look."

His eyes were wide, dubious, but he released my hands and let out a shaky breath.

"Wait." I withdrew and pushed back my hood, and fumbled with my scarf, pulling it from around my throat. One last look into his eyes, I lifted the scarf to cover mine. His fingers grazed my temples, pushing back my hair as I tied the scarf behind my head. His fingertips ran down my throat, down my collarbone and arms.

The world was dark when Black Knife lifted my hands to his face.

He'd taken off his mask.

I slipped one hand to the back of his neck, my fingers sliding into strands of soft hair, and pulled him close.

Our lips touched with soft, hesitating movements, and for a moment, I thought he might pull back again. But Black Knife sighed my name as he kissed a trail of sparks down my cheek and throat, and I lost myself in memorizing the curves and contours of his face. His cheekbones, sharp and prominent. His nose, aristocratically strong. His jaw, angular and firm. When we kissed again, a low moan vibrated in his throat.

His arms wound around my waist, pulling my hips closer to his. His hands splayed out on the small of my back; the very tips of his fingers dug against my clothes.

I touched his throat, his chin. Pressing upward, I explored the ridges of his brow and temples. The soft fan of his eyelashes breezed over my palm. He was forbidden to look at, but I mapped his features with my hands.

And when he kissed me again, all warm invitation, my thoughts swirled away, like drops of ink in water. I wanted more and more.

"Wait." His breath came in short gasps as he took my wrists

and pulled my hands away from him. "I need a moment." He rested his forehead on mine and breathed. Breathed.

I leaned back against the window. His chest expanded under my palm; his heart raced like mine.

Then came the susurrus of his mask going back on. "Can this really work?" I whispered, pushing up my blindfold to look at him. Black silk covered his face, like always. "Neither of us knowing the other's real name? Both of us wearing masks all the time?"

He touched his mask, a distant look crossing his eyes. "Just because I wear a mask doesn't mean you don't see the real me." He took my hands and squeezed. "And just because I don't know your real name doesn't mean I don't know who you truly are. I've seen you rush to help the people you love, and the pain you feel when you're afraid they're hurt. I saw the way you raced to help that boy, and made sure all your friends were safe before you left that night."

I'd been right to be wary of this boy. He paid attention to everything.

"But can this really work?" He gazed beyond me, and a frown creased between his eyes. "I don't think so. No. We both have obligations we won't be able to ignore when masks come off."

Or go on, in my case.

Those were unappealing thoughts. "Are you going to tell me how you chose your name? Are we good enough friends for that now?"

His tone was a smile. "So you're admitting that we're friends?"

"We're something." I smoothed my hair off my face and

sighed. "In some ways now, you know more about me than my own best friend."

"She doesn't know you're a flasher? A radiant?" His eyebrows drew in; I could see just the tips of them through the holes in his mask.

"No," I whispered. "Nor how conflicted I am about it now."

He moved closer to me, so our bodies were just a breath apart. "I'm conflicted, too."

I stepped into his embrace and rested my cheek on his shoulder. His heart beat against mine.

He spoke into my hair, muffling his voice. "I was worried about you."

"Optimistic Knife didn't have complete faith I'd return in one piece?"

"I did. Until you weren't back when you promised. You have no idea how relieved I was to see you earlier." He squeezed me a little. "I wanted to collapse with gratitude."

"I'd have picked you up."

He gave a soft snort. "No, you'd have laughed, and I'd have deserved it." He kissed my temple. Once. Twice. Then, with a soft groan, he pulled away. "It will be dawn soon."

"I bet you look wonderful in the sunlight. Very . . . inky."

He captured my jaw in his hands, turned my face up, and kissed me again. "Come here tonight."

I lifted an eyebrow and glanced at his mouth, hidden beneath that mask.

The cloth shifted, and I could almost *see* the grin beneath the blackness. My hands could half feel the way his smile would move under my fingers. "Bring your new things." He tilted his head toward the packet of gifts that I'd dropped earlier. "Bring your sword, too. I'll show you how to do more than just jab it into scorpions' eyes."

"My way is just as effective as yours." But in the back of my mind, I wondered whether he'd seen me use magic on the scorpion's chains, or what he'd think if he knew what I'd done in the wraithland. He might not trust me so much then.

I slipped away from him and knelt to pick up the mask and gloves.

"I'll see you tonight, nameless girl Will." He pulled open the trapdoor to let me out, but when I knelt beside him, he touched my cheek, my hair, my lips. "I think about doing that all the time."

Pleasure and guilt and uncertainty coiled inside me. Without another word, I left.

Dawn lit the sky in golden tendrils as I reached the palace and climbed up to my balcony, barely avoiding being seen by one of the guards.

Black Knife still didn't know about the other times I'd used my magic. Already there were so many secrets between us. What were a few more? Even if he did find out, surely he wouldn't begrudge my safety.

Except now the wraith was alive. Now it was searching for me.

I glanced over the violet city, half wondering if I'd see Black Knife climbing over the wall, too, but saw only indigo-coated guards changing shifts below, maids leaving grand mansions on early morning business for their employers, and delivery carts rumbling down the streets, making stops at all the prominent houses. Cathedral bells tolled with the dawn.

Exhaustion dragged at me as I hauled open my balcony door and slipped inside. Curtains covered the glass, blocking out the light; cool darkness cloaked my bedroom, with only faint embers in the fireplace to see by.

I crossed to my bed and laid the package from Black Knife on the corner, and changed into my nightgown.

He'd been right when he said it wouldn't work. We both had our obligations. He was a distraction from my duties to the Ospreys, and I was a distraction from whatever his real life was. Nevertheless, as I climbed into bed and drifted, it was with the scent of him still on me, and the memory of his mouth on mine.

Distraction or no, I wanted him. I wanted the nighttime, and the justice, and the way he trusted me even though I didn't deserve it. I wanted *him*.

The light shifted, brighter through the curtains now, and a nearby bell clanged.

Melanie threw herself into my room, wide-eyed as she heaved open the curtains. "Hurry. Get dressed."

I toppled out of bed and into a wine red day dress, and let Melanie coil and pin my hair into a bun. "Where are we going? Why's the bell ringing?"

"It's an emergency bell."

That shocked me into motion. We hurried into the hall, following the crowd of people making their way downstairs. Rumors rippled through the hallways like water: the queen's sister had killed a man; the prince's bodyguard was imprisoned; Black Knife had been caught.

I grabbed Melanie's hand and followed everyone into the throne room.

Light from the open windows shot through the wide space, illuminating dust motes and gold filigree and crystals on the chandelier. Hundreds of people pushed their way in, forcing everyone to crowd closer. The room grew hot with anticipation.

Minutes passed. Guards in their Indigo Order uniforms pushed their way around the perimeter of the room, their expressions hard and cold. A child cried somewhere. Older lords and ladies grumbled.

At last, the doors beside the throne opened, and out walked Crown Prince Tobiah, shadowed by James and a handful of other bodyguards. Both Tobiah's and James's eyes were rimmed with red, with deep shadows hanging like half-moons beneath. Their postures were stiff, as though held up by stubbornness alone.

Tobiah lifted a hand, and the crowd's chatter dulled and ceased. The only sounds were birds tweeting outside, wind chimes clinking in the breeze, and someone's sneeze.

"Thank you all for coming." Roughness edged the prince's voice, and he wore last night's tailcoat and trousers, hastily thrown on over a rumpled white shirt. His normally perfect hair was wild and half hanging in his face. "As you're all aware, this morning brings terrible news."

The chamber was achingly quiet as Tobiah gazed across the crowd. Our eyes met, held for a moment, and he moved on.

"It is my greatest regret," he said, "to inform you of a

murder. An assassination." His voice grew heavy, and cracked. "My father, His Majesty Terrell the Fourth, House of the Dragon, Sovereign of the Indigo Kingdom, is dead.

"Be reassured that the Indigo Order and the police are on full alert and are investigating every lead and scenario. No arrests have been made yet, but a list of suspects is being compiled. Please return to your apartments or homes this morning. Palace staff will be permitted in the halls, once they've been questioned, and all of you will receive meals in your rooms today. All events and festivities for this month have been canceled."

TWENTY-NINE

THE LORDS AND ladies of Skyvale Palace were sent back to their rooms, like children who'd only be in their parents' way if they stayed.

Breakfast was served late, and in spite of the lockdown, rumors still managed to spread from room to room. Black Knife had killed the king; the prince had murdered his father; one of the royal guards had too much to drink and lost control while demonstrating a sword technique. The rumors were wild and frightening, and so was a deep part of me that looked on this development with a sense of wonder.

King Terrell was responsible for my parents' deaths. They'd been slaughtered by his men, there in the courtyard, their blood spilled across the cobblestones. And everyone just watched, too frightened to take a stand.

I remembered catching Prince Tobiah's eye then, the fear and pity in them. "Don't look," he'd mouthed, but it was too late.

I'd already seen.

They were already dead.

"I can't believe it." Melanie dropped to the sofa and took a book from an end table. "Murdered. Not just dead from whatever sickness he had."

I wanted to feel something more, some sense of amusement of the irony, like Melanie did, or relief at the idea of King Terrell *finally* leaving this world, after he'd plagued mine for so long. But all I could summon was this strange sense of pity, like whatever Tobiah must have felt when he urged me not to look at my parents' bodies. Though my parents' men had kidnapped Tobiah, he'd still tried to comfort me when they died. Now, our positions were reversed.

A little after lunch, I rang the servant bell and asked to speak with Tobiah.

"He's part of the investigating team," said the maid. "He's coming to everyone's rooms personally."

I thanked her and shut the door.

While Melanie read aloud from a book describing the One-Night War and King Terrell's part in it, I checked that all of our Osprey things were in hiding places we'd agreed on. Everything was in secret compartments, beneath mattresses, and inside little-worn gowns. Papers, notebooks, map—

"Mel?"

"Yes?" She was still in the sitting room, lounging on the sofa.

"Where is the map?" It wasn't with the rest of the papers or shoved between the drawings I'd been working on as part of our disguise.

The book thumped to the sofa cushion, and a moment later,

Melanie stood in my doorway. "I gave it to Patrick while you were gone. It was finished."

I touched the faded bruise on my cheek and met her eyes.

"No," she whispered. "He wouldn't."

"It wasn't long ago we'd have said he would never hit any of us in anger, either."

"No," she whispered again. "He wouldn't."

"We have no proof, obviously. But we need to speak with him tonight."

She shook her head. "I will. Alone."

"That night we went together, he wanted me to kill someone, remember?"

"But not the king!"

"We don't know who it was. He wouldn't tell us after I said no."

"Let me ask before we start accusing."

I nodded. "Find out what you can." Black Knife had wanted to meet me tonight, and while I wasn't going to tell him about Patrick, he would certainly be interested in the king's assassination. Maybe I could learn something from him. Or help him. Or . . . I wasn't sure.

Being here in the palace was confusing my feelings and goals. This wasn't my home. I had no reason to care that the king was dead—I should rejoice—but I couldn't help but remember how he'd wanted so badly to improve his kingdom. He wanted the best for everyone. Maybe even me.

A knock came at the sitting room door just as I was hiding Black Knife's gifts under my mattress. I opened the door to admit Crown Prince Tobiah, James, General Fredrick, and a handful of other men in Indigo Order uniforms. Bodyguards, no doubt. Both the king's and the prince's.

"Your Highness." I curtsied low, that strange sense of pity gnawing on my heart as I invited him to sit. He took a place at the table and laid out a few sheets of paper. James and the general sat to either side of him, while the rest of the guards took up posts around the room, their hands behind their backs, and their expressions as hard as stone. "My deepest condolences. Losing a beloved parent is one of the worst things in the world. I'm sorry you must endure this now."

I *was* sorry. Having seen him with his father, having witnessed their strained argument last night—it was easy to see they'd loved each other.

"Thank you, Lady Julianna." The prince had washed and changed clothes since this morning, but stress lines pulled at the edges of his eyes and mouth, and grief made dark hollows below his eyes and cheekbones. He looked exhausted as he glanced at a list: reminders of what he needed to say. "I am conducting this investigation myself, with the help of James and my father's best men. We've been at this all day, so please forgive any gruffness to our questions. We want this solved as quickly as possible. I'm sure you understand."

"Of course I do."

He nodded. "If you'd like anything to drink, a maid is waiting outside with a cart of wine, as well as some herbs for stress and anxiety. May we call for anything for you?"

I glanced at Melanie and we both shook our heads.

"Very well." The prince turned the first page of his notes facedown on the table and focused on a sheet of paper with a list of questions on it. "Tell us where you were last night, from the second hour until dawn."

"I was in bed, sleeping," Melanie said. "So was Julianna. We came straight back after the ball."

"Is that true?" Tobiah lifted an eyebrow at me, and I nodded. "Very well." He made a note on his paper and moved to the next question. "Did you notice anything suspicious as you were leaving the ballroom? People you didn't recognize? People behaving strangely?"

"We're still new to Skyvale Palace society," I said. "There are many faces I don't recognize." Not quite true. After spending weeks here, I'd learned many faces, as well as their names and stories and deepest fears, where I could. But everyone I'd seen last night seemed to belong. No, the best attacker would have been one who could have made himself appear to fit in. Unless he'd waited and come after, entering and leaving the palace in the same way Melanie and I did. Once we'd learned the guard routines, the palace was laughably easy to sneak into. Of course, the Indigo Order put a lot of faith in no one untoward being able to cross the wall.

"No one behaving suspiciously?" Tobiah asked again, and both Melanie and I shook our heads. "What time would you say you each fell asleep?"

"One, perhaps?" Melanie cocked her head. "Half an hour following? I was tired after the ball."

"Same for me," I said. I'd gone to bed at the same time; I just hadn't stayed there. "My recent illness causes me to tire very quickly."

"I see." Tobiah asked several more questions, most in the

309

same vein, and after ten or so minutes, the prince handed the papers to Fredrick, who slipped them into a folder marked *Julianna Whitman*.

"That's all we have for now," said the general. He stood and started for the door, but as the prince and his bodyguard began to follow, I leaned forward.

"What happened to His Majesty? We've heard so many rumors."

Tobiah winced. "We'd rather not say for—"

"His throat was cut," said James. "Sliced clean open in his sleep, using a serrated blade. The assassin is right-handed and strong. It's hard to gauge his height, since His Majesty was obviously already lying down, but we know he must be someone with incredible stealth to have slipped past the four on-duty bodyguards."

"James." Tobiah's scowl pulled around his mouth. "That's enough around the ladies."

Belatedly, I remembered to be horrified by the details; I forced my expression to shift into slowly blooming alarm. "Why would anyone do that?"

Tobiah stood and looked at me. All traces of the sullen, bored prince I'd come to loathe were gone. Now, he just looked empty. "People always want to kill kings. That is why they have bodyguards."

A few minutes later, the men were gone, and Melanie and I sat at the table with our chins balanced on our fists.

"You lied about where you were last night." She plucked a petal from one of the flower arrangements on the table. "Where were you really?"

"Getting air."

"For five hours?" She flicked the petal across the table; it fluttered and fell to the floor.

So she'd heard me come in after all. "Well, I wasn't fighting crime with Black Knife." I said it like a joke. And it was true . . . this time. Admitting my relationship with Black Knife would be an even worse betrayal to Melanie. Saying no to Patrick was one thing. Spending a week as Black Knife's partner was unforgivable.

And kissing him, maybe falling in love with him—

I changed the subject. "What do we do about Terrell?"

"Nothing. We're not part of this. Let them handle their own problems."

"And if Patrick is responsible?"

She licked her lips and glanced toward the balcony door. "He must have had a good reason. Like revenge. Like keeping the Indigo Kingdom distracted while we return to Aecor."

None of those things was a good reason for *murder*. "Find out if he did it anyway. And tell him we aren't done here, either. I need to tell the wraith mitigation committee what happened in the wraithland. It might help their efforts against it—and help us, ultimately."

"It might not matter, once we return to Aecor and your identity is revealed. Why would they believe anything you said?"

With a sigh, I strode across the room and found the stack of drawings I'd been working on. My fingers itched for a pen. Working, even on something small, would ease the uncomfortable buzzing in the back of my thoughts.

"The Pierces and Indigo Order might not believe me." I

flipped through the pages and found a half-finished drawing of Black Knife. "But I know someone who will."

Torches burned around the palace walls, pushing back the shadows as dusk fell. The guards had been tripled and soldiers were placed all around the courtyard, gardens, and front drive. Everywhere I looked was evidence of the city lockdown.

Hawksbill was silent. The streetlights blazed, but no laughter drifted up from the mansions. Wind chimes had been torn down so none of their cheer would sound on this dark day. A hush blanketed the whole city in a wraithlike chill.

"Can you do this?" I asked.

Melanie watched the guards below, studying their patterns. Typically, escaping the palace was no problem, but now, with all of the Indigo Order on high alert, I wasn't so sure.

"I think so."

Melanie and I stayed on the balcony as the night grew deeper, two distraught women who'd lost yet another king, now seeking something bigger than them for comfort. As cathedral bells tolled, we huddled together in our shawls and simple dresses, the picture of mourning. The guards never looked up.

An hour before midnight, we went back indoors, and Melanie headed into her room to change. I slipped into the black hooded sweater and trousers from the night before.

"Where are you going?" Melanie asked from the doorway.

"I thought I'd check with some of our contacts about the king's assassination."

Her lips peeled back in a sneer. "It's still not our problem."

"It is if anyone here gets suspicious of us." In which case, both of us leaving tonight wasn't a good idea. *Neither* of us should leave. But I needed to know if Patrick had assassinated the king, and I wanted to hear Black Knife's thoughts. "Lady Chey is having the scribes and records-keepers look over our papers. We're already under scrutiny."

Melanie hissed. "They won't catch us. Your documents were flawless. We'll be out of here before it's an issue."

I couldn't go to Aecor until I'd figured out what I'd done to the wraith, but I wasn't ready to tell her that truth yet.

"Be careful," I said.

"Say it again." She opened the balcony door and descended into the frigid night.

I watched her go, tracking her movements as she slipped from shadow to shadow, avoiding all the guards as they marched through the courtyard. When she was out of my sight, I armed myself with daggers and Black Knife's gifts, and slipped out on my own.

Pressing myself into the deepest shadows I could find, I eased from balcony to rooftop to the ground, keeping my breaths long and deep and silent.

A cold wind kicked up, bringing droplets of water and a sharp wraithy scent, but I suppressed the urge to gag and crept along a hedge until I reached a walled garden near a mansion boasting the House of the Sun crest. From there, I took the most deserted paths possible, hyperalert of every sound and scent.

It took twice as long to reach the Hawksbill wall, and even more time to find a place to scale it. But I managed, and stole into Thornton as quickly and quietly as I could. There were extra patrols here, as well, but there were also more places to hide.

I ran a long route to the breezeway where Black Knife had taken me last night, but I found it and the trapdoor without trouble, and climbed in.

He wasn't here.

The Hawksbill clock tower chimed the second hour. Black Knife hadn't specified a time, so I curled myself into a corner and waited, letting my eyes drift shut for a minute. The taps of light rain against the glass lulled my thoughts. I hadn't slept last night, except for an hour or two when I got back to my room, and the day had been too busy to rest.

I shivered awake when the clock tower struck five. Black Knife hadn't come. He'd asked me to meet him, and then hadn't come.

Then again, everything had changed. Who knew what else he'd had to do, especially if he was part of one of the noble houses.

Dawn was still hours away, but I needed to hurry back if I wanted to avoid the new security.

Yawning, I let myself out of the trapdoor and hurried through the market district streets. My mind was foggy with sleep, but the icy air and run helped. The light rain stopped as I crossed the wall, more quickly this time, so I peeled off the mask and began fitting myself into the shadows of mansions and fountains and anything else I could find.

Footsteps approached from behind. I ducked toward a tall statue, but it was too late; I was too slow.

"Julianna Whitman?" A man wearing the Indigo Order uniform brandished his sword. "Please come with me. You're under arrest for impersonation of Liadian nobility and under suspicion of assassinating King Terrell."

THIRTY

THIS WAS *EXACTLY* why I'd warned Melanie to be careful.

And here I was.

"Just come with me," said the guard. His gaze flickered down as I rested my hands on my dagger hilts. "This will be much easier if you don't resist."

Easier for him.

I set my jaw and drew my daggers. Steel glinted in the light of gas lamps hissing all around us. Cold wind gusted. Conifers rustled.

"Just come with me," he said again, voice low and wary.

I ducked to his right side—so he'd have to swing backward to hit me—and attacked. He staggered and shifted his sword to block my blades at the last second. The clash of steel threw me off balance, but I corrected and struck out with my blades again.

"Found her!" shouted my guard. He foiled another strike,

then another, not bothering to fight me. All he had to do was wait for help.

I sheathed my daggers and dropped to the ground, braced myself, and kicked his knee. Bone shifted and crunched, and I rolled out of the way just as his sword came down. The tip buried itself in the ground as the man screamed and clutched his broken knee.

There was no reason I should feel bad for defending myself, even if he was just some third-born lord without better options than to join the Indigo Order. Still, I winced with a little sympathy as I kicked him in the face, careful to avoid shoving his nasal bones up and into his brain.

Screaming in pain, he fell aside. I stole his sword.

Dawn caught on the northeastern horizon, shining gold above the mountains like a beacon. If I got over the wall I could escape the city and get back to the old palace.

I peeled away from the garden where I'd been sneaking, and made for the wall. My footfalls were silent as I raced down a street, keeping as close to the shadows as possible. In the distance, other guards shouted and called orders.

Someone demanded a physician; their newly crippled friend had been discovered.

I pinned the stolen sword under my arm and took out my grappling hook and line. Boots thudded on the pavement behind me.

I switched the line to my left hand, grabbed the sword with my right, and swung around just as two men in crisp uniforms ran up.

They reeled back, away from the tip of the blade arcing toward them, and one brought up his weapon to block. Our swords clacked and he pressed hard enough to shift mine back toward me; he was stronger.

I snaked my sword around and slung his from his hand. It landed in a rosebush several feet away, and when he ran to fetch it, I hurled my own sword at the second guard's face.

When he scrambled away from the flying blade, I caught my grappling line with both hands and hauled myself up as quickly as I could. Hand over hand. Feet planted firmly on the wall.

Arms wrapped around my waist. My muscles burned as I tried to hang on to my weight and the guard's, but I wasn't strong enough; neither was the line.

I let go, thudding to the ground as I landed on top of both guards. They grunted and grabbed at me, but I elbowed them each in the face and rolled off, leaving behind my grappling line as I took off farther along the wall. Eventually, I'd reach the gate. I'd just have to be fast.

Lights hung down from the wall, illuminating my path. Shouts and cries from the nearby patrols spurred me onward, and my breath heaved in the cold air as I pushed myself. Mist trailed behind me and I gave up all pretense of stealth as two, four, ten guards joined the chase.

I wove between buildings and statues, ducking and dodging as quickly as I could. The crash of men through brush and evergreens chased me. Their boots thumped on the ground.

All over Hawksbill, lights flared from houses and people peered out from windows and over balconies, their faces pale and frightened. I recognized Chey and a few of her friends as I hurtled past her immense mansion.

Cold wind tore at my face, making tears prickle in the

corners of my eyes. Everything blurred, even as dawn began creeping through the Indigo Valley, lighting the city with shards of gold and copper.

The gate to Thornton was just ahead.

My thighs ached as I drove myself faster. My lungs burned. My vision swam.

When I blinked away cold-born tears, dozens of indigo-coated soldiers stood between the gate and me. Dozens more appeared on either side of the road, armed with swords and crossbows.

I thrust out a foot to help me turn without losing momentum—I'd have to go deeper into Hawksbill and hide—but even more men stood behind me.

I staggered to a halt and turned in a slow circle as the men of the Indigo Order began closing in. I was surrounded. Trapped.

There were no tricks or tools in my belt, no surprise escapes. A hundred or more men bore down on me. There was no way I could fight them off.

Heart thrumming, I unhooked my dagger sheaths from my belt and laid them on the ground. With empty hands lifted to my sides, I surrendered.

A young man kicked his horse through the crowd of soldiers, his face red with cold or anger. He dismounted and hopped off, and took several long strides toward me, ahead of the rest of the Order.

Lieutenant James Rayner stood with one hand on his sword, the other fist planted on his hip. When our eyes met, there was no friendliness in him. Only a look of deep disappointment and resignation.

"Lady Julianna Whitman, ward of the kingdom," said James, "you are under arrest for the impersonation of Liadian nobility, and under suspicion of the assassination of King Terrell Pierce the Fourth. Please don't resist, or we'll have no choice but to use deadly force."

I swallowed back a surge of terror as I offered my wrists and held my ground.

James motioned to one of his men, who unhooked a pair of cuffs from his belt and strode toward me. The guards' crossbows were all loaded and aimed; they wouldn't miss if I attacked their comrade.

The cuffs were cold around my wrists, and too tight.

The jail cells beneath the palace reeked of vomit. Rat droppings littered the floor of my cell.

Shortly after being thrown in here hours ago, I'd wiped off the bench so I could sit. Besides a bucket, there was a threadbare blanket and lumpy pillow, and a torch burned on the other side of the bars, throwing in flickering orange light too bright to let me sleep.

Not that I could sleep now anyway.

I sat in the corner of my cell, feet propped on the bench, and leaned my head back to stare at the ceiling. Water tapped somewhere nearby, steady and stately like the beat of a pavane. My bruises throbbed in time.

They were new bruises, shaped like the rough hands of soldiers. The men had grabbed and groped down my arms and legs, searching for hidden weapons. They'd been thorough—too thorough—until James began to shove them aside. He'd called

319

them off, threatening them with dishonor as he reminded them that I was still a lady.

I'd kept my head high. I hadn't so much as squeaked when strange men prodded my chest and stomach.

But as soon as the cell door slammed shut and I was alone, I lost everything into my bucket.

Now what?

There was no helping Aecor from jail. I could escape, but how would I tell the mitigation committee what I knew about the wraith if I was a fugitive?

Then again, was being a fugitive so different from being an Osprey?

I hadn't killed the king. I had to believe they'd learn that. As for impersonating Julianna Whitman . . . what *was* the punishment for pretending to be a duchess?

What if the pretender was actually a princess?

Of a conquered kingdom?

With an army slowly building in the background, ready to take back the kingdom in her name?

Melanie would find out I'd been caught. She and Patrick would figure out what to do. Meanwhile, they'd send word to all our contacts in Aecor that the Indigo Kingdom was holding me prisoner. The resistance groups and former army would rally. They'd come to get me.

Unless Patrick decided a dead Wilhelmina was easier to handle than a defiant Wilhelmina.

No. He wouldn't.

"Julianna?" James stood at the bars, silhouetted by the torch at his back. "I have a few questions for you."

I pushed up to my feet and mimicked his posture: hands behind my back, shoulders straight, and feet hip-width apart. "I have a few questions for you, too."

"This isn't a game." His mouth curled into a frown. "Who are you really?"

Wasn't that what we were all trying to figure out? "A nameless girl."

He glanced at someone outside of my line of sight, but if there was any communication in the look, I missed it; his expression remained impassive, and mostly in shadow.

"Well, nameless girl, I have another question for you."

I didn't move.

"Are you the vigilante known as Black Knife?"

"Do I look like Black Knife to you?"

"Maybe." James pulled a piece of black silk from his pocket—my mask—and held it between two fingers, as though it might contaminate him. "Where did you get this?"

"I stole it."

"So you're not Black Knife."

I held my hands out, gesturing at my empty belt. "Do you see a sword here? A crossbow? Silk cable to bind up my enemies? Obviously, I'm not Black Knife."

"You have the same taste in clothes." He motioned at my trousers and black sweater.

"Black is definitely my color."

"Do you know who Black Knife is?"

I rolled my eyes. "Everyone knows who Black Knife is."

"I mean his true identity."

I shifted my weight to one hip and crossed my arms. "What

about the mask is confusing to you? He wears it so no one will know who he truly is." I let out an exaggerated sigh and rolled my eyes. "I thought being a lieutenant meant you were smart."

He let that slide by. "So you don't know his identity."

"Clearly."

"Are you protecting him?"

"I don't think he needs my protection."

"Very well." James stuffed the mask into his pocket again. "Let's talk about your alias. You're not the real Julianna Whitman, so where is she?"

"Dead, I assume. In Liadia with the rest of her people who couldn't escape the wraith."

"And you forged her residency papers."

I paced across the cell. Of *course* I'd forged the papers.

"What about your friend, Melanie? Is that her real name? Where is she?"

I kept pacing, and the questions kept coming:

"What was your objective here?"

"Where did you learn so much about Liadian history?"

"What kind of information were you after? Was your mission complete? Who are your contacts outside the palace?"

I answered all of his questions with silence and the occasional raised eyebrow, and finally he moved on to the king's assassination.

"Where were you that night?"

"Sleeping."

"We found weapons in your room and on your person."

"But not like the knife you described. Serrated blade? Strong assassin?" I pushed up my sleeve to reveal the slender muscles of my arms, and the pale blue bruises from his men's hands. "Do you think I'm physically capable of cutting clean through someone's throat?"

James glanced at my arm, and his expression tightened for a heartbeat. "You might be."

The truth was, while I *was* strong from years of fighting and training, I had no idea how much pressure or strength it took to cut a man's throat, with a serrated blade or otherwise. It probably wasn't much, but I needed to sow doubt. I was guilty of impersonating a dead duchess, but I *hadn't* killed their king.

"I found your drawings."

I picked dirt from under my fingernails.

"As well as pages and pages of nonsense writing in different hands. Signatures written over and over. Forgery practice, I assume. So you could learn their handwriting. What were you doing with that? Which one is yours?"

"You're a very determined young man, James Rayner."

James ran through his questions again, pressing harder this time, so I stopped speaking altogether. I returned to my bench, propped my feet up as before, and covered my chest with my arms.

James's shadow vanished from my cell. "She won't speak." His voice was low, distant. "Except with sarcasm. She's a completely different girl."

"That's what I expected." The other voice faded before I could tell who it was. A general? The prince? The men were leaving the dungeon.

I closed my eyes and sat in silence, only the *drip drip drip* for company. Desperately, I wanted to be hard. I wanted to be the girl I'd shown James just now—strong, sarcastic, and uncrackable.

But the bruises throbbed and, alone now, my mind took me back to the street in Hawksbill, soldiers all around. My wrists bound. Fingers digging into my flesh.

My stomach turned over again, but there was nothing left to throw up. I took long, deep breaths to clear the taste of bile from my tongue. My hands itched for my notebook and a good pen; writing had always calmed me.

A new shadow fell in front of the torch, blocking the glare from my eyes. "I don't think you killed my father."

"That makes you smarter than everyone in the Indigo Order."

Keys jangled and the bars squealed open. Boots crunched rat droppings and a moment later, the crown prince sat on the bench next to my toes. "Please don't try to escape. There are guards in the hall."

I cracked open one eye. "How many?"

"Five."

"That wouldn't be enough to stop me."

Exhaustion lined the prince's face, and red rimmed his eyes, but he studied me and nodded. "You strike me as a dangerous person, my lady."

"I've been told that before."

Drip drip drip.

"If your name isn't Julianna, what shall I call you?"

"Everyone is so interested in naming me." I slipped my feet off the side of the bench and sat straight.

The prince didn't flinch at my sudden movement. He sat, half trapped in misery, and I knew too well how he felt. Lost. Confused. Betrayed.

"I wasn't lying yesterday," I said. "I know what it's like to lose a parent. I lost both of mine years ago, and their deaths still haunt me."

He dropped his gaze and didn't speak.

"Sometimes I wake up and wonder if I'm back in my real life, where they're alive and everything is as it should be. But I never am. It makes me feel so alone." I swallowed hard and watched the torchlight play across his features. "But I'm not alone. They loved me, and that love doesn't go away just because they're gone. The same goes for you. Your father *loved* you. He would have done anything for you. The pain may never go away, not wholly, but never forget that you meant everything to him."

"You pretended to be someone you're not for weeks. How do I know anything you say is true?"

"You don't." I glanced at the cell door. Closed. The keys must have been in the prince's pocket. "You don't know if anything I just said about my past is true, but you do know that everything I said about your present is. You know how your father felt, in spite of your unfortunate personality. Everyone does."

Tobiah glanced at me and frowned. "And why offer comfort when you have such a low opinion of my personality? Do you think I'm going to let you out?"

I couldn't stop the faint smile that crept up on me. "Because when my parents were murdered, someone I barely knew offered comfort. He had no reason to do it. I used to resent him for it, because as far as I could see, he'd lost nothing when I'd lost everything." I dropped my gaze to my knees, trying not to slouch beneath the weight of old memories. "Now, I wonder if his kindness is part of what kept me human all these years."

He raked his fingers through his hair and leaned back. "Tell me again where you were the night my father was killed."

Back to the questions. I struggled to build up my defenses again, but I was exhausted. My whole body was heavy. "Sleeping."

"You have *no* alibi?"

"I suppose I don't."

"Then I guess I'm done here." He stood and shoved his hands into his pockets. Weariness made his shoulders curl inward. "Unless you want to tell me what to call you."

"You have so many options. I still answer to Julianna."

"James said you called yourself a nameless girl."

"It's what a friend calls me. Affectionately, I think. He doesn't know my real name, either. Don't imagine I'm going to tell *you*."

"A friend, huh?" Tobiah was watching me, his dark eyes filled with grief and regret and a spark of familiarity. He knelt in front of the bench and pressed something small and silky into my fingers. "Oh, nameless girl." His voice shifted deeper. "*When* will you learn to trust me?"

I turned my hand over to find the Black Knife mask.

My heart tumbled and twisted. "You?" *Tobiah* was Black Knife? How? When did he find time? Had his father known? What about James? Or Meredith? And why had he not revealed me as an impostor the first day Melanie and I walked into his father's office?

"But you're so sour and he's so—" I clamped my mouth shut. "Sorry." Maybe.

Oh no. *No.* I was in love with the boy who was the reason

for the One-Night War. The reason my parents were dead.

His mouth turned up in a pale smile. "I'm not a good alibi. You're right."

"Especially when people think Black Knife did it." Fighting to keep a steady hand, I let my fingertips touch his cheek, his chin. The sensation of his skin under mine, the planes and ridges of his face, and even the way he gasped and closed his eyes at my touch: I'd felt all of this before.

This couldn't be real.

"That's why I didn't come last night. I'm sorry you got caught. I couldn't think of a good way to warn you to stay in without you finding out."

"But you told me just now."

"Did I?" With that same tired smile, he took my hand and kissed my fingertips, but drew back when my sleeve slipped up to reveal my forearm. "Oh, *Will*. What happened? The guards?"

"It's nothing." Just the memory made my stomach turn over, but I hardened myself against it. I refused to show him— or anyone—how those men had hurt me.

"I know the way you lie. I've lived with it." He checked my other arm, and his expression fell into something hard and dangerous. Shards of Black Knife manifested: his tone, the way his body tensed, the angle of his head. My heart pounded as he trailed his fingertips across my flushed skin. "Is it like this everywhere?"

I pressed my mouth into a line as I yanked away my arm. "It doesn't hurt."

"Will, you—" He shook his head and slumped. "I was going to suggest you don't have to lie to me—to pretend to be someone you're not. But I suppose I can see why you might not believe that."

"How can I believe anything you do or don't say? How can I believe your actions?" I curled my hands into fists and stared at them. There was no reason he should trust me, either; I was a thief, and an impostor. And worse. I shifted my tone, filling it with more regret. "You said it wouldn't work for us. That you have other obligations."

He exhaled. "That night in the breezeway—that was the truth of my feelings."

"The truth of your actions doesn't forgive the betrayal in them. What about your fiancée? What if you'd already been married? Would you have done the same?"

"Of course not." He pulled back, indignant.

"There's only one side of you I want." I lifted my eyes to his. "And I'm willing to gamble there's only one side she wants, too. You have to choose who you are."

"I know." Tobiah stood and stepped back, one graceful movement. "I have to go now, but you'll be out of here soon."

How had he fooled me for so long? How had he been so *completely* different? "You're going to let me go?"

"I know you didn't kill my father." Grief pierced his words. "You aren't a murderer."

"I tried. Once. You stopped me. It wouldn't be a stretch to believe I might try again."

"But you didn't commit this murder. We were together." For a half second, his eyes dropped to my lips. "You know where to find me. I'll have your things." Our eyes met again briefly, and then the cell bars squealed and he was gone.

THIRTY-ONE

ALONE AGAIN, I sat back and struggled to breathe. Black Knife was Tobiah. Tobiah was Black Knife.

The boy I loved was my enemy. The boy I couldn't stand to be near.

It also meant Tobiah had known who I was from the very beginning—from the moment I stepped into the king's office and our eyes locked. I'd been so worried he would know me from Aecor. It had never occurred to me I should worry that he'd know me from all of his crime fighting.

He didn't know I was Wilhelmina, though. That secret, at least, was still mine.

I sank lower onto the bench, and sank deeper into my confused emotions.

But how—*how*—could they be the same? One boy smiled all the time, even if I never saw it, and the other was so thoroughly unimpressed with everything and everyone. One boy sought me out and fought for my attention, maybe even my affection, and the other ignored my existence except when manners forced him to acknowledge me.

And he was getting married. Tobiah was engaged.

They couldn't be the same. They needed to be different boys so I hadn't fallen in love with a boy I couldn't have.

He'd tried to stop me, though. And he'd stopped himself, when I was ready to lose myself.

While I'd been quietly falling in love, it had never occurred to me he might already have someone. Even if he didn't love her, they'd be married as soon as he set a date. How very *human* of him to fall for someone with such a perceived low rank.

Shame, betrayal, and longing seeped through me, filling every pore. Black Knife became a whirlpool that sucked at my thoughts.

At least knowing it could never work meant I didn't have to stay the hurt boiling inside of me. I just had to contain it for now, and figure out my next moves: what to do about Patrick, and what to do about the thing I made in the wraithland.

Drip drip drip.

Soon, regardless of our actions tonight, our kingdoms would be at war. After all, he couldn't just *give up* Aecor to me. Could he?

But why would he? Kissing wasn't a good enough reason, and I couldn't think of any political advantages to releasing a valuable piece of land, even if it was to stop a minor war. He'd be viewed as a weak king from the start. His uncle, the *Overlord* of Aecor Territory, would be furious. Tobiah wouldn't be able to do it.

No, tonight would be the last time I'd see him. If I ever did again, it would be from across a battlefield.

Nightmares chased me for hours.

Only the occasional thump of boots and the steady drip of water kept me from drowning in memories of the wraithland: white mist swirling all around, lonely whispers breathing my name, and something intangible reaching for me.

What was I going to do about the wraith that knew my name?

A heavy gown swished in the hallway, jerking me from uneasy sleep.

"My lady!" a guard cried. "You can't go down there—"

"I can, and I will."

I sat straight and wiped my face clean, trying to look as though I'd been waiting for my visitor.

A minute later, Lady Chey stood outside the bars, her hands behind her back and a satisfied smirk on her lips. "Well, this is exactly what I've been waiting to see."

I didn't move to greet her, or curtsy, or even change my expression. I put on my silence like armor.

"I knew you weren't Julianna." She shifted her weight to one hip, making her russet gown sway. "I knew Julianna years ago, when we were children."

My expression remained neutral.

"I traveled to Liadia with my family," she said, "and she and I became friends. We wrote letters for years before the kingdom went under martial law. Before the wraith ate up her land. In that last letter, she was so afraid of what was happening. She talked about being imprisoned in her own house, with guards leering at her from the halls. She said how the king had gone mad with his victory over the wraith—even though no one thought the barrier would hold. She wanted to leave, to come here and stay with me, but she couldn't escape her own rooms." Chey swallowed hard, and blinked away evidence of her sorrow. "There were tearstains on the paper. It smelled of wraith. She must have written the letter just days before their barrier fell."

My eyes ached with grief for that girl. Terrified. Alone. Having visited the wraithland myself, I knew how horrific it could be.

"And then *you* came. When I heard Julianna was here, I was thrilled to think she might have escaped." Chey dragged in a long breath. "Imagine my disgust when I found you instead. Pretending to be my friend. Stealing the identity of a dead girl."

I gave a slight nod. "I imagine you were furious."

"Everyone knows what you are now. I've made sure of that."

Certainly, she had tried. "Good-bye, Chey."

"You don't get to dismiss me." She stepped closer to the bars. "You don't get to do anything ever again, except sit there and rot. Oh, and I brought you this."

She tossed a small wooden object into the cell, followed by a lump of white clouds, and then strode off, as regal as ever.

Only when the swish of her dress and stomp of her footsteps faded did I get up to see what she'd left for me.

It was a spindle and wool.

A guard fetched me. The sky was black as I was escorted to the city gates and kicked out with the refugees.

Maybe it was my imagination, but there were fewer people here than usual. Many of the refugees wore backpacks; some had ponies with clothes and supplies dripping from overstuffed saddlebags. Hooves stomped. Bridles and halters clinked.

I stood there, dressed in all black, clutching my mask inside my pocket, and dithered. Tobiah had said he'd bring my things to the breezeway, but the sooner I returned to the old palace, the better. Besides, did I really want to face him now? Black Knife and Tobiah had been separate people for so long; how could I just make them into the same person? How could I talk to Black Knife anymore, now that he was also Tobiah?

Then again, *Tobiah had my things.* There was no reason to believe he hadn't looked at my notebook yet, but if he did, he'd know who I was, as well as what I'd done in the wraithland. I needed that back. And my daggers. I was naked without my weapons.

Shivering in the cold autumn wind, I looked up to find a growing crowd of refugees staring openly. They pointed and gawked, a few of them daring within arm's reach. "Are you Black Knife?" one girl asked.

I flinched. "No."

"You look like Black Knife." She touched my elbow and leapt back. A man caught her shoulders and nudged her, and they both shuffled closer again. "You dress like Black Knife."

"Well, I'm not him." I edged away, trapped in the torchlight that illuminated the wall and the cook fires scattered about the camp. The refugees' shadows grew long and distorted in the jumping light.

"Are you going to save us from the wraith monster?" asked

the girl. "Everyone is leaving because of it."

The packed horses and ponies drew my attention again. On the far side of the camp, several people tore down their lean-tos and rounded up children. The clatter of dozens of people preparing to move out finally pierced my haze, and I narrowed my eyes at the little girl. "What wraith monster?"

Her eyes grew so wide I could see the whites all around her irises. "The one that screams for a lady."

The thing I created. I'd assumed I would have time to think and plan. But no.

It was coming for me.

My heart thundered in my ears, deafening. I had to get back to the old palace. I had to stop the wraith. I had to do *something*—I just didn't know what.

"Are you going to help us, Black Knife?" The girl and her father approached again. She reached for me, fingertips brushing my thigh.

I curled my hands over my hips; only the spindle and wool were in my belt, meant as a gift for Theresa, who'd enjoy it. No daggers. No weapons. "I'm not Black Knife."

"Please stop the wraith." Others grew bold, moving toward me with halting steps. They were afraid of me, but not frightened enough—or simply *more* afraid of the wraith closing in on the Indigo Kingdom. And who could blame them, after what they'd been through?

But now, they came closer, pressing at me on all sides to touch my hair, my clothes, my face. One took the spindle and wool.

"Black Knife," someone murmured. "You're really here."

"Black Knife is a girl!"

"No." I tried to ease my way through the mass of people, but they crowded and their hands grew more demanding, landing on tender bruises. Someone grabbed my wrist. Another touched my throat.

Something in me snapped.

I yanked myself away, shoved someone, elbowed someone. I pushed myself through the crowd of dirty strangers, heedless of their anguished cries, and hurtled into the night as quickly as I could.

"Wait!" someone shouted. "The wraith is coming!" Footfalls thudded behind me. A trail of desperate men and women came after me, pleading for Black Knife's help.

"My daughter is missing!"

"My husband is hurt!"

"Find my sister in the wraithland!"

Everyone needed Black Knife's help. Not mine. I couldn't solve their problems when I didn't even know how to deal with my own.

Strangling back a sob, I threw myself into the forest and let instinct and years of practice take over. I leapt over roots, stones, and streams, dodged the familiar trees of this forest. Birds took flight around me, and at the harried crashing and cursing that pursued me. Brush snapped and someone cried out, but I couldn't stop.

"Stop the wraith, Black Knife!"

I wasn't Black Knife. Why couldn't they *see*?

My flight through the forest turned into a fast walk and climb as the ground sloped upward, toward the mountains. The voices grew fainter as I outran the refugees and their pleas.

Finally, I collapsed to the ground in a heap of shivering and dry heaving. I could still feel their hands all over me, the phantom pressure of their groping.

"Will?"

I snapped up and scanned the area, fingers grasping for daggers that weren't where they should be. But Black Knife stepped out of the shadows, breathing hard as he lifted his gloved hands. One was empty; the other held a small lamp, illuminating his assailable state. A full bag hung off one shoulder.

"I wasn't sure you'd meet me," he said. "So I followed your escort out of the city, just in case you decided not to come back."

Still shivering, I lowered myself back to the ground and shook my head. "You couldn't have had them leave me somewhere more convenient?" My whole body ached with terror and cold and the flood of adrenaline that hadn't quite faded. Even breathing hurt.

"No." He dropped the bag and sat down next to me, angling the light to fall directly in my eyes. "What happened?"

"What do you think happened?" I turned away and breathed in the damp, earthy scent of the forest. "I stood there like an idiot, trying to decide whether I would meet you, and people mistook me for you."

"And then you panicked. Why?"

My heart pounded with memory. Trapped. Hands grabbing. Fingers biting into my flesh. "I don't want to talk about it." That wasn't my voice, so wispy and weak. I tried again. "Just forget it."

"All right." He rested his palm on my shoulder.

I tensed, and he paused, and slowly—slowly—I forced my muscles to relax one by one. I forced myself to breathe.

Black Knife gave me a moment, then stroked my arm over and over, as though he could smooth out the wrinkles in my heart. "What had you decided?" His voice was gentle. "Were you coming to see me?"

"Yes." I rolled over, away from him, and let the breeze cool the sweat off my throat. He wore his mask, as if that could rekindle the familiar anonymity between us, but now that I knew who he was, I couldn't help but see Tobiah's shape beneath the black silk and jacket and polished boots. I'd wanted to know his identity; now I wished I didn't. "I had to get my notebook back. Did you read it?"

He dropped his hands into his lap, shoulders curled inward. "You didn't steal my secret before I was ready. You deserve the same consideration."

I exhaled relief. "Thank you."

"I did go through your rooms. I wanted to make sure no one else found your belongings first." He elbowed the bag he'd brought. "It's all in here. The things I thought looked useful. Or incriminating."

"Oh, Black Knife, how you've fallen." I stared up at him, taking in the tilt of his head, the angles of his body, and the weariness in his eyes. This boy was not like Tobiah at all. "Now you're helping criminals."

"Just one."

"Why?"

"I'm not sure you're a criminal."

I lifted an eyebrow. "I steal things. I impersonate duchesses. I am a flasher, and I've used my power." More than he knew. Much more.

"Are you confessing? After all the work I did to get you out, should I take you back to jail?"

I recovered some of my earlier haughtiness, wielding it like a knife. "That filthy place? Absolutely not."

Black Knife grabbed the silk at his throat and tugged his mask off his face. Brown hair curled downward, just brushing his eyebrows. I'd been a fool not to see it before: the sharpness of his chin, the lean body, the dancer-like movements. But I'd never have thought a prince would care enough to become a vigilante for his city. Particularly not a prince who gave the impression of perpetual sullenness and boredom, and was well-known for being a poor swordsman.

It had all been an act, though. It had been his real mask.

It didn't matter. None of it. Tobiah was already taken. I couldn't have Black Knife.

If only they'd been separate boys.

"The truth is," he said, "a long time ago someone helped me—someone who didn't have to, and probably shouldn't have. But for some reason, she thought I was worthy of saving. Not because of who I said I was, but because she believed I'd been wronged and she needed to make things right. She had the ideals and morals of a young child; I have always admired that." Tobiah slipped his hands into his mask, frowning at the black silk. "While I thought I was doing the right thing as Black Knife, it's true that I ended up hurting people. I didn't wonder what happened to flashers in the end. I don't have a solution, but I do know that throwing them into the wraithland is wrong."

I pushed myself up, half sitting now, leaning on one arm. Cold wind breathed up the mountain, making the forest shiver. I shivered, too.

"Here." Tobiah dug through a side pocket of the bag and pulled out the gloves he'd given me. "Let's put these on before you freeze."

"I have to go," I said, shifting to sit straight. But against my better judgment, I held out my hands. He still looked like Black Knife, with those knee-high boots, the black shirt and trousers. If I didn't look at his face, I could imagine . . .

Gently, he slid the first glove over my hand, careful to make it fit right; his fingertips breezed over the hollow of my wrist. "There's a safe place for you in the city." He swallowed hard, his throat working, and he began fitting the second glove over my fingers, over my palm. Even with layers of leather and wool and silk between us, my hands had never felt so alive.

"I can't." My hands stayed in his, feeling like an impostor again. All of this, the wraith and war, was my fault. "There's something I have to take care of."

He watched me, expression impassive. "Can I help?"

I closed my eyes against the harsh lamplight, and turned my head against the strengthening wind. "I did something bad," I whispered. "Something awful. I tried to run from it, but I'm realizing that I'll pay for things I didn't do if I don't take responsibility for the things I did do."

He squeezed my hands, and a deep undercurrent of fear filled his voice. "What happened? What did you do?" He sounded like Black Knife. Like my friend.

"I want to be someone good. Someone worthy." The confession was for Black Knife, not Tobiah. It was easier to imagine the boy in front of me as the vigilante. "For so long I've felt trapped by my parents' legacy. I thought I had to be just like them, even though I had no idea how. And lately, I haven't known how to reconcile what I've always believed was true and what I'm learning might *be* true. I spend so much time confused now. I miss the clarity and certainty that used to drive me."

My hands dropped to my lap, and a heartbeat later, cool leather touched my cheeks as he cupped my face in his palms. He kissed me, sweet and sad and full of longing. When I drew back and looked at him, unshed tears glimmered in the corners of his eyes. "You could be telling my story."

Thunder rolled in the distance, almost a voice. I could half hear my name in the sound, so much evidence of what I created.

I touched my lips, the leather gloves cool against my skin. "Don't kiss me again."

Hurt flashed across his face, but he nodded. "I won't."

"I said before that there's only one side of you I want. But that's not the side that matters. You're promised to someone else, and you will need to give your whole self to her, and to your kingdom."

"I know. I haven't forgotten what I promised my father." His voice turned cool. A little bitter. "I wish things were different."

"Wishing has never changed anything for me." When I climbed to my feet, he followed.

"Where are you going?"

I pressed my lips together. In the prison, he'd asked when I would learn to trust him. After what he'd hidden from me?

Maybe never. Not fully. Then again, I'd hidden so much from him, too.

One of us needed to make an effort to be honest. "I'm going up the mountain. To the old palace. East Pass Watch."

A combination of a smile and grimace pulled at his mouth. "The Ospreys live there?"

"Yes." I glanced toward the ancient castle, concealed by rock and trees and distance. "I'm coming back to Skyvale. Tonight. But in case I'm not fast enough, or if something goes wrong, you need to be ready."

Darkness veiled his tone. "What do you mean?"

"Skyvale needs you right now." I placed my palm on his chest, felt the quickening of his heart as I stepped back. "They need *you*. Their prince. Their future king. Not Black Knife. Not this time."

"What's going to happen?" His features softened as he gazed toward his city below.

"I'm not sure," I said. "But you'll need your army."

He nodded, somber. "Before we go, are you ever going to tell me your real name? Or will I have to call you a boy's name forever?"

"My name is Wil." I heaved up the bag filled with my belongings. "One *L*." Was it stupid to tell him? It was too late to take back the truth.

"Wil." The way he said my name now was different. Softer, more real, more . . . hopeful. "Please tell me that's short for something."

"Good-bye, Your Highness." I started up the mountain, leaving behind Tobiah and his light.

I WAS THERE *when the war began.*

I was seven, chased out of bed by thunder shaking the panes of glass in my window. When I went to find my parents, they weren't in their rooms.

Frightened, but not admitting it, I hurried, barefoot, to Father's study, where light spilled from the crack below the door and a pair of red-jacketed soldiers stood on guard duty.

Mother's high, angry voice pushed through the corridor. "Do you really want to throw the kingdom into war?"

"War is inevitable after what General Lien has done."

"Not if we get rid of him and return—"

"Regardless, I'm not signing the Wraith Alliance. Magic might not be the answer, but it should be considered as an option." Only thunder rivaled the boom of Father's voice.

They were fighting. Which meant I wanted to be somewhere else. Anywhere else.

I sneaked back the way I'd come so the guards wouldn't notice me.

Maybe I'd find Melanie. She wouldn't mind if I woke her up, and we could easily sneak past her parents.

As I walked by a study door, someone groaned. I halted, listened until the sound came again, and peeked inside. Only a low fire lit the long room; a curtained window loomed at the far end.

I shivered. This was General Lien's office. I did not

want to run into him, especially in the middle of the night. But . . . it didn't look like he was inside. And if someone was hurt, I had to help.

I'd help before the general came back and caught me.

Quickly, I checked the hall. No guards. There was hardly anybody around. Sandcliff Castle was so empty tonight.

Thunder cracked again and I slipped into the room, shutting the door after me.

Another moan came from a chair close to the fire.

"Who's there?"

When only frantic humming answered, I considered going out to find a guard. But then I saw him.

The person on the chair was just a boy, his nightclothes rumpled and dirt stained. A piece of cloth filled his mouth, and his hands and feet were tied with ropes.

I rushed forward and tugged at the gag. "Who are you? Who did this?" Maybe he was visiting from Northland with his family. The duke had a son about my age. Or maybe he was a merchant's son, and some of the castle boys were playing a prank on him, like they used to do to Patrick Lien because of his bruises. Before he learned how to fight back.

The gag came loose and the boy scrunched his face, like he could push the bad taste from his mouth. "I'm Tobiah Pierce, House of the Dragon, Crown Prince of the Indigo Kingdom."

An unladylike snort escaped me as I tried to pry loose the knots in the rope, but the rope was too prickly and hurt my fingers. "Sure."

"I'm not lying. Who are you?"

"Wilhelmina Korte, Princess of Aecor. And I'm not lying." I showed him the signet ring Father had given me. It was an exact copy of his, only smaller. "Hold still." The knots were too tight and the rope too rough. I darted over to the desk to look for shears or a letter opener. Anything sharp.

Papers, pens, wax for sealing letters: there was nothing useful on the desk.

"If you're the princess, why are you freeing me?" asked the boy who couldn't be Tobiah Pierce. "After all, your father had me kidnapped."

"He would never!" I marched back to the boy and crossed my arms. "Take it back. He would never kidnap anyone, not even Prince Tobiah. My father is a good man. Besides, if he had kidnapped you, I wouldn't be freeing you." It was a trick, like the time Melanie and some of the others had hidden inside my wardrobe one night, tapping on the wood and groaning like they were ghosts.

"If you say so." The boy glanced at my empty hands. "Didn't find anything to cut the rope with?"

"No, but it's not a problem. This counts as an emergency." I touched the rope. "Wake up. Straighten out. Carefully." If the prickly bits hurt my fingers, they must have chafed his skin fiercely.

At my command, the ropes shivered to life and slithered so the knots loosened around not-Tobiah's wrists and ankles. He gasped and shoved the ropes off him as the lengths moved on their own. "Was that magic? You can't use that. It's illegal."

I frowned at the bruises around his wrists and the raw skin where the rope had cut. "Magic isn't illegal. You just have to be careful to use it for emergencies only. Don't you think getting the ropes off you was an emergency?" Whoever tied him up was going to be in big trouble. There were a few boys who might have thought binding a visitor was funny, but I didn't like bullies. This—this awfulness would be punished.

The boy jumped off the chair and over the ropes as the loops and knots vanished. It was doing as I'd instructed: straightening out.

I knelt and touched the rope. "Go back to sleep." And then it was dead again, just a scratchy length of fibers.

"You're an animator?" he breathed. "That's incredible."

Not really. My mom was an animator, too. Anyway, I hardly ever got to use my power. Not that I'd tell him that.

"Who are you really? I guess I've got to take you somewhere." No need to get a soldier. If we involved grown-ups, the teasing and pranks would just get worse for him; I'd seen that much when Patrick Lien tried to tell his father about the tricks. General Lien's response had been cruel, and the other boys getting back at him . . .

I'd have to deal with this myself. And fast, before the general returned.

"I'm Tobiah Pierce, and your father's men really did kidnap me. My father's men won't be far behind." Thunder shook again, and he glanced at the chair and gag and ropes. "The Indigo Army was following your people. They might be here already, coming to get me."

"Right." He needed to stop blaming my father or I'd tie him up.

He glanced at the door I'd entered by. "Didn't you see the guards? There were two earlier."

I shook my head. If there ever were guards, which I doubted, they'd taken a break. Tobiah—or whoever he was—had been all tied up, unlikely to escape on his own. "Well, come on. We can't stay here. This is General Lien's study and he doesn't like people poking around."

The boy's voice went low. "I know all about General Lien."

Voices in the hall startled us, making me jump and press my palms to my mouth. The boy's eyes grew wide.

"We can use him to stop the fighting," a man said.

"Not yet." General Lien's harsh voice stilled me. He'd never hit me—I was the princess—but I'd seen enough of Patrick's bruises to know I needed to protect this boy. "His Majesty wants the Wraith Alliance pressure stopped, and this will ensure we are taken seriously in the future."

"His Majesty never approved this—"

"Stuff it." General Lien made a noise like a growl. "Move the boy to a more secure location."

I gasped and glanced at maybe-Tobiah. General Lien wanted to move him? Where? And why? I couldn't believe this was really the Crown Prince of the Indigo Kingdom—my father would never have an eight-year-old boy kidnapped—but neither could I deny that something bad was about to happen.

Unless I took action.

I raced for the window and fumbled with the latch. "If you really are Tobiah, I shouldn't help you." I swung the windows wide open. "But I don't want General Lien to find you, no matter who you are. If you are Tobiah, then I'll figure out what to do when he's gone."

"What are you doing?"

"There's a ledge. We'll hide outside."

Tobiah offered a hand to boost me up just as the study door creaked open.

Behind the heavy curtain, we scrambled onto the ledge, me first, then Tobiah, and he shut the window behind him.

Cold air whipped around us, stinging my hands and face as I sidled along the ledge, Tobiah next to me. The air smelled sharp, acrid. We were high up, high enough to make the city look like a toy. But tonight, everything was different.

Everything was chaos.

Fires burned in every district of Aecor City. People fought in the streets. Screams floated upward. Huge wood-and-metal machines trundled up the main road to Sandcliff Castle, bearing torch-carrying men. They were going to get into the castle. They were going to set fire here, too.

Horror tangled up inside me, pulled tight into a knot. "No. This isn't real."

Arrows rained from slits in the castle walls, falling on the tower men. Bodies fell, torches dropping with them, and then there was nothing left of them but their mangled corpses far below.

My stomach flipped. I was going to be sick. I'd give

anything to be in my room, sleeping. My parents and their guards would come looking for me soon. What would they think when they found my bed empty?

"Are these people here for you?" I said, but wind snatched away my words. My eyes watered with the reek of smoke and disgust at what my father had done. "You really are Crown Prince Tobiah."

"You won't turn me in, will you?" His expression was twisted with fear and sadness.

It was hard to tell from our ledge, but I didn't think it was my people we had to worry about. His were burning up the city. A wheeled tower filled with people banged against the stone wall of the palace, and men jumped onto balconies and through windows. Were my parents safe? What about Melanie and my other friends?

"Wilhelmina?"

I met Tobiah's eyes and tried to ignore our great height, the stink of fires, and the cold in my toes. "No. No matter what our fathers are fighting about, General Lien never should have taken you." Kings and queens were supposed to be good and fair. They always were in stories.

I shivered as thunder crashed again. But it wasn't thunder. It was buildings exploding in the city.

It hadn't been thunder that had awakened me.

Tobiah took my hand, his fingers warm around mine. "If my side wins and they ask who you are, don't tell them your name. Lie. You don't want to be the Princess of Aecor when they're coming to retrieve the Crown Prince of the Indigo Kingdom."

He was right. I didn't want to be me.

I squeezed his hand and watched as my world burned down and men in indigo slaughtered men in red. When the Indigo Army found us on the ledge, they put me in a group with other castle children. I told them my name was Mina and Tobiah told them I'd saved his life.

I was spared. My parents were not. My kingdom was not.

I was there when the war began.

And when it ended.

THIRTY-TWO

MY BODY ACHED as I approached the gloomy old castle. The bag strap dug into my shoulder, all my belongings weighing me down. Clouds covered the sky, leaving the world in heavy, palpable blackness. The wraithy wind that blew in from the west bore breaths of freezing and destruction.

I had to hurry.

I whistled the four-note signal as I walked through the outer curtain, a hulking, mossy shadow in the darkness. While I waited for someone to disarm the traps around the state apartments door, I knelt and groped through my bag. Black Knife hadn't lied when he'd said he found all my things. There was the shape of my notebook, my grappling hook and line, my daggers, and several other weapons. Even my stolen sword.

"You're a pretty poor vigilante these days, Black Knife," I muttered as I hooked my weapons to my belt and slipped my other supplies—lockpicks, matches, a coil of silver wire—into my pocket. "Though I suppose you probably paid for my sword."

For a whole three heartbeats, I entertained the image of an ink-cloaked boy approaching a terrified blacksmith, flinging money at the counter. But I remembered our inevitable war, Lady Meredith, and magic: things that would always come between us.

"Wil?" Melanie's voice came from the doorway. Candlelight flickered as she shoved the stick at someone else, and boots thudded on the ground. Her arms wrapped around me, squeezing tight. "Wil, you're safe."

All my aches forgotten, I hugged her back and breathed in the familiar scent of my best friend. "I was so worried about you."

"You too." She squeezed and stepped back, holding me at arm's length. "What happened? I got out of the palace, but couldn't get back in without being spotted. There were *so* many guards. I waited around for a while, until I heard they caught Black Knife—a girl—and that she'd killed the king, and she only got caught because she went back to kill the prince, too."

Who made up these rumors?

"I'll tell you everything later. But first, there's something I have to say to everyone. Are the Ospreys all here?"

"Yes." She grabbed my bag and leaned into me again, voice low. "It was Patrick. You were right."

My stomach tumbled, and I wished I didn't know Black Knife's identity. Then I wouldn't have cared as much that Patrick had killed Tobiah's father. Though I had no love for King Terrell, my feelings toward his son were . . . immeasurably different. Immeasurably complicated.

I dragged my gloved fingertips over my daggers as Melanie led me to the state apartments door. Connor waited there, wide-eyed and pale.

"Wil!" He thrust the candle to one side and hugged me with his free arm. "I was so worried. You stopped writing to me."

"I know. I'm sorry." Pretending I didn't hear his hiccup and sniff, I smoothed back his hair and whispered, "I missed you, too. Have you been strong?"

He gave a stiff nod. "Even when I thought I couldn't be, I made myself strong. Looking at your old notes helped."

"Good." I kissed the top of his head, too exhausted and relieved to hold back affection. "I'm proud of you."

On the way into the common room, I met several other Ospreys. I traded embraces with Theresa, Oscar, Ronald, Carl, Kevin, and Paige, and finally, as I entered the common room, lit with a roaring fire and candles all around, I found Patrick staring out the window, his hands clasped behind his back.

"Welcome, Wilhelmina." He didn't turn around. The fire threw splinters of light and shadow across his back and the short crop of his hair. The set of his shoulders said he was displeased, and again I wondered if a dead queen was easier to fight for than a defiant one. Was he disappointed I'd been set free?

"You assassinated Terrell."

Patrick turned his head, giving a view of his sharp profile. Light flared, casting his eyes deeper into shadow. "He deserved to die."

"We're not murderers, Patrick."

He said nothing.

"Was this your plan all along?"

Patrick turned and strode around the table. Behind me, the Ospreys scattered into groups of two and three, closer to the hot fire or to the opposite side of the room. "Your mission was more than you knew, Wilhelmina. Yes, I wanted the soldiers freed, the locations and information, and a map of the palace, but anyone could have gotten those. Why do you think I sent *you* to the palace when I could have sent Oscar or Ronald as soldiers or lords and accomplished everything you did *without* that detour into the wraithland?"

Behind me, Theresa gasped and whispered, "She went to the wraithland?"

"Hush, Rees," muttered Melanie.

Patrick wasn't finished. "Sending you was always a risk. You're going to be our *queen*. If they'd discovered your identity, everything would have been for nothing. But I sent you because *you* deserved to take revenge for what he did to our families."

He said it as though he'd tried to do me a *favor* by asking me to kill someone.

"You intended to assassinate King Terrell all this time," I whispered.

"I intended for you to do it, but when you betrayed the Ospreys that night in the Peacock Inn—"

"You *killed* someone, Patrick." My heart pounded in my ears, deafening, and my fists ached at my sides. "You went behind my back to kill someone because you knew I didn't approve. You hid the truth because you knew it was wrong."

"You should be happy." He made his voice a growl. "Terrell was responsible for the fall of Aecor, and now the Indigo Kingdom will be in chaos while the throne changes hands.

This is the perfect time for us to reclaim Aecor. The Indigo Kingdom is in ruins: one ruler murdered in his sleep, and now a city on the verge of collapse. I've seen the refugees fleeing. They say a wraith beast is coming, that it's shouting *your* name."

I couldn't breathe.

"How did that happen, Wil?"

As if I would ever tell him anything again.

"Regardless, we can use this to our advantage. Imagine what they'll say now." Patrick advanced, his glare unwavering. "Even the wraith knows of Wilhelmina Korte's right to the throne. Even the wraith wants the Indigo Kingdom punished for what they did to her." He drew a deep and steadying breath. "Wilhelmina, your army is waiting for you."

Wind tore at the castle; somewhere above, a loose board creaked and banged.

"We'll leave Skyvale tonight," said Patrick. "All of us. We'll return to Aecor and gather our army. We'll strike the Indigo Kingdom when they're most vulnerable."

I relaxed my hands at my sides, let the tension fall from my shoulders as I strode across the room toward the dark windows.

"For almost ten years, the only thing I've wanted was Aecor. Patrick"—I turned to find him watching me, confidence shining in his eyes—"you made me believe that Aecor would be returned to us one day. You inspired me to work hard, to become something no queen has been before: a warrior. And for all these years, I thought I'd be willing to do anything to take back my kingdom."

The eight other Ospreys around the room shifted, looking between Patrick and me with wide, round eyes. I couldn't remember ever fighting with Patrick in front of them—at least not before the night in the Peacock Inn when he told me Quinn and Ezra had died. Only Theresa, Connor, and Melanie had been present then. Now, all that remained of the Ospreys watched.

I addressed all of them, too. "Recent events have opened my eyes. I've become aware of lines I will not cross, not even to take the vermilion throne." I drew a shaky breath and pulled myself straighter. "I will not murder. I will not sacrifice my own people for a mission. I will not *use* people and let them suffer the consequences of something I did; I will take responsibility for my own actions."

Patrick stepped forward. "Wilhelmina—"

I lifted a hand, cutting him off. "Patrick Lien, you have given us years of service. You rescued us from the orphanage. You found food and shelter for us. You trained us. But your methods can't be ours. You lead rebellions, not kingdoms. Leadership of the Ospreys must shift."

Rustling and whispers sounded around the others, but Patrick just stared at me without expression. "What do you propose?"

"From now on, the Ospreys do things differently. When we take action, it will be to help people, not hurt them."

"How will you take back your kingdom like that?" he asked. "War is inevitable. War has casualties."

I swept past him to where my bag waited in the doorway. "If we Ospreys are to be good leaders of a resurrected Aecor, we must reclaim the kingdom in a way that doesn't involve war or casualties."

"And I suppose you're just going to ask for the kingdom?"

Patrick shook his head. "Don't be naive. They will never hand it over to you."

No, they wouldn't just *hand* it to me. I'd have to work for it. Earn it. "I'll sign the Wraith Alliance."

"And ban magic in Aecor?" Connor asked, his voice tiny.

I touched his shoulder. "Magic is already banned in Aecor. It has been for almost ten years." Thunder rolled in the west, rattling the windows in their frames. "I know my parents wouldn't sign it, but it makes no difference to me anymore. I've been to the wraithland. I've seen firsthand what kind of danger it poses, not just to the Indigo Kingdom, but to us. Unless the wraith is stopped, the Indigo Kingdom won't be here to shield us from it forever."

Patrick shook his head. "If you think you can peacefully take back Aecor, you're delusional. It's not going to happen. People there have lived under the tyranny of a false king and overlord for a decade. Our men have been sent to the wraithland to fight battles not theirs. But this battle *is* theirs: they want to fight for you."

"They won't have to." I lifted my chin and addressed the Ospreys. "Come with me. I'll take you somewhere safe while I negotiate for our kingdom."

"There's a monster down there," said Paige. "It'll be in Skyvale soon, if it's not already. We could just let the city burn."

I closed my eyes, remembering the drawings on walls and fences: charcoal-colored knives with messages written beneath them, begging for help, or gratitude for a life. I remembered the refugees outside the city, pleading to be saved from the beast that must have followed me here.

I remembered the fiddler I'd rescued, the neighborhood I'd protected by killing the wraith cat, and the nights spent wearing Black Knife's mask as the two of us helped everyone we could find. I remembered how *right* it felt to help them, to give them hope.

"No," I said. "We can't just let the city burn. There are good people there, and they don't deserve to die simply because they aren't *our* people."

"We can't stop a monster, though." Melanie glanced from me to Patrick, and back. "We shouldn't have to."

No, the Ospreys shouldn't have to, but I did. I'd have to face what I created—and soon. "I don't expect you to stop it. I expect you to get to safety and help others there, as well. Skyvale has two armies and a police force, and tonight, they'll have me. I've been to the wraithland. I've killed wraith beasts before. I can help with this one."

"This one is screaming for you," Melanie said. "It'll kill you."

"Maybe. That's a chance I'm willing to take, in order to enter peaceful negotiations to reclaim Aecor."

"I can't allow you to do this." Patrick narrowed his eyes; the scar over his eyebrow stood out white in the flickering light.

I turned my still-bruised cheek toward him. "Will you hit me again to stop me?"

Patrick flinched. It was small, only for a moment, but the other Ospreys saw it, and they gasped. Connor and Theresa edged toward me.

"You're my princess," Patrick said. "My future queen. No matter what you do, I will never again strike you."

"Will you follow me tonight?" I forced myself to breathe evenly, to not show the way my heart pounded and my head spun with terror. I was challenging Patrick. Asking him to bow to me for once.

"Not tonight," he said. "Not when I know you're wrong."

"I'll follow you." Connor's voice was small, frightened, but he stood at my side with his chin high.

"So will I." Theresa closed the distance between us, and a moment later, Carl and Kevin joined them. The Ospreys were voting.

Oscar, Ronald, and Paige crossed the room to stand by Patrick, leaving Melanie in the middle, pale and still.

"What will you do, Melanie?" I kept my voice soft, and our eyes met for a heartbeat. "Whatever you feel is right."

Melanie gave a slight nod. "Thanks." And with hesitating steps, she walked toward Patrick.

"Mel," I breathed, shivering against the chill of all the blood draining from my face.

"Sorry." She took Patrick's hand and kept my eyes. "I just think he's right. There's no peaceful way for you to get your throne back. I know you're going to try, and they'll protect you when you need it." She nodded at Connor, Theresa, Carl, and Kevin. "And while you try it your way, we'll build your army."

Tension snapped between the ten of us, the Ospreys split down the middle.

"I can't believe this is happening," Theresa whispered.

I touched her hand. "It's all right." I cleared my throat and spoke louder. "It's all right. Be safe on your way to Aecor. Put a cushion on the vermilion throne for me."

Patrick's eyes were steel on mine, a sword or knife or thunder-cloud sky. "Until we meet again, my princess."

With that, I gathered my half of the Ospreys, and hurried them out the door.

THIRTY-THREE

I RUSHED MY Ospreys through the old palace, into their rooms to grab their jump bags—packs filled with a change of clothes and all their most important possessions: notebooks, childhood toys, or miniatures of their parents.

There was only one thing I needed to find: a signet ring, far too small for my finger now. My father had given it to me on my seventh birthday, after I'd made a few too many attempts to take his much larger one. I'd been wearing it when I'd awakened that night, and since then I'd kept it on a chain, hidden among my most personal belongings.

I squeezed the small ring in my hand, the ridges sharp even through my leather gloves, and then looped the chain over my head. The ring thumped on my breastbone. "Let's go!" I called.

Rain misted across the bailey as we lit candles and tucked them inside rusted old lanterns. As quickly as we dared in the dark, in the storm, we hurried down the mountain and raced toward Skyvale below.

On a ridge overlooking the city, I halted, breath steaming in the cold air. The other four stopped at my sides. Hands fell into mine as they gasped. Theresa let out a sob.

Flames lit the western sky, all red and orange and gold as they reached toward the swirling clouds. Sparks scattered like stars. The forest was burning, whipped into a blaze under the shrieking wind. Heat billowed over the valley, brushing the mountainside, bringing with it the stink of smoke and wraith, a miasma that coiled up the back of my nose and made my head spin. Even from here, I could hear the roar of the fire, and the screams that wouldn't be drowned out.

Every streetlamp glowed in the city below, as though it, too, had been set alight. Though the mirrors of Skyvale faced away from us, the glow of the fire's reflected light shone all around them like a halo. Streams of people flowed from the city gates, pouring into the refugee camps and toward the mountains.

"What's happening?" Connor shielded his face with his forearm.

"They're fleeing." I urged the Ospreys onward. "I need to hurry. You four don't have to go with me. You can help people to safety in the woods. Try to organize them and find others who can help you. I'll find you after it's over."

"After *what's* over?" asked Kevin. "Are you going to fight the wraith beast?"

I glanced at the lit city, the palace, the clock tower, the darker patches of the Flags and Greenstone. "I'm going to find it, any-way. It's calling my name. I'm the only one who needs to go."

"I don't want to leave you," said Connor. "What if you get hurt?"

I squeezed his shoulder. "It's all right. Help people. I'll find you at one of our usual spots in the city. You know them, Rees?"

Theresa nodded. Smoke, or something else, made tears glimmer in her eyes. "Be safe."

I hugged each of my friends and left my bag with them; I wore my weapons on my hips, my notebook in my pocket, and my ring around my neck. Black Knife's mask waited in a belt loop.

Gravity pulled me down the mountain. I ran as fast as I could until I hit the first wave of refugees—they were all refugees now—and stopped to point them toward where I'd left my Ospreys.

"There are people who can help you find shelter." I had to shout over the wind and rain and roar of fire devouring the forest beyond the city. How long would this side be safe? Even the driving rain wasn't dousing the fire with the wind stirring everything so thoroughly.

Wet and shivering, the refugees thanked me and pulled one another farther up the ancient road.

I ran, pausing to urge people onward, promise them hope waited just above.

The minutes stretched longer. My flight down the mountain seemed to take twice as long as the hike up, but every time I spurred myself faster, my feet caught roots and tangles of brush, as though the mountain conspired to keep me up here.

"Wilhelmina!" The unearthly voice boomed from somewhere below, louder than thunder. *"Wilhelmina Korte!"*

The sound of the wraith screaming my name made me

shudder, but I didn't stop. I didn't slow. I didn't let anything break my stride until I finally reached the base of the mountain where a thick mass of people pushed and shoved their way into the forest.

Babies and children wailed as their parents pulled them along, urging them not to look up or behind, or anywhere but the road straight ahead. People carried baskets and bags of clothes and supplies. Others attempted to herd horses and cows with little success. Screams and sobbing blended into the terrible cacophony of Skyvale falling apart.

"Stay on the road!" I cupped my hands around my mouth as I moved along the edge of the crowd. "There's help on the mountain. There's shelter. But stay on the road."

My shouts were hardly worth it. No one listened. People pushed and shoved, trampling one another to reach the safety of the mountains. What could I do? I had to get into the city, but this exodus was on the verge of becoming a riot. But who was I? No one to them.

Unless I was Black Knife.

I pulled his mask over my head, immediately enveloped in the soft musky scent of boy. With my sword out, I stepped into a shard of light.

Someone pointed. "It's Black Knife!"

Immediately, people began to crowd me, reach for me, and touch me as they had before, but I shouted for them to back up and brandished my sword.

"You, you, and you." I pointed to a handful of people who looked my age. "Gather everyone you know and get this crowd under control. Get people back on their feet. And you four"—I nodded at a clutch of children, maybe Connor's age—"tell everyone that Black Knife is promising safety in the mountain, but they must stop fighting one another. No one dies tonight."

The children and teenagers ran off, and I moved down the mob of people, giving others the same instructions. I couldn't tell whether the crowd was calming, and I couldn't hear much over the din of voices and fire and roaring thunder, but I hoped with everything inside me that the people I'd recruited to help would be successful.

At last I reached the city wall. The gate was blocked, too many people trying to escape, so I hurled my grappling hook over the parapets and climbed up.

"*Wilhelmina!*" The deep voice came from everywhere, rumbling through my head until it pulsed behind my eyes.

I gasped as I grabbed hold of the stone parapet, hooked a leg over, and finally rolled onto the walkway.

There was no time to catch my breath. I scrambled to my feet and looped my climbing line, and once it was secure, I began to run along the edge of the city. Guard tower doors hung open, leaving my path unblocked.

My sword in one hand, a stolen torch in the other, I rounded the easternmost district, sparing only glances for the chaos that waited inside.

Red Flag burned, homes and shops and inns. Wraith wolves and bears lumbered through the streets, fighting, chasing people as they ran toward the city gates. People cried out for help, splashing through blood in the streets. A wraith cat yowled and pounced on a fleeing man, who threw his young son out before him. The boy tumbled to the ground, froze, and reached for his father, already half disappeared into the beast's jaws.

I hesitated, struggling to decide whether to leap down and help, but this was far from the only horror happening in the city. Somewhere, my wraith creature screamed for me.

Trumpets stole the decision. Indigo-coated men raced into the street, brandishing swords and crossbows and torches. They fell on the wraith beasts without mercy, slicing and stabbing the howling creatures. A few men hurried to pull the boy away from his father's corpse.

I continued onward, uncertain where I was going. Somewhere high. Somewhere I could defend myself.

Rain poured down my face and neck, making the mask stick to my skin. I pushed myself faster through the wet night, coughing against the smoke and stink of wraith.

"*Wilhelmina Korte!*" The voice came from deeper within the city, and I pursued it through the drowning city of mirrors. Glass gleamed and glowed with the blaze to the west, illuminating the city as surely as sunlight. My heart was thunder in my ears, matched by the beat of my boots on the stone ramparts. My sword weighed me down, bouncing on my thigh, but I didn't throw it off; I might still need it.

Who knew what waited for me down there?

I kept running.

More gruesome scenes played within neighborhoods below, people fleeing the prowling wraith beasts. Glowmen ran rampant through the city, urging the beasts onward. Several buildings were gutted, hollowed out by *something* rampaging through them. Stone and wood and bricks littered the cracked streets. Here and there, it looked as though the pieces crept toward one another, as though to reassemble; but that might have been the mist and rain playing tricks on my eyes.

"*Wilhelmina!*" The keening that followed pierced the noise of fire and screams and rain. Pitched higher and higher, the voice shrieked and rang in my ears.

From Hawksbill out, every mirror in the city shattered. Glass blew from windows and frames and walls, and rained into Skyvale in gold-glittering shards.

I threw my torch in front of me and collapsed into a ball on the walkway, covering the back of my neck with my linked hands. Sparks of pain flew across my back and hands and head, coming from the mirror I'd been standing next to. I squeezed my eyes tightly shut, clenching my jaw against the fire of glass slicing open my skin. My gloves and clothes took the worst of it, though; I was lucky.

Moments of deafening silence chased the ear-numbing scream. The clatter of glass hitting the ground was faint, far-away.

My skin felt on fire as I grabbed my torch and sat up. The flame wavered in the rain, but didn't die.

All around me was a shining field of glass shards, bright in the firelight. The blaze in the west blew closer, billowing heat and sparks.

Aching, I climbed back to my feet and ran through the glass, which crunched under my boots, making me slip where slivers lodged into the soles. A few times, I had to stop and pry out pieces that sliced through, scraping my feet. My fingers throbbed from the pressure it took to remove the glass.

Finally, I found a good place to leave the city wall. A wash line had been stretched from a cheap housing building to the wall—illegal, but not enough of a problem anyone cared to do anything about. I tested the line's strength—it would hold—and held my sheathed sword above my head, over the line. I abandoned my torch and zipped downward, onto the eastern side of a building.

I sprinted toward Hawksbill, gasping at the reek of fire and smoke and wraith. The odor only grew stronger as I leapt from rooftop to rooftop through Thornton. Everywhere in the streets, I saw bloodied people carrying one another to safety. The Indigo Army was spread thin, but there were always at least two indigo-coated men in sight. Though many of those men now lay dead in the streets.

The Hawksbill wall stretched before me, lamps still burning even with the windshields blown out. I took my usual route onto the wall, wincing when glass cut through my gloves and trouser knees as I reached the top.

I couldn't see much farther than the mansions nearest the wall, thanks to smoke and mist, but I had enough visibility to tell that the rich district had been devastated. Blackened gardens, shattered glass, toppled statues: that was only the beginning. Nothing was how I'd left it just hours ago.

"*Wilhelmina!*" It came from so close now. Hot wind cut through the rain, and I couldn't help but imagine it was the beast's breath on my cheek.

"I'm coming!" The words ripped from my throat before I could consider the wisdom. But maybe if it knew I was here, it would stop this destruction.

Wind tore at my mask and pushed between my fingers; if I

lifted up my arms, I might be able to fly.

Tendrils of heavy, white mist wove around the cracked columns and statues of a nearby mansion, and the screaming became a whisper. My name fell into the cracks of other sounds: between the splashes of a fountain, the crackles of the fire, and the gasps of my breath.

"Wilhelmina. Wilhelmina. Wilhelmina."

The whole world was calling my name.

No, not the whole world—just the wraith I'd brought to life.

All this mist was here from the wraithland, and it was *alive*. Sentient. I hadn't created a beast, but *living wraith*. It stank, sharp and acrid and toxic, and even as I watched, the stone statues twitched and began to move, while rose beds—those that hadn't yet burned—began to petrify.

Wraith was everywhere in this city, and it had come to find me.

I stretched out my hands to encompass the whole area, just as I had in the wraithland. *"Go back to sleep."*

"No." The world spiraled into a thousand voices. *"Please. We'll die."*

It was going to *argue* with me?

But even as I was about to give the order again, feathers of mist began to break off and sink to the ground, lifeless but still toxic.

No—no, this was a bad plan.

"Stop!" I shouted. *"Wake up! Stay awake."*

The air shimmered and thunder struck, and life crackled down the tendrils of wraith.

"Become solid!"

The odor of wraith seared my nose so that my eyes watered and I couldn't see straight, but when I wiped at my eyes, the white mist was coalescing in the street. Heavy, pained groaning came from the wraith as wisps of mist flew at it from all over the city.

"*Wilhelmina.*" Its voice grew less wild, more contained as the wraith amalgamated into a single, solid mass.

Head spinning, I hooked my grappling hook onto the wall and began descending to the street. If this corporeal thing was just as destructive as the incorporeal, I needed to be ready to command it—or fight it.

Powdered glass crunched under my boots when I landed and took a few tentative strides toward the swirling mist. My hand stayed on my sword. My glare stayed on the wraith. Distant were the sounds of flames and screams and thunder; my focus tunneled on the pitiful cries the wraith made, the desperate way it said my name as though I'd save it from this torture.

The last of the mist sucked into the new form, and I gasped.

It was a boy.

A corporeal, wraith-white boy who shivered in the rain and wind. His wiry body was hairless, unclothed, and when he looked up, his eyes were wide and round and as blue as the midday sea.

He climbed to his feet and turned a complete circle, inspecting the demolished area. Shattered fountains. Statues in a terrifying state of almost-movement. "Where is Wilhelmina Korte?" Glass dug at his bare feet, but he didn't seem to notice. "I must find Wilhelmina Korte."

I ripped off my mask and drew my sword. "I am Wilhelmina Korte."

The wraith boy stared for a heartbeat, then dropped to one knee. His body folded like a sheet of paper. "My queen."

I squeezed the hilt of my sword and took a step toward the boy. He was real. Alive. A *person*. Wind tugged at the mask in my left hand, a small black banner. "You're what saved me in the wraithland," I said.

The boy looked up and met my eyes. His body didn't move, though. His shoulders stayed curled toward the ground, so the way he lifted his face made it look as though his neck were broken. "You commanded me, Queen Wilhelmina. You commanded me, and I will do anything you desire."

Cold spiraled through me, freezing every sliver of awe I'd held only a moment ago. He wasn't a person. What had I made?

"But there will be consequences." His teeth shone when he smiled wickedly. "There are always consequences."

"What are you?"

"Yours to command, Queen Wilhelmina Korte."

A quiet gasp alerted me of an audience. Lights in the windows of the surrounding mansions brightened and dimmed as people pressed to see us, staring down at the wraith boy and me. They'd seen what I'd done. Who I was.

"Wil?" The voice made my heart pound. "Wilhelmina?"

I turned to find Crown Prince Tobiah in an Indigo Order uniform, James at his side, and an army at their backs. My name rippled down the ranks.

"The lost Princess of Aecor is Black Knife," someone said. "Wilhelmina Korte."

"Wil?" Tobiah stepped forward.

At once, the wraith boy was on his feet. His fingers elongated, his spine lengthened, and he lunged for Tobiah with uncannily strong, fast legs.

"No!" I took off at a run, several paces behind. "Stop!"

Tobiah and James whipped their swords up to guard, and the men at their back echoed the motion, but it wasn't necessary.

At my cry, the wraith boy halted and spun to face me, his body back to normal proportions.

The prince's army wasn't so easily stopped, though. Dozens of men rushed toward the wraith boy, their boots stomping the street like drums. They were going to kill him.

I threw myself in front of the boy, my arms out wide, my sword pointed at the ground. "Don't!"

In the space of a breath, Tobiah's expression shifted from confusion to fear, and he stepped in front of me, his sword lifted to defend me. James hurried to protect Tobiah.

The army stopped; the men wouldn't lift their swords against their prince. Ragged breathing filled the air.

"Killing him will only release the wraith again."

Only as I spoke did I realize the wind had died and the thunder had faded. Steady rain thrummed down on the city, and on the fire in the west. The blaze was slowly retreating. Even the screams in other parts of the city had fallen silent, as though all the wraith from those beasts had been sucked into this boy.

What were they now? Confused deer in the streets? Panicked kittens? Or were the beasts all dead?

Tobiah moved first. "Stand down. Lower your swords. No one will harm Princess Wilhelmina." If anyone else noticed the way his voice trembled over my name, they didn't show it.

"How do we know she's Princess Wilhelmina?" one of the soldiers asked.

I pulled the signet ring from around my neck and handed it to Tobiah.

He held the ring up to the light, inspecting the engravings in the metal. "Two ospreys in flight. The Korte crest." He offered the ring back to me. "She is who she claims to be."

"She might have stolen it," muttered a soldier I half recognized. "It wouldn't be the first time."

"No." Tobiah's throat jumped when he swallowed, and he turned to face me. Our eyes met, memories filling the space between us. "This is Princess Wilhelmina of Aecor. I remember her from the night she saved my life." His voice softened. "Wil. Of course."

"And this . . . creature?" asked one of the men. "What is it?"

I stepped aside to regard the wraith boy. He stood there, looking mild and awaiting instructions.

I could almost see the consequences of his creation buzzing around him like gnats. The way he smiled sent shivers through me, but I held myself tall. Of all people—and things—he seemed the most dangerous to reveal fear to. That he was mine to command meant nothing; he was dangerous.

Tobiah shrugged off his coat and shoved it at the boy. "Put this on."

The boy glanced at me, and accepted the coat only when I nodded. He was *naked*. Heat rushed up my throat and cheeks.

"It was wraith before," said James. "I saw it change."

I tried to smooth the shaking out of my voice, but shivers

wouldn't quite let me. "He's human now. He's still wraith, but he's human now, too."

"What do we do with him?" asked a guard.

I didn't know. Pressure pounded through my head; I didn't know what I'd done, how I'd made him, or why he followed me here. I didn't know anything, let alone what to do with him.

The wraith boy leaned close to me and whispered in my ear: "Come to the changing lands with me. Come back with me."

No, no, no. I shifted away from him.

"More important," said another man, "what do we do with a princess who just used magic?"

Everyone looked at Tobiah.

His voice perfectly even, Tobiah said, "I'm well aware of Her Highness's ability. She and I have been experimenting with magic to—" He staggered back as James shoved him aside.

The lieutenant's face crumpled with pain as he clutched his stomach, where a crossbow bolt protruded. Blood soaked his shirt and jacket.

"James!" I grabbed under his shoulders as he began to drop.

Men shouted, scanning the area. "There!" Someone pointed at a dark figure leaping off the Hawksbill wall, into Thornton. The silhouette was familiar and moved with mountain lion grace.

"Go!" Tobiah pointed toward the wall. "Find him."

A handful of guards raced toward the would-be assassin, while others jostled me aside to tend to James. Someone helped him lie down; another checked his back to see whether the bolt had gone all the way through. A few ran for the palace, bellowing for a physician.

I stepped back and turned to the wraith boy. "Find whoever shot James. Then bring them to me. Alive."

With a too-wide smile, the wraith boy dashed into the night, outpacing the soldiers within moments. I watched him as he leapt the wall without trouble, and then I dropped to my knees beside James.

Sweat streaked the lieutenant's face, and his breaths were harsh gasps. "Tobiah?"

"I'm here." The prince knelt next to me. "I'll make sure you get help."

"Your Highness," one of the guards said. "We need to get you indoors. The assassin could return."

Tobiah touched James's shoulder and stood. "Very well. I want Lieutenant Rayner taken to my guest quarters, once he's stabilized. And Princess Wilhelmina assigned new apartments. Make sure—"

"Your Highness!"

There was no more discussion. A guard took my elbow and hauled me after the prince and the guards dragging him.

I took one last look at James on the ground, but he hadn't moved.

THIRTY-FOUR

RAIN DROWNED THE fires in a matter of hours, leaving plumes of heavy smoke rising in the west for days after.

The city was in ruins, buildings gutted and forever *changed* by the presence of the wraith. Every glass mirror on the west-facing walls had shattered. Sweepers filled the streets as dawn broke, steadily removing the dangerous shards that glittered in the banners of gold sunlight.

Maybe mirrors weren't so useless after all, if the wraith had broken every single one in the city.

When paths opened in the streets, bodies were gathered, identified, and buried. Dead wraith beasts were burned. People returned to the city and began restoring their homes and shops, and searching for missing loved ones.

Restoration of Skyvale would be a long, slow process, especially with winter closing in. Even the food stores in Greenstone had been demolished. But the Indigo Army was called in to help, as well as men from all of the surrounding cities and towns, and they brought food and blankets and clean water. A more than fair compensation had been promised for their assistance.

I wasn't allowed out of my new apartments, and I was permitted no visitors. In the days following the battle, the only person I saw was a young maid who was terrified of me.

I was not a prisoner, but neither was I a guest.

I'd been writing in my notebook to calm my nerves, when a boy knocked and offered a card with a note written in unfamiliar handwriting.

> *Her Highness Princess Wilhelmina Korte,*
> *Please join me at James's bedside, located in the guest quarters of my suite. I require your assistance. Come at your quickest.*
> *In hopeful friendship,*
> *Tobiah Pierce*

What did that mean? Was James better? Worse? Dead?

I abandoned my open ink jars and left my pens on the desk, uncleaned. With only my notebook in hand, I hurried after the boy. My silver gown swished around my ankles, hampering my strides. But as visiting—or captive—royalty, and being lately identified as Black Knife, I wasn't permitted to sneak about in trousers and a belt full of daggers. I wasn't even given knives at mealtimes.

My new apartments were in the Dragon Wing, not far from Tobiah's quarters, as it turned out. They must have wanted to keep a *very* close eye on me, if I'd been placed in the most guarded area of the palace.

The young escort knocked on a door, and when I was given entrance, he vanished down the hall.

The crown prince's suite was expansive, with a parlor, a music room, and a private dining room. These were inhabited only by guards now, indigo-coated men with grim expressions and hard eyes they trained on me, as though I'd been the one to attempt to assassinate their prince. As though all this were my fault.

In a way it was.

Tobiah met me in the parlor. He wore his mourning suit, all gray, and dark circles hung under his eyes. "Your Highness." He offered a slight bow and motioned me toward a closed door. "Please join me."

I followed him. "How is James?"

"See for yourself." He turned on the gas lamp, even though light shone through the window.

My ridiculous dress swished as I approached the bed where James lay on his back, breathing regularly. His eyes were closed, as though he were sleeping. I looked up at Tobiah.

"His healing is miraculous." Tobiah offered a chair, but I shook my head. "The bolt hit his gut, but the wound is gone. No scar, even. None of the physicians can explain it."

I frowned. "Can *you* explain it?"

"How could I?" There he was—the prince I disliked so much. But immediately, Tobiah's countenance softened. He tilted his head and gazed at his friend. "I'm sorry. No, I can't explain it. I have suspicions, but I'd rather not say right now."

"I see. You said you needed my help."

"Yes." He took a long, steadying breath. "You have every reason to dislike me. I behaved as though I had no prior obligations, and I will never be able to make up for my indiscretion. Not to you, and not to Meredith. I am thoroughly embarrassed by my actions."

Our time in the breezeway was the last thing I wanted to discuss. "You said you needed my help," I repeated, colder.

He flinched, but nodded. "James hasn't . . . He's healed, but he hasn't awakened. I was hoping you might use your power of animation. I remember seeing you use it when we were children. You said, 'Wake up,' and the rope immediately came to life."

The room grew very quiet between us.

"You know I can't." My words came like chips of ice. "Even if my power brought true life, it would have no effect on a living man."

Tobiah closed his eyes.

"Second, you heard the wraith boy. There will be consequences for what I did to him—consequences I can't even imagine. Don't you think it would be even worse if I tried to use my power on James? He's already real. Alive."

"Wil—"

I held my fists at my sides, barely keeping hold of my notebook. "You've ignored me for days, trapping me in apartments that feel smaller every hour. You've permitted me no visitors. You didn't even come to me yourself and find out what I know. And when you do want to see me, it's for something you know I cannot do. Will not. I won't use my magic again."

Tobiah glanced down at my hands; they were shaking.

"Wil." His voice was soft, almost like Black Knife's. "What happened in the wraithland? Where did all that wraith come from? Why did it come for you?"

"*Now* you ask? It's been *days* since the battle, since we knew each other's identities. You could have asked me anytime."

"I did ask you before. As Black Knife."

I swallowed hard. "And that was why I didn't tell. I didn't want him to be disappointed in me."

He stepped closer. "What happened?" he whispered. "What do you know?"

Outside, the clock tower chimed nine.

"I'm sorry I didn't come to you." He moved back, giving me space to breathe. "I should have come to find out what you knew, and to update you on James's progress. I should have given you freedom of the palace and allowed you visitors. I should have realized I had effectively trapped you here, without access to your friends or anyone else.

"But I was caught up in everything I needed to do, because my father was just assassinated, and my city demolished by something I don't fully understand, and—" He dropped to the foot of James's bed, and all the breath whooshed out of him. "I suppose you know how that feels better than anyone."

"When my city burned, there was someone with me, holding my hand. I wasn't alone."

"And I made myself alone." Tobiah looked up at me. "Because I was embarrassed. Because I thought I had to be alone to think and plan. Because I thought no matter who was with me, I *was* alone. I wasn't thinking about you suffering, too. I'm sorry."

My hand twitched, as though I might touch him, comfort

him, but I caught myself and pressed my palm to my thigh. "I'll tell you what happened in the wraithland," I said. "But not for you. I'll tell you because I need to stop the wraith, and the only chance I have of accomplishing that is with your help and cooperation."

"I understand."

When I'd dragged a chair closer to the boys, I opened my notebook to the sketches and entries I'd made during my time in the wraithland. I indulged a moment of hesitation before I handed it to him. Voice dropped low, I told him how I'd slipped out of West Pass Watch and stolen down the mountainside. He turned the pages along with my story, never looking up.

"I collected several pieces of the barrier from beside Mirror Lake. I don't know if they will be useful, but I wanted to offer them to your committee for study."

"Thank you."

"Did you already know that Liadia had broken the Wraith Alliance by pouring magic into the barrier?"

He shook his head. "We heard the same rumors you investigated, but there was no proof beyond refugee claims. But with the pieces you brought back, it can be verified." He dropped his eyes to the notebook again and brushed his fingers over a drawing of the locust-covered village. "What happened here?"

My voice tightened as I described the blackening sky, the bugs falling to their death when they flew too close to the lake's reflection, and the pattering of their bodies all around me.

"The locusts were everywhere, smothering me. They were in my hair, my mouth, and even my nose. I couldn't get away, so I used my power."

Tobiah's fingers clenched around the notebook. This was why I hadn't told him, even as Black Knife. I didn't need to see the disappointment in his eyes; no one was more disappointed in my weakness than I.

Ignoring his reaction, I continued. "Usually, I have to touch things, so I reached out for the air. I told it to wake up and save me, but it wasn't the air that I awoke."

"It was the wraith." He stared at the sketch of the field of dead locusts, and the clear sky above.

"Yes." I rubbed chills off my arms. "It drained me to use so much magic. I passed out for at least a day, and when I woke up, it was gone. The whole area was clear of wraith, because the wraith I'd brought to life had left."

"But when you returned to the Indigo Kingdom, it followed you."

"It followed me through the mountains, but then the mirrors on West Pass Watch frightened it away. It must have found a different path later, since the castle is still standing."

"When you found it in Skyvale, why didn't you tell it to go back to sleep?"

"If I had, the wraith would have stayed here and corrupted the city. I thought by making it solid, I could take it back out to the wraithland. I didn't expect it to become human." No, not human. Too easily I could remember the wraith boy's body stretching, growing claws. Too easily I could imagine how quickly he'd have killed Tobiah before James or the other guards had been able to move at all. "Human shaped," I amended. "I don't know what he is, really. My power isn't supposed to work like that."

"What do you mean?"

"When I was young, before I understood, I animated my toys to play with me. I thought I was bringing them to life. But I wasn't. Not *life*. Rather, I gave them the ability to do what I wanted them to do."

"But not life. You say 'wake up,' but you don't really awaken it." He glanced at James, finally understanding why I couldn't help his cousin.

"What happened in the wraithland was different, and I don't know why. I don't know how. Just that I've created this *thing* and I don't know anything about it or what to do with it. I wish I hadn't." But giving life to the wraith boy—like this sudden and uncomfortable confession to Tobiah—was something I couldn't take back. It was done. And I would have to deal with the consequences.

The wraith boy wanted me to go to the wraithland with him. In the spaces between breaths, I could still hear his whisper in my ear: *Come to the changing lands with me. Come back with me.*

Tobiah closed my notebook, and his fingers stroked the worn leather cover as though it were a pet. "Do you think what you did mitigated the wraith's approach any?"

"I don't know."

"Could you do it again?"

"Possibly." Probably not. Just the once had nearly killed me; I'd never animated anything so large before, and giving *life* to something was completely new. "But I don't know if it would help. I don't know what the consequences would be."

He nodded and studied the front cover of my notebook, as

though deciding whether to open it and start from the beginning. What would he think, seeing the writing of a nine-year-old girl there? But he didn't open it. He handed it back to me, and seemed suddenly unsure what to do with his hands. No notebook, no weapons, no one safe to touch. "I may be able to modify the language of the Wraith Alliance to allow for experimentation. It would cover what you did in the wraithland and the other night."

"Would the other kingdoms sign it?"

"There aren't many left. They're as desperate as we are. They'd sign it."

We sat in awkward silence for a minute before I said, "I know who killed your father."

Tobiah jerked straight. "Who?"

"The same man I suspect tried to assassinate you."

"Who?" The prince flashed a desperate look at his unconscious cousin.

"Patrick Lien, the son of the general who kidnapped you." I rested my hands on my knees, forcing my voice even. "Patrick confessed that he assassinated your father, and that he intended to have you killed, too. The last time I saw him, he said he was heading to Aecor to amass an army. In my name. He'll claim you're holding me hostage."

Tobiah stared at me.

I slumped, exasperated. "Obviously, this isn't something I asked him to do."

"Then he's a traitor not only to the Indigo Kingdom, of which he is technically a citizen, but a traitor to the vermilion throne as well." Tobiah rubbed his temples. "The guards I sent after the shooter never found anyone. You've heard nothing of your wraith boy?"

I swallowed hard. "I don't know why he hasn't returned yet." There were too many options I didn't like: that the wraith boy didn't have to do my bidding, like I'd thought; that Patrick had been able to outrun the wraith boy; that the wraith boy had been captured. . . .

"Melanie is with Patrick. She'll get word to me before he does anything else." I hoped. I'd trusted her when she took that step toward Patrick but held my gaze, but I couldn't forget how passionately she'd felt about him before.

"I'll have my men begin searching for him. If I asked whether you know where he might be, would you tell me the truth?"

"I don't want anything bad to happen to my people. Not the Ospreys who went with him, or whoever might be sheltering him. If you can promise their safety—"

"My orders will be to spare them." Tobiah met my eyes. "I cannot promise more than that."

It was better than I'd expected. "I'll give you the locations I know about, but he might not go to them."

Tobiah rose and pulled out the chair to a writing desk. "I want us to work together, Wil. I know you're angry with me, and you have every right to be. I'm angry with myself, too." He pulled out a few sheets of palace stationery and a writing box. "But I am willing to do whatever is required for my kingdom's security, and I think you are, too."

"I am." I took the desk chair he offered and arranged the writing utensils. "Rather, I used to be. Now, I find myself butting up against lines I won't cross, but Patrick will. *He* is the one who will do anything for Aecor. Revolutions. Regicide. Revenge. The end justifies the means for him. He sees the most direct path to his goal, and he takes it. He sheltered me from those decisions for so long; I never understood doing *anything* for one's kingdom until I realized the lengths he was willing to go."

Tobiah leaned on the corner of the desk, absorbing my words as I dipped my pen and began writing locations in his handwriting.

"How—" He shook his head. "The note I sent earlier."

"You should be more careful about your messages, Your Highness. You never know who is paying attention to the way you write flourishes on your name."

"First my vigilante identity, and now my handwriting." He gave an exaggerated sigh, and a smile pulled at the corner of his mouth. "You are incredible."

I capped the ink and began cleaning the pen. "You should hear what else I've done in my time here."

"I'm afraid to ask." He took the list and studied it for a moment. "I'm going to have men sent immediately. I'll be right back."

When he left the room, I sat on the bed next to James and touched his hand. "You're missing all the excitement."

James's fingers jumped, and he opened his eyes. "Julianna?"

I stood, stepped back, and my palms brushed my empty hips. "It's Wilhelmina."

He sat up and shook his head. "Of course . . . I'm sorry. Is Tobiah all right? Where is he?"

"He's fine." I forced myself to relax. "He stepped out for a moment, but he'll return soon."

"How long was I unconscious?"

"Three days." I wanted to ask how he'd healed, and how he'd awakened, but he looked so dazed and concerned for his cousin, I couldn't bring myself to speak the words. "I'm sure Tobiah will tell you everything you need to know."

James nodded. "Yes, I'm sure." He flashed a strained smile. "I'm sorry about the way I treated you in jail. I suppose you know it by now, but it was for others' benefit."

I took the chair I'd abandoned earlier, and placed my notebook over my knees. "It's fine."

"You didn't give him up."

I raised an eyebrow.

"Black Knife. You said you weren't protecting him, but you were."

"Maybe. I didn't know his real identity any more than he knew mine. But you knew his. And that I wasn't who I claimed to be. Or who others assumed me to be."

James let out a soft chuckle. "What a tangled web of identities you two made together. Yes, I knew. He's my best friend. I know everything about him."

"My best friend doesn't know everything about me." And now we were even further apart.

He offered a sad smile. "Well, there's no way Tobiah could have slipped past me all those nights. I trusted him to come back in one piece, and he trusted me to go along with the mask he wore for court."

"You think that Black Knife is the real Tobiah?"

"Yes. He's a lot more fun like that. And not as poor of a swordsman as I claimed. He did chew with his mouth open that once, though. I wasn't lying about that."

"And I'm still scandalized." I hesitated. "Does Meredith know? The queen regent?"

"No, no one else knows. I'm not sure what Prince Colin and Prince Herman would do if they even suspsected."

"Well, everyone thinks I'm Black Knife now. And I've heard them calling me the 'wraith queen,' because of what I did during the battle." It had only taken one night's work to corrupt the symbol Tobiah had worked so hard to create. "I'm certainly not helping Tobiah's image by being here, but I can't leave, either. Well, I could—"

Tobiah's voice came from behind me. "Why are you always trying to leave me?"

James surged to his feet, but before he could bow or perform any kind of genuflection, Tobiah rushed in and hugged him tightly.

"You're awake," he rasped. "I can't believe you're awake."

I made myself appear busy while the boys laughed and hugged and pounded each other's backs. After a few minutes, they pulled away and mussed each other's hair.

Tobiah combed his fingers through his curls. "James, put on some real clothes. There's a clean uniform in the wardrobe. I'm going to need you on the balcony. You too, Wil. My mother and Meredith should be here any moment."

While James and Tobiah were in the dressing room, Francesca and Meredith arrived. We didn't speak to one another, even when the boys emerged and Tobiah motioned us all toward a balcony door.

Like the apartments Melanie and I had shared, this balcony

had two doors, one from his private room, and one from the guest room. It overlooked a garden, though now the area below held blackened foliage and a crowd of protesters, shouting about me.

"Kill the wraith queen!"

"Punish the wraith queen!"

Beyond the forever-changed gardens and courtyards of the King's Seat, Hawksbill rose in a statelier glory than it had any right to, but the nobles living in those mansions could afford to repair their homes more quickly than anyone beyond the wall.

Below, someone pointed up at us, and the crowd grew quiet.

Tobiah lifted his hand. "People of the Indigo Kingdom."

Others below joined the crowd, coming from the nearby mansions or the destroyed fountain by the palace steps. Maids, builders, governesses: they all stopped what they were doing to look up at their prince.

"I know what you've been hearing these last few days, since the Inundation." Tobiah gripped the balcony rail and dragged in a heavy breath. "You're afraid of the wraith beasts that attacked our city three days ago. The assassin who murdered my father. Rumors of war from the east.

"I won't tell you *not* to be afraid of those things, because I don't know what the future will bring. But I have made some decisions that I hope will restore your faith in your leaders and heroes." The prince motioned James forward. "You all recognize my cousin, Lieutenant James Rayner. Effective immediately, I am promoting him to the rank of captain. He will oversee security for the entire palace."

Color rose to James's face, but he knelt and bowed his head.

Tobiah bade James rise before turning to Francesca. "My mother will continue acting as queen regent for the time being. After the mourning period and memorial, my coronation will be held in Skyvale Palace. This ceremony will be witnessed by my dear and trusted friend, Princess Wilhelmina Korte of Aecor."

Muttering spread out below, but that was all.

"Princess Wilhelmina, Prince Colin, and I will begin immediate negotiations to determine the future of Aecor and the Indigo Kingdom. War from the east is *not* inevitable." Tobiah touched my elbow, drawing me forward to stand beside him. "It is because of Her Highness's intelligence that we have identified the assassin who killed my father, and who likely attacked me. And it is because of Her Highness's quick action that the wraith beasts were stopped during the Inundation. Together, we are devising a plan to stop the wraith's approach. Princess Wilhelmina is a true friend to the Indigo Kingdom."

"Thank you, Your Highness." I lifted my voice. "I look forward to repairing the damage of the One-Night War and the years since."

The prince took my hand and kissed it, lingering just a second too long. My heartbeat throbbed as he whispered, "I'm sorry," against my skin.

Sorry for what?

He drew back, squaring his jaw. "The last item I would like to share with you is this: my father's death has convinced me of what must be done. I am moved to act for the benefit of this kingdom and the people within it."

The crowd below was absolutely silent.

"I've already announced my engagement to Lady Meredith

Corcoran." He motioned the duchess to stand next to him, and she did. They were beautiful together, his darkness and her lightness, regal in the way they complemented each other just as King Terrell had said they would. "My lady, I humbly apologize for the delay in setting a date."

She nodded, all forgiveness.

"It was my father's dream to see us married. Though he's gone now, I must believe his spirit is still with us. Immediately following my coronation, I will begin the preparations for our wedding. I hope the winter solstice is soon enough."

Meredith hadn't taken her eyes off him the whole time he was speaking, and now her face lit up with a smile. "It's perfect." Daintily, delicately, she lifted onto her toes, and kissed him.

Below, the crowd cheered and celebrated. Tobiah's mother and cousin smiled approvingly.

Only years of disguising my emotions saved me from the urge to stagger back, to press my hands against my heart or mouth. He was really doing it. He was really going to marry her.

I shouldn't have felt betrayed. He'd been promised to her from the start, and *I'd* been the interloper. I hadn't even liked Tobiah. Only Black Knife.

But maybe that didn't matter.

As the cheering crescendoed, I gazed across the courtyard, praying my expression was cool and unaffected by the prince holding his duchess in his arms.

On the rooftop of a nearby mansion, a figure moved. A man. On the next rooftop over, another shadow lurched up, frighteningly graceful and unusually long. The wraith boy?

The first shadow lifted something in front of him, and aimed.

"Get down!" The words were out before I realized, and everything happened in quick succession.

The shooter on the roof loosed his crossbow bolt.

I grabbed Tobiah's shoulders and pulled him back.

The wraith boy surged across the rooftops with a thunderous roar.

Screams erupted in the courtyard below.

The bolt struck Tobiah in the stomach, rather than his heart where it had been aimed, and the prince collapsed to the balcony floor, half in my arms.

Uniformed men rushed through Tobiah's apartments and onto the balcony, shouting and creating a barrier of bodies.

Francesca and Meredith were pulled inside, even as they reached for Tobiah.

Blood poured from the wound in Tobiah's gut, filling the air with an angry scent of copper. I was already sitting over him with his head cushioned in my lap when men began cutting away the bloodied shirt to inspect the wound.

"Trust Wilhelmina." Tobiah's order came out weak, but the men exchanged glances; they'd heard. "Protect her."

Gently, I cupped his cheeks in my hands and tried to meet his gaze, but his eyelids kept drifting shut. "When are you going to learn?" I rasped. "I don't want to be rescued."

His mouth twitched into a pale smile. "I don't want to fight."

Then he closed his eyes.

ACKNOWLEDGMENTS

LIKE REVOLUTIONS, PUBLISHING a book is a team effort. Many thanks to the people (more than I could ever name!) who helped get *The Orphan Queen* out into the world.

My dear ladies in the palace of publishing:

Lauren MacLeod, my agent with an arsenal of highlighters and soothing words. I could never have stormed this castle without you.

Sarah Shumway and Laurel Symonds, my editors who wield red pens like swords. Ladies, songs will be sung in your honor. They will tell tales far and wide of your editorial wisdom.

Katherine Tegen, the queen of KTB. I am ever honored that my books are worthy of holding your logo on their spines.

Alana Whitman, Lauren Flower, Onalee Smith, Rosanne Romanello, Aubry Parks-Fried, and Margot Wood: an extraordinary and supportive team of ladies who can talk books like no one's business.

Amy Ryan, Erin Fitzsimmons, and Colin Anderson: costumers extraordinaire who understand that authenticity is key to any disguise.

Lots of love to the Ospreys in my life:

Adam Heine, who understood immediately where I was aiming with this story.

Christine Nguyen, who code-named this story Batprince. How you read entire first drafts in little chat boxes, I will never understand.

C. J. Redwine, a terrific writer, critique partner, and friend. Sorry I'm not sorry that your street smells like pee. It's out of love.

Gabrielle Harvey, who didn't disown me for what happened to that violin bow. I probably don't deserve you, but I'm glad you stick around anyway.

Jaime Lee Moyer, one of the strongest people I will ever know.

Joy Hensley, my friend, fellow writer, and surprise fifth cousin by marriage (totally a legitimate relationship). Remember that time I trapped you in the car for two hours and made you listen to my mad plot ramblings?

Jill Roberts, my mom, who gasped, "That's a *terrible* ending!" when I explained my plan for revising the first draft. Thanks, Mom. Your horror let me know I was heading in the right direction. Sorry to make you sad, though.

Jillian Boehme, a wise and generous friend who will one day come around to properly appreciating Batman. (I'll keep loving you even if you don't.) Thanks for reading all my stories. And for the Batman T-shirt. I wear it all the time.

DATE DUE

APR